STRIKEFORCE
LIGHTNING

ALSO BY MARK AITKEN

Arctic Floor

STRIKEFORCE
LIGHTNING

MARK AITKEN

ARENA
ALLEN&UNWIN

This edition published in 2014
First published in 2013

Allen & Unwin
83 Alexander Street
Crows Nest NSW 2065
Australia
Phone: (61 2) 8425 0100
Email: info@allenandunwin.com
Web: www.allenandunwin.com

Cataloguing-in-Publication details are available
from the National Library of Australia
www.trove.nla.gov.au

ISBN 978 1 74331 758 7

Typeset by Midland Typesetters, Australia
Printed and bound in Australia by Griffin Press

10 9 8 7 6 5 4 3 2 1

For Elsa

7. . . . some uncertainty is inevitable in any country-wide technical verification process that aims to prove the absence of readily concealable objects, such as components of centrifuge machines or copies of weapon-related documentation, or activities such as small-scale enrichment or weaponization experimentation or computer-based studies. Thus, although IAEA has assembled a technically coherent picture of Iraq's clandestine nuclear programme, there is an inherent uncertainty in the completeness of that picture deriving from the possible existence of duplicate facilities or the possible existence of anomalous activities or facilities outside the technically coherent picture . . .

LETTER FROM UN SECRETARY-GENERAL KOFI ANNAN TO THE PRESIDENT OF THE SECURITY COUNCIL

PROLOGUE

Baghdad, 2003

The convoy of people movers made fast time through the bombed-out streets of Baghdad's financial district. Explosions lit up the night sky, illuminating the bands of looters operating before the Americans had even forced a surrender.

'Scavengers,' snarled Saeed. 'Scum.' He was sitting beside his nephew Tookie in the back seat of the Kia van. Growling curses, he lowered his window, drew a handgun from its holster. An arm reached back from the front seat, grabbing Saeed by the wrist.

'Please, sir—the bank first, yes?' said the intelligence man from the Republican Guard, his face respectful but forearm rigid with insistence. 'These dogs can wait.'

Nodding reluctantly, Saeed reholstered the gun but continued to spit insults out the window as they drove past a line of thieves loading computer hard drives from an insurance office into their pick-up trucks.

Tookie was silent, choosing not to antagonise his furious uncle. Three hours earlier the family bunker had been hit by a string of American missiles, collapsing the concrete roofs on the living areas where the women, kids and servants had been sleeping. Tookie had been lucky to escape—he'd followed his favourite uncle outside for a cigarette just minutes before the missiles started dropping in like whistling skyrockets.

Escaping over a flattened garden wall, they'd been intercepted by the intelligence men and taken to the old underground reservoir where the only truly safe bunkers in Baghdad were hidden. There, in angry whispers, Uncle Saeed had discussed what sounded like a mission, though it seemed not all of Saddam's men were in agreement.

His mother and sister lost to the air strikes—his father long dead to Saddam's secret police—Tookie now tried to stay calm as small-arms fire broke out at an intersection where a six-storey building was now a pile of broken concrete and reinforcing steel. Tookie wondered about the prospect of a future Baathist Iraq. Before he'd been taken by the police, Tookie's father used to say that the Arabs and Persians could cause enough mayhem in the Tigris–Euphrates basin without the Americans and British pouring gasoline on the situation.

And now the evidence was all around them. With Saddam running from palace to palace, the thieves, hijackers, ransomers and pirates who'd inhabited this region forever were back and working without fear. It was hard sometimes to choose between fear of the Americans or shame for the Iraqis—the once-proud Arab nation and last bastion against the Zionist entity.

The van slowed as they turned through rubble and roadblocks onto Rashid Street, the centre of Baghdad's financial district, then stopped behind a series of army pick-up trucks and Kia vans. Tookie knew he was witnessing the end of something as he stared at the damage to the Central Bank building.

'Wait here,' said Saeed, and moved into the night, gun drawn, to meet another man in an army jumper and black beret on the steps of the bank.

Radio traffic crackled and barked in the front seat, the intelligence men calm but determined in their responses to what were panicked questions and demands from the radio. From what Tookie could make out, they were talking about the bank visit, while trying to organise an exit for their own families as the Americans closed on Baghdad's international airport. If Saddam surrendered, Iraq would be no place for the families of anyone in intelligence, secret police or military.

Tookie watched his uncle mount the steps to the Central Bank with the man in the black beret, both of them falling to their knees as another missile whistled over the building. They stood quickly and continued up the steps towards two men who opened the large security doors. Then the man in the black beret walked halfway down the steps, issued orders to the soldiers and ran back inside as the pick-ups drove around the bank and into the side street.

Speaking into the radio handpiece, the intelligence man driving Tookie's van gestured out the window with his arm and the other Kia vans pulled out and followed the trucks into the side street.

'What are we doing here?' asked Tookie, feeling vulnerable without his uncle close by.

'Making a little withdrawal,' quipped the intelligence man in the passenger seat before the driver told him to shut up.

Saeed emerged from the Central Bank's main doors and glanced around nervously, an aluminium canister the size of a small rocket under his arm. He ran down the stairs to the van.

'Side entrance,' commanded Saeed as he slid back onto the seat, panting slightly. 'News from the airport?'

'Americans holding off,' said the driver, accelerating. 'Republican Guards want to redeploy but are being told to remain where they are.'

Feeling his uncle stiffen beside him, Tookie knew this to be a moment when Iraqis simply shut their mouths and avoided stating the obvious: that Iraq's Republican Guards had been the some of the best-paid of Saddam's employees for years because of their loyalty. Yet when it came time to do their duty and defend the airport—the same airport from which the Americans were expected to enter Baghdad— the Republican Guards didn't want to fight.

'Redeploy?' asked Saeed.

'Yes, sir,' said the driver. 'They want to leave it to the militias.'

They waited at the side entrance to the underground garage of the bank, all the men smoking furiously as the sky ignited with flashes of phosphorous. Eventually the first of the army pick-up trucks emerged from the garage, a large white tarpaulin covering the load in the back.

3

A second pick-up followed it into the street and the army man in the black beret jumped off the back of the vehicle as it came to a stop. Walking to Tookie's van, the man in the black beret leaned in the window and whispered something to Saeed.

They drove through the night, the canopy of dark lit up every few seconds. Doubling around freshly bombed suburbs, and taking tips from intelligence sources about the safest routes, they drove north along the Tigris until they finally found an intact bridge and crossed it. On the other side was a large public park where families went for picnics on the weekend; they stopped and Saeed got out and spoke with other men from the army and intelligence.

Tookie watched the meeting and felt a sense of time itself slowing: the men bent over as one, holding their hair as the air tore open with the famous whooshing sound they'd been hearing for the past four hours. And then the hits came fast; the first landed on the river bank, shaking the ground and covering the parked convoy with water and sand. The second landed in a government building over the road from the park, making the air shudder and debris fly like a hurricane of building materials.

Tookie lay on the back seat of the van as the glass blew in, unable to breathe, crying for his mother and praying for Allah's mercy.

Then there was a third whooshing sound that came closer and closer, and a man's voice said, *Curse of Allah!*

And all was black.

CHAPTER 1

Fourteen minutes into the third period Gallen found the watcher. He was sitting five rows back and about seven seats south of the halfway line at the Sublette County Ice Arena. From his vantage point in the visitors' team box Gallen had a direct line of sight on the guy across the floodlit hockey arena. The yells of the hockey fans filled the Wyoming night but the heavy-set African American who'd stalked to his seat early in the first period breathed shallow through his nostrils and showed more interest in the visitors' box than the game between Sheridan Hawks and Pinedale Glaciers, two high school teams.

Taking his eyes from the watcher, Gallen got back to the job and refocused on Dave McCain, the Hawks' star centre, who sucked on a water bottle as Gallen crouched at his right shoulder.

'This Houseman prick ain't such a genius,' said Gallen, hoping the coach, Billy Higgins, couldn't hear him cussing about the Pinedale centre who'd been causing so many problems for the Hawks. McCain's momma was a Christian and Billy didn't want her having an excuse to pull Dave out of the team. 'He's letting his left wing drift in front of him with the puck, and when the winger gets checked this Houseman is taking the puck forwards with momentum and there's a hole up the middle.'

McCain, a high school senior with college potential, nodded. 'Maybe I'll hold back, let someone else make the check on Houseman, right, Mr Gallen?'

'And make sure your right wing is man-on-man with their left.' Gallen stood and patted McCain on the shoulder. 'Just wait for Houseman to accelerate into the channel and come forwards, knock that little prick on his ass.'

A whistle blew above the yells and a roar of approval rose from the home fans. The ref had called a hooking penalty on a Hawks player and the 4–3 advantage to the Glaciers was starting to look strong.

Billy Higgins moved adjacent to Gallen. 'Shit, Gerry. We're getting killed by the calls—this ref from the Blind Institute?'

Dwayne Marsh came in off the ice to start his penalty and sat on the bench heaving for breath, questioning the ref's relationship with his mother. The rest of the Hawks told him, 'Way to go, Dwaynie,' and, 'Forget that blind cocksucker.'

Gallen stamped his feet to get some warmth into his boots; the game clock said four minutes to go. He turned back to Higgins. 'We need to stop Houseman. *He's* killing us more than the ref.'

Higgins' moustache moved up and down with his gum-chewing. He was a cattle farmer who dressed in a suit every Saturday night to coach the team. 'You told Dave that?'

Dave McCain turned in his seat and looked up, sweat pouring out of his helmet, down his face. 'Sure, Coach—we gotta use man-on-man with their left wing, and I'll hold back, make a run at Houseman when he comes through.'

Higgins gave Gallen a knowing look. They'd played high school hockey together twenty years ago and while Higgins was a classic grinder—the hard-working defenceman on which a team was built— Gallen had been coached by his dad, Roy, and his style was inventive, cunning and a little dirty.

The Glaciers were changing two players so Higgins clicked his fingers at Dave McCain. The centre spat between his skates and stood.

'Marty,' screamed Higgins at the ice, his big face purple with exertion. 'Come in.'

The players swapped mid-flow as the power play started: five players now on the ice for the Sheridan Hawks against the full six for the Glaciers. A scuffle started against the boards before Pinedale could properly use their advantage, and as the ref broke it up, Gallen watched the mystery man in the crowd stand and edge along his bleacher, the hockey fans leaning back and forth like metronomes to keep their eyes on the ice.

The crowd booed as the referee sent a Pinedale player to the penalty box. With both teams down to five players, the game restarted with a quick face-off in the Hawks' defensive zone. Dave McCain swooped on the spilled puck, beat one man and drove up the ice, offloading to his left winger who swerved towards the boards and squeezed past a too-brutal attempt on him.

'Oh no,' said an elderly woman behind the Hawks' box as Dave McCain received the puck and slapped a shot at goal without even pausing to line it up. It hit the back of the net and Gallen whooped as he felt Billy Higgins' heavy arm slap around his neck. The scoreboard said 4–4 and three minutes to play.

'Shit, Gerry,' said Higgins, jumping on the spot. 'Shit!'

Higgins had taken over the high school squad for the Hawks having had a mediocre season with the bantams the previous season. He was hated by some of the hockey faithful in Sheridan because he came from Clearmont, which meant he may as well live in Gillette. With a 0–2 start to the season, he needed this game, which was why he'd talked Gallen into being his assistant coach, and why Gallen had accepted.

The crowd built to a hometown roar as the ref brought the puck to a centre ice face-off, and Gallen felt the old excitement grip in his jaw and clench in his fists. There was nothing in the world like going into the last couple of minutes of a tied hockey game and for a split second he wanted to be out there.

The Hawks sitting on the bench thumped their sticks into the boards as the crowd yelled and the puck spilled out of the face-off. Two boys chased it to the boards and a Glaciers defenceman got behind a Hawk and rammed him chest-first into the plexiglass. The ref called play on and Billy Higgins had a meltdown. 'You see that, Gerry? That was a minor, right there.'

A voice bellowed from Gallen's right; it was Ernie du Toit, the Pinedale coach. 'Nothing wrong with that check, Billy—nothing a bunch of girls couldn't handle.'

Gallen stopped Higgins moving towards du Toit, pointed him back at the game.

'Plenty of time for Ernie,' said Gallen.

Patting his old friend on the shoulder, Gallen cast his eyes across the opposite bleachers. The watcher was nowhere to be seen.

'Charlie, get ready.' Higgins slapped one of his players on the back.

The boy called Charlie didn't acknowledge. The entire bench was leaning forwards as the Pinedale Glaciers moved up the ice from their defensive zone, their signature move about to be executed by Darren Houseman. The Pinedale left winger took the puck from Houseman and angled back to centre ice as Houseman skated in behind him. Gallen was about to yell at McCain to pull back but the Hawks' centre was already slowing up, pulling back from the line and calling in his right wing to make the check on his opposite number. Houseman accelerated towards the puck that was laid back by his left wing and poured through the hole in the line as Dave McCain skated straight at him at full speed. Houseman, who'd already made this move work several times in the game, looked up to see the white Sheridan jersey filling his vision. The crowd gasped as McCain dropped his shoulder and swung his hips, sending Darren Houseman into the air, mouthguard flying, and landing on his helmet with a sickening crack.

Seeing the puck at his feet, McCain slapped it to his left wing and skated up the ice, taking back the puck in front of the Pinedale goal and, having wrong-footed the goalie, edged in what looked like an effortless goal.

Beside them Ernie du Toit was screaming at the ref for a penalty as the Pinedale players helped Houseman off the ice.

'Nothing wrong with that challenge, Ernie,' yelled Billy Higgins through cupped hands. 'Nothing a bunch of girls couldn't handle.'

The locker room looked like a battlefield as Gallen went from boy to boy, giving each a few words of analysis and encouragement. It was the role Billy wanted him taking with the team, so the head coach could work on strategy and administration. One of the last on the visitors' benches was Dave McCain, his mouth slack with exhaustion, down to his thermals and nursing a big ice-pack on his left shoulder.

'Nice tip with Houseman,' said the eighteen-year-old.

Gallen smiled, seeing himself in this plucky kid. 'You handled it perfectly. It was a totally legal hit.'

'Glad the ref saw it like that, 'cos du Toit don't.'

'The only thing that matters is that scoreboard, Dave,' said Gallen. 'Du Toit don't mean shit.'

'Coach didn't think so,' said McCain, swigging on a Gatorade.

'What do you mean?'

The kid shrugged. 'Du Toit came to the door while you were in the john. Coach left with him.'

'Christ,' said Gallen, standing.

There was a crowd of beer drinkers in the car park as Gallen burst out of the players' entrance, the cold hitting him in the V where his Bauer down jacket fell open. Pushing through a ring of rednecks in Carhartt jackets and lace-up boots, Gallen was in time to see a spritz of blood fly through the night air and Billy Higgins stagger against a ten-year-old Silverado. Du Toit—his suit jacket draped on a car hood—moved surprisingly lightly on his thick legs and threw a big right which Higgins ducked before swivelling to his left and throwing a fast overhand left punch into du Toit's ear.

The Pinedale coach sagged slightly, his hands rising to cover up, and Higgins regained his balance, grabbed the bigger man by the shirt collar and started an old-fashioned hockey pummelling: no art or style, just a cattleman's right hand pumping back and forth into his opponent's face.

After nine unanswered shots, Higgins stopped and left Ernie du Toit with his hands on his knees, blood cascading onto the wet concrete, steam shooting from his busted mouth. Grabbing his jacket from one of the drunks, Higgins saw Gallen and made for him, checking his own nose for blood as he walked.

'Sorry 'bout that,' said Higgins. 'Ernie needed my opinion on something.'

A tall cowboy with a Willie Nelson beard tried to drop a shoulder into Gallen, saying something about 'Clearmont homos' and 'Sheridan County faggots'. Giving the bearded guy a smile, Gallen tried to push through with Higgins in tow but the cowboy reached for Gallen's collar. Reacting instinctively, Gallen slapped down on the man's elbow crook, pulled his wrist back in a twist and brought the man to his knees in a fast ikkyo. Hearing the tendons snap in the man's forearm and wrist, and the gasping screams begin, Gallen knew he'd overreacted. He'd been trying to detune from life in the field but it wasn't always easy—even the basic Aikido self-defence moves taught to recon Marines were not intended to score points at a tournament; they were designed to incapacitate.

Letting go of the man's useless wrist, Gallen turned to face the crowd: at least nine, some sober enough to fight, others drunk enough to try. A beer can sailed over his head and Gallen felt Coors splash his face as his assailant's sobs echoed around the car park.

'This is over, fellas,' said Gallen, in the voice he used to use when the men had been drinking. 'Let's shut it down, huh?'

Snowflakes drifted through the floodlight beams and Gallen knew it was time to go. As he turned towards the locker room with Billy, he sensed movement before he saw it properly. Something rose out of the parking lot floodlights and seemed to be flying—this one more than a beer can. Too late, Gallen realised a trash can was being swung in an arc at the back of Higgins' head. Grabbing at his friend's head to protect him, there was a dull thudding sound and the trash can came no further.

Someone had intercepted the can and a fight was starting. Pulling Billy around behind him, Gallen looked for the danger and saw two rednecks unconscious on the concrete. A figure pursued another man around the prone form of the cowboy with the busted wrist while the rest of the beer drinkers turned and fled.

Panting for breath, watching for the next missile, Gallen kept his eye on the man who'd come to their aid. A man who knew exactly what he was doing. When the crowd had dispersed, the man walked back between the two unconscious men and stood in front of Gallen.

'You're Gerry Gallen,' said the watcher from the fifth row. 'Can I buy you a beer?'

CHAPTER 2

The Corral Bar seemed okay for a meeting. Gallen remembered it from his teenage years when he'd travelled with his hockey team and Pinedale's Corral Bar had let the drinking age slide. He arrived early, saw the ID cards on the security guy, the security cameras and the signs that warned of breaking the law, and he knew none of the Hawks high school players would be sneaking in here. Then he checked the pool table area, the washrooms and noted a kitchen with saloon doors. If he stood in the right place he'd be able to check the kitchen when a waitress hit those doors.

College snowboarders and cowgirls were filling up the place, so Gallen bought a handle of Bud and took a stand-up table that wrapped around a pillar near the pool tables. The Blackhawks–Maple Leafs game was into the second period on the plasma screen but there was no commentary because the biggest screen in the honky tonk played gangsta rap videos loud enough to shake the walls.

The man who called himself Daly walked into the place at nine pm, as promised, and seeing Gallen he pointed to the glass.

'Bud,' said Gallen, keeping his eyes on Daly as he turned towards the western-themed bar. Daly was about Gallen's age—mid-thirties—and wore jeans and ice boots that had been on a shop shelf the day before. So the dude wasn't from the area, which supported the LA accent.

Daly placed two handles of beer on the table and a wooden bowl with a large packet of peanuts inside it. He sipped at the beer and looked around at the skiers and western girls, a smirk on his face. 'Man, these white folks sure like their gangsta music.'

'The tourists like it.' Gallen raised his glass and clicked it with Daly's.

'What they play in the local bars?'

Gallen shrugged. 'Waylon, Johnny, Merle.'

'Shit,' said Daly, still casing the room. 'Sounds like a law firm.'

'They've been called worse,' said Gallen, sipping. 'Thanks for that before, in the car park.'

'Not a problem,' said Daly, waving it away. 'Saved them boys from a real beating.'

'Yeah?' said Gallen, knowing that the fighting he'd seen from Daly was the kind of thing he'd been taught in the Marines.

'Oh yeah. That boy of yours hits like a steam piston.'

Gallen laughed, the beer relaxing him. 'Yeah, Billy and Ern been at it since they was hockey midgets.'

Daly widened his eyes. 'Midgets?'

'Hockey midgets,' said Gallen. 'Fourteen-year-olds. One year they both made state and fought on the bus all the way to their game with Montana. Been at it ever since.'

'Sure, Gerry,' said Daly, shaking his head. 'But grown men in car parks?'

'Yeah, what I said,' said Gallen. 'So, Daly. What do you want?'

The big man eyeballed him for a moment and then softened. 'Direct. They said you were direct, Gerry.'

'Like I said.'

Daly put his glass down on the table and tore the top off the peanuts, poured them into the wooden bowl and pushed the bowl to Gallen. 'Gotta job for you, Gerry.'

Gallen took a small handful of nuts and fed himself methodically as he scanned the bar for back-up or eavesdroppers. The Marines Force Recon career was history now but he still found it easy to slip into the focused and adrenaline-charged state that had kept him alive in the field for eighteen years. Washing the peanuts down with the Bud, he returned Daly's stare. 'I gotta job, Daly.'

'Sure, Gerry, but you do contracts, right?'

'I'll take your hay off for five dollars a square bale, twenty for a round,' said Gallen. 'That's the only contracting I do and you'd better be old or a widow to ask me in the first place.'

'Not what I meant.'

Gallen breathed out through his teeth and looked away. The one thing they didn't teach you in special forces was how to handle life after the Life; what to do when you were turned out yet still couldn't look at a bed without cringing at its crappy corners. The Marine Corps had invested hundreds of hours of intel staffers telling them what they could never say to the media or their friends, but they never told people like Gerry Gallen that once they were trained and battle-hardened they'd be sought after for private work. 'Who sent you?'

'Chase Lang,' said Daly, in a tone that suggested the whole conversation had just changed.

'Why would Chase want me? I'm out. He knows that.'

'Mr Lang said you're suited.'

'Suited? Shit—this a dating game?'

'Suited to delicate assignments.'

Gallen wanted to blow this horse shit out of the water, but he didn't want Daly going back to LA and creating the impression that there was any disrespect in the equation. Chase Lang was a former US Navy SEAL who ran a large PX operation for military contractors in Longbeach. The military supply business was his public face; Chase Lang was also a mercenary contractor who supplied what was known in the Pentagon as 'Live Solutions'. Gallen had been bailed out by one of Lang's operatives during a stand-off in Canada and he wanted to reject this offer without implying ingratitude.

'Delicate?'

'I saw your file, Gerry.'

Gallen snorted. 'Which one?'

'Captain in Force Recon; tours in Mindanao, A-stan. Silver Star, and you turned down the Pentagon three times for a promotion to DIA. Told the man to fuck himself.'

'Wasn't like that,' said Gallen.

'Really? They offer you oak leaves and a chance to put your feet up, you say no?'

13

'I said yes to farming,' said Gallen, annoyed that he had to talk about his military days. 'Went back to the family farm. That'll be in your file.'

'Says you did some private PSD up in Alberta.'

Gallen finished his beer. 'Don't let me hog the limelight, Daly. Tell me something about yourself.'

Daly smiled. 'Army for thirteen years. The end.'

'Where?' said Gallen.

'Iraq eventually. But Mindanao forced the divorce.'

'Mindanao is shit duty,' said Gallen, nodding. 'Mindanao is where I'd send any politician who wants to wage a war on terror.'

'Hah!' said Daly, beer spilling from his bottom lip. 'Might take the adventure out of it.'

Gallen thought about it. 'Rangers?'

'Yep,' said Daly, draining his glass. 'After a couple of easy years in Iraq, we were rotated back into Mindanao. Half my unit resigned— fuck that shit.'

The waitress approached them with her tray, picked up the empty handles and wiped the table. Daly ordered two more Buds.

'I warn you,' said Gallen. 'I'm only here for the beer.'

'Mr Lang said you'd pass,' said Daly.

'Read me like a book.'

They watched the hockey for a minute, neither speaking. The waitress delivered the beers and Daly hit her with a ten, told her to keep it.

Daly dragged a stool to the table and sagged onto it, a man who was no longer on the clock. 'At least I made the trip, right? Anyways, Spikey can ride some other sucker—you wanna play pool?'

'Sure.' Gallen looked at the table, his temples thumping with surprise. 'You say Spikey?'

Daly walked to the pool table, fed in some coins to release a rumble of balls. 'Sure—Terrell Holmes.'

'I know who he is,' snapped Gallen, annoyed that he was being played. 'What's he to Chase?'

Daly racked the balls and Gallen selected a cue, chalked it.

'Spikey's the gig,' said Daly, grabbing his own cue.

*

14

It was 2005 and Captain Gerry Gallen's platoon of Force Recon Marines were fresh out of Mindanao hell and into the mountains, valleys and snow of Afghanistan. The ongoing problem for the Special Operations Command war planners in Kabul was actual ground movements and the flow of commerce. It was one thing for SOCOM heavies to colour zones on a briefing room map and declare the entire area 'cleared' and 'uncleared', but the role of the Marines special forces was to infiltrate areas and take the photos, assess cargos, count freight movements, crosscheck local intelligence, follow suspects and report it back to Kabul.

It was late November, the snow was flying and after a month of acclimatisation tours with the outgoing Marines, Gallen's platoon was on their second tour out of Bagram Air Base, patrolling the roads between Khost and Jalalabad into Pakistan. The leadership of the Taliban had fled into Pakistan in late 2001, but they'd continued to supply their cells inside Afghanistan with firearms, matériel, money and intelligence.

On a lonely mountain pass, Gallen's men had picked up a truck from Peshawar which used an abandoned road to Gardez. The truck had stopped overnight at a roadside depot: a depot with no gasoline or diesel. On a hunch he'd decided to tail the truck, taking confirmations from the US Navy reconnaissance drones overhead.

After spending most of the morning following the old Mercedes truck in their Humvees, Gallen told SOCOM he was tailing the truck, but the majors and colonels nixed that because the registration plate matched with a pan-Arab humanitarian operation and Gallen's commanders didn't want to look anti-Muslim.

By lunch, Gallen decided SOCOM's directions were irrelevant and told the men to pull the vehicle over; the truck was not being driven by professionals. Staff Sergeant Terrell 'Spikey' Holmes wanted to take the high ground and cover the unit and Gallen reluctantly agreed. Holmes had grown up hard in LA orphanages and foster care. He'd been a middleweight boxer before joining the Marines and he didn't like or trust the Afghanis. He didn't like or trust anyone and Gallen worried that his trigger finger was too itchy.

Gallen and Spikey had formed an uneasy alliance in Mindanao where the group needed a hard-ass figure of authority in the jungles and islands of the southern Philippines. But Afghanistan was different duty: there were Europeans always tut-tutting at the Americans, accusing anyone who spoke English of being culturally insensitive. There was more paperwork and more cultural background briefings in Afghanistan than in any other war Gallen had ever heard of and Spikey Holmes—an able soldier and hard boy from South Central—had never fit in. For Spikey there were friends and foes, good guys and bad dudes; my crew and the rest. He didn't see race or religion or skin colour: he saw threats and solutions, and his own government didn't always appreciate him for it.

As they closed on the humanitarian truck that day, Spikey had taken one other operator to the rocky outcrop over the road. Gallen greeted the truck driver as he climbed down from the cab and the passenger had walked around to join them. It seemed friendly enough until five rifle shots rang out, sending Gallen diving into the mud and slush of the road.

When he stood again, the driver and passenger were dead in the mud, both of them victims of headshots.

Gallen remembered screaming at Spikey as the staff sergeant slid down the scree slope to join the platoon.

'The fuck, Sergeant?' Gallen had cried. 'You killed a couple of truck drivers—who asked you to do that?'

The rules of engagement for US military were very clear and a bunch of serious pen-pushers had warned that murder charges awaited any officer who put his men outside the ROE. Spikey had already cost Gallen a heap of paperwork over a village clearance that ended in several deaths. Now this.

'What's that?' Spikey ignored Gallen's question as he walked to the fallen Pakistanis.

'What?' said Gallen, following Holmes's M4 rifle muzzle, which was pointing at a cheap Nokia cell phone sitting in the mud five inches from the driver's open hand.

'That, cap'n,' said Holmes. 'Cell phone in the man's hand when there ain't no cell coverage.'

'Oh shit,' said one of Gallen's men, and they eased backwards as one.

'And see that driver chest?'

'Yep,' said Gallen, seeing the bulge under the man's jacket.

'Them Pakis wearing ski vests under their clothes now? That the fashion?'

'Get back,' said Gallen to his men as he joined Spikey. They kneeled in the mud, pushed back the driver's jacket and unbuttoned his shirt. Beneath it was a beige canvas fisherman's vest with six bricks of explosive across the chest, above a detonator switch and a radio receiver.

'Shit,' said Gallen. 'They the only occupants?'

'Check,' said Spikey, suspicious eyes scanning the truck and the area for a possible third man with his own Nokia.

'SOCOM told me this was a humanitarian load,' said Gallen, anger welling in his belly. 'Let's check the truck.'

Ramirez, the unexploded-ordnance expert, took thirty-five minutes to check the rear swinging doors of the three-axle, ten-wheel truck before they opened it and found three hundred and twenty-seven improvised explosive devices, most of them in the shape of vests but also bombs disguised as student backpacks, briefcases, cell phones, laptops and five baby strollers packing enough C4 to flatten a brick building.

'I still have to write a report about these poor innocent Pakistanis,' said Gallen as they conferred in the back of the truck.

'Driver drew down,' said Spikey, all gum-chewing and attitude. 'I took the shot before he killed the boss.'

'There was a gun?' said Gallen.

'Is now,' said Spikey with a smile.

'I didn't see no gun, Spikey.'

'Look again, cap'n,' said Spikey. 'The old Makarov I found in Khost?'

Gallen nodded. 'What about it?'

'That Paki bitch's now, see what I'm sayin'?'

The crack of pool balls broke Gallen's reverie. It seemed a lifetime ago that they had stood on that road, constructing the report that would help them to avoid the pen-pushers' debriefings and keep them from the military lawyers who wanted to be the first to pin a murder charge on one of their own soldiers. Spikey Holmes was irreverent, a bad drinker and a problem gambler. And his South Central tough-guy act was the direct opposite of Gallen's redneck slow-talk. But when it came down to it, Gallen owed the man his life. A second's hesitation and that truck driver would have detonated his vest and felled almost an entire platoon.

Gallen was going to say no to Daly, and then he was going to walk away. But he had to hear what had happened to Spikey Holmes. He owed the man that much.

Daly's break fanned the balls to the corners of the table.

'So, Spikey's the gig?' said Gallen, watching two overs drop.

'Spikey wants to be back in LA.' Daly lined up a long rail shot to the far left pocket. 'We want you to help him.'

'We?' said Gallen.

'Columbus Enterprises—Mr Lang,' said Daly, tossing his leather jacket on a stool and flexing soldier's arms under a thick cotton sweatshirt.

'And you?'

'Client manager,' said Daly, concentrating on the cue ball.

Gallen felt himself falling further into the story when he should have been out on the pavement, lighting a smoke and walking back to the Comfort Inn. But combat had been a profound experience and the kind of alliances you made on a battleground were not the kind you shrugged off. 'Where is he?'

'Jordan,' said Daly, missing the shot.

'Jordan?' said Gallen, unsure. 'Jordan, New York?'

Daly smiled as Gallen lined up an easy shot. 'No, Gerry—Jordan as in Hashemites, mint tea, bad drivers.'

Gallen made the shot and stood, looked Daly in the eye. 'So, Chase Lang—who does contracts for the CIA—he wants a Wyoming cattle farmer to go to Jordan and pick up a former staff sergeant of his? This doesn't seem strange to you?'

Daly shrugged. 'Mr Lang don't ask for my opinions on much.'

'And don't tell me—the pay's too good to refuse?'

'I can offer you two thousand a day, two crew and a delivery bonus of twenty thousand,' said Daly, like he'd rehearsed it. 'And full death, disability and hospital cover—consular grade, Swiss insurer.'

'And I gather Spikey is having problems leaving Jordan?'

'Could say that.'

Gallen nodded. 'Who wants him back? Who's putting up the dough?'

'Mr Lang.'

'Who's he doing the contract for?'

Daly shrugged.

'I won't tell Chase you told me—I just want to know the deal now, 'cos if I was to do this and then I found out the truth later, maybe I wouldn't be happy.'

Daly laughed, teeth glinting in the Coors neon above the cue rack.

'Something funny?'

'The boss told me you's one of them quiet rednecks, but you don't take shit.'

'So who's the job for?'

'You didn't get it from me,' said Daly, 'but I think it's the Graham brothers.'

Gallen breathed out through his nose and leaned on his cue, the game forgotten. 'The Grahams—the LA gangsters?'

'They run games . . .'

'Games?' said Gallen.

'Poker, mainly.'

Gallen stomped the cue too hard. 'Fuck!'

'Yeah, I know,' said Daly.

'How much?'

'Around two hundred, but that's guessing,' said Daly.

'Two hundred!' yelled Gallen, making a couple of cowgirls turn and stare. 'You let a soldier get to two hundred thousand on marker?!'

'Not me, my brother.'

Gallen's mind spun but he couldn't see any way out of it. 'You want me to grab an old war buddy so he can face the Graham brothers?'

'No, no, Gerry. It ain't like that,' said Daly. 'Spikey got the money, but he's got a situation in Jordan.'

'Situation?'

'He's holding cash, but he's got some people in Amman who want that cash, see what I'm saying?'

'Why aren't you going?' Gallen wanted some reason to say no.

'You know Spikey . . .'

'Yeah, I know Spikey,' said Gallen. 'So why ain't you doing the gig?'

Daly shrugged. 'Spikey's been drinkin', and it's messing with his mind.'

Gallen remembered some of the scrapes he pulled his staff sergeant out of. Terrell Holmes worked dry but when there was leave or an R&R rotation, he was like a wandering tomcat, powered up on whisky and beer, in the middle of any fight and with a terrible weakness for gambling, cards in particular. Holmes had fought some Golden Gloves as a teenager and when he was hammered he thought nothing of taking on three or four men in a bar fight. But with the drinking came paranoia and Gallen could envisage Spikey Holmes in a drinker's funk, making it impossible for anyone to help him.

'So you know he's drinking? Who did you send already?'

'Mr Lang sent a contractor he knew in Baghdad,' said Daly. 'Spikey put him in the hospital—thought he was CIA, Mossad, that shit. The man's not well.'

'So Chase thought Spikey would respond to his old CO?'

'Once he trusts you, he'll be out of there. He knows he has to get out of Amman.'

'Why would he trust me? I'm bringing him back to the Graham brothers.'

'Let's say he'll speak to you, won't break your jaw.'

Gallen's stomach felt acid, he craved a cigarette. 'I'll need a work-up on this. And a crew.'

'Work up all you want, Gerry,' said Daly. 'But we need you there quick smart.'

'How quick?' said Gallen, thinking about the horses and the cattle.

'You're booked on the five-twenty out of Denver.'

'I'm booked?' said Gallen. 'When?'

'Monday.'

'It's Saturday night,' said Gallen.

'Sure is—want another beer?'

CHAPTER 3

The Hawks' bus pulled into the Sheridan Ice car park a little after one pm and Gallen got off with Billy Higgins, stood by the front door of the vehicle as the boys filed out and into the arms of their mothers.

Mrs Davidson, an eligible mom, bounced beside Gallen, craning her neck for a sight of her son, Patrick. Looking at Billy, she stopped her bouncy act and stared at his black eye and swollen nose. 'You bin fightin', Coach?'

'Walked into the hotel door,' said Higgins as he slapped his goalie on the back, thanked him for a good job.

Having debriefed the players and returned the hockey equipment to the lockers under the Sheridan Ice stadium, Higgins put on his hat and walked with Gallen to the Dodge Ram, the two men lighting their smokes before they got the doors open. They picked up coffees from the Starbucks on Brundage and crossing I-90 onto US 14, Higgins took it easy as the outskirts of Sheridan fell away and then pushed the big diesel to seventy-five mph as the famous highway took them south into some of the best scenery in the world. The skies were slate-grey, flat light bouncing off the snow against the low cloud. It had been a mild start to winter, which to Wyoming farmers was simply a warning to keep the water running in their pipes.

'Your mom ever come back for Christmas?' said Billy Higgins as the one-thirty news finished and 'Green River' by Creedence started up on the radio.

It took Gallen by surprise. He'd been so lost in thoughts about Spikey Holmes and Jordan, and whether he'd take the retrieval gig, that he'd barely heard Billy leading up to that question.

'Umm,' he started, and lit a cigarette, cracked his window slightly, felt the cold December air cut through the smoke. 'That's a good question.'

'Sorry.' Billy took his coffee from the holder. 'None of my business.'

Gallen thought about it. 'No, actually—you guys grew up around Mom, so you have as much right as anyone to ask if she ever comes back.'

They watched the white valleys and iced-over rivers as the truck motored across the wet surface of one of the United States' original long-distance highways. The US 14 started at Yellowstone and ran eastwards to the outskirts of Chicago. Gallen remembered the weekend he drove this road with his father and brother Tom to see the Blackhawks play the Boston Bruins at the old Chicago Stadium. Roy got them second-tier seats—up there with the true hockey maniacs—and eleven-year-old Gerry Gallen was transfixed by a sport where the walls and bleachers shook from the noise of the fans. Walking back to their motel that night, a drunk from Chicago, seeing a Bruins cap on Gallen's head, had roughed with him, and when Roy had stepped in a fight started which Roy won very quickly.

Gerry remembered his mother sulking for a whole week after they returned on the Sunday night, her husband with a missing tooth, one son completely repulsed by the weekend of hockey and the other son wide-eyed with the wonder of it. Gallen's mother walked out on Roy four years later, but the damage was done years earlier.

'I used to go out to Hawaii for Christmas with Mom when Roy could afford it,' said Gallen. 'But she never came back to the farm, or to Clearmont.'

Higgins nodded, lit a cigarette. 'Was it something we said?'

Gallen laughed, feeling the tension unlock in his thighs. 'This life ain't for everyone, right? Mom gave it a shot, she just wanted more.'

'What more could you want?' said Higgins. 'Haul water in the winter, bale hay in the summer. Enough for most folks.'

'She weren't afraid of the work, she just . . . I don't know, she once told me she wanted to live in a place where you say "French mustard" and you're not talkin' about the bright yellow bottle.'

'Nothing wrong with French's, Ger.'

'No, Billy. Can't fault it.'

Higgins nodded, eyes on the road. 'You handled it well, Ger, 'cos I sure do miss my momma.'

Higgins' dad had died twenty years earlier in a round-baler accident, and his mom had passed from cancer the year before last. Higgins farmed alone, lived alone on the family property and had shut himself down to all but a handful of old high school friends. Gallen felt for him, but he didn't want to discuss his own mother.

'Mom and me—we get along good,' said Gallen, flicking the cigarette and closing his window. 'We're just not close.'

Higgins dropped him at Sweet Clover, the Gallen family farm on the Line Draw road outside of Clearmont. Kicking off his boots in the mud room, he made his way through the dusty two-storey place, past Roy's hoarse old dog and into the messy living room where Roy watched hockey on a big screen, eating baked beans in front of the wood-burner.

'Son,' said Roy, not looking up.

'Dad,' said Gallen, moving through to the kitchen.

'Bring me one, thanks,' yelled Roy before Gallen had even opened the refrigerator and reached for a beer.

Throwing his father a can of Blue Ribbon as he sat beside him on the sofa, Gallen stretched his legs and opened a can of his own. The NHL broke for a State Farm commercial and Roy turned to him, big hard jaw and smashed cheekbones fairly much as Gallen knew them as a child.

'Package came for you last night,' said Roy, licking a piece of bean from an incisor. 'From Sprint. Guess it's your new phone?'

'Hope so,' said Gallen, who'd been without his trusty Nokia since he'd dropped it in the well during the week.

'How'd your boys do?'

'Won by a goal,' said Gallen, slurping. 'That youngster McCain is going to college at South Dakota if that's what he wants.'

'Any fights?'

'Only in the car park,' said Gallen. 'Billy hammered Big Ern.'

'Hah!' said Roy, genuinely amused. 'Ern is living proof you cain't beat sense into a man.'

'Billy got 'im good,' said Gallen as the game returned, all organ pipes and the clash of sticks.

'Good for Billy.' Roy sucked on the beer and turned back to the screen.

'Carters pick up the hay?'

'Yep, at sun-up.'

'They pay you?'

'Only had five hunert.'

'And you let them walk for four?'

'Three fifty,' said Roy. 'Bank's bitching about the mortgage.'

Gallen let it go—Roy's attitude to money and farming was a little too elastic for his liking. 'I'll bring the cattle in first thing. The feeder's looking okay?'

'Ready to go, just like this game.' Roy pointed at the screen.

Leaving the warm room, Gallen went past Roy's study, where his Silver Star was hanging in its presentation case on the wall after Roy retrieved it from the trash. At the top of the stairs he turned right and into his childhood room that was now his adult room. Picking up the Sprint package from his bed, he tore the new phone out of its wrappings. It was a shiny new thing—an iPhone 4, according to the box—but Gallen would be happy if it made calls without hassle and kept its charge for more than a day. He pushed the SIM card into it and plugged it into the wall, deciding to do the set-up later.

Lying on the bed, letting his eye drift around the posters that had been left there from his high school days, he saw the obsessions of his youth: the red Chev Camaro; a poster for *Terminator 2: Judgment Day* and the promotional poster for the Suzuki RM250—the dream bike Gallen never got to own.

Rolling onto his belly, he fished under the bed, dragging out a small maple officer's chest he'd used in the Marines. He fished through the badges and ribbons he'd amassed between joining the

US Marines straight from high school and when he left at thirty-six. Stuck into a felt pad were his gold Combatant Diver breast insignia, a dull pewter Navy Parachutist badge and a Distinguished Marksman insignia. There were ribbons for combat tours and a set of his silver Captain bars.

Pulling out the felt pad, he lifted a package of black notebooks held together with a rubber band: his field notebooks from one tour of Mindanao and five of Afghanistan. Recon captains had to prepare detailed reports for the intel staff and they kept notebooks to keep track of details, events and notes along the way.

He rolled onto his back, pulled a notebook from the middle, flipped it over and fanned through the dirty, yellowed pages which still smelled of the spring thaw in the Kush. The handwriting was his, but from another time and place, almost like another person had written it; he recognised the fine black ballpoint lines as the hotel pen he took from the Aden Mercure during a two-day R&R which was supposed to be about drinking and womanising but mainly involved sleeping in and trying to work out what hurt him more: a winter in Peshawar or his wife leaving him for a dentist. It was a lost two days.

Finding the date on the top right of the page—3 March 2005—Gallén stared at what he'd written: *s.sgt Holmes saved unit with expert direct action. Secured large cache of IEDs bound for Kabul. Disrgd own safety. Men very happy—morale lifter! Recommend S. Star.*

The note went on, but Gallen felt his breath becoming laboured. He swigged at his beer, which refluxed. He remembered it all; his first report was handed back by an ambitious asshole called Major Anderson, who was jammed so far up an ambitious colonel's ass that he needed night-vision goggles to say hello. Anderson was nervous about war and terrified of the Afghanis; mostly he was scared for his own prospects. Anderson refused to have any recommendations for honours questioned by the board because of Spikey's reputation, and then have that query reflect on his own ambitions. So Major Anderson asked him to tone down the report and not make any waves.

It was a tough time for Gallen, with Marcia announcing the separation with a Dear John and some battle fatigue starting to mess with his personality. And what with one thing and another—and because Spikey Holmes was a tough black boxer from South Central who had no connections among the officers—Gallen went along with it. The second report made the incident sound like a routine stop and search, which ended in a shoot-out and luckily revealed the cache of IEDs. Spikey Holmes was written out of history.

Throwing the notebook across the room, Gallen rubbed his face in his hands. He'd chickened out when he should have told Anderson to shove his career up his ass. He'd let Spikey Holmes dangle—and he wasn't going to do it again.

CHAPTER 4

Grabbing his British Airways boarding pass, Gallen smirked when the girl asked him if he knew where the business-class lounge was at Denver International.

'That obvious is it?' he said, turning towards the coach class queues for BA, Air Canada and Lufthansa. Gerry Gallen may have been comped a business-class fare but he wasn't going to sit in a business-class lounge, just as he wasn't going to check his luggage.

Pushing through the families and their trolleys, he slung the leather overnight bag's strap across his shoulder and went in search of a coffee and sandwich. It was four-fifteen pm, enough time to wander the concourses and see whose eyes weren't so casual, see if he could pick a pattern. Some airports didn't feel like they had eyes—but Denver International did. It was set up for surveillance of the type Gallen was trained to do in civilian environments: every public transit area had a vantage point that looked down on it, and the natural light coming from the transparent ceilings discouraged people from looking upwards. He'd heard some of the conspiracy ideas about how Denver International was a front for an Illuminati plot, but the real creepiness of the airport was in how much everyone was allowed to see, rather than what was hidden. Denver International made a professional like Gallen feel like a rat in a maze, not like a traveller.

Finding a cafe on the mezzanine level, he ordered coffee and sat at a table for four, sipping and watching, face hidden beneath his Bruins cap. Growing up in northern Wyoming, with no local team to support in the NHL, most of his teenage friends had gravitated towards the Detroit Red Wings or the Chicago Blackhawks, but Gallen had gone for his old man's team, the Boston Bruins, which meant Bobby Orr and Terry O'Reilly. Like many things in his life, it was an old habit that he stuck to without much questioning.

There were businessmen and corporate women all around him, tapping on keyboards and speaking too loud into their BlackBerries, a little self-consciously in Gallen's opinion. Old Roy used to say that a man who talked too much ain't thinking enough, and that bit of wisdom had stuck with Gallen.

He scanned the faces, watched for gait and walked himself through the arrangements he'd been given once he told Daly he was in. He was staying at the Amman Ibis where a work-up pack awaited him, complete with details of where to find Spikey and suggested ways to exit Jordan with him. There was also a Columbus Enterprises credit card waiting for him in his room and the first five days' pay sitting in his bank account—a promise that Gallen had checked at an ATM as he drove through Casper.

He fished in his windbreaker pocket and dragged out the new phone. On the drive down from Wyoming he'd wrestled with the design of the thing, and placed calls to his first choice of crew, but no one had answered.

All he had for Kenny Winter, a Canadian veteran of the Ghan, was an old cell number, but Winter hadn't customised the voicemail so Gallen couldn't tell who he was leaving a message for. The other was an Aussie former navy special forces operator, Mike Ford. The only contact Gallen had for Ford was a Honolulu dive operation—Molokai Ocean Salvage—where the Aussie spent most of his post-military time. His first call, driving south in the truck, had been made too early, since Hawaii was three hours behind Wyoming and Colorado. Now he tried again.

The phone at the other end rang four times and was answered by a sweet-sounding woman.

'Hello, ma'am, could I speak to Mike Ford, please?' said Gallen, lungs wanting to smoke. 'It's Gerry Gallen.'

There was a pause. 'Sorry, sir, Mr Ford no longer works at Molokai Ocean Salvage.'

The girl didn't sound too certain so Gallen pushed. 'Is he still in Hawaii? This is pretty urgent.'

'Umm, I can't really give out that information.'

'Yeah, yeah, I get that,' said Gallen. 'Can I leave a message? Is there someone there who knows him?'

'Okay,' said the woman in a comical whisper. 'You give me your number and I'll tell him, okay?'

'You will?' said Gallen. 'Ma'am, I need this message to get through.'

'I'll tell him,' said the girl. 'What's your number?'

Gallen gave her his number and disconnected, wondering what Mike Ford was up to and the odds of him being interested in a gig in Jordan. And he wondered if the international roaming was going to work as well as the Mumbai call centre worker told him it would before he left the farm.

He tried Kenny Winter's number again. It went to the generic voicemail and as he sat back and wondered who he could get to replace either of his crew, a throat cleared beside him.

Looking up, he saw two men in dark suits. One of them—a skinny white guy—had his hands on his hips in a dominance pose and the other one, an athletic black male, crossed his hands at his crotch, making ex-jock muscles bulge through the Brooks Brothers suit. The white guy wore sunglasses inside, which given the tent-like roof of the terminal was technically okay from a daylight perspective, although it made him look a little desperate for respect.

'Gerard Gallen?' said the man wearing sunglasses, showing some chewing gum.

Gallen looked at each man and settled on Mr Sunglasses. 'I'm assuming that's not a real question.'

'Sorry?' Sunglasses leaned forwards facetiously.

'You know my name, so why ask?' said Gallen.

'Oh,' said Sunglasses, turning to his colleague. 'We have a comedian.'

'For laughs I can't compete with that belt buckle.' Gallen turned back to his coffee.

'Belt? What did you . . .'

From the corner of his eye he watched the black dude calm his colleague.

'Your buckle doesn't go with that shirt,' said Gallen, feigning amusement while he tried to assess these people. They looked official and they carried handguns in right-side hip rigs.

'Oh, really?' said Sunglasses with a sneer. 'And some redneck with elbow patches is going to give me fashion tips?'

Gallen looked down at the left elbow of his old Tough Duck, patched by Mrs Higgins before she passed. 'Thought you could hardly notice.'

'Looks like shit.'

Gallen shrugged, smiled. 'Guess that makes us even, with the belt buckle 'n' all.'

Sunglasses leaned his knuckles on the table, giving Gallen some face. 'Let's just say I ask some questions and you provide some answers, eh, Mr Gallen?'

'Okay.' Gallen felt the man's breaking point coming nearer. 'If you're asking about those Mentos, the answer is—go back to Tic-Tacs.'

The black dude tried to stop his offsider lunging but it was too late and the thin guy's right hand made it to Gallen's shirtfront. Which was too bad, because Gallen was waiting for that and, grabbing the fingers, he pushed them towards the inside of the man's forearm, stabilised the wrist with his other hand in a classic Korean wristlock and pushed down to the ground. The man in sunglasses gasped and went straight to his knees in front of Gallen, who remained seated. The black guy thought about going for the handgun in his hip rig, but decided against it.

'I'm not going to kill him,' said Gallen with a smile, calming the situation. 'Just defending myself against an assault by a man with a firearm. Okay?'

Annoyed, the black man nodded briefly, looking around in professional scans, maybe not wanting his back-up team seeing this cluster.

'Hurts, don't it?' Gallen kept his voice low as he turned back to his assailant, whose face was a rictus of pain.

'Yep.'

'What's your name?'

'Jim.'

'Been following me, Jim?'

Jim nodded, in too much pain to speak.

'So what's going on, Jim? You walk up with your weapon hanging on your belt, give me shit and then grab me?'

'Sorry,' hissed Jim through white lips.

'Ready to talk like grown-ups?'

Jim nodded vigorously and Gallen let him go.

Jim stood slowly and wiped his forehead with a sleeve. Gesturing to his colleague, he sat at the table, gulping slightly as his breathing normalised.

Gallen sipped his coffee. 'So, what can I do for you gentlemen?'

'Special Agent Jim Barrowman, FBI,' said Jim, gesturing at his own chest. 'This is Special Agent Matt Cole.'

'Pleased to meet you.'

The FBI men swapped glances.

'Where are you off to today, Mr Gallen?'

'Jordan, via London.'

Barrowman paused. 'What's happening in Jordan?'

'I hear it's a nice place for an American citizen to exercise his right to travel wherever he wants to without the government wanting to know.'

'You're not helping, Mr Gallen.'

'My job is to do my job, not to do your job.'

Barrowman sagged back in his chair. 'For a decorated soldier you sure are a smart-ass.'

Gallen shut his mouth, looked around the mezzanine.

'Okay, Mr Gallen,' said Barrowman, sitting up again. 'You're flying into Amman?'

'Yep.'

'Why?'

'My sinuses.'

'Don't fuck with me.'

'Cheap cigarettes.'

'I'm warning you!'

31

Gallen smiled. 'Why don't you start by telling me your story?'

'We work on Middle East terror funding,' said Special Agent Cole, changing the tone. 'Money into cells in the US; money from the US into the Middle East.'

Gallen nodded.

'We work with Homeland, Defense and Treasury—try to work out why the money's moving, who's getting it and for what.'

'Fair enough,' said Gallen, preferring Cole's style. 'So where do I fit in?'

Cole stared into him. 'You know Ahmed al-Haq?'

'No.'

'Never heard that name?'

'Like I said. What's this about?'

Barrowman interjected. 'Thing is, Gallen, you don't know al-Haq, but he sure as shit knows you.'

Gallen's mind roared. 'Who the fuck is Ahmed al-Haq?'

'Big-time money launderer and private banker for some very bad Arabs,' said Barrowman, enjoying himself. 'Works out of Detroit.'

'What's that got to do with me?'

Barrowman smiled. 'This morning he cabled an associate in Beirut, telling him that you're on your way.'

'To where?'

'Into Amman via London, originating Denver.'

'Why would he do that?' said Gallen, confused.

Jim Barrowman smiled like a lizard. 'I guess you're about to find out.'

CHAPTER 5

The bus from Heathrow's Terminal 5 arrived six minutes after Gallen lined up at the kerb. He let the thirty other passengers get on before him, keeping his eyes to himself in the morning sleet that raked London's most dismal yet popular landmark. He hadn't slept on the flight from Denver, thinking about who or what was waiting for him in Amman. Now he wanted to change a few things, the entry point to Jordan foremost among them.

The bus dropped them at the security apron of Terminal 3 and, allowing the other passengers to walk in front of him and up the escalators, Gallen looked for the Royal Jordanian desks. The transfer from T5 to T3 was a controlled transit as per international agreements of customs and immigration, and Gallen knew that if he wanted to rebook on a different airline to a destination outside of Jordan, he'd be forced to enter United Kingdom territory and therefore go through the customs, immigration and security gates. In his last gig there had been problems with his passport and he didn't want delays again.

The woman behind the desk dealt patiently with the passengers and after thirteen minutes Gallen was in front of her, cap in his hand.

'I just had a good look at my ticket,' said Gallen, slow as you like. 'They booked me into Amman—but I'm supposed to be in Aqaba. Is there anything we can do?'

The woman was a young and beautiful Jordanian, who gave nothing away as she asked for his ticket and passport.

'You're lucky—the Aqaba flight leaves at around the same time as the Amman flight,' she said, tapping on her keyboard. 'But when you change a ticket in transit, you're supposed to go out into the public concourse and buy another one, then come back in. So you have to clear customs and immigration.'

'I know,' said Gallen, slumping. 'But it's still Jordan and it's the same airline.'

The woman looked at Gallen with liquid dark eyes. 'We have seats in business, Mr Gallen, but I'll have to get this cleared, okay?'

Gallen's heart beat hard in his chest as he took a seat and waited. Dark suits mingled with ghutras and Arab women in brightly coloured crushed silk accompanied women in long black sacks. People milled and there were too many eyes on him: he hadn't dressed properly for business class and now he'd made himself stand out even more with a strange request. He was getting soft—this wasn't how he was taught to travel as part of his intelligence training, where the anonymous guy was the one telling stories at the bar and the hero was worm-food.

On the television set in the departure lounge he could see CNN's coverage of another truck bomb in a Baghdad souk, and the body language of the Arab travellers watching it. In a bar in Wyoming, it was about US soldiers and the price of oil; in the departure lounge for Royal Jordanian, they watched their culture being torn apart.

A middle-aged Arab with receding hair and a moustache walked to Gallen's check-in girl and his gaze was soon levelling on Gallen. Moving away from her, the man inclined his head and smiled and Gallen got to his feet, went to the counter.

'Mr Gallen, my associate says you're aware of the transit rules?'

'Sure,' said Gallen, looking at the man's name tag. 'Thing is, Hassan—I didn't book the ticket. I'm still going to Jordan, but it should be Aqaba.'

Hassan looked through him like he was a pane of glass and Gallen held the stare. 'What kind of business are you in, exactly, Mr Gallen?'

'I'm a farmer,' said Gallen. 'Cattle, northern Wyoming.'

'Ah,' said Hassan, displaying some good teeth. 'Jackson Hole, right? My daughter is at the UCLA, and she goes skiing in Jackson Hole for the—how you say—winter holiday?'

'Winter break,' said Gallen. 'Jackson's a few hours away by car, but yeah, that's my country.'

Hassan looked away, bit his lip. 'It may not be so perfect in Afghanistan, yes? But at least you tried.'

'Well . . .' started Gallen, before catching a half-smile from Hassan, suggesting he was about to get a lecture about being an American. But Hassan's smile turned real and then he was holding out a Royal Jordanian flight folder. Gallen checked it, found a new ticket and boarding pass for the Aqaba flight.

'The world is not a perfect place, Mr Gerry, but we need our idealists.'

Gallen waited for the smile to become a sneer, the way so many Arab men were brought up to do. But the sneer didn't come.

'Thanks,' said Gallen.

'Enjoy Aqaba,' said Hassan. 'The farms should be to your liking.'

The Royal Jordanian Airbus pitched over slightly and an English accent told the passengers they were about to begin their descent into Aqaba. Snapping out of his half-sleep, Gallen reached for the water bottle he had stashed, and then thought better of it. He'd dozed and anyone could have tampered with the bottle. Standing, he took his leather overnight bag out of the overhead and made for the toilet. Taking a seat, he rummaged through the clothing compartment and then the toilet bag he'd packed. The words of the FBI agents in Denver had ruined any chance he was going to have of an anxiety-free trip. Seeing nothing amiss he returned to his seat and asked the stewardess for another bottle of water. Then he shut his eyes and tried to relax: he was not, he reminded himself, in the field anymore.

The dry air tore at his lungs as he walked down the stairs and across the floodlit tarmac towards the terminal. It was 11.14 pm by his G-Shock and bugs swirled in the columns of light.

Making straight for the customs and immigration stations, Gallen walked through quickly, his paperwork in order and his bag small enough to attract no attention. There was a cell phone kiosk in the terminal. Gallen bought a cheap Motorola with a pre-paid card. He scanned for eyes as he waited for a taxi, the queue annoying him: at a foreign airport he didn't like the taxi driver choosing him—he preferred to choose them.

Gallen was feeling jumpy by the time the Toyota minivan stopped beside him and a keen young man named Davi leapt out to help him with his bag. Gallen sat in the back and asked for the best local hotel in Aqaba—not a Marriott or Holiday Inn. They went through some of the names as they drove into the ancient city, moths and bugs swirling in the coppery light against profiles of minarets and sandstone walls. When Davi hit on the Aqaba Gulf Hotel, Gallen told him to drive there.

At the hotel, he paid off Davi then, blinking dust out of his eyes, walked up the stone steps and into the late-1960s foyer. As the heavy glass doors slid open, he turned back to the minivan and gave a quick smile. Gallen's heart was starting to pound slightly; he was getting the jitters about the driver and the ease with which he allowed the foreigner to nominate the hotel. Arab cabbies had arrangements with the hotels that made driving cabs worth their while, but Davi had gone along with the Gulf without even warning about the size of the rats or how many of the maids were thieves.

The desk clerk smiled, eyes tired. 'Good evening, sir.'

'Evenin',' said Gallen. 'I need two rooms—one on the ground floor, that's for my mother-in-law. She hates heights.'

'Okay,' said the clerk, bringing up a screen.

'And I'd like something as far away from her as possible,' said Gallen, winking. 'That possible?'

The clerk smiled, his long tan face revealing a bright set of choppers. 'I understand perfectly, sir.'

'And for my taxes, let's have my room in my name and the mother-in-law's under "Mrs Smith".'

Taking both sets of keycards, Gallen watched where the clerk indicated his rooms on the hotel map and set off for the elevators, heading for his room on the sixth floor. In the elevator he pushed 'M' and got off at the mezzanine level, where the reception rooms were, the air buzzing with the hiss of a sleeping hotel. Walking the length of the mezzanine, he found the fire exit and descended, emerging at the far end of the swimming pool. An Italian couple in their late twenties splashed and giggled in the sapphire pool as Gallen closed the door to the fire exit and waited in the shadows.

Controlling his breathing he scanned the layout: low bushes in front of him, a dried-tree fence surrounding the pool, the tower block of the main hotel looming above and a building pushing out from the tower block to his right which looked like the foyer and turning into something advertised as the 'Gulf Snack Bar', adjacent to a covered eating area at the other end of the pool.

Stalking around the pool, in the shadows, he made it to the covered area at the end as the cavorting Italians got out and ran to their room. Gallen surveyed the ground: the room in Mrs Smith's name looked out on the swimming pool and there was no one in the shadows or behind the trees. Taking a seat, he realised he could also see into the foyer and to the area in front of the desk. It was empty.

He stayed silent for ten minutes, smoking duty-free Marlboros and observing the coffin-shaped pool, developing a feel for the place. In his career he'd spent thousands of hours doing this: creating an OP—an observation post—and waiting for the convoy to come through, for the HVT to arrive at the depot or for the HiLux load of guns to arrive at the souk. That's what recon was: waiting, documenting and reporting. The other tasking that they made the movies about—direct actions—was a much smaller part of the true special forces community, and US Marines Force Recon was no different. The truth of it was that military intelligence found the shoot-'em-up troops annoying and counterproductive. They preferred what Gallen had trained for and provided as a Force Recon captain: the capture and retrieval of illicit field intelligence, to order and on time.

He stood and entered the tower block, using the keycard to enter Mrs Smith's room on the ground floor. Checking the room, he turned off the lights and let the ambient illumination from the pool light the good-sized room.

Opening the cheap Motorola phone, he programmed his own number into it and rang himself. Hanging up as soon as there was a connection, he slipped out into the hallway, checking both ways before heading for the stairwell again. He was sweating as he got to his room. Ear against the door, he listened. It sounded empty, so he slipped the key in the slot and let himself in.

The room was exactly the same as the one on the ground floor. Checking the wardrobe, Gallen pulled an ironing board from it and laid it on the carpet, its blunt end towards the door. He pushed the legs up against the wall behind the arc of the door and then placed the phone's back sideways against the skirting board, its 'call' button leaning on one of the ironing board's legs. Pushing the door back and forth in a trial run, he was satisfied that when the door was opened, it would push the ironing board's leg against the phone hard enough to make it call the 'last number dialled'.

Gallen padded back to the elevators and went to the ground floor, letting himself back into Mrs Smith's room. He would have loved a shower, but he didn't want the distraction. Instead, he found a can of Miller GD in the fridge and opened it with a reassuring hiss. Sitting in the shadows, the pool casting a strange dappled light across the ceiling, Gallen sipped and pondered what the hell he was going to do. A bunch of Arab money launderers from Detroit were awaiting his arrival in Amman and he'd been unable to contact his preferred crew. He was in the wrong city and still a hundred and twenty miles from Spikey Holmes.

In the morning he'd have to get his work-up pack and credit card from the Ibis in Amman and he'd have to do it without being caught. But that was in the future. Right now he wanted to get some sleep without a visit from unfriendly locals. He mulled it over and was satisfied he hadn't imagined it: the taxi driver had a little Koran on the dashboard, sitting on its own little crocheted mat. He also wore a kufi, the little white skullcap. As far as the Arab world went, Davi was advertising the fact he was pious. And while modern Islam had certain accommodations, the Prophet was very clear on men and jewellery: they don't mix.

So why, thought Gallen, did Davi have an earring in his left ear?

He sipped again and decided to keep his boots on.

CHAPTER 6

Gallen woke and for three seconds didn't know where he was. He was lying on a double bed in the dark, a light flashing slightly brighter than the pool dapples and a buzzing beside his left ear. Turning he saw the iPhone skipping across the bedside table, its screen blasting white light on the ceiling.

'Yep,' he whispered as he pressed the green button, expecting to hear shuffling sounds from a set of boots as whoever worked with Davi pushed into his room on the sixth floor. He propped on his elbow and froze, wanting to hear every nuance. Gallen didn't like being tailed or watched and he was prepared to send a very strong message to whoever needed telling.

'Gerry?' said the male voice, in good English.

Gallen breathed through his nostrils feeling his pulse bang in his neck, waiting for more.

'Gerry, that you?' said the man at the end of the phone, his accent American. 'Gerry Gallen?'

Slumping back on the bed, he looked at his watch and matched a name to the voice. 'Kenny?'

'You called,' said Kenny Winter. 'You broke?'

Gallen laughed, wished he could smoke in his room. 'I'm a soldier who became a farmer—broke about covers it.'

'Where you at?' came the slow, deep voice of his former colleague, a man who'd played pro hockey and fought in Afghanistan.

'Can't say,' said Gallen, sitting up and running a hand through his short hair.

Winter hawked and spat. 'You lost?'

'No, I'm compromised.'

'Need help?'

Gallen stood, walked to the window. 'Well, maybe. But more like I'm offering you a gig.'

There was silence on the other end of the line. Winter had done a lot of assassination work for ISAF and the CIA during his time in Afghanistan and he'd retired with his own pension stash. He didn't need to work, but he might want to.

Gallen tried the window but it wouldn't open. 'Thousand a day, full insurance cover.'

Winter sucked on a smoke, exhaled. 'How you been, Gerry?'

'Fit,' said Gallen. 'You?'

'Got access to my boys, so I bin busy. You remember my hometown?'

Gallen thought about it. 'Yeah, I do.'

'That's my Skype, if you wanna get off the air.'

Gallen figured it was just past five in the afternoon if Winter was on his home turf of Saskatchewan. 'Gimme ten minutes,' said Gallen, hanging up.

Making for the bathroom, he washed his face in cold water and slapped himself twice to make the blood run into his head. He was exhausted and jetlagged but he wanted to stay alert, so he grabbed a bottle of water and his iPhone headphones as he slipped out.

The hallway was hot and airless compared with his air-conditioned room and he felt a headache coming on as he walked the dark carpet towards the business centre, located above the reception area, at one end of the mezzanine. It was shut down and he peered through the windows; the place was dead, none of the computers switched on. Trying the door, he pushed through into the darkness.

He found a computer with a cubicle divider in front of it, hoping not to project too much light and be disturbed by security. Powering up the black machine he watched a Windows system announce itself

40

before showing him a desktop with a Skype icon on it. Gallen double clicked then entered his user name and password. Guessing that Kenny Winter was talking about his home town of Maple Creek, Gallen input it as one word into the search box and a list of possible matches came up. One claimed he came from Baker Lake, which was a reference to a gig they'd done together. Deciding it must be Winter having a joke, Gallen clicked for a phone call and plugged in his headphones.

The weird ringing sounded for a few seconds and then Kenny Winter was on the line.

'Being followed?'

'Think so.' Gallen tried to keep his voice down.

'Where are you?'

Gallen laughed. 'I'll tell you when you say yes.'

'What's the gig?'

'High-Value Target, wanted back in LA,' said Gallen. 'He's surrounded by unfriendlies, too scared to move.'

'HVT a snatch, or a friendly?'

'Friendly,' said Gallen. 'Least, he will be with me.'

'Why?'

'We served together, he made me look good.'

'You owe him, huh?' sighed Winter. 'Why can't old soldiers just let this shit go?'

''Cos then we'd be old accountants,' said Gallen.

Silence held between them and Gallen could sense a man wanting to slip back into the suburbs but not being able to change who he was. Something occurred to him. 'You shacked up, Kenny? That it?'

'Fuck,' said Winter. 'That obvious?'

'Only when you change your tampon.'

Gallen heard a shriek and a belly laugh booming down the line. 'Shit, boss, I sure missed you.'

'Shouldn't be longer than a week—twenty grand delivery bonus split three ways.'

'Three?'

'Looking for Mike—got any ideas?'

'Ford?'

'Yep.'

'Working salvage out of Honolulu.'

Gallen told him what he knew. 'I'd like to have three on this, considering the ground.'

'Where you at?' said Winter.

'Aqaba.'

'Jordan?'

'Yep.'

'We got any weapons?'

'I'm working on it,' said Gallen.

'Got an exit?'

'I'm working on it,' said Gallen. 'So, you comin'?'

'You're in trouble, aintcha?'

'Looks that way.'

'I'll be there touts.'

Unplugging the headphones, Gallen listened for noises and switched off the computer. Standing in the dark room, he shoved the headphones into his right pocket. As he pulled his hand away he realised the screen of the iPhone was illuminated. Holding it up, he saw someone had called him while he'd been speaking to Winter and he hadn't heard the alert.

Opening the messages folder it said he had one missed call. He didn't need to dial for voicemail. There was none. The number that had called him was the one belonging to the Motorola he'd jammed against the ironing board on the sixth floor.

His watchers were in the building.

The door hinges had been oiled lately, Gallen noticed as he got the sixth-floor fire stairs door open one inch. The door to his room was closed and there was no movement. As he was thinking of walking into the hallway, the familiar sound of the elevator 'ping' rang out and he could see at least two sets of shoe heels disappearing into the opening doors.

Shutting the fire door, Gallen skipped down the stairs three at a time, trying to remain silent enough that security didn't send someone out to see about the commotion in the stairwell. He was panting and sweating as he reached the ground-floor fire door. Gulping for breath, he opened it slowly and recoiled from the brightness of the gold- and marble-lined lobby.

He looked across the lobby and couldn't see past a small abutment. Swallowing hard as sweat ran off his forehead onto his lip, he heard the ping of the elevator and a hiss of doors opening. One of his visitors wore rubber-soled shoes; Gallen could hear them squeaking across the marble floor as the doors slid open and the sounds of the night rushed into the lobby.

Thinking fast, Gallen realised he had a choice. Because he had no weapon, he could let them go and count himself lucky; or he could do as he'd been trained to do in the Corps: make the recon, get the intelligence, make it easier for someone to plan a next move. As the doors shut again, Gallen decided he'd have to find out who'd sent Davi the driver and who wanted to visit him at almost three am in Aqaba. He didn't know anyone in Aqaba—it was hardly a friendly visit.

Pushing out of his hide, Gallen padded into the lobby and along the wall that turned into the front desk, giving him the best angle to stay hidden from the men if they were waiting on the front steps. There was no one at the desk as he walked by in his boots and jeans, eyes peeled on the blackness of the sliding front doors.

Moving to the side of the doors, where he was concealed by a big ficus pot plant, he pushed his face against the glass to cut out the reflection. Across the set-down area, out in the dusty palm-lined boulevard of King Hussein Street, two athletic men circled a white Toyota and made to get in. Beyond them the Red Sea glinted in the half moonlight and the lights of Eilat—on the Israel side of the Gulf of Aqaba—glowed yellow.

Running to the door, Gallen tried to keep his eyes on the two men as they launched sideways into the car and slammed their doors. Outside, he sprinted along the inside of the set-down area to a point where he could hide behind a palm and collect the registration of the Toyota. Committing the rego to memory—an old habit from his Force Recon days—he realised the car hadn't started and the lights hadn't been switched on. Then he saw it. On the other side of the avenue, an arm extended from the open window of a black SUV. The hand was pointed at Gallen. As he assessed his chances of disappearing back into the hotel, the men in the Toyota were turning their faces to him and the doors of the car opened.

Backing up from his hide behind the palm tree, Gallen turned for the hotel entrance, but the black SUV had come to life and squealed across the light traffic in a wide U-turn for the set-down area, heading off Gallen's escape.

The men from the Toyota closed on him and Gallen decided to take them first and then deal with the SUV. Looking around for a weapon, he saw a dead branch in the palm tree above him that hadn't fallen to the ground. Leaping slightly, he caught hold of it and pulled, the eight-foot length of the branch coming free in his hands. He could hear the Arabic chatter of the men coming across the hotel's lawn and the area around him became bathed in headlamps as the SUV stopped with a squeal of brakes.

Putting one foot on the dead palm leaves, Gallen pulled up on the branch and tore the foliage loose, the branch making a heavy club in his hands. There was a tree and some shrubs in front of him and he crouched into them as the men got closer. Something he'd learned in the jungles of Basilan Island was that darkness ruined depth perception around foliage and by moving forwards at an adversary you could confuse their timing.

Running at a crouch through the chest-high shrubs, Gallen aimed at the man on his right—the one in the white polo shirt from the passenger seat. The man moved too confidently, too upright to be truly focused, and this was the one Gallen would take unawares. If he could disarm the man, the fight would even up. The men slowed to surround the palm tree and its shrubs, but Gallen continued to run, bursting out of his cover at the man in the white shirt, surprising him. As the man turned to face him, Gallen realised he had no firearm. He drove the branch tip-first at the man's throat, lifting him off his feet. Gallen swivelled his hips, readying to swing the palm branch to his left. Turning with the arc of the branch he saw the second man—a large Arab in a dark red business shirt—reaching for a holster on his right hip.

'No,' said the man, but it was too late. The palm branch hit him in the side of the head, too fast for his rising left-hand block. Staggering backwards the man in red looked up in terror as Gallen leapt on him, grabbing the gun wrist and wrenching it back as they hit the lawn.

Using the momentum of the tackle to roll him over, Gallen threw a fast elbow into the man's forehead, stunning him, and simultaneously reached for the hip holster. Panting like an animal, Gallen tore out the pistol and turned back to cover the SUV.

'We done?' came an American voice from the set-down area.

Gulping for oxygen, Gallen looked down at the handgun. It was a Motorola walkie-talkie handset.

'Shit,' he said to himself, looking at the two groaning shapes on the lawn around him.

'One way of sayin' it,' said the man from the SUV, stepping onto the lawn.

'Daly?' Gallen squinted into the hotel lights.

'You bin drinkin'?' said Daly, putting a smoke between his teeth. 'Look like shit, Gerry.'

CHAPTER 7

Twenty minutes out of Aqaba, Gallen pointed to a Jopetrol gas station in the dust and rubble at the side of the road.

'Can we?'

Daly pulled the silver Toyota Land Cruiser into the forecourt, said he'd tank.

Wandering inside out of the hundred-and-ten-degree heat, Gallen went for the small rack of sunglasses beside the cash register, tried on a set of wraparounds and paid for them in Jordanian dinars. He'd forgotten to bring his sunglasses and he felt a headache coming on from all the squinting. Making for the toilet out the back, he pulled out his iPhone and sent a simple text—*Amman Ibis*—to Kenny Winter. He had agreed to the gig on the basis that he'd be running his own crew, but now he had Daly assuming leadership and Daly's sidekick, an Arab called Adib, along for the ride.

Daly was paying for the gas when Gallen came out, the atmosphere between the two men still testy.

'Sprite okay?' Daly pointed to the cans in front of him.

'Sprite's good,' said Gallen, grabbing the cans and heading back to the Land Cruiser.

They drove north to Amman on Highway 65, thankful for the air-conditioning, listening to a Michael Jackson CD. The events of the night before had been an embarrassment. Gallen had overreacted, become paranoid, and put that poor sucker on the ground with a whack to the throat. The other man Gallen had attacked outside the Gulf Hotel was sitting in the back, arguing with his wife on a cell phone. His name was Adib, and the former Syrian intelligence officer's linebacker frame would have made Gallen hesitate if he hadn't been hyped on adrenaline and fear.

Adib finished the call.

'Okay there, buddy?' said Daly, smiling in the rear-view mirror. 'Still got an ear?'

'Life could be fine if I do just what she say,' said Adib.

Turning to face the big man, Gallen saw the black eye and butterfly clips across his left eyebrow. 'Sorry about the misunderstanding. I was tired, reacted badly.'

Adib shrugged, a small smile erupting from his big round head. 'Hit by a palm tree—my first time ever.'

As they passed a brown tourist sign advertising the site of baptism, Gallen groaned.

'Got a problem?' said Daly, lighting a new smoke. 'With John, I mean?'

'No,' said Gallen, reaching for one of Daly's smokes. 'Just, wherever I look I'm seein' billboards of my Sunday school career.'

'Hah,' said Daly, who'd pointed out a turn off to a King Solomon landmark. 'You too?'

Gallen sucked on the smoke, looked out at the passing desert.

'Wasn't tailin' you, Gerry,' said Daly after an awkward pause. 'Just worried about you.'

'Just checking on me?'

'I put out feelers, man,' said Daly. 'Like I said back at the Gulf, I got braced by them FBI agents and the alarm bells rang. I couldn't raise you on the phone, you weren't at the Ibis and when I checked through Adib, I found out you were landing in Aqaba.'

'Davi? The taxi driver?'

'My fault.' Adib leaned between the two front seats. 'Davi works for me, in the old times and now too. I ask him to keep eyes on you, tell us where you stay.'

Gallen turned to Daly. 'So you hit my room?'

'Night manager wouldn't put through a call at two in the morning,' said Daly, frustrated. 'But, shit, man—why'm I asking you to believe me? You the one flew into the wrong city, started with all the Rambo bullshit. I was tryin' to look out for you.'

'Didn't want to fly into Amman,' said Gallen, who'd almost turned and walked to the nearest airport on three occasions, his paranoia about Daly and Chase Lang and this whole Middle East snafu growing. 'Not after what the FBI said.'

'Then you made the taxi driver?' said Daly. 'How'd you know he was ours?'

'Didn't know,' said Gallen, finishing the smoke and flicking it out a cracked window. ''Cept no devout Muslim man wears an earring, right, Adib?'

'Mohammed says no to men dressing like lady,' said Adib. 'That mean the earring too.'

'Really?' said Daly. 'Must have missed that culture session.'

'So, this gig still on?' said Gallen, looking at Daly.

'Ain't goin' to Amman for no holiday.'

'What about this al-Haq in Detroit?'

'What about him?'

Gallen let his neck go soft, rolled it a few times to stay relaxed. 'He knew where I was going, and he cabled into Beirut to alert his associates to my arrival.'

'The FBI claimed that, sure,' said Daly. 'Don't make it so. Might be they're messing with us for other reasons.'

'Other reasons?' said Gallen, unconvinced. 'You heard of al-Haq?'

'Mr Lang has.'

'And?'

'And al-Haq is not exactly a terrorist.'

'No?'

'He's a businessman,' said Daly. 'An associate of Khashoggi, did things for Arafat, worked for Iraqi intelligence for years out of Lebanon and Jordan. Tell 'im, Adib.'

'Al-Haq,' said the big Syrian, as if thinking about a good wine. 'He has the official life as the banker for Arafat and the emissary for Saddam. But he also the financier for the terrorist.'

'Emissary for Saddam?'

'I'm thinking Kofi Annan called him this,' said Adib, thoughtful. 'But perhaps not your CIA or Pentagon, yes?'

Gallen snorted. 'So, one of Saddam's spooks has ears in Chase Lang's office? Why would . . .?'

Daly bit his bottom lip and something clicked for Gallen.

'Shit, Chase ain't the only person after Spikey, that it?'

Daly sucked on the last of his smoke, flicked it out the window and grabbed at his Sprite. 'We're on a clock, Gerry. Spoke with Mr Lang this mornin' and we've got til midday tomorrow to lift Spikey.'

'So, it's a lift now?' said Gallen, slightly too snappy. He was annoyed at the rush and the intel leaks and now the story was being subtly changed. 'What happened to Spikey wanting to get back to LA? I thought we had a cooperative target?'

'I told you, Gerry—the man's not well. You two kiss and make up, and we get him on the plane, then I'm good. But he starts swingin', doin' all that Compton hard-boy act, and he travels in a hood and straitjacket, get my drift?'

'*We?*' said Gallen. 'You say *we*? This is my gig, Daly. I don't get managed.'

'Think I like this?' said Daly. 'We got till midday and you hidin' out in Aqaba, no crew, no vehicle, no weapons, no contact with Spikey.'

'Yeah, well Chase changed the game,' said Gallen.

'Understand something,' said Daly, taking an off ramp to Amman. 'Chase Lang *is* the game.'

Gallen surveyed the ancient skyline of Amman as the afternoon light bathed the sandstone buildings in gold. He was on the top floor of the Grand Hyatt, listening to the murmurs of Daly talking behind the closed door of the master suite while Adib caught the five o'clock news on Al Jazeera.

The suite was enormous, containing three bedrooms and three bathrooms. It was a cut above the Ibis and Gallen was secretly glad that they'd cased the first choice of hotel and been spooked by the black Lincoln Navigator parked across the road from the set-down area.

Defaulting to the Grand Hyatt with Daly's alternative passport and Visa card made Gallen comfortable that at least he'd get some sleep. But he wasn't comfortable about the Navigator: its thick, short aerials reminded him of something. He couldn't place it. He was exhausted and on edge about the new deadline and the appearance of Daly and Adib. He didn't like timelines and personnel changing—people got hurt with too much of that. And while Syrian intelligence had as good a reputation as any in the region, he didn't know Adib and had never worked with him. He pulled a can of Coke from the bar fridge as Daly emerged.

'Just remembered,' said Gallen. 'My work-up pack is at the Ibis.'

'Don't worry about it,' said Daly, nodding at Adib. 'Let's go through it.'

Sitting at the large dining table, Daly took a satchel from Adib and unfolded a tourist map of Amman, plunging a finger into the cat's cradle of streets that spread across the ancient city of hills.

'Al Hashimi Street,' said Daly, lighting a smoke. 'You know it?'

'Walked down it once, six or seven years ago. Went to a Roman theatre. That close?'

'Here,' said Daly, pointing to one end of Hashimi. 'Al Hashimi is the proverbial Arab street; if some reporter on CNN wants to tell you he knows the vibe of the Middle East, he stands in Hashimi and tells everyone what they think. It's loud, it's crowded, it's Arab.'

'I remember,' said Gallen. 'Chased a couple of bag snatchers who were harassing a Japanese couple.'

'Hashimi Street is where criminals go to disappear,' said Daly. 'There's a strong police and intel presence because of the tourists, but you get into the laneways and alleys, and it's run by old Hamas commanders.'

Adib cleared his throat. 'Amman was once head office of Hamas for the whole world. If we want to know where the next bombing or assassination was to be, we had to have our informers. Hashimi informers was one time a good career.'

'Okay.' Gallen turned to Daly. 'So where's Spikey?'

'Spikey's here.' Daly pointed to a slight bend in the road and then reached for a stack of black and white photographs. 'He's in a place called the Araby Castle Hotel.'

Gallen took the proffered photos. They showed what Americans understood to be a 'local's hotel'. About five floors, bland concrete front, old neon sign in Roman and Arabic. Gents sitting on picnic chairs out the front, smoking; people loitering; a sinister compound at the back, spilling onto a rear laneway that Jesus might have walked down.

'Charming.' Gallen peered closer. 'Video surveillance?'

'One camera above the reception desk inside; one wide-angle over the compound in back.'

'Spikey's room?'

'Three-oh-eight. North end of the third floor, beside the fire stairs. One mortice lock in a steel door.'

'Doorframe?'

'Looks to be steel too. Haven't tested it.'

'Lock you recognise?'

'First guy we sent says it's a Schlage.'

'Access to the third floor?'

Daly didn't know. 'There's a stairwell and elevator. I don't know which one is locked down or when.'

'Security?'

Daly cleared his throat, looked at Adib. 'Good question.'

'Well?' said Gallen, sucking on the Marlboro.

'There's a duty manager and a porter,' Daly told him.

Gallen sensed something. 'And?'

'Well, it don't need security like we need it back home.'

'Why?'

'It's a Hamas hotel,' said Daly, averting his eyes.

Gallen stared. 'That's a big detail to leave out, don't ya think?'

Daly looked up slowly. 'Seemed like a detail we'd get caught on.'

'No, we wouldn't get caught on that—I'd pass at that.'

Daly shrugged, like, *What could I do?* Adib kicked at nothing on the carpet.

'Seriously?' said Gallen, his ears roaring with the predicament. 'You send me into Amman to lift an unstable target, and you want me to do this at a Hamas-controlled hotel, in a Hamas-controlled part of Jordan?'

Daly deadpanned.

'I'm an American for Christ's sake!' yelled Gallen, incredulous. 'I'm ex-Marines! They'll have me in a basement and on YouTube before I get anywhere close to Spikey.'

'We have Adib,' said Daly.

Gallen looked at the big Arab. 'Adib? You got a plan?'

'These people I can talk to,' he said. 'Maybe they listen and they become our friends. Maybe they friendly when they see the greenback.'

Gallen nodded, his nostrils flaring and jaw clenching. He felt trapped and vulnerable. All his education about Hamas was via the US Marines, where they were reviled Palestinian militants and terrorists. They'd also been taught that Hamas was a far-reaching social and political entity which counted lawyers, bankers and police among its numbers. Hamas had once used Amman as its home base, and it still controlled many neighbourhoods.

'Look,' said Daly, 'listen to the set-up, and if you don't like it, you can walk. Pay you for three days, and you walk away.'

'I hate it,' said Gallen.

'Ain't heard it, Gerry.'

Gallen got up from the dining table and slumped on a large sofa, sipping on the Coke. Like most old soldiers, he was superstitious, and of all the small things he chose to do in the field—always write his initials when he pissed, say a quick grace for even small snacks—his major superstition was to always give in to instinct when it was strong enough. And his instinct about this gig was negative; very negative, as in doom.

'You're only here because Mr Lang named you as the man,' said Daly, walking to the large windows that looked out over the city. Evening was creeping up. 'I could try this with Adib, I guess, but I need to have it done by midday tomorrow.'

'Why?' Gallen kicked himself for being lured back into it.

'Got an aircraft exfil at a field out of town, they'll wait till two.'

'Where?' said Gallen, standing.

'East of here.' Daly unfolded a larger map of Jordan and planted his finger in the middle of the eastern desert of the country, a desolate swathe of land that extended all the way to Iraq's western border.

'Two hours to drive out there?'

Daly nodded. 'Maybe two hours fifteen.'

Gallen thought about it. If he was going to do this, he wanted to take back the initiative. He'd been a special forces captain for too long; he no longer worked under micromanagement.

'If you have to be here,' said Gallen, lighting another smoke, 'then you're working for me. You and Adib—you're the crew.'

Adib smiled. 'Okay.'

'Okay.' Daly looked genuine. 'What's the plan?'

'Need the work-up kit back from the Ibis,' said Gallen. 'When we pull this off, I don't need some hero cop putting the pieces together and hunting us down.'

'Okay,' said Daly.

'Also want that P9 you promised me,' said Gallen. 'And the credit card.'

Daly nodded.

'Well?' said Gallen.

'Should we go now?' said Daly.

'Take Adib,' said Gallen. 'I need you back here inside an hour with the kit.'

Daly frowned. 'We're in a hurry?'

'We'll do it tonight.'

Daly hesitated. 'That a good idea?'

'We'll know in a couple of hours, won't we?'

Daly checked his pockets, held up his iPhone. 'On this, if you need me.'

'I won't,' said Gallen. 'From now on, ROE is radio silence, okay?'

The three of them synced watches.

'Okay.' Daly moved for the door. 'Be back in an hour.'

'Good,' said Gallen. ''Cos if you're not, I'm pulling the plug.'

CHAPTER 8

The old Peugeot cab pulled up a block south of the Araby Castle at twelve minutes to eight. Paying the cabbie, Gallen turned and walked away from it with the early evening foot traffic of Hashimi. Most Jordanian cab drivers were informers for either the Israelis, the Iranians or Hamas, and Gallen didn't want the word going out that an able-bodied American was interested in a local hotel.

When he judged the taxi would have blended into the crowded traffic of the famous street, he turned back towards the hotel and found the alleyway they'd identified on Daly's map. It was hot in the confined space, motorbikes against the left wall and a small cafe to his right. Taking a seat at a tiny round table, he raised a finger and asked for one coffee as the young owner approached him. In the cafe, two middle-aged local men stopped their talking and turned, a fug of smoke around them.

Gallen smiled and lit his own smoke as he adjusted his hips so that the P9 handgun remained hidden under his windbreaker, giving himself a good line of sight on the alley and the passing pedestrians of the main street. The coffee was hot and strong, and a perfect accompaniment to his cigarette.

Sipping he looked to his right, up the slight slope where the alley led into darkness. The plan was to use Adib as a decoy on the ground floor, while Gallen slipped up the fire stairs to Spikey Holmes's room on the third floor. His first choice was to knock on the door and persuade Spikey to open up, talk to his old captain, without his Hamas watchers knowing that a couple of American ex-servicemen were interested in Akh Spikey. If it went smoothly, Gallen would flip the room light on and off three times, Daly would drive the Land Cruiser to the front entrance and leave the motor running.

If it didn't happen the easy way, they would draw down on the small security numbers, force entry to Spikey's room, and attempt to be out of the Araby Castle before the local Hamas soldiers were dispatched. Adib had a fallback safe house a fifteen-minute drive across town, and Daly had a rendezvous site in the desert, either of which would act as a staging point for getting out of Jordan.

It wasn't perfect, but neither were the timelines or the Hamas complication. Whatever happened, Gallen would know very quickly how it was going to play out once Spikey recognised him through the door. That's when the stopwatch started—that's when Gallen would know what the booze was doing to his old sergeant.

When he was sure no one was watching him from the street, Gallen checked his G-Shock: 7.57 pm. Paying for the coffee, he turned right into the ancient laneway and walked slowly up the flagstones, past young children playing and men smoking in groups, crossing their legs at impossible angles. He'd been trained to blend into foreign environments, but his old Wranglers, cowboy boots and light windbreaker singled him out as an American.

After ninety seconds Gallen came to the rear loading dock and laundry area of the Araby; the old painted signage above the loading dock was in Arabic script but the picture of a fort was the same as the one out the front.

Slowing in the darkness that spilled away from the hotel's floodlit rear compound, he made out two heavy-set local men in trop shirts waiting at the gate into the hotel compound. They whispered between themselves and Gallen was about to clear his throat when a dishevelled man with dark skin staggered out of the compound, obviously drunk. Stopping near the two men, Gallen's heart sped up: the drunk was Spikey Holmes. Before he could react, the two men standing at the gatepost turned and closed on Holmes, the shorter of the two flicking his cigarette as he made to grab his quarry.

Eyes wide at the approaching men, Spikey got a right fist in the face from the shorter man.

'Hey!' yelled Gallen, without thinking.

The taller man looked briefly over his shoulder with a look that said *don't get involved* and lunged at Spikey.

As Gallen moved towards the melee, he watched Spikey recover his balance and whip a fast left-hand hook at the taller attacker, connecting with him flush on the right jawbone. It was a perfect shot which left him positioned for the shorter man's kick, which he took in the floating ribs with a loud expulsion of breath.

Leaning into the kick, Spikey lashed out with an elbow, busting his assailant's nose, and followed it with a savage left-hand body rip to the kidneys. As the shorter man's legs gave way beneath him, the tall man was on his feet again and pulling a pistol from his belt. Hitting the tall guy with a flying shoulder charge, Gallen watched the tall man lose his feet, his pistol clattering over the paving stones.

Heaving for breath, Gallen stood up straight as a third man with a big moustache came from the shadows, swinging a handgun. Shrugging his face away from the arc of the weapon, Gallen felt the butt of the black gun drive down into his right eyebrow, an explosion of light flashing as his eyes involuntarily squeezed shut. Staggering backwards, not knowing if he was standing or falling, Gallen lost his balance. His last sensation was the feeling of cyclone fencing jamming into his shoulder blades.

A voice echoed from somewhere. Gallen felt hands under his armpits and he blinked, his eyesight okay if he squinted. The three thugs' shouts echoed down the alley, the shorter man yelling threats as they limped and staggered away.

Beside him, Spikey Holmes shoved two handguns into the back pockets of his shorts. 'That you, cap'n?'

'It's me,' Gallen groaned with the exertion of speech. 'And it's Gerry now.'

'Be fucked?' said Spikey, smiling and investigating Gallen's facial wounds. 'Been a few years since we kicked us some Towelie ass, huh, boss?'

'My head.' Gallen felt his eyebrow spasm and gently touched the golf ball on his forehead. 'Holy shit.'

'Let's look,' said Spikey Holmes, like he'd never left the Corps. Gallen could smell old booze on his breath and saw a good-looking man, late thirties, who could have done with a shower and a shave.

'Been pistol-whipped is all, cap'n,' said Spikey, his drawling Compton accent loud in Gallen's shocked ears. 'Let's get some ice on that.'

They found a table in a cool, brightly lit room that looked like the hotel restaurant if hotel restaurants had lino on the floor. Gallen sat, wondering where Daly and Adib had got to, while Spikey walked to the kitchen area yelling for something.

Around the walls was a gallery of portraits and mural art, showing various soldiers and generals, Arab, Persian and Anglo. It was a military wall of fame, complete with a case of crossed scimitars with Arabic script underneath and another display with two crossed AK-47s, a black beret mounted between the rifle stocks. There was a large poster of Yasser Arafat—a signature scrawled across it in black texta—and a huge official portrait of Saddam Hussein in his army greens. Gallen's phone buzzed against his leg, a text message from Kenny Winter: *at heathrow—connecting now.*

Quickly responding with *Hussein Mosque 12*, Gallen turned back to Spikey, who had returned with a bucket and made an ice bag out of a white table napkin. Taking the ice, Gallen eased it onto his throbbing eyebrow and winced with the pain, his eyes shutting involuntarily.

'Mustaf!' yelled Spikey. 'Two cold Heinekens. Now.'

'You too drunk already, Mr Spikey,' came an older Arab's voice. 'I bring you the apple juice.'

'Don't you be bitching on me, Mustafa,' said Spikey with a growl. 'That what you doin'? You fucking bitchin' on me?!'

'No,' said the man, and Gallen turned his head slightly so he could see past the ice bag to an old man in a waistcoat standing beside the maitre d' station. 'It's no good for you to drink the more alcohol.'

'I'm sick of this fucking shit . . .' said Spikey, scraping back the chair as he stood. Gallen whipped out a hand, holding Spikey lightly by a muscled forearm.

'Can we just have the apple juice for now?'

Reluctantly Spikey sat down, still engaged in a lingering stare-out with the hotelier. 'You're in luck, Mustafa—my old captain here would like an apple juice.'

Spikey crossed his legs and put a smoke in his mouth, considering Gallen with a knowing squint. 'So, I'm guessing the visit ain't social, right, boss?'

'Thought you'd like a hand getting out of here.' Gallen took a cigarette from Spikey as Mustafa arrived with a glass pitcher of appleade and two glasses.

'Hah!' said Spikey, smiling as he lit their smokes. 'So I need help from a man who gets hisself rabbit-punched like that?'

Gallen felt the insult. 'Wasn't ready for the third dude. Wasn't even ready for the first two.'

'So, who sent you, cap'n? Chase Lang, right?'

Gallen put the ice bag on the table and poured a glass of the apple drink. 'Does it matter?'

'When the debt collector is a big-time contractor, it matters,' said Spikey. 'You know what they collecting?'

'It's none of my business.'

'Got in deep on a game, cap'n. Ran it up and put my house up as security.'

Gallen was about to wave it away, but the revelation pulled him up. 'Security? I thought you owed two hundred grand to the Graham brothers?'

'I do,' said Spikey, amused at Gallen's lack of knowledge. 'But I signed over my house down in Huntington.'

'House?' said Gallen, his pulse thumping in the golf ball. 'I don't follow.'

'They don't want to take my house, cap'n. Maybe they don't want me able to pay them back.'

Confused, Gallen shrugged. 'I'm lost.'

'Maybe they think they'll get more if I have to give up some-thing else.'

Gallen had heard enough. 'Chase wants me to help you get out of Jordan and back to LA. Apparently you have the money. That's all I know.'

At one end of the dining room a scuffle sounded and male voices rose above the whirr of the ceiling fans. Looking up, Gallen saw Adib and Daly being pushed into the restaurant area by several Arabs, guns in their backs.

'Well, well, well,' said Spikey, sucking on the smoke. 'If it ain't Lang's bitch.'

'Shut it, Spikey,' said Daly. 'You okay, Gerry?'

'I'll live.'

'Call off your dogs, will ya?'

'Not mine, Daly.' Spikey was enjoying himself. 'You gotta stop harassing me, man. You go tell Chase I ain't got nothing for him.'

'You got plenty, Spikey.'

'They got my house—I loved that house.'

Gallen raised his hand, happy for the P9 in his waistband. 'Will someone tell me what the hell is goin' on?'

'Chase thinks I've got a stash somewhere in Jordan,' said Spikey. 'Told the Grahams they can split it, call it a repayment of my debt.'

'Stash?' Gallen looked at Daly.

Spikey kept with the story. 'They've been at me for a few weeks, but they've been standing off given the owners of this hotel and all.'

Gallen shook his head. 'You've got it wrong, Spikey. My job is to take you home. We're getting out of here.'

Spikey laughed. 'Oh really? So why's Chase Lang in Amman?'

'Chase is here, in this city?' said Gallen, his pulse becoming erratic. 'I don't believe you.'

'Okay,' said Spikey, 'so how we getting out of Jordan?'

'Exfil by private plane from the eastern desert.'

'Only thing in the eastern desert is a Chase Lang training camp for Jordan's special forces. You won't be taking me to a plane—you're delivering me to Lang.'

Gallen looked at Daly. 'Well?'

Daly shrugged. 'Okay, so Mr Lang is in-country. Big deal.'

'Big deal?' said Gallen, feeling betrayed. 'Chase Lang is sittin' out there in the desert?'

'Oh boy,' said Spikey with genuine laughter. 'This is good.'

Gallen looked from Daly to Adib. 'Adib—you know what the fuck's goin' on here?'

Adib looked at his boss, and Daly nodded.

'Mr Spikey thinking it funny, about Chase Lang being in Jordan.'

'It's not that funny,' said Gallen, anger replacing confusion.

Adib creased his brow. 'No, but thing is—Chase Lang is not in the desert.'

'No?'

'No,' said Adib, embarrassed. 'He at the Hyatt.'

CHAPTER 9

Gallen thought about the situation. He had no fight with Spikey Holmes and the fact that Chase Lang was staying in the Grand Hyatt was annoying but not dangerous or even dishonest. He wasn't on one side or the other of the argument between Daly and Spikey. He was the hired hand and the opportunity to take a fee and leave—as outlined by Daly back in the hotel—was starting to look attractive.

He decided to keep the P9 in his belt. There was no point in encouraging the big-talk to turn into something serious.

'So,' said Gallen. 'We goin' to LA, Spikey?'

'Not with Daly, I ain't,' said Spikey, nursing one of the pistols he'd confiscated. The henchmen who'd pushed Daly and Adib into the restaurant had taken seats against the back wall, which left the American and Syrian standing.

'What about me?' said Gallen.

Sliding the breech on the black handgun, Spikey inspected the chamber and eased it back into place. 'I'm comfortable here for now, thanks, cap'n.'

Spikey nodded at the seated henchmen and they stood, escorted Daly and Adib out of the restaurant. Gallen stood to join them, but Spikey raised his hand.

'You don't have to go, cap'n.'

Gallen paused. 'You holding me, Holmes?'

Sniffing, Spikey Holmes grabbed the other pistol and then gave both of them to Gallen. 'I'd rather talk, boss. I need some advice.'

Looking at the handguns, Gallen handed them back. 'Berettas—some people got no class.'

The roof garden of the Araby Castle had once been a garden with flowers and a fountain, but now its centrepiece was a glass-topped steel table with matching chairs, surrounded by sand-filled flower boxes crowded with cigarette butts. Gallen pulled up the collar on his jacket; the night temperature in Amman was not exactly balmy.

'So, you a prisoner here, Spikey?' Gallen flipped the top off the Bud with his cigarette lighter. 'Those henchies of yours didn't look like friends.'

Spikey crossed his ankle over his knee, laughed softly. Behind him, the lights of Amman twinkled in the golden atmosphere of the city at night. Gallen had attended intel briefings in Damascus, spent a week in Baghdad and overnighted in Cairo. They were all great, ancient cities but Amman had something extra. Known as Philadelphia in the ancient world, Amman felt like Jerusalem—a thing unto itself, not belonging to any race or religion or dynasty.

'Cap'n, I ask you a question?'

'Since you asked so nicely.'

'Lang's payin' you, but you still owe him, right?'

Gallen thought about it; the concept about owing something other than money to another man seemed childish in the real world, but it was still currency among soldiers. 'Man saved my skin last year up in Canada. Sure, I owe him.'

'I have a proposition where you help me and Lang can be happy too.'

Gallen nodded, sucked on his smoke. 'I was contracted to help you, but double-crossin' ain't my thing, Spikey.'

'I know, I know,' said Spikey, big arms stretching out of his T-shirt until he was leaning on his knees. 'You signed on to help me, cap'n—said so yourself.'

'True,' said Gallen. 'I had no idea Daly and Lang were in-country. I thought it was my gig until this morning.'

'So?' Spikey sat up and opened his palms to Gallen.

'So?' said Gallen. 'What's the deal?'

Spikey looked over his shoulder at the doorway that gave access to the roof garden. The man was nervy. 'Deal is, we pick up my stash and you keep a third.'

'A third?' said Gallen, not expecting that.

'Thirty-three per cent, cap'n—yours to hand to Chase Lang, or yours to keep. That ain't my fight.'

Gallen sipped on the Bud, laughter coming up.

'What's funny?' said Spikey. 'You laughing at me?'

'Shit, Spikey,' said Gallen. 'I took a job to help you out of a bind and now I'm going to help you pick up a stash. Why can't retired Marines just stay out of this kinda shit?'

'Just bein' straight.'

'Really?' said Gallen. 'Then be straight about your friends in the restaurant. Who else claims an interest in this stash of yours?'

Spikey sat back in the chair, picked at the beer label. 'It's complicated.'

'So's *Jeopardy*. Out with it, or I'm gonna finish this beer and walk.'

They stared at one another, Gallen hoping Spikey would wave it all away, let him drift back to the farm.

'I once saved your lily-white, cap'n.'

'You sure did, Sergeant,' said Gallen. 'That's the only reason I said yes, and that's the only reason Chase asked.'

'I'm in a situation where I can't trust anyone.'

'The owners of this hotel?'

'Mustafa el-Masri runs the place. His brother—Baba—is a Hamas commander. Baba owns the Araby Castle.'

'Baba political Hamas, or military?'

'Baba's political, but he's crewed up,' said Spikey, rubbing his temples. 'He's got his own soldiers and he has connections in Jordan's intel and police.'

Gallen let it sink in. Visitors to the Middle East who operated slightly below the squeaky-clean level usually ended up with the protection services of a group like Hamas, Hezbollah or the Quds. They handed a foreigner his safety, like it was a gift, and then owned that person for the rest of his life. Gallen knew from his colleagues at DIA that any American who'd ever spent more than a week in a Middle East jail was tracked forever because the likelihood that he now owed his life to Hamas or Hezbollah was so high that even when he returned to the States, he would be asked for a favour.

'Hamas keepin' you alive?'

Spiky gulped. 'Could say that.'

'Why would they do that?'

'See, I klept some money and a bunch of local criminals decided I should give it to them.'

'Okay,' said Gallen, although it was far from okay.

'And Baba el-Masri heard about this . . .'

'How?'

'I was holed up in a police station out by Hussein Mosque,' said Spikey. 'These local criminals were chasing me, and I ducked in to get protection from the cops.'

'And?'

'Cops made a call. Mustafa el-Masri turned up half an hour later, and the other gang backed off.'

Gallen sipped. 'So what's the deal?'

'Safe haven.' Spikey indicated the area around him. 'But they want a cut of the stash.'

'They keep this criminal gang at arm's length so you can pay them off?'

'That's about it.'

'Will they let you live?'

Spikey shrugged. 'Like I said—it's safe haven with the devil.'

'How much?'

Spikey cleared his throat. "Bout six mill in greenbacks, some jewels and some other shit.'

'They won't let you live, not for six mill.'

Spikey made a face. 'Like I said, cap'n—I got a situation, and Chase Lang's goons ain't exactly the solution.'

'You wanna grab the stash and run to where?'

'First up, I was lookin' at Israel. But Hamas got long arms, and who's to say they ain't got soldiers working as border guards?'

'So, not west. South, into Saudi?'

'Too American,' said Spikey. 'Too many CIA assets currying favour with al-Qaeda.'

'Then where? Egypt? Lebanon?'

'Iraq,' said Spikey.

Gallen finished his beer. 'Iraq? That's shit duty.'

'That's where I got an exfil, and no double-crossers, no last-minute baksheesh.'

'Okay, so you got a friend in Iraq,' said Gallen. 'But you got six, seven hundred miles across a desert, one road, a border crossing and then the world's most lawless territory outside of Somalia.'

'I could do it with you, cap'n.'

'Don't kid yourself, Spikey,' said Gallen. 'I'm a farmer now.'

'Will you help?'

Gallen sighed. He felt the same sensation of drifting towards a waterfall that he'd felt the time he furloughed out of Afghanistan back to Denver, where he'd set up house with his wife, Marcia. The letters and phone calls had not been encouraging but he'd made himself take leave back home, knowing that when he asked her for the truth she would lie, and it would break them. That furlough was the worst ten days of his life and a week after returning to Afghanistan—where the winter swept down from the Kush like God's punishment—he'd received his Dear John, and a Houston dentist had received his wife.

'Six mill in cash? That's not small,' said Gallen. 'We can carry this between two men?'

'There's seven bags,' said Spikey. 'Three-man crew would work.'

The first crack sounded like one of Amman's million pigeons clucking in its sleep. The second was unmistakable as a bullet ricocheting off the stairwell walls.

Spikey ran to the edge of the roof garden, while Gallen moved to the roof door. It was outward opening and as Gallen turned back to grab one of the steel chairs they'd been sitting on, automatic fire sounded in the stairwell along with men's shouts.

'Shit,' said Spikey as Gallen jammed the chair under the door handle.

'Who?' Gallen joined Spikey at the parapet. On the street below, a ten-year-old red Mercedes sedan was surrounded by three Arab men in jeans and windbreakers, machine pistols in their hands.

'Trouble,' said Spikey.

'They're in the hotel,' said Gallen, heart banging like a trip hammer. 'You got any ideas?'

Spikey walked the parapets, looking for escapes, Gallen taking his six, the P9 cocked and held in cup-and-saucer. Looking over the wall, he saw a white BMW 4x4 pulled up behind the red Mercedes. A tall Arab in a dark blazer and a white shirt buttoned to the throat stepped from the BMW and pulled on black gloves. From the hang of the blazer, Gallen could see he was carrying a suppressed machine pistol in a large shoulder holster.

Pulling back, he looked at Spikey. 'You ever dealt with a tall Arab dude, drives a white BMW?'

'Don't know who he is, but I seen him.' Spikey looked around. 'He got Saudi plates?'

Peering over the wall at the BMW, Gallen saw a white plate divided into four rectangles. As he ducked down, the tall Arab looked up.

'Shit,' said Gallen. 'He made me. You must have thought about this, right, Spikey? You had an escape route planned?'

'I had one in the basement,' said Spikey, eyes wide and his breathing strained. 'Didn't think about being caught up here. *Shit!*'

'Those Hamas dudes going to hold?'

'Have no idea.' Spikey focused on a rooftop on the other side of the alley that ran down the side of the Araby Castle. 'Depends what's in it for them.'

Gallen saw an electrical cable traversing the alley to the other building, but nothing else. 'You're not serious?'

'Got something better?'

Gallen looked over the edge again, and into the eyes of a man who aimed his machine pistol at the roof and fired. Leaping back as concrete chips sprayed across the roof garden, he was pulled to his feet by Spikey.

'Tell me about the basement exit,' Gallen panted, the sound of Arabic voices echoing up the stairs.

'Garbage exit, for the trucks,' said Spikey. 'Leads into the alley.'

'How do we get to the basement?' said Gallen, reassessing the rooftop of the neighbouring hotel. It now seemed more sensible than trying to make the basement.

'Umm.' Spikey scratched his jaw. 'I guess there's one way.'

'Forget the stairs, Spikey—I ain't doin' no shoot-out against machine pistols.'

Spikey nodded. 'Okay, so there's a garbage chute on each floor of this hotel.'

Gallen couldn't believe what he was hearing. 'Six floors down a garbage chute? You may as well break my neck now.'

'Remember we used to train to go down air-conditioning chutes?' said Spikey as the automatic slammed into the parapet again. 'Boots out against the walls of the chute, fists front and back?'

Gallen remembered. 'Sure, Spikey, and you had someone like me holding a rope around you.'

Spikey nodded. 'That's the best I got—'less you wanna go over the side?'

'Show me.' Gallen pushed Spikey to the roof door.

Pulling the chair away, Gallen opened the door two inches and listened. Men shouted, feet padded and scraped. 'They're on their way.'

'Where?'

Gallen listened again. 'Third floor, fourth maybe. Where's the garbage chute?'

'Gotta go down this flight of stairs, turn left onto the sixth-floor landing, and the chute's just to your right, beside the service elevator.'

'Okay,' said Gallen, easing into the darkness of the stairs. 'See if you can let that chair fall back against the roof door when we close it—at least give them something to play with.'

Spikey eased in behind him. He kept his arm wrapped around the door and, as he pulled it shut, let the chair fall back beneath the door handle.

'Got it?' said Gallen.

'Got it, boss.'

They waited in the blackness, listening to the shoes turning at each landing. 'Those shit-heel Berettas,' said Gallen, moving down the stairs. 'You got them on you?'

'Sure,' whispered Spikey.

'Pass me the oldest, shittiest one.'

Spikey nudged Gallen in the ribs as they reached the landing of the sixth floor. One landing below them, someone hit the stairwell light which bounced up to where Gallen and Spikey stood like statues.

'What're we doin'?' said Spikey.

'Old Berettas turn into hair triggers, right?' Gallen cocked the pistol and threw it down the concrete stairs. As the handgun bounced, the trigger let go, shooting several times as it clattered down the stairs.

Pushing through the stairwell door, they emerged into light. The hallway was deserted, except for a middle-aged tourist, wide-eyed, dressed in nothing but his shorts.

'Back in your room, sir,' said Gallen, and the man withdrew immediately.

'There,' said Spikey, pulling the handle of the garbage chute. In the stairwell the automatic gunfire reached deafening levels as the thugs made it to the sixth floor.

'Go,' said Gallen, and Spikey put one leg into the chute and then the other. And then he was gone.

The doorframe splintered and a bullet whizzed past Gallen's head as he opened the garbage chute and squeezed himself in.

It smelled like old fish and an outdoor latrine. Pushing one boot against each side of the steel chute, Gallen eased in.

The last thing he saw before he let himself go was the door springing open and the tall Arab in the blazer aiming the suppressed machine pistol at his face.

CHAPTER 10

The garbage sludge ran down his neck as Gallen found a foothold inside the dumpster and attempted to follow Spikey into the loading bay. The light was dim, a dull reddish glow from an engineer's light, but he could see Spikey crouching against the far wall between canisters of cleaning fluid.

'Cap'n,' said Spikey in a loud whisper, the sound of footfalls and slamming doors closing on them. 'Over here.'

Rolling over the side of the stinking dumpster, Gallen moved to Spikey's hide, his feet sliding in the wet detritus he'd picked up on his boots. He felt like a shit-house mop.

'Ten rounds.' Spikey slapped the clip into his borrowed Beretta. 'What you got?'

'Full clip—seven, I think,' said Gallen, removing the thin pistol from his belt and ejecting the clip. The Heckler & Koch P9S had a single stack of bullets in the clip, making it thinner than the double-stacker Glocks and Berettas which had up to fifteen loads in the magazine.

Spikey pointed at the service doors. 'We gotta move.'

'They had men posted outside the hotel,' said Gallen. 'We have no idea what's on the other side of those doors.'

Spikey gulped down a breath. 'They know we took the garbage chute by now, cap'n. We don't have no choice.'

Something smashed in the adjacent kitchen, and Gallen knew they were about to be collared. 'Let's go.'

Standing, he ran toward the swinging service doors, Spikey sweeping the rear. Slipping the inside bolt that held the doors together, Gallen took a big breath and exhaled slowly—an old special forces trick for overcoming a racing pulse and frantic breathing.

'They're here,' said Spikey in Gallen's ear, as voices increased at the kitchen access door. They were about to storm the garbage room.

Gallen pushed the doors and realised the trash storage opened onto the rear compound where he'd met Spikey. The fully lit area was vacated, but as he opened the door further, he saw them. Three motorbikes with riders, engines off, in shadows beyond the floodlights. Gallen recognised the man on the closest bike: the short one from the crew that had attacked Spikey a couple of hours earlier.

'Shit.' Gallen pulled back and looked over Spikey's shoulder at the kitchen access door. 'Your friends are back.'

'Lemme see,' said Spikey, pushing into the gap between the two doors. 'Yep, it's them.'

A boot hit the kitchen door, and the door burst inwards as Spikey pushed out of the garbage room into the rear compound, Gallen covering him with the P9. Following closely, Gallen's heart raced as his former colleague walked straight towards the short man on the bike, Beretta held cup-and-saucer.

Gallen didn't understand what Spikey's rushed Arabic was communicating, but the short man and his two thugs raised their hands as the Americans approached. Shrugging, the short man dismounted from the blue Suzuki 250cc and stood back, gesturing for Gallen to take the bike.

'You ride one of these things?' Spikey grabbed the pistol from the short man and gestured to the others, who dropped their weapons.

'Sure.' Gallen threw his leg over and checked the ignition key. Hitting the starter button, he felt the machine roar to life.

Spikey kicked at the dropped pistols and was reaching for the keys in one of the other motorbikes when a bullet hole appeared in its tank.

'Shit!' Spikey ducked as men poured into the rear compound, firing shots. The short man's henchmen threw themselves to the laneway's paving stones as Gallen revved the bike and found first. 'Get on, Spikey.'

Feeling Spikey's arms clasp around his waist, Gallen ducked into the handlebars and let the clutch out, feeling the bike surge into the darkness. A slap hit him in the right thigh as he changed to second and flew down the ancient laneway, shots bouncing off sandstone walls.

'Right, *right*,' Spikey yelled in his ear, and Gallen touched the foot brake, changed down to first as he leaned the bike over and hit the gas. The motorbike lurched forwards, Spikey's body weight unbalancing them slightly, and as Gallen tried to right the machine the bald tyres let the bike slide until the wheel hit an old gutter—not much higher than two inches—sending them upright and towards the wall of a commercial laundry.

'Fuck!' said Spikey, as they scraped against the wall, tearing the arm off Gallen's jacket and taking the end off the rubber grip under the clutch lever. 'You said you could ride, cap'n!'

'Hold on.' Gallen hit full beam on the lights, illuminating a long, twisting laneway where every resident and business owner seemed to be coming onto the street to see what the commotion was about. Finding his balance, Gallen felt the bike's limitations and accelerated into second gear again, trying to keep one eye on the wing mirror as he dodged children and laundry racks, apple crates and parked motorbikes.

'Left here—left,' said Spikey as they emerged into a narrow but well-lit part of the laneway network. 'And slow down. It's a main street.'

Gallen was ready this time, dropping down to first gear well before the corner and taking it in a smoother arc because of the bald tyres. Accelerating into the lane, Gallen rode into the back of a tiny delivery van, the type powered by a motorcycle engine.

Gallen felt Spikey slam into his back, heard his headlight smash.

'Hey,' said a local man, arms waving as he walked out of a bakery, yelling in Arabic.

'I'm sorry,' said Gallen, trying to get his feet on the ground and reverse the bike. The motorbike wouldn't cooperate and he played with the clutch, trying to find neutral.

'You pay,' said the man, up in Gallen's face. 'Fuck-een American. This my van—you pay now.'

Spikey dismounted and Gallen swung his left arm backwards, grabbing at Spikey.

'No, Spikey,' Gallen hissed, his leg aching and shit sliding down his back. 'We'll pay him. Just smile and let's enlist this guy.'

Spikey tensed a little and then sat back down as Gallen fished in the inside pocket of the Tough Duck, pulled out his wallet.

'I'm sorry,' said Gallen, as another man in baker's whites filled the doorway, holding a length of steel pipe against his thigh. 'Hundred enough?'

Gallen held out the five twenties, watched the van owner try to stay tough, and then smile as he tenderly accepted the money. 'US dollar!'

'Nice place you got here,' said Gallen, replacing the wallet and trying to push back his feet. He couldn't get a grip on the paving stones. 'Gimme a pull, Spike.'

Spikey dismounted, slower this time, and pulled the Suzuki back to the intersection.

Looking back the way they'd come, Gallen saw a motorbike headlamp careening down the alley, two men on the back. Revving the engine, he put it into gear and looked at the man counting his money. 'These people chasing us? They're IDF.'

Letting out the clutch, Gallen launched the bike down the alley, now without lights. The chasing bike's lights cast an eerie shadow as they rode into a dark part of the laneway and then the shots started. Gallen and Spikey ducked as the single pistol shots pinged off stone and echoed in the crowded spaces, sending locals into doorways.

Gallen felt Spikey twist on the pillion seat, and he could hear him shooting back as Gallen found a clear run and changed up to third.

'Not too fast, cap'n,' said Spikey in his ear.

'What?' said Gallen, not totally understanding.

Spikey yelled something that Gallen couldn't hear, and then the bike was slewing, as if it was wagging its tail.

'Shit,' said Gallen, trying to keep the bike in a straight line despite its flat rear tyre. 'We're hit.'

Slowing to twenty miles per hour, Gallen made to slide the bike on its side, and use the position to draw down and shoot back at their pursuers. He'd been taught the technique at an escape-and-evade course he'd done with the British SAS regiment, way back when he was a young Force Recon officer. The driving and riding they'd done out at Hereford with the 23 SAS had been amazing, but some of the Americans had scoffed at the SAS's use of a controlled motorbike crash to spring a surprise on the enemy.

Now Gallen saw its application. 'Hang on,' he yelled over his shoulder as he tapped the foot-brake pedal to get the rear wheel sliding.

'Cap'n!' came the screamed voice in his ear, as the dark part of the alley gave way to the light, and the ground gave way beneath them.

'Shit!' said Gallen, realising he'd been powering towards a long, steep series of steps. Gripping the handlebars as tightly as he could, he aimed straight as the front forks dipped violently and the shuddering from the front wheel on the old steps transmitted directly up into his neck and head. Shaking as they accelerated downwards, Spikey pressed up against his back, Gallen left the throttle off and let gravity pull them down to the first landing, where tourists flattened themselves against the walls as the motorbike careened.

'Again,' said Gallen, out of breath and scared. He'd fought in some seriously dangerous parts of the world, in conflicts where many highly trained soldiers were killed or maimed. He hadn't gone through all of that to be shot like a rat in an Amman alleyway.

The second set of stairs—about fifty of them—seemed to go on forever and Gallen felt like he'd been hit repeatedly in the guts by Sonny Liston by the time they reached the flat. Exhausted, Gallen stopped the bike. 'Time to run, Spikey.' Grabbing his P9 from his belt, he dismounted and turned to the stairs, where he saw the two men coming down as fast as they could, guns drawn. There was time to run—it didn't have to be a shoot-out, something Gallen had been trained to avoid around civilians.

Grabbing Spikey, he turned to run but his right leg stalled. It didn't want to move and it seemed to be sliding. Worried he'd picked up a big piece of crap from the dumpster, Gallen looked down to see

73

what the problem was. A pool of dark liquid grew around his right boot and the jeans around his thigh was slick with blood.

'Spikey,' said Gallen, trying to drag the leg as he hobbled after his old sergeant. 'Leg's gone.'

Stopping, Spikey turned and saw Gallen's leg, his face dropping as he focused on the wet thigh.

'Took a bullet,' said Gallen with a grimace, bolts of pain rocketing down his leg as he acknowledged the injury. 'Can walk, but no runnin'.'

'Gotcha,' said Spikey without hesitation, stowing his pistol and opening his arms as he crouched down. Leaning forwards, Gallen reached over Spikey's right shoulder and allowed the bigger man to lift him and clutch him with a right arm across the back of his legs.

'Shit, cap'n,' said Spikey as he turned and started to jog down the alley. 'You bin hittin' that fried chicken since you got out?'

'Ribs and beer,' said Gallen. They were moving down the alley towards what he thought was the heavily populated Hashimi Street. Looking towards the steps they'd just crashed down on the bike, Gallen saw their pursuers on the landing that separated the two sets of stairs. He raised his pistol, but given the bouncing of the fireman's lift and the presence of civilians, he decided not to shoot.

They ran that way for thirty seconds, Spikey not wavering. In the Marines, anyone wanting to make it into special forces had to endure the fireman's races in which one man carried his buddy for a hundred yards, then his buddy carried him back over the same hundred yards. The timed event was designed to highlight psychological weakness as much as physical; it was a test that Gallen hadn't appreciated until he'd seen combat: knowing that another platoon member could carry you at a jog, and that you could carry him, was a priceless morale-builder.

'Hang on, cap'n,' said Spikey, his steps sure. 'Almost there.'

The pain in Gallen's leg was so intense now that he was grinding his teeth, and before he could answer Spikey, they were into the roaring bustle of Hashimi Street.

'Food poisoning,' said Spikey. Gallen couldn't hear the answer. And then there were hands on him, and he was being laid flat in a vehicle, and a door slammed as he drifted close to unconsciousness.

An engine turned over and Spikey said, 'I gotcha, cap'n,' and there was darkness.

CHAPTER 11

The Jordan version of a breakfast talk show played on the radio, two rooms away. Gallen lay on starched white sheets, the half-open venetian blinds showing morning light on Amman. He guessed it was after seven am and before seven-thirty.

Sitting up he felt light-headed and then the dull ache of his leg wound started in waves, hitting his pelvis and then his knee and then his ribs and his feet. Breathing to cycle the pain, Gallen wanted to outlast the first waves without panicking and try to find its equilibrium. He'd once broken a small bone in his foot thirty-six hours into a four-day route in Afghanistan, and he'd found that once he knew the parameters of pain—and there were no more surprises—he could work within those parameters. Didn't like it, but he could work with it.

The pain eased slightly and he pulled back the sheet, seeing a professionally strapped thigh sticking out of a surgical gown. He checked for locks on the windows, deadlocks on the door and security cameras on the walls. Ixnay on that—he was patched up and this place wasn't a prison. It wasn't a bad start.

Rolling so he was facing the window, he searched the bedside commode. No clothes, but his watch, wallet, passport and iPhone were lined up on the top shelf. Opening the cupboard beneath, he found his P9.

'It's all there,' said the American voice.

Starting slightly, Gallen turned, covering his exposed backside with the sheet. The woman stood in the doorway, leaning on it with her left shoulder, assured but casual.

'I wasn't . . .' started Gallen, and the woman laughed.

'I was kidding,' she said, moving to the bed, clipboard in her hand. She was honey blonde, about five-nine, mid-thirties. Gallen noticed a pair of Levis and a T-shirt under a white clinic coat. 'Dr McIntyre.'

'Doctor?' said Gallen. 'What a pretty name.'

'Alison,' she said, shaking his hand.

'Gerry Gallen,' said Gallen, shaking soft. 'Where am I, Doctor?'

'South Amman,' said McIntyre. 'The WJ Clinton Medical Center.'

'As in Bill Clinton?' said Gallen.

'William Jefferson to you, Gerry,' she said as she pulled a small flashlight from her coat pocket. 'You mind?'

Gallen opened one eye and then the other as McIntyre checked his pupils. She held up a finger, made him try to follow it with his eyeball, then pushed her finger towards the bridge of his nose, asking for him to say when he could no longer see it. Gallen missed the point—he was too busy looking for a wedding band.

'You patch me up?' he asked, after she'd asked him the day and the year.

'Yeah, wasn't a big deal,' she said, putting the flashlight in her pocket and making a note on her clipboard. Gallen saw fast, accurate movements, wondered if she was a big-city surgeon slumming it.

'Not a big deal?'

McIntrye shrugged. 'Single nine-mil slug, intact. No bone contact, no arterial perforation, just a lot of muscle tears. You got lucky.'

Gallen smiled at her ease around gunshot injuries. 'Lucky, huh? You ex-army?'

'Fuck off,' she said, releasing the butterfly clips on the leg bandage. 'Med Corps, US Navy.'

'And now?'

'And now, five years at Boston General, one year with Médicins, and somehow I fall in love with Jordan and take a job at an American medical centre, patching up mercenaries and oil workers.'

'Hey, just a second.'

The doctor gently peeled the bloody gauze pads away from the wound. 'Sorry. It's just a joke among the doctors—we have poverty all around us and the only people we treat are the foreigners with guns and international health cover.'

'I'm a contractor, not a mercenary,' grinned Gallen. 'The cover comes with the job.'

'Lucky for you. What does a contractor do that a mercenary doesn't?'

'Don't tell war stories in bars.'

'Thought drinking and boasting was part of the job?'

Gallen felt tired. 'Real soldiers drink with people who don't ask.'

McIntrye flashed a set of naturally white teeth, cupped her hands around his knee joint. 'Can you bend this? Take it really slow.'

Gallen eased his knee up slowly, the pain dull rather than acute. 'Does that hurt?'

'Only when you bite.'

'Watch it, Mr Gallen. That hurt?' She let go of the knee joint and pressed around the dark circular puncture wound five inches above it.

Gallen managed to squeak a quiet *yep* as the agony took hold.

'Okay, put it down,' she said as a local nurse entered the room and Gallen exhaled in a heap. 'Nurse, dress this wound.'

'That's it?' said Gallen, regaining his composure.

'No, I'll let you have a bulk pack of T3s, on the house.'

Gallen laughed. 'I get shot with a machine pistol and you send me home with a bottle of Tylenol? Man, you're cold.'

'It's a nine-mil, short slug,' said the doctor. 'Gunshot wounds cause more damage the larger the projectile and the greater its velocity. A nine-mil slug from a machine pistol is a small projectile and low velocity.'

'So you'd be okay with a nine-mil round from a machine pistol?'

'I'm a doctor, Mr Gallen, not a mercenary. But I'll throw in a three-day course of metronidazole. That should stop the bacteria growing in the wound.'

'Okay,' said Gallen, sick at the thought of a bacterial infection. 'Where's Spikey?'

'The man who brought you in?'

'Yeah.'

'He ducked out. Said he was coming back in an hour.'

'When?'

'Hour and a half ago.'

When the doctor had gone Gallen had a shower. A set of temporary clothes lay on the bed when he came out, the doctor's business card lay on top. Dressing slowly, he thought about the previous night and the sudden violence. He was no longer ready for that kind of escalation—didn't have the instincts or the fitness and the training was just a memory. He didn't even like the sound of firearms anymore: old Roy had dragged him out one night to go shooting coyotes, and Gallen had taken a back seat, let Roy and his buddies take the shots. It was no longer in him.

When Spikey was no longer in danger, he was going to walk away. He owed Holmes that much, but he was going to start negotiating himself out of the picture. He was done—all washed up.

Through the window of the private room, Gallen saw movement as he belted a pair of borrowed jeans around his waist. Ducking slightly, unsteady on his right leg, he tried to hide as a vehicle whisked up the medical centre driveway.

Pushing himself against the wall, his heart walloped against his chest. He carefully leaned down to the commode, opened the cupboard and grabbed the P9. Checking the clip and cocking the slide, Gallen moved barefoot to the door. He'd seen the vehicle before, and didn't like it then either: a black Lincoln Navigator, two short black aerials.

Gallen pulled on his boots, slipped out of the room, and walked to the lobby of the medical centre, wobbly on his leg. The black Navigator had stopped outside the glass sliding doors, under the awning. Pulling back, Gallen scoped the lobby: a receptionist answered a question on her headset, a middle-aged Anglo couple spoke quietly on the vinyl sofas, and across the lobby Gallen could see the corridor continuing.

Looking back the way he'd come, a running shoe emerged from an open door—a man was leaning into a room . . . talking to someone?

'Spikey,' hissed Gallen, but the heel didn't move. He raised his voice. '*Spikey.*'

Spikey Holmes pulled back into the corridor and stared at him.

'We got company, Spike.' Gallen pointed to the door.

Walking to Gallen's position, Spikey took a quick look, then moved towards Gallen fast. 'This way.'

As he got his arm around Spikey's shoulders for support, Gallen saw the doors of the Navigator open. He turned and hobbled with his old sergeant for three strides before Spikey threw his body weight into a side door marked *Switch Room: Authorised Personnel Only.*

Gallen felt the humidity grab at his throat as he followed Spikey into the dim room filled with generators, fuse boxes and control boards. He couldn't breathe, couldn't walk.

'Know who they are?' said Spikey, as they moved across the switch room.

'They were camped outside the Ibis, so we went to the Hyatt. Now they're here.'

'They don't look friendly, anyhow.'

'Where we goin'?' said Gallen, gasping as they reached a steel door on the other side of the switch room. 'Need air.'

'Car park,' said Spikey, opening the door. 'So you don't know 'em?'

'Know those aerials from someplace,' said Gallen.

Squinting into the sun, they emerged onto a steel gantry with two sets of switchback stairs that led to a parking lot. It was too open.

'Don't like this, Spikey. We got a car?'

'Not yet.' Spikey swung his arm under Gallen's ribs and aimed him towards a group of cars parked against the main building—in the spaces reserved for employees.

As they closed on the vehicles, Gallen saw a head of blonde hair bouncing over the level of a car roof.

'Hey, Alison,' yelled Spikey as they got to the hood of her Chev SUV. 'Can we talk?'

Stumbling to keep up, Gallen saw the look on Alison McIntyre's face and knew what she was thinking before she said it.

'What's going on?' she started but Spikey had already opened the passenger-side rear door and beckoned for Gallen.

'Do this nice and easy, Miss Alison,' said Spikey, grabbing Gallen by the bicep and propelling him into the Chev. ''Tend like there ain't nothin' doin', then we walk away, awright?'

Lying across the back seat of the SUV, Gallen could see Alison putting on a brave face as Spikey ran in a crouch to where she stood at the driver's door. Through the glass Spikey's voice was muffled and then the door was opening beside Gallen's head and Spikey was in the vehicle.

The driver's door shut and Alison turned the key, the beeping from the dashboard telling her to put on the seatbelt.

'I hope you two know what you're doing,' she said, head shaking slightly as she found reverse and turned. Looking up, Gallen caught her eye briefly: she was handsome more than pretty, brown-eyed and calm for someone who probably felt like she was being car-jacked.

'There's a picnic blanket back there, if you want to hide.'

As the car stopped reversing and she put it into drive, Gallen looked out through the windscreen, along a concrete parking apron that ran uphill slightly for fifty yards, where it split into an exit driveway and the entry drive-through. The black SUV sat in the shadows, a man in a polo shirt and chinos walking behind the vehicle, talking into a walkie-talkie and looking around. His gaze seemed to fix on Alison's car, and Gallen slid to the front of the rear seat, knelt on the carpet and allowed Spikey to throw the blanket over both of them.

'Be cool, sister,' said Spikey, pistol at the ready. Touching Spikey's gun hand, Gallen shook his head.

'You get us outa here and I'll buy you lunch,' said Gallen, his flexing leg triggering a fireworks display behind his eyeballs. 'Jarhead to Pecker Checker.'

'Marines, huh?' said Alison. 'Since when do you guys do lunch?'

'He's a captain,' said Spikey, coiled behind her seat. 'Don't lick his fingers—nuttin' like that.'

They accelerated up the apron, Gallen's heart rate rising as they closed on the black Navigator. Their car hit third and Gallen thought they were home free, when the man with the polo shirt stepped out of the shadows and raised his hand at Alison.

'Shit,' said Alison, the nerves now evident in her voice. 'Shall I stop?'

'Yes, stop,' said Gallen. 'Be cool.'

Ducking under the blanket, Gallen smelled the old booze on Spikey's breath. Alison's window whirred down and Gallen could see Spikey's face pushed up against the driver's seat-back, his eyes wide, the pistol by his cheek.

'Well, if it ain't our favourite ex-pat doctor,' came the voice of an American who thought himself particularly charming. 'How you doin', Ali?'

Gallen's hair rose on the back of his neck. He knew that voice.

'Doin' well. You got over the consulate's barbecue yet?' said Alison.

'He could've told me it was goat—that's all I'm sayin', right?'

They laughed together and Gallen sweated, the adrenaline churning in his gut. He was waiting for a clear break in conversation, a signal that Alison was pointing in back, that the man was moving to the rear door.

'So, what's up, James?' said Alison, and Gallen knew who the voice belonged to.

'Looking for someone—you treated a Gerard Gallen? An American. Ex-soldier, rough-looking.'

'Sure,' said Alison, nice and casual. 'Slipped over when he was drunk—nasty cut.'

'He still here?'

'Where?' said Alison. 'The clinic?'

'Yeah, we need a word.'

'He's in three-oh-three, about to have lunch last I checked.'

'Thanks, doll.' James tapped on the roof.

Alison said her goodbyes and they accelerated away, the rising window returning the SUV to quiet and cool as they all exhaled.

Spikey didn't pull back the blanket until they were into the traffic and heading north. He clambered onto the back seat as Gallen tried to get his leg into a place where it wasn't going to make him pass out.

'Where we going?' Alison reached for a bottle of water in her cup holder.

82

'Thanks for not squealing,' said Gallen, finally getting onto the back seat and leaning into the front.

'Maybe I should have,' said the doctor, terse. 'You're obviously trouble—you know James is FBI?'

'Yeah.' Gallen remembered a man at Denver International who needed to learn some manners. 'We've met.'

CHAPTER 12

The call to sunset prayers from King Hussein Mosque started grating on Gallen about thirty-seven seconds into it.

'You got a place underneath the speakers, Spikey?' he said, pacing the stone balcony overlooking a narrow street that led to the mosque. 'Think we got the sub-woofer.'

Jordanites wandered towards the mosque, a mix of Western and Arabic dress, in no hurry. The evening was brilliant, the sky pale purple and the city glowing in a soft caramel light.

Holmes lit a cigarette, handed the pack of Marlboros to Gallen. 'Why I went to live at the Castle—this dude is the original psy-ops. Beer?'

'Sure.' Gallen's eyes scanned the apartment across the street, the tables at the cafes and the strollers. The previous two days had been a blur and he needed some space to sit down and work out what he had to do to help Spikey and how likely it was that he'd get killed.

There seemed to be at least three crews who wanted Spikey's cash. There was the FBI, who'd announced themselves at Denver and were now hunting him in Amman. The Hamas group headed by Baba el-Masri had hooks in the deal. And then there were Chase Lang's boys: Daly and Adib.

There was also the crew that came into the hotel, shooting up the place. Were they with Daly? Gallen had to find out.

Holmes, flipped the lids on two Millers and handed one to Gallen. They sat at the coffee table and clinked bottles. Gallen fished the Tylenols from his pocket, popped two in his mouth and washed them down with cold beer.

'How's the leg, cap'n?'

'Sore,' he said, pushing one of the antibiotics out of its foil and swallowing it.

He could see Spikey's leg bouncing as he drank. It wasn't a good sign—in the field, when Sergeant Holmes had the fidgety leg, it meant he was looking for action.

'Shouldn't have let the doctor go,' he said, looking over the city. 'Not fair on us—not fair on her.'

'She dropped us three blocks away,' said Gallen, who also harboured fears about Alison McIntyre's friends in the FBI. 'We should be fine.'

'We got soft, cap'n.'

'I don't know what we got till you tell me somethin'.'

Holmes turned to him. 'Tell you what?'

'What the fuck's goin' on?'

A small burst of beer spurt from Holmes's mouth. 'Shit, cap'n.'

'Well?'

'It's a little embarrassin'.'

'You'll live.'

A knock sounded at the door of the small apartment. Spikey walked into the kitchen and peered into a small security screen on the counter, then went to the door.

'Meet Captain Gerry.' Spikey returned to the balcony with a ten-year-old boy in tow. 'Cap'n, this is Sami, my friend.'

'Sami,' said Gallen, shaking hands with the waif. He wore a Manchester United FC shirt and an LA Lakers cap.

'Hello, Captain Gerry,' said the boy, all smiles. 'Mr Spikey is back.'

'Sure am, my man,' said Holmes, producing a US ten-dollar note. 'Same deal?'

'Same.' Sami snatched the money. 'Got some Coke?'

'Sure,' said Holmes. 'Two in the refrigerator—your granma got any of that goat stew?'

When Sami had left, Holmes brought two more beers to the table. 'Sami is the landlord's grandson. Lets me know if people are nosing about, brings me food.'

Gallen's head swam with the T3s and the beer, but he took another Miller and drank. He noticed that Spikey was still in shape, his thigh muscles bulging through the military shorts as he sat in the balcony chair. In the Corps, Holmes had revelled in his resemblance to the boxer Marvin Hagler, although he used to say he was 'Hagler with a haircut'.

'You was saying,' Gallen prompted.

Holmes lit a smoke, tossed the soft pack to Gallen. 'I was out of control in LA—had the Corps pension, which I put into a house, but I was in my own way all the time.'

'Drinkin'?'

'And fightin' and wherever I went I was in a card game. Shee-it.' Holmes sucked on the smoke and looked into the sky. 'I was almost there. Was hittin' the mortgage, and I was shacked up—with Betty, you know—but I couldn't keep away from the tables.'

'Goin' up to Vegas?'

'Started that way. It was ,"Ooh, baby, I's gotta go work for a few days," and I'd be hittin' the no-limit games at the Palms for sixteen, twenty hours at a time.'

Gallen sipped the beer. 'You workin'?'

'Drivin' some bond runs LA–Vegas, and Phoenix, mainly. But then the drinkin' started, and some shit started and I dropped the manager.'

'Dropped?'

'I swear I only hit that boy coupla times, cap'n, but when I sobered up, he was in UMC with a tube in his mouth and I was in the sheriff's lock-up.'

'Shit, Spikey,' said Gallen. 'Really?'

'I know, I know.' Holmes raised his hand. 'No excuses, cap'n. I own it all.'

'So?'

'So the duty attorney points out to the judge that the manager was armed with a handgun at the time, and that's all she heard, 'cos she let me walk on no surety but now I got thirty-six days to get me an attorney and get my life together.'

'Back to LA?'

'Yeah, back to no Betty. She left, but I have this message on my voicemail from an Arab dude called Ariq.'

'You knew him?'

Holmes blew smoke into the night sky. 'Apparently I drove his cash from Phoenix to Vegas a few times. Now he wants me to ride shotgun when his security guy makes a pick-up and takes it to Jordan.'

'Shotgun? Why an American?'

Holmes shrugged. 'Lots of these Middle Eastern dudes have trouble with the help. Even the people closest to them will try to kill them, steal from them. He thought me and Faidh would even each other out.'

'So?'

'I told him to take a hike. But I still needed the money for a lawyer, for my trial in Vegas, and so I found a game . . .'

'Poker?'

'Blackjack, up in Newport,' said Spikey, crushing the cigarette in the ashtray. 'I was ahead for a ten hours and then—'

A knock came from the door. Sami, with a tray containing two bowls of steaming stew.

They ate quickly, both of them hungry. Gallen burped when he'd finished, wiped his mouth with a small white napkin. 'So, I guess the game you found in LA was the Graham brothers, right?'

'Yep.' Holmes leaned back and put a cigarette in his mouth.

'Is it true they let you go to two hundred grand on marker?'

'Eventually, yeah,' said Holmes. 'After two days I was fifteen grand down and Don Graham turns up at the house, tells me we gotta go for a drive. I thought I was dead—but he tells me I can try to climb back if I put up the house.'

'Shit, Spikey!'

'I know—almost twenty years of shit duty, and the one thing I got to show for it, my house, and I'm staking it at a blackjack table.'

They smoked and watched the street. There was nothing to say to Spikey Holmes. He knew what his life had become.

'Four days later Don cut me off at two hundred grand, told me I had a month to clear the marker or he'd take the house, even though he didn't want to do it.'

'So you ring the Arab?'

'I call Ariq and tell him I'm in—at this point, I need to make money and I figure this Ariq is bad enough that there might be some big paydays for someone like me.'

'What happens?'

'Well, it turns out me and Faidh are cool. The man's funny, and we do our pick-ups, but then we get into Aqaba and it all goes bad.'

'What happened?'

'We come in from Kuwait, across Saudi, and up into Jordan from the south. We thought we'd be doing one last pick-up in Aqaba and then delivering to Amman.'

'But?'

'But we're met at the hotel by Ariq's Jordan crew, and these dudes are not friendly,' said Holmes, finishing his beer. 'And Faidh has no sense of humour with these guys. There's a lot of Arab banter that I can't follow but, basically, they insult Faidh, take the keys to the Suburban and leave us with two bags of cash.'

'They paid you?'

'Twenty grand—greenbacks,' said Holmes.

'That's not bad.'

Holmes smiled. 'I'm like, "This isn't too bad," and Faidh says he knows where the goods are going, and why don't we take it down?'

Gallen slumped. 'Tell me you said no.'

'I said no, cap'n. Swear to God.' Spikey sat forwards, wide-eyed. 'I'm like, "I'm taking my twenty K and I'm going back to LA."'

'But?'

'Faidh and I have become friends by now, and he knows my troubles. He says to me, "Mr Spikey, there's more than twelve million US dollars in those bags we've been picking up—don't you want to pay these gangsters and keep your house?"'

Gallen shook his head.

'I ain't no thief—honest, cap'n,' said Spikey. 'I thought, one take-down, from bad Arabs, and I square it wit Don Graham, pay off the house, maybe I get Betty back in the crib.'

Spikey Holmes told Gallen how they hired a car, beat Ariq's crew to the drop-off point at the trucking depot in Amman, waited for the crew to leave and then hijacked the cash. He told it like a Marine: without the fear or the doubt.

'So,' said Gallen. 'Let's grab the money and get out of here. You said you had an exfil in Iraq?'

'Sure, cap'n, but we gotta go back in.'

'Back in?' said Gallen, eyelids drooping.

'To the depot—that's where the cash is at.'

Stifling a yawn, Gallen focused on his former sergeant. 'You just told me you hijacked the cash.'

'We did, but after we split it, I got separated from Faidh and then the place is being locked down and all the floodlights come up.'

'Faidh set you up?'

'I don't know,' said Holmes 'I got six mill outa there, so I haven't dwelt on it too much.'

'So where's your money?'

Holmes grabbed a smoke. 'I hid it in the depot—made a run for it.'

'The cash never left the drop-off?'

Holmes shook his head.

'Where's the depot?'

'Five blocks north.'

'What was the plan?' said Gallen.

'I wanted to talk about that,' said Holmes. 'See, the way this city works, we can't be here by morning.'

'You telling me this now?'

'Needed to hide from the feds. But we can't be in the neighbourhood come daybreak.'

Gallen winced as he moved his wounded leg. The T3s took the edge off, but they didn't kill the ache. 'That kid?'

'Sami's cool. But he tells his granma, and she gets talking to the fish dude at the souk, and then he talks to the fruit guy . . . and once the souk is talking, then the Hamas man knows, 'cos the Hamas man runs the souk.'

'Your business is everyone's business?'

'Welcome to Amman.'

Gallen blinked hard, a little woozy from the beer. 'I need some sleep.'

'Alarm set for midnight.'

Gallen took the spare room, slumped straight on the bed. His eyelids drooping from fatigue, he thought about the coming night's work and what he was going to do about Kenny Winter, who he was supposed to meet at midnight at the Hussein Mosque. The break-in at the depot would take precedence, but he wanted Winter close. He thought carefully about the text he should send, and then wrote *Hussein meet cancelled. Busy. Standby.*

As he dozed off, his iPhone buzzed. Answering, he heard Winter's drawl, hovering between lazy and menacing.

'Busy, huh, boss?' said the Canadian. 'Need me?'

'Can't involve anyone right now,' said Gallen. 'I'll call you later.'

'Where you goin'?'

'Don't know,' said Gallen, whispering. 'I'm doing a favour. No addresses.'

Winter hissed out a lungful of smoke. 'You're on that Tactical NAV thing, right?'

'Sure.'

'So when you do have an address, send it,' said Winter, 'and like the boy from Wyoming says: no heroes, okay?'

'Got it,' said Gallen, disconnecting.

He drifted to sleep, worried about the depot, worried about Spikey, but his biggest concern went deeper: that he no longer had the heart for this life.

CHAPTER 13

Gallen opened his eyes two minutes before midnight. Limping into the tiny kitchen he found Spikey drinking water, nodding at someone on the other end of his cell phone.

'Yep, yep,' said Spikey, standing. 'Ready to roll.'

Gallen found his T3s and then popped an antibiotic, washed them down with his bottle of water. The heat of the day had given way to a chilly night. 'We okay?'

'We got Charlie Basa as a driver—heard of him?'

Gallen cocked the breech of the P9, counted rounds in the clip, looked for obstructions in the barrel. 'Who's Charlie Basa?'

'Ex Jordanian intel—trained with the SAS, useful dude if you wanna get around.'

Gallen never liked last-minute additions to a team, but he also wanted this gig to be over. He shrugged as he pulled his fleecy sweater out of his bag. 'This Charlie our ticket to the exfil?'

'The desert express.'

The street was well lit and empty. Gallen held to the shadows as Spikey made for a Chev Yukon that was idling on the other side of the ancient street. He looked like any local of Compton Beach: military shorts, Nikes and a flannel shirt over a T-shirt. He didn't look to Gallen like a man who was risking his life to steal six million dollars. Holmes reached the Yukon and spoke to the driver, turned back to Gallen, motioned him over.

The Yukon smelled of Old Spice and Camel cigarettes. Gallen sat in the back seat, waited for the two men to make their greetings in Arabic, while Charlie Basa eyeballed him in the mirror, didn't take his eyes off.

When the hellos were done, Charlie reached out with a handshake and Spikey took it, before looking back at Gallen.

'Cap'n—meet Charlie.'

The Jordanian turned and looked at Gallen. He was a large, bald man in his early forties, his eyes steady and unimpressed. Gallen noted driving gloves and a dark windbreaker.

'Mr Spikey give me the mission, but I make the decisions. You understand this, Mr Gallen?'

'I get it,' said Gallen, his leg starting to throb. 'It's your ship.'

'Yes, *captain*. It's my ship.'

They drove a circuitous route, Basa taking smooth corners and doing his best to keep moving. When a traffic light went red he'd slow to a crawl and wait for it to go green. He pulled over to let following traffic go past and maintained obvious spatial awareness. Gallen did not know where he was but he felt they were heading in a general north-west direction.

Spikey and Basa murmured quietly, the Jordanian very cool but clipped in his questions.

'Okay, Mr Gallen.' Basa talked into his mirror. 'The way this work is that I give you ten minutes exact to go in and come out. Then we go to eastern desert.'

'Okay,' said Gallen, his leg refusing to find a non-agonising angle of rest.

'If I'm made, I go to Bravo—at the rear of the building.'

'There's another gate?'

'No,' said Spikey. 'Mezzanine offices open onto a roof that extends to the wall. Charlie waits under that.'

Gallen murmured his assent without meaning it. The Plan B—the Bravo—was a jump into an alley. With his leg, it was going to hurt. And with the way the Middle East worked, there was no guarantee that Charlie Basa would wait for his passengers once the bags had been thrown into the alley.

'What about the entry, Spikey? We got a way in?'

Holmes turned, a white plastic access card in his hand. 'We go in the way everyone goes in, cap'n.'

'That an entry card?'

'Yep.' Holmes lit a smoke and handed the pack to Gallen. 'After Faidh left, I was going through a bag he left at my apartment.'

'That's Faidh's?'

'Well, yeah. He worked there.'

Gallen wasn't convinced. 'It wasn't cancelled?'

Spikey smiled. 'While I was staying at the Araby Castle, I got friendly with the cook's son—twelve years old, one of them computer geeks. He hacked the access control database for me: this card and this number are still active. I'm betting we can walk in the front door.'

Gallen had been a special forces captain long enough to know that any set-up that looked too good to be true was probably a trap. From the jungles of Mindanao to the mountain passes of Laghman Province, Gallen couldn't remember anything being handed out free. The way he remembered it, free lunches came with ambushes, landmines and IEDs in cell phones.

'How do we know it's not a trap?' said Gallen.

'Why would it be?' said Spikey. 'Ariq's people didn't know I left the cash inside.'

'What about Faidh?' said Gallen. 'He see you leave?'

'I don't know.' Spikey stole a quick look at Basa. 'Didn't stick around to ask him.'

'What do we know about security in this depot?'

'Nightwatchman in the mezzanine office—only thing he watches are pirated DVDs.'

Charlie Basa slowed in a dark side street and came to a stop. Eighty yards away, on the other side of the cross street, was the entry gate.

'That's it,' said Spikey.

Leaning between the two front seats, Gallen eyed the depot: its stone walls ran for most of the block, broken by a closed wooden gate, a blue sign over it.

'What's that say?' he said, reaching for Basa's binoculars on the centre console.

Adjusting the night-vision field-glasses, he focused on the white Arabic script. Below it was smaller Roman letters. It said *al-Haq Transport*.

Sitting back, he felt the blood racing into his neck. 'Spikey. al-Haq?'

Holmes pulled a black baseball cap hard over his eyes. 'What about it, cap'n?'

'Is that Ariq's name?'

'al-Haq. Yep, that's him,' said Spikey, checking and rechecking the clip on his Beretta, two spares going in the chest pockets of his shirt.

Gallen massaged his face. 'Shit.'

'Problem?' said Spikey, turning.

Gallen ignored him—he was sick of Spikey's shit-magnet. 'Charlie, you know about the al-Haqs?'

'What can I say?' said Basa.

'The fuck is goin' on here?' said Spikey, but Gallen ignored him. 'Charlie, look at me.'

Basa turned in his seat and faced Gallen. 'Yes, I know about the al-Haqs. But there is always myth and truth, yes?'

Spikey stopped, became still.

'So tell us, Charlie, before we go in there.'

Charlie put a Camel between his teeth, flicked his lighter. 'Where should I start?'

'Start at Denver International, forty-eight hours ago,' said Gallen, feeling his nostrils flare. 'I was approached by a couple of FBI dicks who warned me about flying into the Middle East.'

'Didn't tell me about it,' said Spikey.

'Didn't think the name was important. They told me a money launderer out of Detroit—Ahmed al-Haq—had cabled an associate in Beirut about my arrival in Amman. So, Charlie, let's start with the al-Haq family. Ahmed and Ariq—they brothers?'

'Yes they are.' Charlie turned back to the windscreen, sucked on his cigarette. A dark green Chevrolet van drove the street in front of the trucking depot. 'I can tell you some things, Mr Gallen, but maybe it is the conjecture?'

'Let's hear it,' said Gallen, wondering about that van.

'Okay, Ariq al-Haq—so they say—is an operative for Saddam.'

'Saddam *Hussein*?' said Spikey. 'You high?'

Basa sniffed. 'Saddam in the 1990s, he had the UN sanctions, and he could not use his oil revenue for anything but the humanitarian goods.'

'Meds, food, school books—right?' said Gallen.

'Right,' said Basa. 'So to get the hard currency from the UN, he pays too much for the Australian wheat, so long as the Aussies use a trucking company in Jordan to take the wheat from Aqaba to Baghdad.'

'So how does Saddam get the hard currency?' said Spikey, confused.

'Because,' said Charlie Basa, 'the trucking company the Aussies had to use was al-Haq Transport.'

Gallen chuckled, couldn't help it. In one of his intelligence programs, back in 1st Recon, they'd spent a week learning the basics of money laundering and trafficking from a bunch of smart-asses from the FBI and Treasury. He remembered a bright-eyed first lieutenant in front of him putting his hand up and saying—with some outrage— that if what he was hearing was true, the world was run by bankers, lawyers and accountants, at which the smart-asses started laughing.

'What?' said Spikey, looking from Gallen to Basa. 'The fuck you two laughing about? Care to let me in on the joke?'

Gallen sighed. 'Charlie's saying that the al-Haq brothers were a front for Saddam, who created a Jordanian trucking company so he could charge a fee for trans-shipping the wheat. But the money paid by the UN to al-Haq Transport was going straight to Saddam.'

Spikey's mouth hung open. 'Did you say that, Charlie?'

'Mr Gallen has it correct. The conjecture is that the al-Haq family is the same family that ran the Iraqi Central Bank and finance ministry. Very close to Saddam, by marriage.'

There was silence in the Yukon.

'So,' said Gallen. 'Saddam is dead, but the al-Haqs are still active. Any ideas?'

The two men in the front seat looked through the windscreen.

'Let me start, then,' said Gallen, annoyed. 'We're in the middle of Hamas turf, about to steal six million bucks from Saddam's gangsters and then drive to an exfil on the Iraqi border. You're a gambling man—what are the odds?'

'I'm sorry, cap'n,' said Spikey. 'I didn't mean for this—'

Gallen held up his hand. 'I told you I'd help you, because I owe you. But here we are in this situation and I'm not happy because I don't know everything.'

'Now you do, don'tcha, cap'n?'

'I know we're in a shit sauna, Spikey,' said Gallen. 'I think we should postpone this until we know more about the al-Haqs.'

Spikey and Charlie looked at each other. 'Actually, cap'n—clock is ticking. Our plane arrives in twelve hours.'

'We're going at midday?'

'Yep,' said Spikey. 'And I can't change it.'

'You up for this, Charlie?' said Gallen. 'I saw your face when I said Ahmed al-Haq knew about my trip.'

Basa winced. 'Ahmed is the criminal in the suit.'

'White-collar criminal,' said Gallen.

'No.' Basa shook his head. 'Saddam's criminal—very rich, very dangerous.'

Gallen breathed out. 'So, you in?'

Basa looked worried. 'We do this now—and if not now, then not again.'

'So,' said Spikey, turning back to face Gallen, 'that's two votes for go. What you wanna do, cap'n?'

Gallen popped a strip of Doublemint in his mouth, felt his mind adopt tunnel vision, his gaze turn into a thousand-yard stare. His officer training and the Force Recon culture emphasised planning, intelligence and above all other factors an exit: the special forces motto was *stupid gets you in—smart gets you out.* The US Marines had no intention of spending all that time and money training a recon Marine so he could get himself caught or killed.

'Here's my worry, Spikey: you swipe that access card and you either get a guard coming down with a flashlight and a shotgun, or you get a bunch of heavies from the al-Haq camp coming in at breakneck, right?'

'If they know I got that card, then, yeah, I see what you sayin'.'

Gallen sipped at his water bottle. 'So my rule is going to be that we do this gig only if we can do it in three minutes. I'm talking about walking in, dropping anyone who gets in the way, lifting the bags, and coming straight back out. One hundred and eighty seconds, go to whoa—can you talk me through that?'

Spikey beamed.

'Oh,' said Gallen. 'And I forgot to add, you're working with a partner who's got a hole in his leg.'

Spikey laughed. 'We're back, cap'n.'

'Can we do it?'

'Set the clock for one-twenty,' said the former staff sergeant. 'I's gonna work you like a private.'

CHAPTER 14

The red light on the access swiper blinked to green as Spikey pulled the card down the slot. Lights came on in the entrance vestibule and the bolts retracted in the security door.

'We're go.' Spikey pushed through the inward-swinging door and headed for his right, into the darkness of the building. As the doors swung back, and Gallen checked that the lock bolted, a yellow Nissan taxi drove past the door, too slow for his liking. He listened to hear if the cab had stopped or slowed. It didn't. Firing up his iPhone, Gallen selected the Tactical NAV app, dropped a pin on his location and emailed it to Kenny Winter. He followed Spikey into the dimly lit hallway, feeling the breath rasping in his throat. The air was dusty, unventilated and the corridor became darker as they jogged down it, past empty office cubicles, frosted-glass office windows and rubbish bins emptied but standing outside their offices.

Gallen's leg ached. Not enough to stop him, but enough to slow him and make him feel uncoordinated.

Spikey stopped at a locked door, its wire-glass panel at head height showing a darkened space behind.

'Mezzanine office is behind this door,' said Spikey, gulping for breath. 'If the card brought the guard out, we should know it soon.'

Listening to Spikey control his breathing, Gallen stood to the side of the glass panel, keeping his eyes glued for movement. His G-Shock said forty-two seconds elapsed.

Spikey reached forward with his access card but Gallen grabbed his wrist. 'Wait.'

A faint splash of light shone through the glass, becoming stronger. They threw themselves to the walls on either side of the glass as the beam of light strengthened and then shone right where they'd been standing. Raising his pistol to his chest, Gallen breathed deeply through his nostrils as the flashlight beam became stronger and closer, until the light was clearly being shone at the glass from a few feet away, the outline of a man's head evident beside it.

Bringing the P9 level with the guard's head, Gallen made a cup-and-saucer grip. If the guard opened the door, Gallen would shoot him. The guard's head remained motionless for a few seconds, then the flashlight beam swung away and began to retreat. Breathing out, Gallen lowered his weapon.

'He's goin' back to the office,' said Spikey, as the sound of boots on a steel staircase rang out around what was obviously a large space on the other side. 'Tell me when he shuts his door.'

They listened for the footsteps: they reached the top of the stairs, walked across the mezzanine floor. A door squeaked and Gallen raised a finger. As the door slammed shut on a spring, Gallen dropped his finger and Spikey swiped the card again, opening the bolts.

Gallen peeked into a large space, faintly illuminated with the glow of engineer's lights. It was the workshop, and in the distance he could make out a dozen trucks parked inside. He assumed there were many more outside in the compound.

'Follow me.' Spikey slipped through the door into the workshop.

Gallen spied his watch as he followed: ninety-five seconds elapsed.

Easing the door shut so it didn't make a sound, Gallen followed Spikey as he skirted a huge inspection pit. Gantry cranes ran overhead for the length of the building.

Spikey took a sudden left-hand turn between two prime movers: a Mercedes-Benz and a MAN. Gallen paused and looked up at the mezzanine office. Now the layout became clearer: the security office looked down on the main parking area for the vehicles, not on the workshop space. As he made to turn away, he saw the guard's head moving across a side window.

He turned to follow Spikey, but was distracted by something on the mezzanine.

'Cap'n,' hissed Spikey. 'You comin'?'

Raising his hand, Gallen focused on the security office window. The head bobbed up and down: was he talking on the phone?

Another head appeared through the window, and then another.

'Shit,' said Gallen, running after Spikey, who he found waiting beside a partly wrecked Mercedes-Benz prime mover with a tarpaulin covering the flat nose. 'There's three up there.'

'Up where?'

'I count three guards in that office—they expecting us?'

Spikey shrugged, his eyes white in the darkness. 'There's always one. Don't know nothin' bout no three. How're we for time?'

'Two minutes down.'

Opening a side hatch on the Mercedes, Spikey pushed his hands in and disconnected the batteries so the interior light wouldn't switch on when he opened the cabin. Then, pulling the door back, he climbed into the cab, Gallen following.

The cab was dark but as Gallen eased his weight onto the driver's seat the creaking sounded like a fog horn. Turning, he looked through the driver's window, across at the mezzanine office. He had a level line of sight into the room. Two men in plainclothes stood over a man in a guard's uniform, who sat at the desk. One of the plainclothes held a pistol.

'Don't like it,' said Gallen. 'Let's move.'

Spikey stood and reached for the storage bins over the driver's position. Pulling a canvas military duffel from the locker, he followed with another, dropping both of them on the floor of the cab beside Gallen. The zips were locked with small combination locks. He pulled another couple from the centre bin and dragged a single bag from the storage bin furthest from the driver's seat.

'That it?' said Gallen. 'Thought there was six or seven?'

'Down here,' said Spikey, turning and dropping to his knees to open another storage bin beneath the bed. Out came two more canvas duffels with strap handles. 'That's it—seven bags. Grabbed them from the Suburban in front of that office.'

Gallen grabbed the two bags closest to him and threw them across his left shoulder and neck, and then reached for the next two.

'That one.' Spikey grabbed at one bag and pushed the other to Gallen, before hesitating. 'I mean, you need the light ones—no offence, cap'n.'

'None taken,' said Gallen, throwing the third across his right shoulder and neck, so he looked like a sherpa. 'Let's move.'

His watch said they had twenty-three seconds to leave the building, jump in the Yukon with Charlie Basa and drive into the desert. Pushing the cab door open, Gallen swung his feet onto the steps and eyed the office window: no sign of the guard or the two plainclothes. They were on the move.

Sliding down the side of the prime mover, the bags grabbing at the door as he descended, Gallen hit the concrete with a jolt to his aching leg. It wasn't feeling strong. Jogging into the lee of the neighbouring truck, he hid in the shadows and waited for Spikey. Drawing the P9, he checked the slide and the clip as Spikey got to him, four bags on his back.

'This way.' Spikey wove through the workshop.

Gallen followed, limping now and wanting to pull up on Spikey, remind him that they had security roaming in the building. They stopped twenty feet from the access-controlled door through which they'd entered the workshop.

Gallen was about to readjust the bags on his bag when the ceiling lights went on, blinding him. Spikey pulled back, almost landing in his lap, and they shuffled into the lee of a truck cab.

'Shit, they're on the mezzanine, outside the office.'

'They seen us?' said Gallen, as a thick Arabic accent echoed around the work bay: 'Come out, American thieves. We see you.'

A burst of automatic gunfire tore across the shop floor, showering them with concrete chips.

'Okay,' said Gallen. 'So they've seen us.'

Spikey turned back, eyes bulging. It would look like fear to many people, but Gallen knew he was figuring out how to get away clean with the loot. 'I got a plan, cap'n.'

More assault-rifle fire ripped through the wall above them. 'Come out, Americans,' said the voice. 'You have something that belongs to us.'

Gallen went to look around the cab they were hiding behind, thought better of it. 'What's the plan?'

'Cover me to the door.' Spikey pointed at the access door. 'I'll slip through, return fire on them, and you make a run to me.'

'You won't make it,' panted Gallen. 'They've got assault rifles. I've got a pea-shooter.'

'Here, take this,' said Spikey, handing over the Beretta he'd taken from the motorcycle riders behind the Araby Castle. 'Just like the OK Corral, right?'

Gallen smiled as he checked the Beretta for action and loads. When Marines in his unit wanted to talk shit about how easy a mission would be, they compared it to the classic movie shoot-out; a gunfight that featured heavy-calibre pistols with no kickback, pinpoint marksmanship with no aiming and men approaching a known ambush by walking down the middle of the street.

'Sure, Spikey. Just like they do it in Tombstone.'

'Remember, cap'n—no heroes, right? They drop me, you run!'

Gallen shook his hand. 'No heroes, Sergeant.'

Spikey counted down from three. Then he started out, and Gallen stood, fired his first and second rounds with his right hand around the corner. The first three shots at the mezzanine security office hit nothing—he'd spent too long out of the military. He shot five more rounds from the Beretta but his targets had already pulled back before Gallen realised he had nothing to shoot at. Automatic fire ripped into the truck cab beside him and Gallen fell back into its lee, pieces of windscreen glass raining on him.

'Cap'n,' yelled Spikey and, turning, Gallen saw him standing in the open doorway. 'Let's go.'

Gallen weighed it up. There was still too much firepower on that mezzanine gantry. He wasn't going to run for it. As he stood, more automatic fire hit his hide, and he ducked reflexively as a wing mirror flew past his head and smashed on the concrete.

'Cap'n,' yelled Spikey. 'Get ready.'

Gallen watched Spikey aim his Beretta at something along the wall—a big white steel box. The switchbox. As the fifth bullet hit the box, sparks spewed from it and the lights wound down like a giant motor had stopped running.

In the darkness, Gallen couldn't even see his hand in front of him. It was an opportunity—perhaps the only one he'd get—to cross the open ground and get to Spikey. Setting out in the direction of the door, bags dragging on his weakened leg, Gallen pulled up short as lights flashed behind the door's glass panel and shots sounded.

Freezing, Gallen listened as the door clicked shut and excited male voices filtered from the other side. He knew those voices from his time in battle: the voices of victory and bloodlust. The sound of men finally getting their hands on the enemy.

CHAPTER 15

Knowing there was nothing he could do for Spikey, Gallen turned away from the side of the truck that faced the security office and moved further into the dark as flashlight beams cut through the inky blackness. He found the side wall of the workshop and started edging along it, hoping that the interest shown in Spikey would distract the ambushers.

He paused for a couple of seconds, feeling dizzy, disoriented. The feeling ended in a near-swoon and he blinked hard, slapped himself to wake up. The air in these places could be stifling.

As the workshop gave way to the parking area of the trucking depot, Gallen realised there was a man-sized opening in the huge retractable doors at the front of the building. He needed to rest again, a general feeling of faintness coming over him—the antibiotics and the beer? Sitting in the lee of a truck, crouched on its step to avoid having his feet on the ground, he noticed that the two flashlight beams had become one. Being up against an assault rifle, he still wasn't in the clear, but one-on-one was something he could work with.

The flashlight moved closer, but towards another truck. His arms and shoulders ached with the strain of keeping the bags off the ground, a burden he could do without when it came time to neutralise his pursuer. Pushing his back against the driver's door of the truck, he kept the bags flat too, squeezing into the shadows to avoid creating a silhouette.

Feet scraped on the concrete nearby, and sweat poured off Gallen's forehead, wetting the band of his cap. His P9 was in his waistband and to reach for it would mean dropping the bags and giving away his position. The feet came closer, the flashlight sweeping in front of them.

Gallen's heart beat hard. The flashlight swept to where Gallen's feet would have been if he was standing on the ground, and then arced away. Gallen breathed out and launched himself in a dive, ripping his right elbow at the man's exposed temple. The guard yelped but the blow felled him where he stood, his M4 clattering slightly on the concrete as Gallen landed on him with the extra weight of the bags.

Panting on the concrete, feeling the warm form beneath him, Gallen waited for the sounds of approaching cavalry. None came.

Pushing slowly to his feet, Gallen made himself breathe deeply through his nostrils, his brain drifting away as if hallucinating. He needed to think, to act carefully. Spikey was gone, but there was a door that opened onto the front parking area of the depot, and Gallen now had an assault rifle.

Jogging towards the door, his leg almost useless, Gallen stopped and looked at his G-Shock: eight and a half minutes had elapsed. Charlie Basa said he'd go to Bravo if the shit started and wait for ten. The gunfire must have been obvious to Basa, which meant he should be in the rear alley.

Padding back towards the office which would take him to the roof, Gallen held the M4 at his shoulder, sweeping for sounds or movement. He reached the steel stairs without incident and paused on the bottom step, checking for movement. There was none, but something caught his attention: below the office mezzanine, parked near the front of the vehicle garage, was a white SUV. He shouldn't have thought anything of it—white was probably the world's most popular colour for SUVs.

Climbing a few more stairs, he looked down again and now got a better view of the vehicle: a BMW, with Saudi plates.

He heard noise behind the main access door and climbed the stairs, the bags growing heavier with every step. He swept the area from the open gantry before walking into the office, now dark, the banks of screens glinting but dead. His armpits and neck were wet with sweat as he reached French doors on the side of the security office, and found them unlocked. He pushed into the night, happy for the blast of cool and noticing the stars in the clear sky. The roof garden area looked deserted and he walked nervously to the brick rampart twenty yards from the office, shouldering the M4 and sweeping the area with it as he approached.

The silver Yukon was parked in the darkest part of the dim alley and it was forty seconds until the ten-minute limit. Seeing a dumpster at one end of the wall, Gallen walked thirty paces and threw his bags so they fell to the garbage, tossing the assault rifle after them. Feeling blood run into his shoulders and arms, Gallen was energised by the reduction in his load, and stood on the rampart, aiming himself at the rubbish bags. He had a soft landing, although his right leg didn't like the impact and he yelled in pain without meaning to do so.

Rolling out of the trash, he heaved the bags on the ground and swept the area with the M4, his heart still beating too fast. He was not only out of shape—he was scared, a bad place to be.

Grabbing the bags, he limped to the Yukon, which idled softly, the exhaust vapour seeming oddly beautiful—his mind was playing tricks on him, creating colours of the rainbow and a New Age soundtrack as he watched the vapour. He decided he must be close to collapse.

Opening the passenger door, he wondered why Charlie hadn't leapt out to help him. But Charlie wasn't in the driver's seat—Charlie Basa sat on the passenger side with a busted nose, while a large Anglo man sat behind the wheel, a sawn-off shotgun held across his crotch at Gallen's face.

Gallen knew the man.

'Hey, boss,' came the slow drawl, fresh off the Saskatchewan prairie. 'Charlie here was gonna leave. Thought I'd persuade him otherwise.'

'Hey, Kenny,' said Gallen, shoving the bags inside the rear door. 'We gotta get out of here.'

'That sounds smart.' Winter shifted the gear lever down to D. 'You always was smart.'

Lights swirled, voices ebbed and flowed, colours seemed wrong and harsh. Gallen was lying in a bed in a small bedroom—one belonging to an Arab family judging by the rugs on the wall.

A local man's face loomed over him, a smile erupting beneath his big moustache.

'It is Mr Gerry,' said the man, standing upright and speaking to someone.

Kenny Winter came into view, long face, big jaw, thinning blond hair. 'Back with us, boss?'

'Where am . . .' he started, but no sound came through the dry croak.

'Here, drink some,' said the Arab man, offering a bottle of Evian and trying to coax Gallen's head upwards.

Gallen drank deeply, choking as he tried to take in too much. 'Where am I?' he said, handing the bottle back to the Arab and trying to raise himself on his elbow.

'This is Zaki,' said Winter. 'He's a scientist. We're in his house.'

Gallen nodded. 'What happened?'

'Don't remember?' said Winter, lighting a cigarette and pointing at Gallen's leg.

Looking down, he saw he was wearing borrowed clothes and a large bloodstain had wet the sheets around his right thigh. 'Shit,' he mumbled, seeing a pile of bloodied sheets in a hamper by the door. 'That me?'

'Sure is,' said a woman's voice, and then Alison McIntyre was sweeping through the door, a large military medic's satchel over her left shoulder. 'What were you doing running around trucking depots when I'd specifically told you to rest?'

Pushing him back onto the pillow, she dropped the satchel, rolled up the sleeves on her blue chambray shirt and clicked her fingers at Winter. 'Water, warm water, lots of it. Now.'

Winter disappeared and she turned to Zaki. 'You got a hat stand?'

'Sure,' said Zaki, intimidated.

'I need it.'

'Okay,' said the scientist, leaving.

'Actually,' said Gallen, his head still light and as close to zero energy as he'd ever felt, 'I did rest.'

'You fool,' said McIntrye, wriggling her fingers into single-use latex gloves, her face annoyed and pretty. 'You've lost *so* much blood. You realise that? You should be dead.'

Gallen looked down at the blood. 'Was I shot?'

'No, that was the first time I met you,' said McIntrye, tearing open a blood-typing kit with her teeth. 'I'm betting this was your wound perforating due to exertion.'

'Sounds like me.'

She squirted a liquid onto the four printed boxes of the typing card. 'Your big friend called and said he found you in the back of the vehicle, sleeping in a pool of your own blood.'

She grabbed his hand, made to spike his thumb, but Gallen pulled back. 'I know my blood type. O negative.'

'You got that from your dog tags, when you were in the military?'

'Sure,' said Gallen.

McIntyre grabbed his hand again and spiked the thumb too aggressively. 'You know dog tags are wrong eleven per cent of the time? Wrong spelling, wrong blood type, even wrong social security number?'

'Learned this in the Med Corps?'

'First thing they teach you,' said McIntyre, squeezing his blood onto the card so it left four samples in a row. 'Never trust a dog tag.'

Zaki dragged a hat stand into the room, set it near Gallen's shoulder.

'So what's this about?' said Gallen.

'Transfusion,' said McIntyre. 'I need an IV pole. But first I'm going to see about that wound.'

It was almost seven pm when he woke to the smells of the family meal. He was in the same room, but he was in a fresh T-shirt and a pair of borrowed shorts. There was no sign of blood and a heavy bandage encircled his thigh.

Sitting up, he looked around. He felt good—better than he'd felt since being shot in the leg at the back of the Araby Castle. Swinging his legs over the edge of what was a child's bed, he eased his weight onto his feet and stood. The leg still ached but there was no dizziness and no swoon.

The living room was empty but he heard voices on the large patio that overlooked the city. Several people, including two children, sat around a long dining table in the cool evening. Winter looked up, chewing a huge mouthful. 'Hey, boss. You hungry?'

Gallen nodded as he sat on the chair beside Alison McIntyre, and hands went to various dishes to ensure he got some food. It was lamb with couscous and a cucumber salad; he ate two plates before coming up for air.

'How do you feel, Mr Gerry?' said Zaki, after he'd introduced a son and daughter who looked like they'd be in junior high, and his wife, a handsome middle-aged woman called Maria.

'I feel good, Zaki—thanks for everything.'

Zaki opened his palms at Winter. 'I owe this man my life. Any friend of his is a friend of this family.'

Gallen poured a glass of water, picked some dates from a silver bowl. 'So, what happened?'

'Picked you up from your interview,' said Winter, pretending to cough into his huge fist. 'We was driving through the city and you was awful quiet back there. When we got to the hotel, you were asleep on the back seat and there was blood everywhere.'

Gallen shook his head slightly. The previous night was a blur.

Winter pointed at Zaki. 'I knew a place I could take you, and when we got you into the house I found a card for Dr Alison McIntrye in your wallet. I called her cell, she came over and decided you needed a transfusion.'

A servant brought a silver tea set to the table.

'Charlie?' said Gallen, remembering the Bravo pick-up in the alley.

'Waiting for us,' said Winter, taking a small glass of mint tea. 'Patiently.'

Alison McIntyre leaned into the table with an arch look. 'Kenny was telling us how you're a farmer and he helps you out with odd jobs.'

'That about covers it, right, kids?' said Gallen, winking at the boy.

Down on the street, just twenty feet below them, three car doors slammed almost at once, and Gallen saw Winter stiffen. They swapped a glance: the doors translated to at least three men, organised.

Lifting his finger to his lips, Winter made the international sign for 'ssh' as he rose silently from his seat. Gallen rose too, wondering where his P9 and the M4 assault rifle had gone. The rest of the diners at the table watched, wide-eyed, as Winter drew Spikey's Beretta from the back of his waistband.

A boot scraped on the sidewalk below them, and then came three fast raps on the door. Gallen froze, stared at Winter. Both of their instincts had been triggered, which usually meant it wasn't paranoia

'What did you hear?' whispered McIntyre.

It was a cool, still evening in Amman, so the entire table heard the next sound drifting from the front door: the sound of a cartridge being automatically flipped into the firing chamber as someone primed the weapon.

CHAPTER 16

Winter moved inside to the head of the stairs while Gallen gestured for McIntyre and Zaki's family to follow him. Like most Arab bathrooms, theirs was a solid concrete arrangement; the walls would stop bullets but the door might not. Gallen ushered them in and asked Zaki to lock up, get the women and children to lie in the bath.

'Where's my M4?' said Gallen, arriving beside Winter at the head of the stairs. There was a fidgeting sound from the front door, which was hidden as the stairwell reversed on itself.

'The rifle's still in the truck—pea-shooter's beside your bed.'

There was another rap at the front door and a small whimper sounded from the bathroom. Gallen ran softly into the room he'd recuperated in, lifted a pile of his cleaned clothes, and grabbed the P9. Checking the clip and the breech as he moved back to the stairs, he remembered the bags.

'Listen, Kenny, these people want the bags. Zaki's people have no dog in this fight.'

'Agreed,' said Winter, the Beretta in cup-and-saucer grip, his face impassive as he edged sideways down the stairs.

'So where are those bags?'

'Truck,' said Winter, moving down the stairs.

'Where you goin'?' hissed Gallen. 'I count three bad guys with at least one assault rifle.'

'Sounds like a glass door.' Winter reached the turn in the stairwell. 'See what I mean?'

'Kenny!' said Gallen, as loud as he could without shouting, but the Canadian was already peeking around the turn and raising the Beretta, drawing back the cocking lever. 'We don't even know who they are.'

An Arabic voice yelled from the other side of the door, followed by yet another rap on the glass. Whatever these people were doing, it wasn't clandestine. Gallen heard a sound behind him and turned to face Zaki. 'What are they saying?'

Zaki scratched his head, confused. 'That's my landlord. You can't shoot him.'

George sat upright in his seat when Maria delivered tea to the balcony table, attempting a coy smile that sat somewhere between obsequious and sleazy. Gallen saw the look sneaking out from behind the big Saddam moustache: from his rural American perspective, the Arabs stared at women way too often for a culture which demanded such propriety between the sexes. He'd been raised in a place where you called women ma'am and kept your eyes off their breasts when you spoke to them. He was glad he'd persuaded Alison to stay with the children.

'So, now I know you're all okay—and there is no danger . . .' said George, turning to his offsider, a skinny Arab with a shoulder holster under his right armpit. The man shrugged at George and then George shrugged too, reaching for his tea.

Gallen took a cigarette from Winter, waited for the punchline. George the landlord had just spent the last seven minutes telling his tenants that he was concerned for their welfare because of some things he was hearing and some happenings in the neighbourhood, and how talk of such things can get people hurt. Gallen kept an eye on Zaki, watched the man nod like a Howdy Doody doll. The conversation was becoming menacing, especially since the third man in the party—the one with the submachine gun—was posted outside the front door.

'So, Mr Gallen,' said George, his tone no longer labouring the bonhomie with his terrified tenant, 'what brings you to Amman?'

'Business.' Gallen sucked on the smoke.

George smiled. 'Business? What business is it that you hurt your leg so badly?'

'I slipped,' said Gallen. 'Fell on a spike.'

'Ah,' said George, shaking a finger. 'Perhaps the spike fell on you?'

'Ah.' Gallen nodded at the joke and smiled.

'There's a trucking company two blocks from here,' said George, smile suddenly disappearing. 'al-Haq—you know of this place?'

'Sure,' said Gallen, pulse pumping in his neck. 'Big place, can't miss it.'

'Yes, Mr Gallen. It was robbed last night, and the people who own this place . . . how can I say it?' George winced in a way that suggested he'd seen too many silent movies in his time. 'These are very possessive people, very particular.'

'You're saying they're scary?' said Winter, his slow gum-chewing making his jaw muscles bulge.

George made a point of shifting in his seat to look at the big man. 'If scary means that the al-Haq brothers will pull the eyeballs from your head for stealing from them, then yes, Mr Kenny—they are scary.'

Winter nodded. 'So, George, how much?'

Zaki stood, worried. 'My guests don't mean it like that.'

'It's okay, Zaki, my friend.' George raised his puffy hand and placed it softly on Zaki's forearm. 'You're not in trouble.'

'I mean, you got a price?' Winter leaned towards George, elbow on his knee.

'Okay, everyone,' said Gallen, wanting to stop the momentum of the conversation before it went too far. Kenny Winter was the wrong person to intimidate with suggestions of violence: he'd been an enforcer in the Western Hockey League and had gone to Afghanistan as an Assaulter, the elite of the Canadian infantry. He spoke slow but he finished conflicts very quickly if he felt threatened.

'No, no.' George held his hands up in the surrender pose. 'Mr Kenny is right—I can help with these matters, for a modest consideration.'

'Help?' said Gallen, trying to keep a lid on it. 'With what?'

'Well, given that most of this city now knows that the Americans who robbed the al-Haq brothers are living in this house . . .'

'Yes?' said Gallen, wanting to keep Winter out of it.

'I can relocate you in a place that is not known or talked about.'

'Where?'

'This would depend on the level of recompense,' said George, with what looked like a small wink. 'I could put you in an apartment that no one would know about.'

'Or?' said Gallen.

'Or I could arrange the return of the goods, ensure that the owners understood that there had been a misunderstanding.'

Gallen's temples thumped and he could feel hot breath streaming from his flaring nostrils. Turning to Zaki, he looked the man in the eye. 'Shit, Zaki. These people Hamas?'

Zaki's eyes grew wide and he stood quickly, addressed George. 'I never said these things, I swear to God,' before stuttering into a stream of Arabic and clutching his hands in front of his chest.

George gestured for the man to sit, like a pained consul who'd grown tired of being worshipped. 'Hamas?' He stared at Gallen. 'They call it this on the TV, they call it that in the American papers—but in Amman, we are just friends, yes, doing the favour for our brothers.'

There was silence around the table. They were in trouble.

'Let's just say, Mr Gallen, that the al-Haqs are not my favourite family, but they employ many people in this city, and I want them to feel comfortable to do business here.'

'Okay,' said Gallen.

'So I'm going to assume that whatever you took from them is gone—am I right?'

Gallen nodded.

'But you have something that must be returned, and for the consideration of fifty thousand US dollars, I will return this item to al-Haq and ensure that you are free to leave this country unharmed.'

'And Zaki?' said Gallen.

'Zaki is my tenant,' said George. 'In Jordan it is considered very rude to evict a man for no reason.'

Gallen nodded, looked at Winter, before looking back at George. 'What's this item?'

'His real name is not important,' said George. 'But you probably know him as Charlie Basa.'

The first thing Gallen noticed as he stepped onto the street outside Zaki's house was the second crew, four of them leaning on a Toyota minibus on the other side of the road. They looked like Russian criminals, all shiny leather bomber jackets, heavy thighs and obvious handguns.

George stopped at the pavement, spoke with a skinny Arab with a large shoulder holster. Gallen took the opportunity to collar Winter.

'Jesus, Kenny!' he hissed. 'The fuck was that about Charlie?'

Kenny cased the street. 'Had to remove him, for safekeeping,' said the Canadian. 'Didn't know where he stood with us.'

'You fricking kidnapped someone from Hamas?' said Gallen, seething. 'In *Amman*?!'

'Ride with me,' said George, walking towards an eight-year-old BMW sedan parked with two wheels up on the sidewalk. Following George, Gallen saw Winter being led to the Yukon by one of the thugs at the Toyota. The skinny dude with the shoulder holster opened the BMW's doors and Gallen got in back with George.

'I'm thinking we should move you out through Aqaba,' said George, lighting a dark cheroot and cracking his window. 'Once they have Charlie back, I can hold the al-Haq crews for a few days, but these are thorough people, Mr Gallen. May I suggest that even when back in America, you are careful, yes?'

Gallen twisted slightly to check on Winter's progress. With his half of Spikey's stash, there was around three million dollars in those military duffels, and even though he wanted to be out of Jordan, the presence of so much money gave him at least a sense of options.

'I'll be careful, George,' said Gallen, distracted as the skinny henchman walked back to Zaki's house. 'I was here to help an old buddy get out of Amman—I got no fight with the al-Haqs or Hamas.'

'You and your Hamas. You Americans read too much *Newsweek*.'

'It got a better name?' Gallen craned to see where Skinny had disappeared to.

'It has no name in Amman,' said George with a cold smile. 'Did you not see Zaki?'

The door opened and Skinny thrust something at Gallen. As he leaned sideways, he realised it was Alison McIntyre.

'Leave me alone, creep,' she said, as her shoulder drove into Gallen's left bicep. 'I'm a US citizen—what the hell do you think you're doing?'

Gallen turned to George. 'She's not in this.'

'Just keeping the military personnel together,' said George.

'Military?' said McIntyre, showing no respect. 'I was a doctor in the US Navy eight years ago!'

A thug from the Toyota arrived at the hood of the BMW with one of the duffels Gallen had lifted from the trucking depot. He opened it and showed Skinny, and neither looked happy.

'I'm warning you,' started Alison, but Gallen squeezed her knee, gave her a *shut up* look.

Skinny handed the bag to George, chattering in Arabic. Opening it, George looked inside, then showed Gallen. 'There's twelve thousand dollars in this bag, Mr Gallen.'

Gallen had a look, saw a loose pile of bound US notes. 'I'll trust you on that.'

George observed him too long and then smiled. 'My expertise is people, Mr Gallen, and you are not a stupid one. Yet smart men do not break into Ariq al-Haq's business and steal from him for twelve thousand dollars. Not even a stupid man would do that.'

Gallen gulped. 'I was expecting more than twelve grand.'

'How much?'

'Three million US, but you only wanted fifty K,' said Gallen.

'It's a good deal,' snarled George. 'So where is it?'

'That's it,' said Gallen. 'What's in the truck—that's what I left the depot with.'

'The bags are shit,' said George, tossing his cheroot. 'Bunch of intelligence papers and blueprints. There's an old pistol and a bunch of keys. Don't tell me you risked your life for this shit.'

116

Gallen looked away, but George caught something in his eyes. Calling Skinny over, he asked something which was relayed back to the Yukon and then an answer given to Skinny.

'It seems, Mr Gallen, that the al-Haqs are missing seven bags, stolen from their depot.'

'So?'

'You have three in your vehicle.'

Gallen looked straight ahead. He wasn't raised to squeal on a colleague, even one as annoying as Spikey Holmes.

George pulled a BlackBerry from his leather jacket, selected a number from his address book and called it. He talked in Arabic and then hung up on a call that lasted seventeen seconds.

'So,' said George, 'my informant tells me that when you jumped in the garbage bin behind the depot, you were carrying a rifle and three dark military bags.'

'Correct.'

'So someone else took the other four?' said George.

Gallen remained silent.

'Hmm . . . I wonder. I don't suppose the former colleague you are rescuing is a US Marine called Terrell Holmes?'

Gallen stared at George, their noses inches apart. 'It would make sense, wouldn't it?'

George lost his hardness, looked up at Skinny. Among the stream of Arabic, Gallen heard mention of Spikey's name, which made Skinny turn his eyes and the palms of his hands towards heaven.

George lit a new cheroot, turned to Gallen. 'So it seems Holmes took all the money, yes?'

Gallen was confused. 'Wasn't he caught?'

George shook his head slowly. 'Not according to Ariq al-Haq.'

Gallen's ears rang: Spikey had set him up? He hadn't been caught, he'd staged it with the security people and made off with the entire six million? And Gallen was the patsy who was supposed to be caught and dragged into Hamas interrogation sessions?

George clicked his tongue. 'Since Holmes is in this, you'll have to meet the boss.'

'Boss?' said Gallen. 'Who's the boss?'

117

'Baba el-Masri,' said George, his cheroot hand slightly unsteady. 'May I suggest you are very silent and very respectful in front of Baba. Let me do the talking.'

'And?'

'And perhaps we'll see the dawn, Mr Gallen.'

Gallen couldn't help a smile. *'We?'*

'The message and the messenger are the same animal,' said George, dragging too hard on his cheroot. 'Welcome to Hamas.'

CHAPTER 17

The room looked like the storage section of a garage. No windows, bare concrete floor, boxes of books, VHS tapes and folded linen along one wall.

'I can't believe this,' said Alison, vacillating between defiance and fear. 'The only thing I know about Hamas is that they bomb Israelis.'

'They only want me,' said Gallen, who'd stopped smoking out of deference to the doctor. 'You won't be harmed.'

'What are they waiting for?' Alison stood abruptly as the nerves cut in again. 'You think they're phoning my parents, seeing how much they'll pay?'

'Can't say for sure,' said Winter, who was laid out on the floor, conserving his energy. 'Seems to me George was after an easier payday than your ransom.'

'Easier?' said Alison.

'No American media, no State Department or CIA—just a couple of thieves with six million dollars in a bag. And they're in your hometown. If you were a Hamas commander, which one would you go after?'

'I don't know,' said the doctor.

'Think about it.' Winter sat up. 'So, boss. Where's Spikey come into this?'

'He's my old staff sergeant, from A-stan,' said Gallen. 'I was contracted to bring him back to the States so he can pay back some Longbeach gangsters. I get over here and realise he's stolen millions of dollars and the locals want their cut.'

Winter thought about it. 'Spikey working with Hamas?'

Gallen shook his head, the naked bulb in the ceiling giving him a headache. 'Baba knew Spikey had knocked over the al-Haq depot—he protected him at the Araby Castle hotel in exchange for a split of what he'd taken, when he could get out and claim it.'

'So where's Spikey?'

'Don't know.'

'But wherever he is, he has six million dollars?'

Gallen nodded. 'I think he staged his own capture. He gave me three bags to carry and he took four. We were separated when the gunfight started, and now here I am: captured by Hamas, chased by the al-Haq brothers and I have twelve grand.'

'Think Spikey got the money?' said Winter, lighting a smoke and chuckling. 'You Marines—never stop scheming for money.'

'Shit.' Alison shoved her hands too deep in her Levis and hunched her shoulders. 'That's all you army guys can talk about: money?'

'And food,' said Winter.

'And women,' said Gallen.

'And Harleys.'

'And Camaros . . .'

'Yeah, yeah, yeah,' said Alison. 'I get it.'

'What I don't get is why you're here, boss,' said Winter. 'You came to pick up Spikey, or the money?'

'Chase Lang paid me to help Spikey grab his money and get out of Amman, back to LA where he can pay his gambling debts.'

'Where's Chase now?'

'I kind of got on the wrong side of Chase's main dude—guy called Daly.'

'Chase Lang is fairly high calibre,' said Winter, confused. 'He'd get involved with someone like Spikey?'

Gallen popped his last stick of Doublemint. 'Well, I guess he did.'

The door swung inwards and George beckoned Gallen over.

'Nothing smart, nothing disrespectful,' said George, as they walked down a tradesman's corridor. 'Maybe Baba's in a good mood and we all walk away, okay?'

Gallen nodded, looked at his watch: almost two in the morning.

George stopped outside a closed door, knocked, and an armed thug let them through into a living room, the lights of Amman twinkling through a long set of windows.

'Here, put them on,' said George, grabbing a folded pair of blue jeans from the table. 'You can't meet Baba in shorts—he would not understand.'

Dropping his shorts, Gallen looked at the sizing on the Lees. 'Thirty-fours? Flattery will get you everywhere.'

For the first time, Gallen saw a sheen on George's forehead that spelled pure fear. He had an idea.

'You were looking after Spikey, at the Araby?'

George rubbed his temples, looked sideways at the thug who was moving away. 'My people were living there with him.'

Gallen sucked his stomach in, buttoned the Riders. 'Then I came along?'

George snorted. 'Do not be on the ego trip, Mr Gallen.'

'It's just that, if we tell this story my way, perhaps things turn out better for us both.'

George turned his back on the bodyguard and leaned towards Gallen. 'What story?'

Baba el-Masri twirled the phone cable in big skipping-rope arcs while creating a creaking symphony with his leather chair. Everything about the man was big: big wrists, big eyebrows, big voice, big belly and the big sausage-like hands of the secret police.

He laughed into the handset while George and Gallen gasped for breath in the fetid atmosphere of sweat and tobacco. Along the walls Gallen counted seven scimitars mounted against murals depicting battle scenes, and on the vast antique desk was a set of what looked like solid gold horse figurines, with mare, foal and stallion arranged as a family. Gallen thought about the horses back at the farm, the bucking herd that Roy contracted to the rodeo companies each summer; he hoped his father had brought them up to the run-in paddock where they could be fed under shelter and kept out of the winter winds. Roy had forgotten to bring them up from the bottom field one year and when a cougar spooked them, they'd run across a frozen part of the creek and dropped through the ice. Eleven of them had drowned. The rodeo contracts were one of Roy's few reliable cash-earners on the farm, and losing that herd of rough stock had almost driven Roy to the point of having to give the farm back to the bank.

The phone slammed down, breaking Gallen's reverie. He looked up, into a set of large dark eyes that looked through him.

'American?'

'Yes,' said Gallen.

'US Special Forces?'

'I drove a truck.'

'Hah,' said el-Masri, leaping to his feet. He was around six-three, with what Gallen would call a 1970s wrestler's body. 'You see that, George? Only the real guys say they are not special forces.'

'Yes, Baba,' said George, his face pale and scared.

El-Masri walked around the desk and sat on the front of it, one foot remaining on the ground. 'So, Captain Gallen,' he said, his English spoken with a French accent in the manner of many middle-class Arabs. 'You were in the Afghan war with Mr Holmes?'

'Sure,' said Gallen.

Baba grabbed cigarettes from his chest pocket, offered one to Gallen. 'You're aware that this man owes me for accommodation, food and protection services at my hotel?'

'I heard that.'

Baba lit their cigarettes. 'Some very bad people wanted some money from him, would torture him for it if my men had not deterred them.'

'Okay.'

'So in exchange for protecting Mr Holmes he agreed to pay me a percentage of his money, when he was able to retrieve it.'

Gallen exhaled smoke at the ceiling. 'Yep.'

'Then you, Captain Gallen, arrive with Chase Lang's men, but you leave with Mr Holmes.'

'Correct.'

'And then you retrieve Mr Holmes's money, which turns out to be hidden in the al-Haqs' depot.'

Gallen looked at his cigarette. 'I suppose.'

'So now Captain Gallen is here, but he has no money,' said Baba, crossing his arms and looking at George. 'The al-Haq brothers have lost their money, and Mr Holmes has gone . . . yet he has *all* the money.'

Gallen realised that Baba el-Masri's overly friendly style was making George nervous.

'So you see, Captain, I have no recompense for myself. My clients—the al-Haqs—are most unhappy. And the al-Haq brothers are not people who you'd wish to make unhappy.'

'Why don't I get it back for you, Baba?' said Gallen. 'I mean, he stole from me too.'

Baba looked at George and then each of his two bodyguards before settling back on Gallen with a face that had lost its friendliness and now exuded the violence Hamas was known for. 'You should be careful about what you promise me, Captain Gallen.'

Gallen's throat felt dry. 'I understand.'

'Do you? *What* do you understand, Captain?'

Gallen held Baba's stare. 'I understand that you have not only lost a lot of money, but you are probably embarrassed by what Ariq al-Haq has said to you.'

'Yes?' Baba sucked on the smoke.

'I know you can alter the lives of me and my friends fairly easily, but you wouldn't do anything too drastic if there was another way.'

'Continue.'

'So I propose that George and I track down Spikey—I mean, Mr Holmes—and retrieve the money.'

Baba slid off the desk so he was standing over Gallen. Crushing his cigarette, he looked back. 'George, yes? You want George to help you?'

'I need someone who knows the city.' Gallen warmed to the conversation. 'And someone who carries the weight of your name.'

The first strike was a blur that made Gallen recoil slightly, and then blink as a shot of warm blood hit his face. By the time el-Masri had lifted the figurine of the stallion for a second attack, George's head was lolling sideways onto his chair arm, a large gash in his forehead suggesting a fractured skull and instant death. The second strike from the figurine hit George's temple so hard that the rectangular base of the gold statue embedded itself in the flesh and bone and Baba had to use two hands to pull it out.

Gallen raised his hands to ward off an attack, but it didn't come. Replacing the bloody, hair-encrusted stallion on the desk as George's lifeless body slumped to the carpet, Baba leaned back on the desktop and looked at Gallen.

'No, George is not right for this assignment.'

'Okay,' said Gallen. He needed a bottle of Pepto.

'He used his traitorous brother, Charlie, to drive you, and look at where we are now.'

'So . . .' started Gallen.

'You don't need my men, Captain Gallen,' said Baba, tearing three tissues from a box and wiping his hands. 'You take that big Canadian—I'll keep the girl.'

'No.' Gallen stood but the phone started ringing and Baba walked back to his chair.

'You've got a week,' said Baba el-Masri as he waved Gallen away and picked up the phone. 'Use it wisely.'

CHAPTER 18

The room was too cool for Gallen's liking and the conversation was not going as he'd planned.

'You see, Gerry?' said Adam Regan, a second secretary with hair that couldn't decide if it was sandy or ginger. 'There's no ransom demand, there's no video on YouTube, no evidence of violence, and she isn't part of a United States government program. This falls outside any consular responsibility.'

'I'm not doin' this for me,' said Gallen, stifling a yawn. 'She's an American doctor. You tellin' me Hamas gets to hold her and Uncle Sam does nothing?'

'Don't lecture me, Gerry,' said Regan, a thirty-something with an expensive shirt. 'You people come here, get mixed up with precisely the wrong people, and then you think you can whistle up the cavalry when you get caught.'

'Look . . .'

'No, you look, Captain. Former soldiers don't get mixed up with Baba el-Masri because they want a Nobel Peace Prize. They do it for money.'

'I'm a contractor.'

'You're a cliché, Gerry. You're hired muscle, only this time you've dragged an innocent into it.'

Gallen looked at the ceiling. 'Just help her.'

'Help her?!' said Regan, making other embassy workers turn in their cubicles. 'I majored in French and politics.'

'I meant, you know . . .'

'No, I don't know,' said Regan. He pointed at his screen. 'You're a former Marine. Why aren't you and your buddies helping her?'

'I shovelled chow in the Corps.'

'Really?' said Regan. 'Your file is classified. I mean, virtually the whole thing.'

'Secret recipes,' said Gallen.

'You don't look like a cook.'

Gallen nodded. He needed sleep and he needed someone to take the case of Dr McIntyre. He worried that if it wasn't a consular operation it would become a Kenny Winter operation, and he didn't know if he had the stomach for that anymore. He'd fired too many rounds, seen too many field injuries and roadside graves. After George was bashed to death beside him, Gallen had felt queasy. Battle fatigue wasn't something he wanted to explain to Regan because he couldn't yet explain it to himself.

'Look.' Regan leaned back in his chair. 'See it from the locals' point of view: they have a king who answers to the White House, a military that answers to the Pentagon and an intelligence service that is basically the CIA. Hamas may not be perfect, but Hamas is Arabs and a lot of locals don't see the problem.'

'You're saying they're untouchable?'

'No, I didn't say that.'

'Good, 'cos when I served my country Hamas was on the terrorist list,' said Gallen, 'and that list came from the State Department, far as I remember.'

'Gerry, you must know that more than eighty per cent of people in the Arab world want the Jews out of Palestine? I mean, fuck, this is Jordan.'

'No, Adam, this is the US embassy and no Jew ever put a bomb on my bus.'

Regan exhaled, concentrated on a Chicago Bulls coffee mug beside his laptop. 'Okay, Gerry, Dr McIntyre's name is now in our watch system. And I'll kick this upstairs: maybe you get lucky, but more than likely someone says, *Wait for a week, see if she gets sick of her new boyfriend . . .'*

'Or?'

Regan looked around the cubicles. 'Got a cell number?'

Gallen wrote the number on a notepad, pushed it over. 'Who sees this?'

'One of the spooks. Deals with kidnappings and ransoms—Hamas know him.'

'He got a name?'

'Yep,' said Regan. 'Now get out.'

Gallen paid the cabbie in greenbacks and walked the two blocks south, feeling the dry afternoon heat on his back, his black baseball cap shading his face and allowing him to check faces and tails.

Taking a sharp right down an old alley, he passed tiny coffee shops and old men playing dominoes, smoking narghile pipes in the shade. At the Wadi Oasis private hotel he stopped at the caged reception desk and the young Arab behind the bars pressed a button, releasing the internal security door and allowing him into the lobby.

He took the stairs, determined to get strength back into his wounded leg, and had to pause on the second-floor landing as the pain spasmed in the wounded thigh muscle. 'Shit,' he moaned, and forced himself to walk to one of only two doors on the level.

Letting himself into the comfortable but not luxurious suite, Gallen staggered to the lavatory and dropped to his knees at the toilet bowl, vomiting hard. When he was finished, he leaned back against the white tiles and liked their coolness.

'You okay, boss?' said Kenny Winter.

Gallen looked up, saw the bottle of water being held out to him, drank deeply. 'Leg playing up—pain went to my gut.'

'That Dr Alison told you to take it easy, boss,' said Winter, sitting on the edge of the bathtub. 'Might wanna think about that.'

Gallen tasted a chunk of food on his bottom lip, spat it out. 'Plenty of time for resting once we've dealt with this thing.'

'How'd the embassy go?'

'Said what you said they'd say.' Gallen drained the water bottle. 'Jordanian Hamas has been normalised.'

Winter smiled. 'So, then?'

'Don't look at me like that, Kenny.'

'Just sayin'.'

Gallen wiped the cold sweat off his forehead. 'I know what you're thinking, Kenny, but the fact is there's two of us and that's not enough to take down Baba's crew.'

'Dr Alison saved your butt three times in one day,' said Winter, biting a Marlboro from a soft pack. 'I'd say you owe her.'

Gallen growled at that. When he was in the field he yearned for the day when the meticulous soldier's accounting of who owed what to whom would be a thing of the past and he wouldn't have to keep tabs on who gave him a new tube of Crest or who gave him a packet of Schicks because he'd forgotten to stock up at the PX. The soldiering world ran on IOUs and it was following him into civvie life. He would never have travelled to Jordan if not for owing Spikey.

'There's another way,' said Gallen, putting his hand out to be helped to his feet.

'What's that?' said Winter, suspicious.

'We find Spikey, return the money, get Alison.'

'Really, boss? Spikey Holmes ain't some law student proving he can rough it in the slums,' said Winter. 'He's a staff sergeant with a lot of combat duty—hard duty—on his sheet. What makes you think he'll be easy to find, let alone capture?'

'I didn't say easy.'

'No,' said Winter. 'Try taking six million dollars off a man like Holmes. Might be easier taking on Baba's boys.'

Gallen limped out of the bathroom into the suite's living area and stood in front of Charlie Basa, who was duct-taped to a dining table chair, a strip of silver tape across his mouth.

'Thirsty?' said Gallen.

Basa nodded and Gallen grabbed a water from the bulk pack, tore the duct tape off the captive's mouth and aimed the water at it.

When Charlie Basa had gulped the contents of the bottle, Gallen gestured to Winter to let the man go free.

'Thank you,' said Basa as Winter sliced the duct tape.

'So, Charlie.' Gallen lit a smoke and tossed the pack to Basa. 'I have bad news.'

Basa lit a smoke. 'What is it?'

'George, your brother—he's dead.'

Basa's face froze. 'George? But . . . how, where?'

'Baba killed him in front of me,' said Gallen, deadpan.

Basa gaped. 'Why?'

'Spikey Holmes—remember him?'

'Sure,' said Basa, his face twisting into a mask of shock.

'He took six million dollars out of that depot, left me with nothing.'

'But you got the bags . . .'

'There was nothing in the bags 'cept for some paper and twelve thousand dollars.'

Basa slumped. 'Baba killed George?'

'George was supposed to be minding Spikey at the Araby Castle. Baba thought George was in on it with Spikey, and he thinks you're part of it too.'

'Me?' said Basa.

'Called you traitorous.'

Charlie Basa grimaced. 'This is not good.'

'No, this is not good,' said Winter. 'Because Baba el-Masri is holding an American doctor until we bring him the dough.'

'And we have a week to do it,' said Gallen.

'What do I have to do with this?' said Charlie Basa.

'You know Spikey, know where he's going,' said Gallen. 'You know the RV out by the Iraqi border, you know who runs the exfil and how it works. You might even know where he'd hide the money, who he trusts.'

'Why would I help you do this?' said Basa, sucking on his smoke. 'Why would I bring six million dollars to the man who killed my brother?'

Gallen smiled. 'You'd do it to get close to Baba. You'd do it to get close to Spikey. Maybe there's change out of that money—enough to split?'

Charlie Basa looked from Gallen to Winter. 'Why wouldn't I run?'

'To where?' said Gallen. 'To Hamas? To the police? You should remember something—I'm now protected by Baba el-Masri. I'm his six-million-dollar payday. You wanna put a bullet in me, you're putting a bullet in your family.'

Basa shook his head slowly, tears running down his cheeks. 'I told George, many years ago, that this Hamas and this Baba were no good. I told him!'

'Spikey said you were intel,' said Gallen. 'We're gonna need everything you've got.'

A cell phone rang. Gallen slapped his pockets and Winter shook his head. They looked at Charlie Basa, who was fishing a Nokia from his dark chinos. He gave Gallen an inquiring look.

'Take it,' said Gallen.

Putting the phone to his ear, Charlie listened and then spoke. In English.

When he'd signed off, he looked at Gallen. 'I have a meeting, this afternoon.'

'Cancel,' said Gallen. 'We're going to the eastern desert, catch Spikey before he flies.'

'Maybe I should go,' Basa said, taking Winter's pack of Marlboros and lighting one.

'Why?' said Winter. 'We gotta get goin'.'

'Because we can move faster if we have the budget and the support.'

'Of who?' said Gallen, standing up and feeling a burst of pain from his leg.

'Of the United States government,' said Basa. 'That was my Agency controller from the embassy.'

'So?' said Winter, restless.

'They need me as a go-between with the Baba el-Masri faction—seems Baba is holding an American doctor.'

CHAPTER 19

Gallen had a good line of sight across Rainbow Street and into the Café des Artistes. The line might change if a delivery van chose to take a park in front of Charlie Basa's sidewalk table, but for now he could see Charlie, see the meeting and most of the street. He would have liked a wire on Charlie—even just an open cell phone—but he didn't want anything to appear amiss. He wanted the US embassy spooks to come into the open, brief Charlie Basa, and then leave. And then Gallen would debrief Charlie Basa. Not perfect but workable.

Winter was positioned on the corner, about thirty yards up the street and elevated slightly.

'Blue Dog, this is Red Bird,' said Gallen into the hands-free cord dangling from his ear to the phone. 'You copy?'

Winter's voice replied, deep and slow. 'Copy that.'

Gallen listened to the crackling of street noise coming through Winter's phone and scanned the set-up: Charlie reading the *Financial Times*; Charlie thanking the girl with the apron for his heated croissant; people milling at the counter of the trendy cafe; a middle-aged Anglo male making his way from the eastern approach to the cafe, magazine rolled in his hand, sand-coloured chinos, polo shirt and Ray-Bans. He could have been any Western tourist but he moved like a pro.

'I've seen our spook,' said Winter, before Gallen could say it. 'Bet you a beer this dude in the blue polo shirt's our guy.'

'Odds are too short.' Gallen looked to see Charlie's reaction. There was none.

The Anglo in the polo shirt walked past Charlie and into the cafe. Emerging two minutes later with a cup of coffee, he pretended to be looking for a spare seat and asked Charlie, who gestured for him to sit.

'Okay,' said Gallen into his hands-free mic. 'That's our guy.'

'Copy that,' came Winter's response and Gallen watched the Canadian leave his position on the corner and start walking downhill towards the Café des Artistes.

Gallen's waiter asked if he wanted another coffee; he asked for a Coca-Cola.

Charlie was now talking with the stranger, but without any of the animation that humans used when they established a social connection from scratch. This was business.

Winter, in a Detroit Red Wings T-shirt and military shorts, sauntered into the cafe, stood waiting for the person in front of him to order. A man in his twenties looked Winter up and down, but when the Canadian turned slightly, the man quickly turned away. Gallen listened to Winter order a coffee and watched Charlie, who sat back and shrugged, as if surrendering. The Anglo in the polo shirt pulled out a phone and made a call, and Gallen sat up straight.

'Blue Dog, the target is making a call.'

'Copy that,' said Winter. He paid for the coffee, walked towards the sidewalk. 'Got a table just inside the window.'

Winter sat down so that Gallen could see his outline through the window. Winter's proximity to Charlie was a precaution rather than a necessity: if the US embassy was going start trouble, Kenny Winter was a good man to be first on scene.

The Anglo finished his phone call and Gallen watched as Charlie made small talk.

'Good coffee,' said Winter. 'Let's remember this place.'

On Gallen's side of the street, two men left the sidewalk and waited between parked motorcycles for a break in the traffic. He couldn't see their faces, but Gallen could see that one was white and of medium build while the other was black and built more like him: perhaps a former football or hockey player.

Walking directly to Charlie's table, they stopped beside the Anglo in the blue shirt. The white guy introduced himself to Charlie, while the black guy went to another table, grabbed two chairs. As he turned and placed the chairs on the sidewalk, Gallen realised the build wasn't football or hockey: it was US Army Rangers. The guy was Daly.

Turning his head into the motorbike magazine, Gallen let Daly and the other dude walk by, watched them climb into Daly's silver Land Cruiser twenty yards from his table and accelerate into the traffic.

'I'll see you back there,' said Gallen into his hands-free, then he stood and walked in the opposite direction to Daly's Land Cruiser, his mind tumbling over the possibilities.

At the hotel room, he cracked a bottle of water, opened the sliding door to the terrace and peeled an orange. The traffic sounds and the smells of the Middle East drifted into the room as he paced and thought about the various strands of the story: he felt stupid for having gone to the US embassy, made a fuss about Alison. He should have dealt with the problem himself, either by finding Holmes and the money, or taking down Baba el-Masri.

Now he had the CIA and Chase Lang's people interested again.

The door lock rattled and Winter and Charlie Basa walked into the room, slumped into the sofas.

'Okay,' said Gallen, when they all had water and a cigarette. 'Shoot.'

Charlie held up his hands in a helpless gesture. 'I meet Amundsen, the Agency guy at the embassy, and he tells me that he wants me to approach Baba el-Masri, see about this American doctor—Alison somebody . . .'

'McIntyre,' said Gallen.

'Yes, that's it,' said Charlie.

Gallen was impatient. 'Yep?'

'Amundsen said I can do limited negotiation, as usual. He tells me that the US government does not pay for the return of hostages but there is a madrassa for the blind in south Amman that needs funds.'

'That how it's done?' Winter lit his smoke. 'Make a donation to a Hamas school?'

'It's how the CIA thinks it's done,' said Charlie. 'Baba? We'll see.'

'What did Amundsen say about my involvement?' said Gallen. 'Negative?'

'He said a US Special Forces captain—Gerry Gallen—is working privately in Amman and is likely to grab the doctor himself if it's not dealt with.'

'That's it?'

'Amundsen said you are deceptively quiet. He said to be careful because you are very dangerous and that you could be working with, um . . .'

'Kenny?' said Gallen. 'He said Kenny Winter?'

'He didn't say it like that.'

'How'd he say it?' said Winter, walking to the refrigerator, cracking a Mountain Dew with a loud hiss.

Charlie fidgeted with his fingers. 'He said Gerry was working with a Canadian assassin who had done some very serious things for ISAF in the Afghan war.'

Winter swapped a look with Gallen. The Canadian's true role was classified and it was unusual for a CIA man to disclose it.

'He told you that?' said Winter. 'He said ISAF?'

'Yes. Amundsen tells me that you two are special forces people with much experience in war and that if either of you make contact—directly or through Terrell Holmes—I must contact the station at the embassy immediately.'

Gallen breathed out. 'He know where to find me?'

'He said you were last seen with Terrell Holmes, and that Holmes has been implicated in a robbery at the al-Haq depot.'

'He ask where I was?'

'No,' said Charlie. 'He asked if I'd met you, given that I knew Holmes.'

'And?'

'And I said yes—I'd seen you on the night of the al-Haq robbery, but when it all went bad I'd left and not seen either you or Holmes again.'

Gallen looked at him, searching for a sign of dishonesty, but he couldn't see one. 'What about Kenny? How did Amundsen bring him into it?'

'He said Kenny Winter had entered at Amman International airport two days ago, that they didn't have a reason or the personnel to tail him but they assumed he was here to work with you on something.'

'And then Daly turns up?'

'Yes. Amundsen says he would like me to meet a person who might have some interests in common. He introduces me to Daly and a man called Bryce.'

'Daly tell you where he's from?' said Gallen.

'No,' said Charlie. 'Amundsen didn't say and neither did Daly. I assumed he was a US government contractor.' Charlie took them through the rest of the meeting, the questions from Daly mostly being about Gallen and Holmes, about timing, about possible exfils and other accomplices in the heist. 'But it was strange,' said Charlie. 'I thought we were talking about Holmes, but Daly was really interested in the bags.'

'You mean what's in them?' said Gallen.

Charlie scratched his temple slowly, sipped on his water. 'Well, he asked me twice what Spikey and you were stealing from al-Haq.'

'And you told him six million US?'

'I said all I knew is that Spikey and this other American were taking something from a depot,' said Charlie, pulling a dramatic Arab shrug and raising his palms to heaven. 'My job was to get them out of Amman and to a meeting point in the eastern desert.'

'Yeah?' Gallen watched Charlie squirm.

'I told these men that I got cold feet when I realised it was Ariq al-Haq, and that Ahmed al-Haq is trying to track you from Detroit. I said I was scared of stealing from this family, but I decided to give you ten minutes to be in and out.'

'Yes, you did, Charlie,' said Gallen, quietly impressed with the man. 'So where did the six million dollars enter the conversation?'

'I told them I found out later about the money: I only knew you and Holmes were picking up something.'

'So,' said Winter, 'it came back to the bags, not the money?'

Charlie nodded. 'The third time Daly asks me, I again tell him about the money, and Daly says, *Six million—and that's it?*'

The three of them shared a perplexed look.

'So I look at him, and I say, "Six million US is a lot of money in this part of the world, Mr Daly," and . . .' Charlie's voice trailed off as he sucked on his cigarette.

'What did Daly do?' said Winter.

Charlie looked at his hands.

'You okay, Charlie?' said Gallen. 'They threaten you? Your family?'

'They offer you money to turn?' said Winter, his voice losing any friendliness.

Charlie looked up. 'Yes, Mr Winter.'

'What'd they offer you, Charlie?'

'Daly said he'd give me half of Spikey's money, and . . .' Charlie looked out the window, jaw clenched.

Gallen crouched in front of Charlie Basa. 'What did Daly offer you, Charlie?'

'He said he could protect me.'

'From Hamas?' said Gallen. 'From the al-Haqs?'

'No,' said Charlie. 'From you two.'

Gallen rose and walked to the windows. The city teemed on the streets below, stores spilling onto the sidewalk, large olive oil cans piled against walls, cleaning fluids, boxes of Coca-Cola and bulk packs of soap on low shelves above the kerbs, so close to the traffic that if a bus door opened it would knock down the whole thing.

'What'd Daly say?' said Gallen, not looking back.

'He said that Kenny Winter was an expert at murdering Arabs, that he saw them as vermin and that he was a CIA assassin used against al-Qaeda HVTs.'

There was silence in the room, except for a large slurp from a Mountain Dew can. Charlie Basa turned slowly to face Winter, who was sitting beside him on the sofa. Winter burped.

'Daly said that if I didn't believe him, I should find out about Sapphire.'

Winter stared at Charlie until the Arab looked away. 'So, Daly thinks you have something to do with us?'

Charlie gulped. 'I said I hadn't seen Gerry since the night at the depot.'

'I didn't ask that,' said Winter, face still, voice heavy with menace.

'What Kenny is saying is that Daly assumes you're in contact with us,' said Gallen. 'Did you let him have that impression?'

Charlie shook his head. 'I said nothing—I said I met you briefly when I drove you and Spikey to the depot, but when the gunshots started, I drove away.'

'How was it left, with Daly?'

'He gave me his card, with his sat-phone number, and he told me to call him if I suddenly remembered something.'

Gallen walked to the television set mounted on the wall, found CNN and cranked the sound. When he turned, Charlie was fishing Daly's business card from his jacket pocket, handing it to Winter.

'So, Charlie,' said Gallen with a wink. 'Let's talk about the original Spikey exfil, down at Tabuk.'

Winter walked to the window, held the white card up to the sunlight.

'It was six o'clock tonight, wasn't it?' said Gallen, talking to Charlie but looking at Winter, who had a penknife in his hand.

'Um, yes, it was Tabuk Airport. Spikey has a friend there with a King Air for charter.'

They watched as Winter carefully sliced the card edge-wise, and then peeled a surface sheet of paper away from the back sheet. Holding up the back sheet and pointing at a small black dot the size of a pin head, Winter gave thumbs-up. He placed the card on the coffee table beside the sofa and walked to his room.

Gallen kept Charlie talking while Winter collected his and Gallen's backpacks.

Winter pointed to the card and then pointed to Charlie Basa, and then pointed to the toilet. Then made a yap-yap motion with his hand.

'Okay, gentlemen,' said Charlie, nodding slowly at Winter. 'I just need to go to the bathroom.'

Winter carried Daly's card to the bathroom, turned on the shower and closed the door on his way out.

'Know what that was, Charlie?' said Winter, checking the clip of his Beretta.

Charlie shrugged.

'It was a micro device, of the type that the Mossad and the CIA use,' said Winter, getting his backpack settled. 'Some can transmit voices, others just transmit location. You wanna hang around, see which one that is?'

'No,' said Charlie.

'Either way,' said Gallen, checking his own P9, 'we're blown. Time to go.'

'Where are we going?' said Charlie.

'To the eastern desert,' said Gallen. 'We need to talk to Spikey.'

CHAPTER 20

The drive north-east out of Amman was smooth even as they stopped twice at gas stations to look for tails. Charlie had dropped his Yukon at a private garage and they were now driving a Nissan Patrol hired from Hertz on Winter's corporate credit card under the name David Ellis. It wouldn't stop someone who really wanted to find them, because someone like Daly would be able to run a search and find a string of Winter's known aliases. But as they took the off ramp from King Abdullah Highway and entered the dedicated road system that led to Amman-Marka Airport, they seemed to be clean.

'Why we passing the entrance?' asked Winter as Charlie took the Patrol past the old 1960s main terminal, now superseded by Queen Alia International.

'My guys are around the back.' Charlie pointed further down the designated road that fed the airport. 'When Marka stopped being the main airport for Amman, it became the airport for regional travel and charter companies.'

The road followed the security fence and Gallen felt his stomach grind with paranoia and hunger. He'd avoided eating on the way out of Amman because of the gnawing in his gut and now he was paying for it. Through the skylight in the roof he watched for helicopters, knowing as he did that it was pointless; this was a charter airport in the Middle East—it would have helicopters the way Manhattan had yellow cabs.

Charlie took a sharp left at a gatehouse and waited in front of the security barriers. The young guard wandered to Charlie's window, asked something in Arabic, looked in at Gallen and lifted his sunglasses to get a proper look at Winter in the back seat.

Pulling a piece of plastic ID from his wallet, Charlie handed it over: Gallen liked that. Nothing cute like handing the entire wallet over.

The guard nodded as he found a name on his clipboard, looked at his watch and noted the time against Charlie's name. Then he looked at Charlie but waved his hand at the Nissan in the international gesture of 'who are your friends?'.

Gallen kept a smile on his face but he didn't like the set-up: a digital surveillance camera looked down on the spot where the vehicles parked, a bad sign given that the new surveillance cameras plugged into data networks and corporate servers—they could be monitored from anywhere, and by anyone, including foreign intel operators who were looking for someone trying to get out of Amman. And judging by the distinct concrete pad that they'd been directed to, he guessed the vehicle was also being photographed from underneath, looking for bombs and other contraband. There was too much information being collected, and if the guard wanted ID from himself and Winter, there'd be an elephant trail for Daly and the al-Haqs to follow.

Gallen could see it coming. He slowly pulled the iPhone 4 from his jacket pocket and held it in front of his chest, pretending to be looking at something.

'Tell him,' said Gallen, as a silence opened between Charlie and the guard, 'that I'm amazed I can get internet on my phone, this far out of town. It's an incredible machine.'

Charlie ramped up the enthusiasm and the guard leaned in the window. Holding the iPhone in front of him, Gallen mucked around with the settings and realised he had a new text message. Clicking on it as Charlie kept up the patter, he sat up: it was from Mike Ford. His heart rate climbing, he read it: *Hey boss. I'm in uq. Need me?*

Gallen fumbled for the reply settings—Mike Ford was in Umm

Qasr, Iraq's Persian Gulf port. He'd been a Royal Australian Navy commando in Clearance Diver Team 4, a heavyweight special forces outfit that wasn't written about much in the newspapers but which turned up in the all the worst warzones. Ford was a very useful Aussie whom Gallen would trust with his life.

The guard was now showing real interest in Gallen's phone as he fashioned a response to Ford, and over the top of the hood Gallen could see him coming around to his side.

'What's going on?' said Winter from the back.

'Guard wants to see the phone,' said Charlie.

Gallen thumbed a hasty text to Ford: *Working jordan. Need you.*

The guard arrived, smiling. 'See this?' said Gallen, flicking the machine to Google and making a search of 'Mustangs'. The search came back with a link that Gallen clicked on, showing a '69 Ford Mustang convertible in its full glory.

The guard's hand went out and Gallen let him have it.

'Okay, that's good,' said Charlie and Gallen could feel him shift the transmission to drive.

'What's good?'

'Your gift,' said Charlie as the guard stepped back, engrossed in the phone.

'You gave him my phone?' said Gallen.

'No, you gave it.'

'Shit, Charlie,' said Gallen. 'I was going to offer him my watch.'

Gallen sighed, looked at the guard. 'Sorry, dude. I need the SIM card.'

Charlie started to translate but the guard held up his hand, directed a loose end on a key ring into the side of the iPhone and fished out the Sprint SIM card.

'Why do I feel short-changed by this transaction?' said Gallen as the micro-SIM was placed in his palm.

The guard waved at his offsiders and the boom went up. Charlie surged forwards and they were onto the dusty concrete aprons that Gallen had spent much of the last decade rotating through.

'Like coming home,' said Gallen. They swung to their right, taking in a series of concrete hangars with private jets and C130s waiting outside.

'And not in a good way,' said Winter as they sped past an unmarked Fokker Friendship for a hangar with a sign reading *Air Services Arabia* across the entrance.

Gallen's leg almost gave way as he stood on the apron. Gasping, he leaned against the front fender of the Patrol, waiting for Charlie and Winter to join him.

'Okay, boss?' said Winter. 'You taking those antibiotics?'

Gallen closed his eyes, shook his head.

'Jesus,' said Winter, opening the back door and grabbing a foil of pills from Gallen's backpack. 'Here, boss. Take one. Don't want that wound infecting.'

Gallen took the pill, the pain flashing from the leg wound up into his groin.

'So,' he said, when he'd composed himself, 'how does this play out, Charlie?'

'We go in, see Johnny, tell him we need a ride to the east.'

'How much money he need?' Winter spat on the ground.

'He owes me,' said Charlie.

They followed Charlie out of the blazing sun and through a side door that led to an air-conditioned office space. There were sofas around the edges and a reception desk with the Air Services Arabia sign behind it. Gallen paused but Charlie kept walking towards the door on the other side of the room that said *Manager*.

Pushing through it, they saw an Anglo man on the other side of a dark desk, tapping on a laptop. As he looked up he recoiled, throwing himself sideways from his chair. Gallen remembered what the rats looked like in the bottom of the corn hopper after a harvest: you'd lift the lid on their eating and they'd run anywhere and everywhere— even upside down—to escape the threat. The man with the name plate *Johnny Eastgate* looked like a hopper rat as he found the far corner of his office and looked around for escape routes.

Charlie was the first to speak. 'Johnny?'

'Why'd you bring him here?' Johnny spluttered in a west London accent. 'Are you mad?'

'Who?' said Charlie.

Jimmy pointed, as if at the devil. 'Fucking Winter. What the fuck is he doing here?'

Winter stepped forwards. 'Hey, Johnny. Nice place you got here.'

'Don't you dare,' he started, a man who couldn't help using management standover techniques even as he shit his pants. 'I'm out of all that now, you hear? You can't just—'

'How you bin, Johnny?' Winter lit a smoke as he looked around the office.

'Someone, please,' said Johnny, looking from Gallen to Charlie and back to Gallen. 'Stop this, please. *Stop* it!' He eyed the top drawer of his desk.

'Don't, Johnny,' said Winter, soft enough that the Englishman sagged into the corner and sat down on the garbage bin.

'What's goin' on?' said Gallen.

'It was a misunderstanding, a long time ago.' Johnny talked too fast. 'I didn't know about Dippy—swear to God.'

'What?' said Gallen. 'Charlie, you know about this?'

Charlie Basa shrugged. 'I know Johnny because we've done work together. I don't know about this.'

'I can explain,' said Johnny. 'You're CIA?'

'No,' said Gallen. 'But you can still explain.'

'Keep him away from me,' said Johnny, pointing a trembling finger at Winter. 'This isn't Afghanistan, you know.'

'He's not going to touch you,' said Gallen. 'Who's Dippy?'

'Dippy Fernandez. Sri Lankan shipping magnate. The Agency decided he was a money launderer and supply conduit for Osama bin Laden.'

'And?'

'And I ran a legitimate air cargo business from Colombo into Oman and Yemen.'

'For Dippy?'

Johnny nodded. 'He was one of my customers.'

Gallen smiled. 'How many customers you have on those routes?'

'I don't need this shit,' said Johnny. 'I was cleared by MI6.'

'You weren't cleared, Johnny,' said Winter. 'They threw you back in the pond, made you their bitch.'

Johnny pinched the bridge of his nose, took a breath. 'Kenny, whatever you decided Dippy was doing, you killed him for it and

143

ruined my life, okay? I'm paying my penance, even though all I did was transport goods.'

'So when you let Southern Nominees buy twenty-five per cent of your Delaware holding company, and then sell their holding in London three years later, you think maybe you partook in an al-Qaeda money-laundering operation?'

Johnny stood and raised his hand at the big Canadian. 'Okay, so Perry Mason wins. You got me. Now I guess you either kill me or you want a favour, that it?'

'We need a ride, Johnny,' said Charlie.

'Okay, you need a ride—I need a deal,' said Johnny. 'I do this thing and I'm square with Kenny. That fair?'

'Kenny?' said Gallen, looking at Winter.

'I ain't gonna kill him,' said Winter.

'That okay?' said Gallen. 'He won't touch you.'

'Where we going?' said Johnny, sitting at his desk.

'Eastern desert,' said Charlie.

'Crossing over?' said Johnny, leaning back in his chair and ripping the cellophane off a new pack of Dunhills.

'Depends,' said Charlie, walking to a large wall map that took in northern Saudi, Iraq and Syria, and showed airfields and their refuelling capability. 'We either pick up the trail of what we're looking for west of Tarbil, or we'll have to cross over.'

Charlie left his finger resting on a point that looked to be about twenty miles inside the Iraq side of the border with Jordan. 'And if we cross over, we'll be aiming for RGW airfield.'

Johnny made a noise in the back of his throat as he stood and looked at the map. 'You sure, Charlie? We're heading for the RGW?'

'What's that?' said Gallen.

'Republican Guard West airfield,' said Johnny. 'Saddam's elite units used it to maintain and check on their missile systems in the desert. Doesn't show up on any maps—the Yanks like it that way.'

'You know how to get there?' said Gallen.

'Oh, yeah.' Johnny looked surprised. 'We flew someone there this morning.'

'What?' said Gallen.

'Who?' said Charlie.

'Woah,' said Johnny, hands up at the surrounding faces. 'He's an American guy. Black, muscular. Trouble.'

'He has a name?' said Gallen.

'Just a sec,' said Johnny, leaning over his desk, looking at a clipboard. 'Holmes: Terrell Holmes.'

CHAPTER 21

The Bell 429 helicopter followed Highway 10 eastwards for half an hour. At the point where the highway turned suddenly northwards to the border crossing, Johnny used his left arm to indicate to the pilot to carry on and veer south.

Turning back to the passenger section, Johnny tapped his watch and mouthed the words 'ten minutes' at Gallen.

Giving thumbs-up, Gallen looked to Charlie and Winter, who had taken the Kevlar vests on offer at Air Services Arabia and were now checking and rechecking their pistols. The retrieved M4 assault rifle sat beside Winter.

Gallen went through the situation in his mind: Spikey had been aiming for an RV at the airfield just over the border, to exfiltrate himself from the area with the money. Charlie's role had been to drive him in the Yukon, direct from the al-Haq depot to the Republican Guard West airfield, where Spikey had made his own arrangements. But instead he staged his own capture, saddled Gallen with the dud bags and stole out of Amman with the money. Spikey must have had a false start getting clear of Amman, or felt the heat coming from the al-Haqs or Daly, and decided to blow some money on a charter flight to the exfil.

Now Spikey had an hour's head start on Gallen and Winter,

in a King Air 200, which had twice the cruising speed of the Bell. There were no official control towers or management at the RGW, according to Johnny Eastgate. Privateers, contractors and deniable elements of the US occupation forces used the airfield, so there was no reliable channel to phone ahead and try to outmanoeuvre Spikey. The opportunity existed to land at the RV as close as possible behind Spikey, find his next destination and surprise him.

A hand hit Gallen's chest and he looked down, took a Marlboro from Winter. The Canadian leaned into Gallen's ear. 'I'll stay in the helo, cover you with the rifle, if that's what you want.'

'I'm not worried about you, Kenny. It's Spikey—I served with him, he's a hard on.'

Winter lit their smokes. 'You gonna talk him down?'

'He's not like you and me,' said Gallen. 'You know when a horse don't wanna be ridden, know how to stand back from a steer that won't be cornered. Spikey—he comes out of that whole Compton Beach foster-care system. You come at him, you better kill him, or he's gonna kill you.'

'Good in battle,' said Winter, nodding.

'He's an ace, but I haven't felt comfortable with Spikey since I got to Amman. If I get the chance I'll explain to him the position he's left us in with Alison, but I don't hold out hope.'

The helo tipped forwards slightly and started a descent.

'That's the Iraqi border we just crossed,' said Johnny, turning and raising his voice. 'You see that in the distance?'

Gallen stood in a crouch, looked over the seats facing him and through the pilot's windscreen. The gold and tawny desert stretched for hundreds of miles into a thick haze. 'That's a lot of desert.'

'Look at the horizon—we got a storm warning, coming through in forty-five minutes. Goggles and scarves are under the seats.'

They opened the bins beneath the seats and pulled out a collection of the type of junk that gets carried around in desert charter planes: flare-gun kits, hypothermia bags, tents that fold into a pencil case and reflectors that get planted in the sand for those lost in the Sahara.

Pulling out what they needed, Gallen and Winter changed from shorts to jeans and pulled on jackets and long-sleeved shirts, buttoned them to the throat.

The helo slowed and flew lower. Through the windscreen loomed the shape of an east–west runway inscribed in the scrub and the sand. The helo came down to two hundred feet and skirted the southern boundary of the airfield, allowing them to see the low air traffic control buildings on the northern edge, concrete domed hangars and what looked like barrack buildings behind the administration blocks.

There didn't seem to be an aircraft at the abandoned base. The helo banked at the eastern end of the standard 3600-metre military runway, and flew back up it at one-hundred-foot clearance.

'No one's here,' said Johnny. 'Jason's trying to get someone on the radio.'

As they flew past the admin buildings and hangars, Gallen could make out two vehicles parked in one of the huge concrete bomb-proofed hangars. The helo flew to the end of the runway and circled back, this time on the northern side of the base, over the barracks and water towers which Gallen could see were partially destroyed. It was from this site that Saddam's western desert defence system of Scud missiles had been administered, arrayed up and down the border and aimed primarily at Israel.

The pilot brought them around and flared in front of the old control tower. The dust rose from the ground so Gallen could barely make out the hangar where he'd seen the cars.

'You'll be on your own once we drop you,' said Johnny.

Gallen paused as he reached for the door release. 'The deal was we get a ride back.'

Johnny pointed to the dust cloud. 'The storm is just starting. We can't leave the helicopter here, it'll never start again. And we can't fly in this once it gets bad.'

'Forget it,' said Gallen, waving his hand. 'I'm aborting.'

'Wait, boss.' Winter grabbed his arm. 'You see that?'

'What?' Gallen squinted into the increasingly soupy atmosphere. The helo touched down on the runaway.

'There—right there! You see that?'

Gallen stared through the side window into a light brown fog. Shapes came in and out, light swirled. And then he saw it: unmistakable.

The runway may have been abandoned but there were blue-white tracer rounds flying through the dust storm.

From their position on the steps of the control tower building, they watched the ASA helicopter leave through the dust storm, the throb of the turbo-shaft engines receding into the gloom.

They wrapped their faces and necks in the special forces scarves and fitted the Oakley goggles which Gallen recognised as US military general issue. As the dust got thicker and the wind grew faster, Gallen wished he'd grabbed the gloves he'd seen in the helo when he had the chance.

By the time Gallen had fitted his goggles to stop the sand hitting his eyes, Winter was crawling around the side of the building towards the origin of the tracer rounds. They paused at the corner and looked at the ground: thirty yards to the first concrete hangar.

'Think I saw those shots coming from around that one,' said Winter.

Gallen nodded. It was the hangar with the vehicles inside.

They leapfrogged from the building to a disused aircraft tug sitting between the control tower and the hangar, the adrenaline pumping hard enough to counteract Gallen's gunshot wound.

Gallen panted. He was out of shape. 'Kenny, you've got the rifle, you take the front: we'll hook round the back.'

Winter gave thumbs-up and crabbed into the storm, disappearing into brown sand after twelve paces.

'Come on.' Gallen led Charlie around the back of the hangar. A shot rang out, followed by a burst of automatic fire. The thwack of bullets hitting concrete, then an engine revved and accelerated away.

The visibility became worse and the wind came in harsh gusts, so the air itself seemed to change from a whistling blizzard to a sudden lull where an entire desert seemed to be suspended in the air. It was intensely disorienting.

Gallen walked with one hand on his pistol, one hand held out in front. He hit the side of the hangar and then turned to make sure Charlie was with him. The hangar gave them slight shelter and Gallen pulled Charlie in, yelled in his ear above the din: 'I'm going to enter from the back, you cover me from ninety degrees, okay? You stay hidden till the shit starts. No heroes, okay?'

Charlie nodded but Gallen could see scared eyes through the goggles. They moved along the hangar wall, pausing as gunshots rang out again, this time further away. Charlie froze.

'You okay?' said Gallen, his leg twitching.

'I can't see,' said Charlie, sounding panicked. 'It's like walking in the dark.' Gallen saw the other man's chest heaving—he was having an anxiety attack. Gallen was reminded that being Arab didn't mean you were comfortable with sandstorms.

'Hold my pack,' said Gallen, unable to stop and talk Charlie through it. He would have to operate without covering fire.

Charlie grabbed the back pocket of Gallen's backpack and they walked around the corner of the hangar, into the howling blast of the sandstorm. It grabbed at his face and throat, lifted the top of his scarf, looking for ways to get through the defences. Tugging the scarf harder around his throat, Gallen tucked it in on his left shoulder and rearranged his shirt to keep the sand and grit off his chest. Moving along the back wall of the hangar, Gallen reached the rear doors after eight paces. Turning, he raised his P9 in front of Charlie, who raised his own Beretta and nodded.

Turning the door handle, Gallen pushed the door inwards and the storm grabbed it, threw it back on its hinges. The space in front of him was massive, naturally lit from the ceiling, and contained several aircraft and vehicles.

Thirty yards away, a man stood over two others. Gallen raised his pistol but the man waved at him. Winter.

Shutting the door, Gallen cased the hangar as the storm howled and thumped against the back wall. 'We clear?' yelled Gallen as he unwound the Tuareg headscarf.

'Don't know,' said Winter. 'Just found these two.'

Winter stood over an Anglo man who was trying to minister to a gut-shot Arab lying in a pool of blood on the concrete floor. Their rifles were stacked behind Winter.

Gallen looked at Winter. 'You do this?'

'Your sergeant.' Winter unwound his headscarf and spat on the concrete.

'You got any meds?' said the man, obviously an American. 'He's bleeding out.'

'Nothing,' said Winter.

Gallen looked around, saw an office. 'I'll have a look. Charlie—stay with Kenny.'

The office had been cleaned out long ago: the filing cabinets hung open, the desk drawers were on the floor along with the papers they'd once contained. The official portrait of Saddam Hussein, president and prime minister, was still on the wall, but with a moustache and hairline drawn on him that made him look like Adolf Hitler. In thick black felt pen, someone had drawn a large kangaroo on the white wall, with the legend *Swanie* written below, the 'i' of which was fashioned from an SAS dagger. It was a reference to the pre-invasion commando raid by the Aussie special forces in the hours before the United States declared war on Iraq in 2003. Several troops had moved on motorbikes through the night, taking out the Scud missile batteries and support air bases before the war had even started. Gallen guessed that 'Swanie' was slang for Swanbourne Barracks, the base for the Aussie SAS.

There was a locker beside a window that looked onto the runway. Pulling it open, Gallen found cans of insect repellent, stacks of floppy disks and what appeared to be a Windows XP manual in Arabic script. At the bottom he found a small first-aid kit.

He went back to the injured man, handed the kit to the Anglo and looked at Winter. 'These our guys?'

'No,' said Winter. 'Spikey was here but he was chased into the desert.'

'This is Bryce.' Charlie pointed at the Anglo. 'From the meeting at the cafe.'

'You with Daly?' said Gallen, as Bryce pulled open the first-aid kit, revealing tiny bandages and a couple of dressing pads.

Bryce didn't say anything.

'No offence, Bryce,' Gallen said, 'but I got the gun so you got the answers.'

Sitting back on the concrete, Bryce gazed at the Arab on the floor. 'He didn't make it. Nice guy.' He looked for something to wipe his hands on.

'So where's Daly?' said Gallen.

'Chasing Holmes,' said Bryce, wiping his hands on the concrete.

'Holmes got the bags with him?' said Winter.

'Oh yeah,' said Bryce. 'That guy's a psycho.'

CHAPTER 22

The tracks the silver Land Cruiser had left through the wadi and the scrub were deep enough that they could follow them in the black Land Cruiser. The sandstorm blasted at the windscreen and exhausted the window washer after forty seconds, leaving a dirty scum of grit over the glass that was added to in constant waves of dust. It was like driving through a waterfall of sand.

Peering through the windscreen, Gallen tried to navigate for Winter, but they drove into small trees, fell into drop-offs and almost toppled twice on termite hills as Winter kept the pedal down and the transmission in 2.

Accelerating through soft sand, Gallen felt the Land Cruiser bog down, go sideways and lose speed until the vehicle wouldn't move.

'Shit,' said Gallen, his country boy ego hurt: townies and eggheads got bogged, not bronc-riding farm boys. Opening his door, he rewrapped the Tuareg headscarf and dropped to the sand, the storm buffeting his face and making it a major effort to shut the door. Lying on his front, he saw the problem: they were in a wallow. It was wet sand and they were jammed to the axles.

As he pushed himself up from the sand, he saw movement to his right. A flash of feet. Pulling his P9 to his face, he thought about it. If they had become bogged then Spikey and Daly would have too. They could be twenty feet away and Gallen wouldn't see or hear them.

Gallen cracked his door. 'Kenny? They're here.'

Winter emerged from the other side of Land Cruiser, nothing but a dark shape in the storm. Gallen moved to him and they dropped to their knees together. 'I saw feet running this way,' said Gallen.

Winter in the lead, they walked quickly in a crouch, until Winter stopped and pointed down: there was a trail, two sets of boot prints in the marshy sand.

'This way,' he said, and they jogged along the trail, the foliage becoming larger and denser until Gallen ran into the back of Winter and they looked down. They were knee deep in a pool, the location of the base suddenly becoming clear: there was a spring here.

The sand and grit seemed to bounce across the water and create an angry surface, the juxtaposition of the coppery sand and the dark pond looking almost artistic. It was the middle of the afternoon, but the sandstorm had made it seem like early evening.

Winter pointed one way and Gallen pointed the other. Pulling back they separated and started to walk in different directions around the edge of the pool. The going was tough, the heavy sand and bog sucking at Gallen's boots, the sandstorm whipping around his face, and the gunshot wound still aching. He strained to hear more sounds of gunfire, hoping for a clue as to where their quarry was heading.

He walked for five minutes, ducking branches and peering into flying sand. As he waded through a mini pond, he heard it: automatic gunfire not fifty feet away. Ducking, he craned for the sign of movement, looking for more tracer rounds. But the gunfire stopped. He headed in its direction, treading more carefully and feeling the strength ebbing from him. It was hot, he couldn't get fresh air through the headscarf and his thigh was aching to the point that the quad muscle wanted to seize. Sweat ran freely beneath his Kevlar vest.

Stopping to regain his breath, Gallen pulled off his backpack and sucked at his water bottle. He was panting, exhausted, his skin already drying to paper in the storm. The bullet split the branch in front of him, throwing splinters into his goggles. Dropping to the ground, spilling his water, he fumbled for the pistol and brought it up cup-and-saucer style. From his low position he could see a flash of feet moving to his right and, standing, he followed them. He found himself on a well-worn track, probably used by herders and their animals judging by the imprints. He jogged through the storm, small trees waving and dipping in the winds, until he saw a dark shape disappearing into the ground thirty feet away. Crabbing to where he last saw the human shape, he found a steel manhole cover with a large handle on it.

Gallen gasped for breath beneath the Tuareg scarf, wanting back-up, wanting radio contact, wanting Winter to know where he was. The wind lashed at his head, the sand making a staccato racket on his rapidly scarring and denting goggle lenses.

The wind was getting worse, the light decreasing as the main body of the storm set in. Gallen reached down and grabbed the handle, pulling the cover upwards with surprising ease, exposing a ladder set into concrete. Whipping off his scarf and goggles, Gallen eased into the hole and pulled the cover shut. The interior was cool and quiet and Gallen remained on the top rungs of the ladder for ten seconds, controlling his breathing. He could smell diesel and rubber, and wet sand.

Slowly easing himself down the ladder, he let his eyes adjust to the inky blackness. When he reached the bottom of the ladder, he looked around and realised there was some light, thanks to a long series of slits along the ceiling of the vaulted structure.

Getting his bearings, Gallen saw some large shapes in the darkness. A noise from further down the hall startled him, and he turned towards it. As he walked along the concrete wall, leaning his hand on it for guidance, it suddenly struck him: he was in one of the secret bunkers that housed the giant Soviet-designed MAZ rocket carrier trucks from which Saddam's Scud missile arsenal had been launched. These trucks were all over the western desert.

His foot slipped on something. Crouching, he touched the concrete floor and smelled his fingers. Blood. Someone was bleeding and, after tapping at his own jeans, he was sure it wasn't him.

The light from the ceiling grew brighter and he could see the end of the bunker, a hundred-yard-long building that had the MAZ trucks parked two abreast, the rockets cut at the two-thirds mark, probably by the US Army engineers during Iraqi Freedom. It was a massive area and at the end he could make out large steel doors and what looked like a diesel dump beside it.

The blood trail was now shiny in the half-light and Gallen saw that it led to the diesel barrels. Sticking to the wall, he moved quietly, his leg aching but controlled by his adrenaline. At the diesel dump, he slowed and stealthed around the corner, ducking beneath the level of a fifty-five-gallon drum with a pump handle screwed into it. Waiting in the dark, his Heckler & Koch cocked for firing, he listened to the groans not five feet from him. His target was behind the diesel drum.

Gallen took a deep breath, stepped out. In front of him, lying on a pile of sacks on a loading pallet, lay Spikey Holmes, groaning like an animal, blood leaking out of his stomach, chest and neck.

'Spikey,' said Gallen, holding the pistol on him. 'The fuck you doin' down here?'

'Cap'n,' gasped Holmes, his hand still on the grip of an M16 rifle. 'You came.'

'Yeah, but you didn't.'

'I can explain.'

'Explain what, Spikey? You left me with the empty bags,' said Gallen. 'You left me to face the al-Haqs.'

Now Gallen could see the four bags that people were dying for. Spikey was lying against them like they were harem cushions.

'You want the money, cap'n? That it? That what you're here for?'

'I came to Jordan to take you home, Spikey,' said Gallen, not wanting his former sergeant to raise the rifle. 'That was the gig.'

'What's the gig now?'

'Get you to a hospital,' said Gallen. 'What you got, lung shot?'

'Don't matter,' said Spikey. 'It's a dying shot.'

Gallen watched Holmes' hand crawl onto the grip of the rifle.

Gallen cocked the P9. 'Don't do it, Spikey.'

'Why not? Chase Lang gets the money anyhow, right?' said Spikey.

'No,' said Gallen. 'That ain't right.'

'Well, it your boy who did this.' Spikey looked down at his blood-soaked shirt. 'Almost on my ride and wham, that bitch Daly lands right on my ass.'

'You shot up that local kid pretty good,' said Gallen. 'He's dead.'

'Motherfucker came at me, cap'n. You know how I feel 'bout that.'

Gallen breathed deep, aimed the pistol at Spikey's forehead. 'Hand off the rifle, Spikey. Let me get you to a hospital.'

'I ain't goin' in,' said Spikey. 'Ask your boy. He won't allow that.'

'Daly?' said Gallen. 'Won't allow what?'

'Daly got his orders,' said Spikey. A glob of livery blood leapt from his mouth, landing on his chest.

'Daly's here to kill you?'

'The money's a sideshow, cap'n.'

'Time to shut your mouth, Holmes,' came a voice from the darkness.

A shape stepped forwards: Daly, shouldering an M4 rifle.

Spikey coughed. 'See, cap'n? Ain't about the money.'

Spikey grabbed the grip of his rifle and lifted it, and Gallen shot him twice in the forehead. Swinging his shoulders, he faced Daly but the rifle was already aimed at his chest.

'Drop it, Gerry,' said Daly, and Gallen threw the gun in the air, lunged into the darkness of the MAZ truck's undercarriage. Landing in a judo roll, Gallen flipped onto his feet and dived again, taking the impact of the fall on the rounded curve of his right shoulder, and using a flick of his hip to gain his feet on the other side of the MAZ.

Bullets zinged and tracer rounds glowed blue in the darkness, one of the massive tyres almost blowing him over as it tore and released a gush of air in his face. Running down the aisle formed by two lines of trucks, Gallen could feel his thigh wanting to seize up. His limp was becoming exaggerated as he got to the ladder that would take him to the surface.

'Gerry,' yelled Daly from the darkness. 'We gotta talk. I'm not shooting to kill—honest to God.'

Gallen was exhausted, he was sore, and now he had to climb the ladder. It took all his effort to reach out and grab the bottom rung and pull himself up, his feet grappling and scraping for grip. He put one hand over the other and clawed his way up the ladder, until he was pushing back the manhole cover.

The worst of the sandstorm had passed; the high winds had abated and the trees were almost standing up straight. As Gallen fell onto the soft sand, he gasped for breath. Getting to his knees, he turned and realised a man was beside him.

'Kenny?' said Gallen, confused by the scarf and goggles.

'No,' said the man, slapping him hard with a rifle stock.

Collapsing to the ground, Gallen fought unconsciousness as the man stood over him and unwound his scarf.

Gallen looked up, groggily trying to comprehend. 'Christ,' he said. 'The FBI?'

'Special Agent Barrowman,' said the fed. 'How you been, Gerry?'

CHAPTER 23

The demountable room was comfortable enough, although Gallen could have done without the lock being on the other side of the door. It was a matter of principle: a person who'd served his country as an officer in battle shouldn't really be locked up by other Americans.

He'd dozed and been checked over by a doctor, then taken a shower and slept, and was now sitting at the small table in the middle of the room—called a Chu in the US military, for Containerised Housing Unit. He ate breakfast while watching the late-night TV news in New York. Lawyers, politicians and bigwigs from the Pentagon were talking about the exact details of the US withdrawal from Iraq, and the power vacuum it might create not only among the orthodox Islamic factions, such as Sunni and Shiite, but also among some of the old industrial and banking interests which had flourished under Saddam's regime. The owners of money knew how to own the military—history had proved it to be so.

As the news switched to a story about a llama 'guide dog', a knock came at the door.

'Sorry, not buyin' today,' said Gallen, shovelling scrambled eggs into his mouth. ''Less you got the refill for my coffee.'

The door opened and Daly walked in with a pot of Bunn coffee and a mug. 'Fresh—made it myself.'

He poured for them, sat on the end of Gallen's bed. He was dressed as if no time had elapsed from that night in Pinedale: blue jeans and a dark blue Carhartt sweatshirt pulled up to the elbows.

'This that thing about the alpaca?' Daly slurped and got comfortable. 'Some wonderful shit.'

'Yeah, it's cool.' Gallen finished the eggs and wiped the plate with a piece of toast.

'You okay there?' said Daly, watching. 'I get you a towel?'

'You can get me some biscuit, since you're asking,' said Gallen. 'Like biscuit with my eggs and coffee.'

'That a Wyoming thing?'

'That's a taste thing,' said Gallen. 'Try it next time you're in a truck stop with some class.'

Daly made a face. The next item was the stock market and Gallen pointed the remote, killed the power. He let the silence settle and he slurped his coffee.

'So, I guess we gotta talk about you shooting at me.'

'Tryin' to make you stop is all,' said Daly, eyes observing Gallen over his mug.

'Holmes said you were there to kill him, that it weren't about the money.'

Daly smiled. 'He's a hard on, Gerry. I warned him—I said, "You shoot at me, Spikey, I'll kill ya."'

Gallen wasn't convinced.

'And when it came down to it, Gerry, I noticed the option you took,' said Daly.

Gallen nodded.

'Great room, shower runs hot and I liked the breakfast. But you can tell Chase that I'm ready to go now.'

'Tell 'im yourself,' said Daly. 'He wants to talk.'

Chase Lang's office and living quarters were in a red forty-eight-foot semitrailer with satellite dishes and aerials sprung from its roof and wind-outs that made it twice as wide as its chassis.

Gallen was shown into the office at the rear of the semi, where a solidly built black man in his fifties stood from an armchair and shook Gallen's hand while continuing to speak into a sat phone. Raising a finger to Gallen in the sign of *I'll be one minute*, Lang turned away, his voice conversational yet authoritative. 'Sure, I can talk with the general, Paul, but it should really come from you. You're the politician—the minister of defence tells the general how it's gonna be, you with me?'

Gallen marvelled that this barrel-chested man in a polo shirt and jeans—someone from his own operational background—now took meetings with various undersecretaries from the Pentagon and congressmen on the House Committee on Armed Services. Chase Lang's military contracting operation had avoided the security and prison work that the Department of Defense was so keen to farm out, and instead had found a niche in what used to be called deniable activities, but which these days were called extrajudicial actions.

'You like it?' Daly smiled at Gallen's reaction to the place as Lang continued to patter with the minister for defence.

'Might get one myself,' said Gallen, looking around. A young man worked in front of a bank of screens, a cordless boom across his mouth; two screens angled from high on the wall streamed video footage of a live mission up what appeared to be a small tropical river; behind the main desk—obviously Lang's—was a collection of memorabilia, including a photo of Lang with George HW Bush and George W Bush, a picture of Lang with Arnold Schwarzenegger and a shot of Lang at a charity golf day in Dubai with Erik Prince, the founder of Blackwater Security.

He leaned forwards to get all the detail of a black and white photograph taken at night of three men in battle dress sitting in a specially built dune buggy used by the US Navy Seals. A younger Chase Lang looked out at the camera from the passenger seat, tactical helmet of the type that looked more like a ski helmet, goggles pulled down to his neck, assault rifle across his lap and pistol hanging on a chest holster. Gallen smiled: the eyes of a tired but winning soldier were the same regardless of the time or the place.

'Kuwait City, February 1991,' said Chase Lang, behind Gallen's left shoulder. 'The man told us to hold the locals back from the US embassy, so that's what we did. Just drove around the embassy all night, while Johnno—that dude on the fifty-cal at the back—fired over the heads of anyone wanna get jiggy.'

Lang put a smoke in his mouth, offered one to Gallen. 'Lesson number one in war: just 'cos some fucker wants to hug your ass, don't mean he's no friend. Johnno didn't wanna fire at no locals waving their red, white and blues, but he did what he hadda, right, Gerry? That's war—that's shit duty, but someone gotta do it, and hell, if the money's right . . .' Lang moved back to the young man monitoring the screens and whispered something in his ear, slapped him on the back. 'Let's walk, Gerry,' he said, heading for the door. 'I'll show you the place.'

The three of them strolled through what was a small military camp, although Lang insisted on calling it a contracting base. Gallen's Tactical NAV app told him the site was slightly on the Iraq side of the border, about a mile south of Highway 10. The RGW airfield was another seven miles further south. Everywhere were the signs of builders fixing what had been damaged by the storm and soldiers digging piles of sand out of where it wasn't wanted. There was a large, shaded, outdoor eating area a few minutes from Lang's trailer and they sat at a picnic table, smoking.

'See, Gerry, I needed to bring you in 'cos maybe there was a misunderstanding.'

'I can see that,' said Gallen. 'I go to the Araby Castle with Daly, and then I leave with Spikey. Wasn't really my call, right, Daly?'

'Sure, Gerry,' said Daly, inscrutable behind aviator shades. 'Spikey's crew came in and you hadda go.'

'But of course, I'm still payin' your ass, Gerry,' said Lang, crooking a finger at a worker who was carrying a tray of chicken wings to the kitchen, telling him to get someone out here, right now, pick up this goddammed trash.

'It's just as well for you, Gerry, 'cos I had a visit from the Iraqi criminal investigators this morning.'

Gallen felt the atmosphere change. 'I see.'

'Yeah, they had some jive 'bout an American soldier murdered another American soldier not far from here.'

Gallen slumped slightly, looked at Daly, who smiled.

'So, Mr Lang,' said Gallen. 'I guess that puts you in a position, given you had me as a guest and all?'

'I'm glad you see it the adult way, Gerry,' said Lang, his big face intent on his cigarette. 'See, I have to do business in this part of the world. I can't have people walking around saying these things about me.'

Gallen knew something was coming and he just hoped it didn't involve any more killing. Shooting Spikey was messing with him: that so many routes and missions had come down to killing a brother Marine in an underground diesel dump just didn't seem right.

'I understand what you're saying,' said Gallen.

'Good,' said Lang, tilting his head at Daly, who produced a foolscap document and gave it to Lang. 'This is an official statement of contract between a registered security contractor—Columbus Enterprises—and one Gerard Roy Gallen, for services in the Republic of Iraq under the auspices of the CPA, the Coalition Provisional Authority.'

Lang slid it across the white plastic table and Gallen trapped it under his fingertips. Picking it up, he flipped through the six pages to the back. 'I didn't sign this, did I?'

'No, but you might want to for one great reason: CPA order seventeen.'

Gallen looked from Daly back to Lang, confused. 'Which is?'

'It's the order that says any person working for a security contractor registered with CPA will be immune from prosecution.'

Gallen smiled. 'Prosecution for what?'

'For anything,' said Daly.

Gallen thought about it. 'Didn't I read the Iraqis had stopped that? It's unconstitutional or something.'

'They did stop it,' said Lang. 'But the Pentagon persuaded them to leave order seventeen active for those already signed up before the change.'

'But I'm signing today,' said Gallen.

'Look again.' Lang lit another smoke.

Flipping to the front page, Gallen saw the dates printed in the preamble: they were predated by three years.

'So when the investigators come back?' said Gallen.

'I show 'em this,' said Lang, big finger landing on the contract. 'We can predate it in the e-lodgement system too. It'll be legit. So, you in?'

Gallen leaned back. 'Why do you need me when Spikey's dead and you have his money?'

'We need you to finish some things, Gerry,' said Daly. 'Loose ends that Spikey left. Another couple of days' work, but you're paid up for the month.'

'Forget the money for a second,' said Gallen, raising his hand. 'Where's my crew?'

'Winter, and that local dude?' said Lang.

'That's them.'

Lang turned and pointed at the large white demountable building behind him. 'In the rec centre, finishing breakfast, playing pool. So, you in?'

Gallen felt the two men looking at him. They had him with the murder, but he sensed he might still have an ace. He just couldn't see what it was.

'I could be in, but I have a loose end that I have to tie up.'

'I'm in the solutions business,' said Lang. 'What's up?'

Gallen told him the story of Baba el-Masri and Alison McIntyre, and how he'd been given a week to bring in the money. 'I have six days. It isn't an option—I dragged her into this and I can't walk away; the embassy are useless and I don't have the men to rescue her.'

'So you need the six mill?' said Lang.

'Yep,' said Gallen.

Chase Lang looked at him as if he might be something very far away. 'That's a lot of money, Gerry.'

'I know what it is, Mr Lang,' said Gallen. 'I helped steal it, I've been chased across the Middle East for it and yesterday I killed for it. Thing is, this doctor saved me when I was bleeding out, she drove me when I needed driving, and now she's in a Hamas cellar because of me. You know how it goes.'

'Yeah, Gerry, I know how it goes.' Lang nodded slowly, as if calculating something. He looked at Daly. 'How much in Spikey's bags?'

Daly rolled his eyes to the sky. 'Um, six million, three hundred and sixteen thousand dollars, and change.'

'Okay, so there's six point three in the bags. Baba gets six, the Grahams get their two hundred and the rest is my overhead, fair?' said Lang.

'You kiddin'?' said Gallen. 'You can't give away six million dollars. What's the catch?'

'Ain't givin' it away, Gerry. You said yourself that this buys back the doctor.'

'And I'm gonna do six million dollars worth of work in two days?' said Gallen, still looking for the ace. 'I was a captain, not a general.'

'You heard Daly,' said Lang. 'I need you to do something for me.'

Gallen was growing exasperated. 'What else is there? The gig was Spikey.'

'The gig is freeing the doctor,' said Lang. 'Let's stay focused.'

'You playing me?' said Gallen.

'Only in a good way.'

Gallen was so tired and there was so much to do on the farm. 'Two days' work?'

'My word on it,' said Daly.

'And Baba gets the six?'

'My word on it,' said Lang, holding out his hand.

Gallen shook hands, grabbed the contract and took a pen from Daly. As he signed, a speeding Land Cruiser pulled up in front of the eating area, dust spraying as the 4x4 slid to a halt. Jim Barrowman, in a hurry and angry, leapt from the passenger seat.

'What's he doing out here?' Barrowman strode to their table. 'He's mine, remember that, Chase? It was my debrief.'

'Sure, Jim,' said Lang. 'But he's signed already.'

Barrowman thrust his hands on his hips, same macho pose he gave Gallen at Denver International. 'Shit.'

Gallen looked up. 'What?'

'Gallen, you're a fool,' said the FBI man. 'Columbus now owns anything you find.'

Gallen shrugged. 'Not the six mill, Jim. That's earmarked.'

'Oh,' said Barrowman, with that snigger that needed wiping. 'So I guess they haven't told you?'

'Told me?' Gallen looked from Daly to Lang. 'What?'

'We needed those bags, Gerry,' said Barrowman, condescending. 'The money had nothing to do with it.'

CHAPTER 24

They travelled in convoy, Gallen, Winter and Charlie in the black Toyota, Daly, Bryce and Barrowman following in the silver Land Cruiser. Gallen had stocked up with painkillers at Chase Lang's camp, but there wasn't much to be done for Winter's hurt pride. He wanted it on the record that he only went along with Daly because they'd already caught the boss. No other reason.

'So, Daly wants the bags that Spikey left you with?' said Winter, smoking, one hand on the steering wheel. 'What's in 'em?'

'Stacks of paper, an old handgun,' said Gallen. 'I think George said blueprints, but I never looked.'

'That's it?' said Winter. 'That's worth six mill?'

'I don't know,' said Gallen, turning. 'What about you, Charlie? Any ideas?'

'Americans,' said Charlie Basa, who seemed upset by the events of the past two days. 'They want more than six million dollars?'

The agreement was not ideal but it was all Gallen could secure. Daly and Barrowman would follow them to Baba el-Masri's office, but they would hold the six million. Daly would hand the money to Gallen as he knocked on the door. Then, Charlie would lead them to the Yukon at the private garage, where Daly and Barrowman would pick up the three bags that were lying in the back of the SUV.

'If you're happy with this, boss,' said Winter, 'then count me in. But I'm not happy with the no-gun bit.'

Gallen nodded. He'd insisted that he have his own vehicle for removing Alison from the scene as soon as she was released. Daly's trade-off for allowing separate vehicles was to disarm Gallen's crew.

'I'm not happy with any of it,' said Gallen. 'I came here to help an old brother from A-stan. But he's dead, and the woman who saved my life is being held by Hamas.'

Winter made a noise in his throat.

'You okay?' said Gallen.

'I'm trying to see how it makes sense,' said Winter. 'This Barrowman dude fronts you at Denver International and tips you off about the al-Haqs?'

Gallen nodded. 'I keep thinking about that. I think he was trying to flush me out, see if I knew what he was talking about. I think they were looking for an easy trail to these fricking bags.'

'So now Barrowman is telling you not to be so stupid—it's not the money, it's the bags. What's that about?'

Gallen shrugged. 'Guess we'll find out.'

'You don't remember what Barrowman said he was working on?' said Winter. 'FBI cover a lot of stuff.'

'He said it was interagency work, tracking money networks, terror financing, money laundering,' said Gallen. 'Maybe if we can prise open some of those old NATO contacts of yours, we can start with Ahmed al-Haq, see why the FBI have a team on him.'

'Well it can't be anything to do with Saddam,' said Winter with a smile. 'They terminated that dude, saw it on TV.'

The lights on the silver Land Cruiser flashed and they pulled into a gas station. They waited in the shade while Daly tanked, then he walked towards them.

'Feel like lunch?' he asked Gallen. 'Think there's a burger in there.'

They sat in the air-conditioned roadhouse, looking out through tinted windows into the glare of the desert sun where peasants herded goats and Mercedes-Benz sedans zipped down the highway. Three men lined up against three men, with Gallen and Daly the ones making occasional small talk. The only thing Daly and Gallen had in common was stints in Mindanao, the one place in the world that any US serviceman preferred not to discuss.

The burger buns were wet and filled with babaganoush and there was a chickpea salad jammed on the tasteless hamburger meat. The milkshake wasn't made of milk and the fries were hard and cold. There was a roadhouse in Nebraska that could do worse if you ate there on a Sunday, but the Jordan burger was probably the worst Gallen had eaten.

'So, Gerry,' said Barrowman, still putting a swagger in his style, 'you wanna bring us in on this damsel-in-distress gig?'

'Nope,' said Gallen. 'Not really.'

Daly snorted, lost a piece of food from his mouth.

'We're back to that, huh, Gallen?' said Barrowman, face flushing. 'The smart-ass redneck all over again.'

'No such thing as a smart-ass redneck,' said Gallen. 'So whaddya need to know?'

'Who's the girl?'

'Her name is Alison McIntyre, and it was my screw-ups that landed her in the clutches of Baba el-Masri.'

Barrowman's food held steady in his mouth as he stopped chewing, his pale eyes burning into Gallen's. 'This a joke?'

''Fraid not, Jim. I've been out in the desert, trying to steal the money to buy her back from Hamas.'

Barrowman turned to Daly. 'This wasn't something you wanted to tell me?'

'Chase told me not to,' said Daly. 'Not our fight.'

'Not your . . .?' Barrowman shook his head slowly. 'Alison's my friend, dammit.'

'Yeah, so it was better to let Gallen and Charlie go do the talking,' said Daly, staying calm. 'Don't wanna go all FBI on Baba.'

Barrowman put his head in his hands briefly, massaged his face. 'Shit, Gallen!' he said, as he re-emerged. 'What the hell did you drag her into? She's a doctor for Christ's sake.'

'She helped me with a wound,' said Gallen. 'Gunshot in the leg.'

'But Baba el-Masri? Really?!'

'She gave me a transfusion at Zaki's house—saved my life.'

'Oh, shit,' said Barrowman, trying to comprehend. 'Holy shit.'

'Yeah, so Charlie's brother turns up and takes us to Baba, see about this money taken from the al-Haqs. Baba says he wants six million back from Spikey, and he'll keep Alison until he gets it.'

'So you just go get it?' said Barrowman, annoyed. 'Just go take six million dollars?'

Gallen shrugged. 'Kenny wanted to take down Baba, but I'm sick of guns. So we went to the desert.'

Barrowman's tone changed to bitchy. 'Sick of guns, eh, Gerry, but you go out there and shoot Terrell Holmes?'

Gallen stared at the man. 'Who said I shot Spikey?'

'Well, I just assumed . . . I mean, he did, right?' said Barrowman, looking to Daly.

Daly shrugged. 'Didn't get that from me, my man. Didn't get that from Chase, neither.'

Barrowman looked for an expression of support, but he couldn't find one.

'Who wants coffee?' said Daly, standing. 'I'm buying.'

When Gallen got to the Land Cruiser, he asked Charlie to drive. As he climbed into the passenger seat, he remembered he needed a new phone. Climbing back out, he pushed into the roadhouse and saw Winter standing over Barrowman.

He bought an unlocked iPhone, paid for it on the Columbus Enterprises MasterCard, and Gallen joined Winter at the door as they pushed into the sunlight.

'Everything okay?' said Gallen.

'Is now,' said Winter, spitting on the concrete, climbing in the back seat.

Gallen put his hand out for the door and heard a throat clear behind him.

'Sorry 'bout that, Gerry,' said Barrowman, squinting even behind his sunglasses. 'You know, 'bout Spikey.'

Gallen nodded. 'Holmes saved my life once, saved the whole platoon, and when it came time to insist on a commendation, I chickened out. I owed him is all.'

Barrowman put his hands in his back pockets, looked away. 'Winter told me soldiers don't discuss killing, and they don't take kindly to being asked about it. I wasn't aware of that—I'm sorry, okay?' He extended a hand and Gallen shook it.

'And I'm sorry about Alison,' said Gallen. 'Let's get this done.'

The late afternoon traffic was becoming heavy as Charlie Basa took a series of turns off Hashimi Street, heading north into the winding lanes that crept up and down the hills that defined Amman.

As the alleyways became narrower, and the eyes of the locals more piercing, Gallen realised he was in a part of the city that tourists were steered away from. He followed the route on his NAV app. But the streets they were now travelling down must have started life as drains built by the Greeks and later covered over, because they didn't show on the map and they didn't have names.

As he tried to find a name that went with the map references, the app asked him if he wanted to send the map ref to a contact, and Gallen sent it to Mike Ford with the cheeky message: *Send three and fourpence going to a dance.* If the operators of the app were telling the truth, the reference would go through a crypting server and only be able to be opened on the device that bore the mobile phone numbers he'd sent it to.

'This where we came that night?' said Gallen.

'Near here,' said Charlie, concentrating on the tight turns and tides of children and animals crammed into the ancient precincts.

'Daly behind us?'

'Yes,' said Charlie, slowing for a large delivery van jammed into a side alley.

The narrows opened into something resembling a normal city street, and Charlie stopped the Land Cruiser in front of two armed men who Gallen thought he'd seen the night George came to dinner.

Dropping the window, Charlie spoke in Arabic and the bodyguard pointed to a rectangle painted in white on the cobbles. It reminded Gallen of the techniques MPs used to control drivers when they entered military bases: make them park in an exact position, take the control from the driver.

They parked and two more men appeared, one with a mirror on the end of a pole and the other with a black and yellow detector

171

wand. It was the regime that Gallen missed the first time around because he was looking at black hessian.

Weapons were primed and aimed in a flurry as the guards turned on Daly's Land Cruiser. Daly heeded the warnings and stopped the 4x4 twenty yards short of the first one, but the distance was worrying to Gallen. He needed control of the money—it wasn't something he wanted a bunch of Hamas triggers messing with when it was supposed to be buying the return of Alison McIntyre.

'Tell 'em, Charlie,' said Gallen.

Charlie rattled a series of commands at the bodyguards, who mouthed back at him. Then Gallen's Land Cruiser was dealt with and the guards gestured for Daly's 4x4 to park on the rectangle.

The skinny Arab who'd accompanied George to Zaki's house emerged on the street, shiny suit with no tie, a small walkie-talkie handset held against his thigh. He motioned to a bodyguard, who asked for Gallen's phone, and then Gallen turned to Daly, asked for the money.

'You know the deal, Gerry,' said Daly with a wink, as he and Barrowman handed over the black bags.

'Got it,' said Gallen. Bodyguards picked up the bags and then Gallen turned and followed Skinny and the bags into the house.

'Take it easy, boss,' said Winter.

Through a series of heavy steel security doors, they progressed further into the cool, sandstone house until they reached a door where a viewing slit moved across and was then opened by a guard with a submachine gun. They were now in the living area, edged with comfortable sofas and the dining table where George Basa had handed him a pair of jeans a few minutes before he had his brains smashed out.

Skinny went into Baba's office and came out ten seconds later, beckoning for the bags to be brought through. When Gallen tried to follow them, Skinny blocked his way. 'You come to Baba when Baba calls.'

His leg aching again and paranoia swirling in his head, Gallen took a seat on the sofa facing Baba's office, tried to stay calm. The situation was not good and he wondered at some of the choices he'd taken in his life to bring him here: the truth was far from the gung-ho special

172

forces image portrayed in the movies. Gallen could have pushed for a hockey scholarship at the University of South Dakota, could have studied sport science and physical education, gone to the WHL or maybe the big show with an NHL team. A hockey scholarship at USD would have suited his educated school-teacher mother as much as it suited his hockey-obsessed dad. But he'd gone for the Corps, signed up for duty, to *serve*, to be a part of something that mattered. The officer school and Force Recon had developed from his love of the Corps—it hadn't been a lifelong dream. And now here he was, a Wyoming boy who just wanted to be back on the farm but couldn't shake this world.

Skinny opened the door and Gallen walked into Baba el-Masri's office, took the armchair he was directed to. This was almost over—not even the most capricious Hamas commander would renege on a deal where he got six million dollars simply for handing back a woman.

Baba came round from behind the desk, shook his hand. 'Captain Gallen, so nice to see you.'

Gallen smiled. 'The money in order?'

Baba waved the comment away. 'Of course, Captain, and Miss Alison is being brought up here.'

'So?' said Gallen.

Baba looked at him and then pointed to a large flat screen on the wall that contained six security camera views within it. Moving a mouse on his desk, he made one of the views take up the whole screen: it was the camera trained on the rectangle outside the front door.

'So, let's look at this, Captain,' said Baba, standing and using a pen as a pointer to identify Jim Barrowman, who was leaning on the hood of the silver Land Cruiser. 'This one here is FBI, an expert in so-called terror groups.'

Gallen shrugged. He knew Hamas and Hezbollah were well connected, but in this case their intel sources were quite impressive.

'And this gentleman right here is DIA,' said Baba, pointing at Daly, who smoked with Winter.

'DIA?' said Gallen, filing that away.

'Yes,' said Baba. 'But this one here, this is the one I want to know about.'

Gallen's stomach flipped as Baba's pen settled on Winter. Kenny had killed a lot of high-level terror organisers and funders in his military career, and Baba el-Masri wanting to know about him was a very bad sign.

'What do you want to know?' said Gallen, gulping at a dry throat. He just wanted to see the girl and get out of that house. And if he ever got out of there he was going to a doctor, see about this acid stomach.

'What's his name?' said Baba, a theatrical lilt to the question. Gallen kicked himself for not coming in hard and doing a take-down of this place; Winter was the expert in these people and these situations and Gallen should have listened.

'Winter,' Gallen croaked. 'Kenny Winter.'

'I knew it,' said Baba with a sudden burst and a stamp of the foot. 'I went to university in Spokane—I remember him playing for Lethbridge. What were they, the Hurricanes?'

'Oh,' said Gallen, feeling sick with the adrenaline let-down. 'Of course, the 'Canes.'

'He was famous. He once put his stick through the plexiglass, you know?'

Gallen thought he might pass out. 'Yeah, I heard.'

Baba looked up at the screen. 'I might ask him for an autograph. Do you think he'd mind?'

CHAPTER 25

The dog got closer and finally took a lick of his face before Winter whisked it away with his boot.

'Thanks,' said Gallen, on all fours, his stomach now drained. 'Think I'm done.'

Standing with the aid of Winter's hand at his elbow, Gallen brushed off and avoided looking at the wet patch in the gutter. A post-trauma puke was a part of life in the field, but heaving because he'd been scared shitless by Baba el-Masri was not something he'd boast about.

'Let's go.' Gallen pulled on his black baseball cap. 'Daly still with us?'

'Right behind us,' said Winter, helping Gallen to the rear passenger door of the black Land Cruiser.

'Sorry, folks.' Gallen wiped his mouth on his shirt sleeve as Charlie took them back into the perpetual fight that was Amman traffic.

'You okay?' said Alison McIntyre. She was looking good for someone who'd been held by one of the world's most dangerous terror organisations. She'd been covered up previously but now Gallen saw what she looked like in her Levis and T-shirt, he wondered why he'd missed it the first time around.

'I'm good,' said Gallen, his leg aching again. 'I'm sorry we can't take you straight home. We made this deal—we'll have you safe and sound within the hour, okay?'

'It's okay, honest.' She smiled at him. 'I'm just glad you came.'

Gallen saw her hand unfold on the seat between them, and he knew he was supposed to hold it. But instead he gave her a pat on the inside of the forearm.

Alison rolled her eyes and hmphed, so Gallen held her hand and Alison smiled again.

'That was the weirdest kidnapping,' she said, relaxing and leaning into Gallen. 'You know Baba's a hockey tragic? I got caught in family squabbles over whether to watch the hockey or *Grey's Anatomy*.'

'Hockey would win in my house, if the Red Wings were playing,' said Winter. 'But the Bruins or Leafs? I'd rather watch Patrick whats-isname.'

'Hey,' said Gallen. 'Don't diss Boston.'

'In my house it was the Blackhawks,' said Alison. 'My brothers were maniacs.'

'In your house?' said Winter, looking into the back seat with a laugh. 'Hear that, Gerry? Our doctor's a hockey nut.'

'Not me,' said Alison, a little embarrassed. 'Where I grew up it's either Blackhawks or Red Wings. I'm over it.'

'And where would that be?' said Gallen. 'Where you grew up?'

'Des Moines, if you must know.'

'Hah,' said Winter, high-fiving Gallen. 'Redneck girl.'

'I am *not*,' said Alison.

'Your secret's safe with us,' said Winter.

'I'm okay about where I come from,' said Alison. 'I just don't go for all that car park barbecuing, yee-haw bullshit.'

'Really?' said Winter. 'You wear that Carhartt jacket of yours in Boston? Hawkeyes hoodie under it?'

'Oh, shut up,' said Alison, whipping her hand away from Gallen's.

'Leave your beer in the snow when you go to doctor parties?' said Gallen. 'Get hammered at the rodeo dance?'

Alison put on a pained look. 'You two look like shit. You might want to find a hotel, take a tub.'

'Thanks, ma'am,' said Winter. 'I'll take that on board.'

Charlie slowed the Land Cruiser to a crawl and pointed to a broken-down building which looked like a mechanic's workshop with a big set of barn doors beside it.

'I parked in there.' Charlie stopped and pulled on the handbrake. 'Let me get the key, then I'll take Daly inside.'

'Everything okay?' said Alison, as Charlie dodged across the road and talked to a mechanic in grey coveralls. They disappeared into the mechanic's office. Daly materialised beside Gallen's window, handed him a backpack.

'Your pieces,' said Daly, stretching and yawning. 'You okay, doctor?'

'I'm fine, thanks,' said Alison.

'This is Daly.' Gallen passed the bag of handguns forwards to Winter. 'Made the rescue possible.'

'Thanks, Daly,' said Alison, a flashy smile becoming evident.

Charlie stood outside the mechanic's office, holding a set of car keys for Daly to see. Daly acknowledged and turned back to Alison.

'You look fine, doctor,' said Daly. 'But was Baba—you know—well behaved?'

'Nothing happened,' said Alison. 'I cooked, I watched TV, talked with his kids.'

Across the road the doors to the storage garage opened from the inside and the mechanic walked out, latching back the left door first and then the right as Charlie walked over to the silver Yukon.

'Time to work.' Daly tapped on the windowsill and gave Alison a small salute. 'Nice to meet you.'

'You too,' said Alison.

Daly walked behind the Land Cruiser and waited for traffic. Barrowman, talking into a cell phone, joined him at the kerb.

Charlie aimed the keys at the Yukon, the indicator lights flashed once and the first thing Gallen saw was the front wheels sag outwards like a cartoon and Charlie flying through the air like a scarecrow in a hurricane. The fireball, when it came, threw the hood up and over the SUV, orange and red flames spurting out the sides and to the garage ceiling. The roof of the structure lifted—firing nails into the air as it did—and then dropped into the garage as the Yukon flew ten feet off the ground.

Gallen grabbed Alison and ducked as the concussion wave crossed the road and swept through the Land Cruiser, rocking it on its suspension and washing the vehicle and surrounding shopfronts with a hail of nails, screws, wood and glass.

The screams started before Gallen lifted his head. Checking that everyone in the Land Cruiser was unhurt, he opened the door and stood on the sidewalk, birds falling dead from the sky and pieces of burning paper and wood floating on the air. Glass continued to fall around him, tinkling like a demented piano. In front of the Land Cruiser, Charlie had come to rest against the flat bed of the light truck parked in front of them. Locals rushed to help Charlie but his back was broken against the edge of the flatbed, his clothes on fire.

Gallen ripped off his denim shirt as he closed on Charlie, threw it onto his chest and around his neck, trying to douse the flames. It was hopeless: Charlie was dead.

A woman screamed and Gallen turned. A man—her husband?—leaned against the florist shopfront, mouthing something as he tried to pull the foot-long dagger of glass from his throat. Blood flowed in a fountain and the woman screamed and screamed, trying to get her kids behind her skirts.

Gallen kneeled beside him and held him up as the life bled out, the woman screaming and crying until Gallen stood, tried to hold her by the biceps in a universally useless gesture as her man slumped dead on the sidewalk.

Turning, Gallen saw Alison and Winter kneeling over Barrowman out on the road. The traffic had come to a stop as people ran everywhere and a fire siren wailed in the distance as the mechanic's workshop went up in flames. Trying to get to Barrowman, Gallen ran into Daly, staggering, without sight.

'Daly,' said Gallen. 'Here, it's me. Gerry.'

Daly's arms went out, grasping like a blind man, holding onto Gallen's forearms. 'Shit, Gerry! My eyes. My fucking eyes, I can't see.'

Gallen tried to get Daly away from the street, where the fire sirens grew closer and the police vehicles were crashing through. Pushing him up against a barber shop which had lost its entire front window, Gallen kicked glass away and sat Daly down. 'Shit, Gerry. It's bad, man, it's fucking bad.'

Daly hacked a cough and tears streamed down his face as Gallen tried to get him comfortable, saying meaningless things they used to tell each other in the Ghan, like, *Vac is almost here, man, just hold on*, and, *They've gotta bed waiting for you, man*.

From behind him Gallen heard the locals muttering. He didn't know a lot of local lingo but he knew that when Arab-speakers used words like *mayet* and *inshallah*, someone had died.

Turning, he saw the barber, blood all over his shirt, pointing his palms to heaven and shaking his head. At his feet was Jim Barrowman, prone. Alison walked away, towards an ambulance, waving her arms at the driver. Gallen wanted to tell her she couldn't walk in open-toed sandals around a bombsite but his throat wouldn't work. Looking back at Barrowman, he realised there was another man, a local, lying beside the FBI man.

Daly groaned and Winter approached through the soot-laden mayhem, carrying a child whose head was lolling on a rubbery neck.

Gallen pointed to the ambulance and Winter aimed for it, running to Alison, who took the child and jogged with him to the back of the ambulance.

The fire trucks arrived and took forever to find a hydrant as the fire in the mechanic's workshop burst through the roof and fanned into the blue sky. Locals aimed garden hoses and threw buckets at the inferno as Alison ran back from the ambulance, a plastic bottle in hand.

Kneeling in front of Daly, she spoke reassuringly as she forced his hands down. 'Hold them, Gerry,' she said and opened the plastic bottle.

'I'm going to clean your eyes with saline,' she said. 'Just relax the eyelids and blink with it, get the tear ducts going, okay?'

Daly nodded, his hands agitating as Gallen held them down. He coughed again, spluttering in the soot-infested air as Alison squirted the saline onto his eyelids.

'Take this,' she said, handing Gallen a large white dressing pad.

Gallen took it, letting go of Daly's hands.

'Your neck,' said Alison, pointing. 'You're bleeding.'

Slapping the pad on the left side of his neck, Gallen looked down, saw his white undershirt had turned red.

A helicopter thromped somewhere and Gallen looked up. The helo wasn't visible but he saw something else: on the roof of an old retail building on the corner of the next block, there was a man standing at the parapet, holding what appeared to be binoculars to his face.

Gallen felt his breath catch as the man reached to a handset dangling from a lanyard on his chest, and spoke into it.

'Kenny,' said Gallen, standing and not taking his eyes off the man on the building. 'You got those pieces?'

'In the truck.'

'Get 'em,' said Gallen. 'Grab those field-glasses too, huh?'

Daly spluttered and shook his face as Alison stepped back, put the cap back on the saline bottle.

'It's okay, it's okay,' said Daly, blinking his eyes and trying to smile through the tear-response. 'You're right, doc. It's okay.'

Winter returned, handed over Gallen's P9 and the Nikon glasses from the glove compartment. Lifting them to his eyes, Gallen aimed the cross-hatched square of the viewfinder at the mystery man and let the auto-focus adjust the picture.

The man looked back at him, his binos perfectly aligned. 'Shit, Kenny,' said Gallen. 'I know this prick.'

Winter stood beside him and Gallen handed over the binos. 'Roof of the shop on the corner, glassing us.'

'I got him, boss,' said the Canadian, who seemed to slow down as the stress went on. 'You want this dude in a bag?'

Checking his Heckler & Koch, Gallen turned to Alison. 'You stay out of trouble, okay? Daly will look after you.'

'The fuck I will,' said Daly, standing and brushing the last of the soot from his eyes. 'I'm chasing this dude.'

'You're in no state,' said Gallen. 'You can hardly see.'

'But I can shoot,' said Daly. 'Let's go.'

They moved to a side alley and pushed into a light jog. The idea was to go around the back of the shop and catch the man off guard.

Struggling to keep up with Winter, his leg in agony, Gallen tried to put the puzzle together. It wasn't the binos that drew Gallen's attention. It was the dark blazer, and the white shirt buttoned to his throat.

CHAPTER 26

They emerged from the alley into a sea of chaos, streams of people running everywhere at once. Looking up, Gallen saw the face of the tall Arab pull back from the parapet.

'He's leaving,' said Gallen, aiming for the crowded street.

Winter led the way into a lane separating the corner building from the neighbouring one.

'I'll take the front.' Gallen split from Winter and Daly, and headed for the front door. The building's ground floor was a pet shop, and Gallen found the owners cowering behind the counter, the wife in tears and the man ashen-faced.

'You are police? CIA?' said the man. 'Is there another bomb?'

'I don't know,' said Gallen, his mind producing colours around the edges of his vision as he tried to repress the pain in his leg. 'There's a man on your roof. How would he get there?'

The man shook his head. 'We have a key to the ground entrance, for our shop. The other level and the roof—they are different tenants.'

'They get in at the back?'

'Yes,' said the man. 'When is it safe to come out? I have to get my wife home.'

'Stay down.' Gallen headed for the rear exit of the shop.

The rear door opened with a creak onto a parking compound, walled in with wooden fences, a gate giving access to the rear lane. Looking around, he faced upwards. The entry to the upper levels had its own staircase which was chained off and locked at the point where it hit the car park.

The sounds of panting increased from the laneway: Winter and Daly.

'He's either still in the building,' said Gallen, moving hesitantly into the compound, 'or he's found another way out. He can't go through the pet shop—they have separate entrances.'

'Nothing in the lane.' Daly looked around. 'Think he's still on the roof?'

'I doubt it,' said Gallen, his leg throbbing. 'And he wasn't dressed for Spiderman action.'

Winter walked to the security gate at the entry to the upper levels, looking for a way over. As he did, an engine came to life, revved, and wheels spun as a vehicle accelerated away.

A white roof moved along the top of the wooden fence line and a vehicle appeared in full as it cut through a gate on the other side of the alley and sped down the laneway.

'That's it,' said Gallen, limping across the compound dirt to the gate and looking down the lane. At the end, forty yards away, the BMW 4x4 braked hard and bounced in the culvert as it turned right.

As the soot fell out of the sky, Gallen saw the rego: a four-part Saudi plate.

He came up from the depths, faster, more out of control until he raced into the light. Gallen blinked and struggled to move his head and arm to reach the phone on his bedside table.

'Hello,' he said with a croak, disoriented.

It was Daly.

'What's the time?' said Gallen, mumbling out of the side of his mouth. He'd taken a long bath at his suite in the Hyatt and then a handful of antibiotics and painkillers before going to bed at eight o'clock.

Daly told him it was around three and asked if he could come up.

'The fuck for?' Gallen shifted his right leg from a tangle in the sheets and felt a blast of fresh pain. But Daly had hung up.

'I think this is it,' said Daly, fiddling with the coffee maker in the suite's kitchenette. Gallen sat in an armchair, dressed in a hotel robe and rubbing the centre of his forehead with the tips of his fingers.

'I'm not gonna drink coffee at half past three in the morning,' said Gallen. 'So quit wastin' your time.'

'We need to get down there before the cops and the intel guys,' said Daly.

He'd been tipped off that the mechanic who stored Charlie's Yukon was alive and had regained consciousness shortly after midnight. 'I don't even want our friend Amundsen getting down there and asking questions before we do.'

'Can't it wait?' Gallen yawned and wished the painkillers would work faster.

'All these cops and spooks start work at eight,' said Daly, tapping at his G-Shock. 'We go now, we can be in there before this boy's family arrive.'

'Take Kenny,' said Gallen, the smell of coffee drifting to his nostrils. 'He loves early mornings.'

'I'm not waking that dude at three in the morning,' said Daly. 'Seen his hands? They're like car doors.'

Gallen thought about it. He was sleepy and tired and sore. In the Corps, you took sleep like a beautiful woman: with a great deal of appreciation.

'Why ain't you down there already?' Gallen watched Daly pour two coffees. 'I'm black with two.'

'You know more than me about certain aspects of this thing,' said Daly, carrying the coffees to Gallen and taking a seat on a sofa. 'You'd seen the tall dude before; you knew what shape the Yukon was in, what was in it. See what I'm sayin'? Right now, I can't be missin' even a small thing.'

'I don't know anything, Daly,' yawned Gallen.

'I think you know more than you think you know.'

'Like?'

'Like, what was it with that dude on the roof yesterday?'

Gallen stretched. 'You know what it's like. Someone glassing you, they need investigatin'.'

'You'd seen him before?'

Gallen considered how he was going to deal with this. 'The night that Spikey had you escorted out of the Araby Castle?'

'Yeah.'

'We were on the roof, having a beer, and this crew attacked us. That's where the hole in the leg came from.'

'Who were they?'

'Spikey didn't know, but there was this guy—a tall Arab—who got out of a BMW four-by-four with Saudi plates. He seemed to be running the soldiers.'

'That guy on the roof had Saudi plates,' said Daly. 'Is he Hamas?'

'No,' said Gallen. 'Baba's boys were protecting Spikey for a cut of the money. I think this tall guy works for al-Haq. The night I went into the depot with Spikey, I saw the BMW parked there.'

'Shit, Gerry. You didn't think to tell me?'

'I was chasing money and chasing Spikey, remember that gig?' said Gallen. Then he saw an advantage. 'You know what? I'll go down there, Daly—but first you answer some questions from me.'

'Do what I can,' said Daly, taking a sip of coffee.

'Baba told me you're DIA. Are you?'

Daly smiled. 'I'm a manager with Columbus. What Baba's sayin' is that Chase never stopped being DIA.'

'So all that mercenary stuff, that's not real?'

'Sure it is,' said Daly. 'Think I'm gettin' paid to do nothin'?'

'But Chase works for the Pentagon's spooks?'

'They trust him, they can deny him,' said Daly. 'I never really get into it with him. They do for him, he gives back. Old-school stuff.'

'So what's in the bags?'

Daly shrugged. 'I don't know.'

'Come on, Daly. You know.'

'The FBI knows what they think is in the bags.'

'And what's your theory?'

'All I can tell you is what Barrowman briefed me with the first time we met,' said Daly.

'Which was?'

'It was a week before I found you in Pinedale,' said Daly. 'Barrowman is vague, but he tells me there's these Arab criminals— the al-Haq brothers—who are based out of Detroit and Amman, with an office in Beirut.'

'Okay,' said Gallen, leaning forwards, holding the mug in two hands. 'What's their deal?'

'Well, Barrowman's a specialist in terror funding, so at first I thought they were involved in that. Then one of our bugs in Spikey's apartment picks up a conversation with you a few days ago.'

'You prick.'

'Well, yeah,' said Daly. 'So then I realise that Barrowman isn't chasing a wire transfer—he's got his eyes on actual bags of dough that Spikey Holmes and his buddy Faidh have picked up and couriered into Aqaba.'

'Where did Spikey and Faidh get the money from?' said Gallen.

Daly laughed. 'Great minds, huh? I go to Chase, ask him to tap someone on the shoulder and get a travel log for Mr Terrell Holmes.'

'And?'

'Spikey and Faidh flew into Athens, took a charter flight to Beirut, hired a Chev Suburban from Hertz and disappeared. They only turn up on the radar because the Chev busts a transmission in Baghdad— Hertz replace the vehicle and the next thing we know, Spikey and Faidh are crossing into Saudi and then crossing into the south of Jordan and driving to Aqaba.'

'So, if we accept the connection between the al-Haqs and Saddam, the pick-up was Baghdad?'

'That's my assumption. Barrowman didn't want to discuss it. He saw me as the hired muscle, and hired muscle too close to DIA.'

Gallen thought about what Spikey had told him. 'And Ariq al-Haq was so sensitive about the bags that he sent another crew to dispossess Spikey?'

'Seems that way,' said Daly. 'But Faidh and Spikey decide to heist it back.'

'The original twelve million explains what Spikey and Faidh were thinking,' said Gallen. 'But Barrowman's a money-laundering expert. Why's he only interested in the bags full of crap?'

Daly finished his coffee and stood. 'Maybe it's not crap in those bags. You comin'?'

'Let me freshen up.'

King Hussein Hospital was in the centre of a massive campus in the middle of Amman. Daly did the talking with the guard at the military gate and they were allowed through.

The ICU was on the ground floor of the building and Gallen followed Daly through the white corridors, smiling at nurses and greeting doctors, until they found the ward they were looking for.

'May I help, sir?' said the young woman at the nurse's station.

'I'm from the embassy,' said Daly. 'Attached to the Mukhabarat.'

She started to argue and Daly withdrew his phone from his pocket and flipped it open. 'I can call them if you'd like?'

'Who are you here to see?'

'Ahmed Khaki.'

'From the bombing? He's not awake.'

'I can get the GID to come down here and wake him. What's your name again?'

The woman led them into a room where a man lay on his back, heavily wrapped in bandages, his open eyes glinting in the night light. The nurse spoke with him softly in Arabic then left.

'Hi, Ahmed,' said Daly, making the introductions and explaining what he was doing there. 'This is Gerry Gallen—a friend of Charlie's. He wants to ask some questions so we can find who killed Charlie.'

Gallen looked down at the injuries. 'Lucky, eh, Ahmed? God must like you.'

The man blinked.

'So, what can you tell me about the men who came to your workshop? Did they ask for Charlie?'

The man whispered, 'No'.

'Did anyone come, want to look at the car you stored for Charlie?'

'No.'

'Do you know who planted that bomb?'

'No.'

Gallen looked at Daly, turned back to Ahmed. 'Did Charlie discuss with you some bags he had in the car?'

'Yes.'

'Did he want them put in a safe place?'

'No.'

'Was he worried that they contained money?'

'No.'

'Was he worried about the guns?'

Ahmed shook his head slightly. 'I was.'

'What?' said Gallen, Daly moving in beside his shoulder.

'I worry about guns.'

'Trouble with the police?'

'Yes.'

Gallen could tell that the strain of talking was getting to Ahmed.

'Did you hide those bags?'

Ahmed's throat seized up but he nodded.

'Where?'

'Inspect—' said Ahmed, and then the coughing started.

Gallen readied for another go but the nurse came in, this time with a doctor.

'Visiting time is over,' said the doctor. 'And if you really want to quote the Mukhabarat, I have friends there too.'

Stepping into the night air, Daly and Gallen lit cigarettes.

'Wanna take a look at that bombsite?' said Daly.

'That inspection pit has our names all over it.'

CHAPTER 27

The explosion had created a fire that burned down half the block. In the panic that had followed the initial blast, the flood of people across the narrow streets had prevented the fire trucks from getting through and now, as Gallen and Daly ducked under the police tape and past two dark vans, there was a scene of blackened wreckage disappearing into the darkness, with a tent-like structure around what Gallen assumed was the destroyed Yukon. A light glowed from inside the tent and silhouettes of people moved against it; police or intel probably.

'Here,' said Daly, indicating the long way around the burnt-out workshop. The neighbouring building had also been burned out, providing them with a stealthy way to approach Ahmed's inspection pit. Daly held his Maglite low and they trod carefully through the neighbouring site, crouching behind a half-toppled brick wall when someone from the forensic team in the workshop pushed open the tent flap and lit a cigarette.

Waiting in the darkness, Gallen got his leg into a comfortable position and asked the question that had hung between them. 'So what do we do with the bags when we get 'em?'

'They go to the client, the FBI,' said Daly, whispering. 'Why, you got an eBay thing goin' on?'

'Just askin',' said Gallen. 'When people are dyin', I like to know what for.'

'Stop you goin' to Mindanao?'

Gallen scoffed. 'You a hippie now all a sudden?'

'Just sayin'.'

The smoking investigator flicked his butt away and re-entered the glowing tent and Daly led the way to a door that opened into the main workshop area of Ahmed's business. The wall between the garage and workshop was mostly intact, allowing some room to work without being discovered.

The inspection pit was a large one, built for trucks as well as cars. Daly held the flashlight and Gallen tried to descend the stairs only to find the pit filled with charred wood, burnt paper and cinders.

'Shit,' said Gallen. 'Like a grease trap for a fire.'

He starting handing out the larger objects to Daly, moving as fast as he could without the leg becoming impossible. They worked quickly and quietly, one of the few military skills he thought he'd ever have to use again. Gallen handed, Daly stacked, until Gallen could get all the way down into the pit.

Daly followed him with the Maglite. Along the pit walls were six steel doors—three on each side. Gallen opened the first one, looked in: the space was the size of a family sedan's trunk, containing grease guns and rags and a set of safety glasses. The next door was padlocked, and shining the light down the wall, they could see that the subsequent door was also locked. They looked in the three storage compartments on the other side of the pit, but they just contained oil trays, filters, goggles and gloves.

The bags had to be behind the padlocked doors.

'There a bar in that compartment?' said Daly, taking a small wrecking bar from one of the open doors: one end with a flat tongue and the other with a split tongue.

They positioned the flat end under the loop that was padlocked and tried to get leverage. The lock wouldn't budge. The latches weren't bolted straight into the concrete: they were welded onto plates which were welded onto the door and dynabolted into the concrete.

'Jesus, what was Ahmed going to stash in here? His cocaine?' said Daly, giving up with a grunt.

'Let's fulcrum it,' said Gallen. There was a half-brick on the floor of the pit and Gallen fitted it under the wrecking bar and beside the padlock. Getting the weight on, Gallen put his arms around Daly's shoulders, got a grip on the bar and they put their combined weight—about four hundred pounds—onto the fulcrum. It wouldn't give.

'We should've brought Kenny,' said Gallen, panting as they released the bar. He pulled a foil of T3s from his jeans pocket, popped two and swallowed them without water. 'Okay, let's think this through. Ahmed has six storage compartments in his inspection pit: there's padlocks on two of them, and not new padlocks.'

'So he locks things regularly,' said Daly. 'Which means he might keep the keys nearby.'

Daly walked the length of the pit, holding his Maglite high so the beam wouldn't escape. 'A mechanic would want the keys close but hidden,' he said, almost to himself.

'He'd use a hidey-hole,' said Gallen. 'Maybe even in the pit.'

Daly kneeled to investigate the stairs that gave access to the pit. There were five steel-grating steps, riding on their own scaffolding. Reaching behind the steel beams that held up the steps, Daly ran his fingers up and down the beams and behind the steps themselves.

'Bingo,' he said, holding up a set of keys. He opened the first door and shone the flashlight inside. There were two black military holdalls, the same ones Gallen had risked his life to take out of the al-Haq depot a week ago. Gallen pulled them out, threw one over each shoulder, and Daly used the flashlight to check if they'd missed anything. The third black holdall was in the other padlocked storage box. They dragged it out and Daly put over his shoulder. As he shut the door Gallen saw a scrap of paper had fallen off the bag, the loop of twine still attached to the handles. Picking it up he saw it was a name tag of some sort and he screwed it up, put it in his pocket.

There was a sound of feet shuffling and Daly killed the flashlight.

Huddling in the dark, they waited for the footfalls to move in the other direction, but they came closer. Instinctively Gallen and Daly turned away so their shoulder blades were also touching and cocked their pistols. Gallen's breathing came heavier as the feet got to the edge of the pit, a wave of cinders falling on the two men. Raising his Heckler & Koch into the darkness, he waited for the intruder to announce himself. And then he was going to shoot.

'Daly, that you?' said an American voice. 'Gerry?'

Gallen turned back to Daly and they faced each other in the dark.

'The fuck?' whispered Gallen, his heart racing.

'Raise your hands and drop it,' said Daly, loud and confident.

'Seriously?' said the American voice. 'That you, Joe?'

'Identify yourself,' said Daly.

'Christ's sake, Joe,' said the voice. 'It's me—Barry Amundsen.'

Amundsen carried a glass pot of coffee and three mugs hooked into one hand, placed them in the middle of the board table. A large black man—introduced simply as David—delivered a small tray containing sugar, cream and cookies and took the chair across from Gallen.

'Mind?' said Gallen, pulling a pack of Marlboros from his Tough Duck pocket.

'I don't,' said Amundsen. 'But Uncle Sam does.'

Gallen dropped the pack on the table, looked around the nondescript office. It was a front for the US intelligence community, which usually meant Central Intelligence Agency and Defense Intelligence Agency, either of which had to be able to operate covertly and illegally while also having legitimate attachés and first secretaries at the embassies. The intelligence staff at this unofficial office was probably larger than the official 'station' at the embassy.

On the table was the junk from the bags that Amundsen had been sorting through. There were reams of paper, some of them stapled together, some fastened onto cardboard as files and others—which looked like bills of lading and freight manifests—floating free. David had flipped through them and translated the Arabic, pronounced them not entirely interesting. David's allegiance had been left vague but, judging by his Westpoint ring, Gallen had him as DIA.

'So, Barry,' said Daly. 'I guess this is the point where I remind you that I'm working for someone else.'

'Sure,' said Amundsen, a round face producing the perfectly

insincere smile on cue. Gallen had always wondered if the CIA taught its field guys how to do that.

'By which I mean, copy all you want, but the FBI wants this,' said Daly.

'I get it,' said Amundsen, standing. 'Won't keep anything from the feds. Scout's.'

The big Agency station chief slurped on coffee and stretched so hard that his back clicked. It was just before five in the morning and he had a face that Gallen recognised as being used to working with broken sleep. Gallen knew the facial tics, the suppressed yawns and the constant blinking as the signs of a man working through fatigue—knew it because it was how Force Recon captains were expected to operate when they took on a combat billet.

'Chase is okay, you bein' here an' all,' said David. 'If that's the thing.'

Daly gave him a look. 'This is the thing, David: what comes out of the bag goes back in. All I'm sayin'.'

Among the items on the table was a grey three-foot-long PVC tube. A screw-on lid at the end facing Gallen featured a piece of white tape with black Arabic writing scrawled on it.

'You mind?' Amundsen pointed at the tube but was looking at Daly.

'Be your guest,' said Daly, over his coffee.

The end of the tube came away with one twist and Amundsen peered inside, pushed his fingertips in. Pulling back on the tube, he dragged out a rolled blueprint which he flattened on the table, David using his coffee mug and the side of the cream tray to hold it down.

'What is it?' said Gallen, curious.

'I have no idea.' Amundsen craned his head as if a new angle might make it obvious. 'I'll hand it on. Some egghead will know.'

'No idea?' said Gallen, stopping short of a sip. 'You don't know what this stuff is?'

Daly swapped a look of confusion with Gallen.

'Should I?' said Amundsen. 'I mean, it looks like a storage facility or something. Probably a missile bunker.'

Gallen and Daly stood, looked down on the blueprint. It showed a triangle-shaped structure inside a mountain—or under a lot of soil—and containing what looked to be its own small town. Gallen noticed a few horizontal wavy lines along the top of the page—perhaps an abstraction of the sky?

'It's a dump or a warehouse,' said Daly, tracing his finger over the paper, the lack of writing making it hard to find a focus for the structure. 'Looks pretty big. Why's there no writing on it?'

'Classified,' said Amundsen. 'You have your plans with no words and a sheet of words held by someone else that you overlay when the two items are in the one place.'

'Like a door that needs two keys?' said Gallen.

'That's what I'm assuming,' said Amundsen, sitting down. 'It's normal for the European military, which means it's normal for the Middle East.'

'So what were you expecting?' Gallen ignored the snide reference to the Russian and French influence on militaries in the region.

'It's not what I was expecting,' said Amundsen, reaching for Gallen's smokes and lighting one. 'I was more interested in where it came from.'

'I don't follow,' said Gallen. 'You were after the bags.'

'We were after the whole chain—' Amundsen pulled up short as David gave him a look.

'Got something you'd like to share?' Daly looked at David. 'This your show?'

David stretched out, put his hands over his belly. He was late thirties, built like a wide receiver. 'It's the FBI's show.'

There was a pause and then they all started laughing, Gallen feeling guilty as he thought of Jim Barrowman bleeding in the street. The FBI had to stick to the rules in a way that the Pentagon and Langley never did, and the idea that the feds would be running an intel operation in a place like Jordan was laughable.

Gallen made the connection as he reached for his smokes. 'When you talk about where it's coming from, you mean this was about the al-Haqs?'

Amundsen scratched his head, turned away. He'd just thrown to David, the real power in the room.

David looked at his hands. 'That's classified, Captain.'

'It's Mr Gallen, and I've just been carrying this stuff around for five days—it's hardly classified.'

David nodded, non-committal. 'Tell me what came out of the al-Haq depot. Tell me everything.'

'I went in with Spikey,' said Gallen. 'He had seven bags—just like these ones—stashed in a wrecked truck.'

'Where?'

'In the storage bins over the dashboard, and one under the sleeper. He took four bags filled with money and I got these,' said Gallen, gesturing at the paper with his cigarette. 'The rest you know.'

'Where did Holmes get the bags from before he stashed them in the truck?'

Gallen tried to remember the story. 'He told me he was a courier for Ariq al-Haq, taking a bunch of bags to Amman. When he got to Aqaba, Ariq's boys intercepted them at the hotel, took the bags into Amman, so Spikey and his buddy decided to heist them.'

'I mean,' said David, leaning forwards on his knees and fixing Gallen with a stare. 'Where did the bags originate from? Where did Holmes get them from?'

'Our guess was Baghdad,' said Gallen. 'But—'

David had raised his hand. 'Sorry, Gerry, but I don't need a guess. Baghdad is the size of Chicago. It's the largest city in the Middle East. The question is where those bags came from, who told the al-Haqs to pick them up, and why now?'

'Shit.' Gallen sat back. 'You don't know any of that?'

David opened his hands like a magician proving he had nothing up his sleeves. 'Tell me about the watcher—dude on the roof after the bomb.'

Gallen sucked on his smoke, poured the last of the coffee. 'Don't know him.'

'But you'd seen him before,' said David. 'That's what set you off?'

'The night at the Araby Castle, when we went around to break out Spikey,' said Gallen. 'I was on the roof when a local crew—not Hamas—stormed the place.'

'This tall guy one of them?'

Gallen nodded. 'I think he was the leader. He drove a white BMW four-by-four, Saudi plates, and he looked like a movie star, one of them Bollywood dudes. You know?'

'No,' said David. 'Tell me.'

'Tall, groomed, white shirt, expensive blazer. You ever seen a Bollywood movie?'

'Enlighten me.'

'A dude like the one I just described—he always gets the chick.'

Gallen thought he saw a flicker of interest cross David's face. 'That ring a bell?'

'No,' said David, flicking a business card across the table. 'But stay in touch.'

CHAPTER 28

The doors hissed open and Jim Barrowman limped into the Royal
Jordanian business-class queue, assisted by Alison McIntyre.

Gallen and Winter stacked their bags, made room for Barrowman,
whose head was wrapped like a wounded soldier's. He was wearing
military shorts, his right leg bandaged from the ankle to mid-thigh.

Kenny Winter wolf-whistled. 'Nice legs, Jimbo.'

Through the bandages, Gallen saw a smile. They got him
seated and Winter went searching for croissants and OJ from the
concourse cafe.

'How you doin', Jim?' said Gallen.

'Half melted,' said the FBI guy. 'The whole thing's like a bad
dream. Alison said you chased a bad guy. On a roof?'

Gallen nodded, raised his empty coffee mug at Winter for a refill.
'Someone glassing us from a rooftop while the workshop went up.
Just chased him on a hunch, but he ran.'

Barrowman's head nodded and his phone went. As he answered,
Alison moved to Gallen's other side and stood too close, a position he
liked. 'You okay, Gerry?'

'I'm fine, blast didn't really hit me.'

'Not that, the gunshot wound. Keeping it clean?' She flicked
some hair which had come loose from her French plait.

'Had a bath this morning,' said Gallen. 'Still hurts to walk on it. What are you doin' here?'

'After that bomb the company pulled the plug on expat doctors, reassigned me to DC, but I've got two weeks in between.'

Gallen's iPhone buzzed in his pocket. Turning away slightly he tapped on the text pending and found a message from Mike Ford, the Aussie naval commando. It said *In honkers, dest ME. Call you then. Mike.*

Gallen responded, caught Alison looking at him as he pocketed the phone.

'You ever stop working?' she said, smiling.

'No,' said Gallen. 'Least, I don't remember it.'

They checked in and made for the departure gates, shepherding Jim Barrowman through the ultra-modern airport. As they moved towards the security zone, a local man with a big moustache and dusty clothes waved at Gallen.

'Friend of yours?' said Alison.

'No,' said Winter, behind them. 'Mine.'

A ten-year-old boy moved from beside the man and walked to Winter.

'Hey, Rashie,' said Winter, shaking the boy's hand. 'How's the ears?'

Gallen could now see big wads of cotton wool in the child's ears, held down by transparent tape. The boy—urged on by his father—held out something to Winter. It was a small stone carving of what looked like the King and Queen of Jordan.

'It's beautiful, Rashie,' said Winter, the slow prairie drawl showing a faint sign of enthusiasm. 'Hey, Gerry—come meet Rashad.'

Gallen said hello to the child and listened to the father trying, in his limited English, to explain that Jordan was a peaceful country and the bombing was the work of outsiders, not Jordanians.

Gallen was humbled. Here was a man who'd almost lost his son in the blast and he was being protective about his country's reputation. The man became excited and Gallen turned away. He was tired.

'Rashie wants to say something,' said Winter, slapping Gallen in the stomach.

'My father say it not Jordan people who bomb,' said the boy. 'He say Jordan people finish argument with deal, or they have the fight, but they don't leave the bomb in the street like coward.'

'I understand,' said Gallen.

The father poked Rashie in the chest and said something before giving Gallen a look. The boy turned back to Gallen. 'He say the people saw you chase the real criminal.'

Gallen's face flushed and the father jabbered at the son.

'My father say all Jordan hope you catch the Iraq son of the whore.'

'What?' said Gallen, interested now. 'You say Iraqi?'

A security guard approached and tried to move the locals on from the departures area.

'Tell me,' said Gallen, walking around the guards to Rashie.

'My father say he saw you chase—'

'Yeah, yeah, Rashie,' said Gallen. 'I get that. How does your father know the man on the roof is from Iraq?'

Rashie spoke to his father and turned to Gallen. 'He says the man you chase is Saddam's family. Everyone know this.'

Gallen's head swirled with the noises of the airport. He was so tired. 'Listen, Rashie, ask your father does he know the name of the man on the roof?'

Rashie turned to his father as a security man became insistent with Gallen.

'My father say he don't remember the name, anyway it is a false one,' said Rashie. 'He say the man is al-Tikriti—the Americans should have killed them all the first time.'

The Atlantic played its red and purple and then blue and green light show as the British Airways 777 sped westwards to New York, two and a half hours out of Heathrow and chasing the sun into dusk. Gallen had slept for an hour on the Amman–London leg and had dozed for another hour as they climbed over the Atlantic. Now he was wide awake and could have kicked himself for it—he was sitting in a capsule seat that lay flat to make a bed, but he couldn't make the most of it so he was watching War Horse and dreading the scene he didn't want to see again.

'Horse movie, huh?' she said, as she sat on the fold-down seat opposite Gallen that also doubled as a footrest for the bed.

'Well,' said Gallen, fumbling for the pause button.

'I'm kidding,' said Alison, stretching and then wrapping her arms around herself and doing an incomplete job. 'You like horses?'

'Sure.' Gallen found the pause button just as the barbed-wire sequence began. 'Like 'em enough to not see that scene again.'

Alison craned forwards to see the screen and he could smell her perfume.

'It's a great movie,' said Gallen. 'There's just a part when he panics and gets caught in the barbed wire in—you know—no-man's-land.'

The plane was dark, everything turned down and people snoozing around them.

Gallen felt a little nervous with her proximity. 'You've seen it?'

'No,' she said, and then he knew she was making fun of him.

'It's about a horse who tries his heart out in the Great War. In Europe.'

'I know where the Great War was fought,' she said, laughing.

Gallen could feel himself blushing. She was either being rude about his movie choice or she was flirting, and he wasn't sure what to do about either.

'And I've never seen the film because my friends know I couldn't handle that scene.'

Gallen's turn to smile. 'You ride?'

'Since I was a child.'

'Showjumping, I bet,' said Gallen.

'You think that's who I am?'

Gallen shrugged.

'Anyway,' said Alison, 'I've got two weeks in Des Moines and I thought I'd head out to Aspen, see a friend of mine.'

'I see,' said Gallen. 'Nice down there.'

'So, maybe . . .'

She let it hang like that, in the way that always confused Gallen. 'Oh, you mean, maybe we could grab a drink or something?'

'Sure, why not?' she said.

'Okay,' said Gallen. 'Shall I call you, or you can . . .'

200

She held up her iPhone, tapped in his number at the farm as he recited it.

'You normally pick up men in planes?' said Gallen.

She laughed. 'Only when I need company to see a horse getting hurt.'

Gallen shifted over, made room, and Alison joined him on the lay-flat bed, pulling an airline blanket over both of them and pushing her breasts into his shoulder. He was surprised how well she fit him and by the fact that for all her curves she also felt muscular, solid.

He turned to ask her what she was going to do about earphones and she kissed him, and Gallen kissed her back. When he came up for air she had her forehead on his and her fingers in his short hair.

'You lose the bet, by the way,' she said.

'What bet?'

'It wasn't showjumping—I was a barrel racer,' she said.

Gallen tried to laugh but she was kissing him again.

He awoke to the quiet roar of the Boeing. All around, people slept and only one television screen was operating, sending out an eerie light around the dark business-class cabin. Edging out of Alison's embrace, he moved two pods down the aisle to where Jim Barrowman endured his vigil as the last television screen still playing a movie.

'What's so important you can't switch it off?' said Gallen.

Barrowman turned the screen so Gallen could see Tom Cruise doing his thing in *Jerry Maguire*.

'You grabbed me at hello,' said Gallen.

'You *had* me,' said Barrowman.

'Don't say it too loud, dude,' said Gallen. 'They'll all want a turn.'

'Shit, Gallen,' said Barrowman, shaking his bandaged head as Gallen giggled. 'You can take the boy out of the Marines.'

'Yes, well,' said Gallen, pushing Barrowman's feet off the footrest, taking a seat. 'And I only had one beer.'

'So, Gallen. A mysterious fireball erupts in the middle of Amman and the next thing I know, our intrepid special forces soldier is chasing down a man on a roof.'

'Sounds like a movie, don't it?'

'Sounds to me like you know who he was.'

Gallen looked around. The BA business-class seats faced one another with a divider down the middle and he wasn't sure who was on the other side. 'I'd seen him before.'

'Who?' Barrowman sat up straight.

'Dude on the roof.'

Barrowman stared at him. 'Where?'

'Jim, I think it's about time the FBI worked with me rather than against, see what I mean?'

'So I show you mine? That's a little clumsy, isn't it, Gerry?'

'I feel like every time I try to join the game, I only get four cards,' said Gallen. 'We should share the wealth, is all.'

'Shit,' sighed Barrowman. 'It's not that simple.'

'I'm going to tell you what I know about the man on the roof,' said Gallen. 'And then you'll tell me what you know about what I know. Fair?'

'Talk away, Gerry. But I can't promise.'

'That's a pity,' said Gallen, standing and moving away. ''Cos I was goin' to spell out the Iraq connection. Enjoy Renee Schwarzenegger.'

'Zellwegger!' said Barrowman, too loud, as Gallen walked back to his pod and the curves of a warm woman. Gallen grabbed the blanket as Barrowman limped up, furious.

'Gallen! I'm sorry, okay . . .' Looking down, he saw Alison sleeping and what Gallen could see of his face went through the full spectrum of emotions before he collected himself. 'Sorry. Didn't realise . . .'

Edging away from Alison, Gallen walked back down to Barrowman's pod.

'I saw this man from the roof when I was at the Araby Castle,' said Gallen. 'He was running a crew that came looking for Spikey, but he was a cut above them in looks, grooming, dress—you name it.'

'You talk to him?'

'No,' said Gallen. 'I ran away from him and his goons, slid down a garbage chute to get out of there.'

'Then you see him on the roof, looking over the bombsite?'

'Yeah, I saw him looking at the flames through binoculars. So I got a set of my own, glassed him back, and realised he was looking at us.'

'Us, or you?'

Gallen thought about it. 'I don't know. Anyway, we lost him, and just before I got on the plane in Amman, a local told me that the tall Arab was an Iraqi.'

'Tell me, Gerry,' said Barrowman, shaking slightly. 'Did you get a name?'

'No, Jim. But the local told me he was one of Saddam's people— al-Tikriti.'

Barrowman grabbed his forearm, held it tight. 'Don't bullshit me, Gerry. How did the local know this?'

'Said everyone knew who he was and that the US should have buried the lot of them when we had the chance.'

Barrowman sagged back in his seat. 'Shit.'

'Your turn to tell,' said Gallen.

'You want me to lose my job?'

'You want my help on this?'

Barrowman's bandage covered most of his left eye but Gallen could see both of them burning out of the dimness. 'The al-Haqs are from Tikrit. That's Saddam's hometown.'

'So?' said Gallen. 'Saddam was executed back in oh-six. What's he got to do with anything?'

'The al-Haqs were Saddam's main money men and fixers around the Arab world,' said Barrowman. 'They ran the scams that got around the UN oil-for-food embargos. They imported Cobra helicopters for the Jordanian air force, but they ended up in Iraqi livery. They even sourced and funded the Saddam nuclear weapon program that the New York Times said didn't exist.'

'What's that got to do with a tall Arab on a roof in Amman?'

'When I approached you in Denver, we'd intercepted a communication from the US al-Haq operation, alerting Ariq al-Haq to your arrival.'

'Yeah, you told me.'

'What I didn't tell you is they knew what Spikey wanted to pick up and that you were going to help him. This package came from Baghdad and is incredibly important to the al-Haqs and other al-Tikriti.'

'I'm not following,' said Gallen.

'The al-Haqs want to return Iraq to the way it was, and something in those bags you were carrying gave them the power to do that.'

'They military people?'

'No,' said Barrowman. 'Worse than military.'

Gallen made a doubtful face.

'These people are a nightmare,' said Barrowman. 'They're Baathists.'

CHAPTER 29

The old sorel waded through the fresh overnight drift, the snow crust sparkling with small diamonds as the sun waited to rise over the Arpan Butte. Gallen lit a cigarette, flicked the collar of his plaid riding jacket up higher as he pressed his wounded thigh into the warm patch on the saddle. Lincoln, the labrador-collie who did a lot of porch-minding for a working dog, plunged and dived through the snow, making more noise than Gallen and the horse, Jessie, put together.

'Easy, Jessie,' he murmured, not wanting the old girl to work too hard in the snow. She'd been spelled most of the summer in the paddock behind the barn, and he didn't want to go back to Roy, tell him his old Jessie had slipped in the snow, injured herself in a bronc chase.

They crested a rise, a bare dome on the bottom sixty that looked down on the creek and across twenty paddocks to the barn and the homestead, where a trickle of smoke drifted like wool twine from the kitchen stove stack. Cattle grazed in the snow off to the right, the butte rising purple and black behind them.

'Whoa, Lincoln,' said Gallen, conversational, and the shaggy black beast stopped immediately. Gallen had argued with his father about using horse commands to run stock dogs, but he had to hand him one thing: you didn't have to raise your voice to get Lincoln's attention.

Looking over the amazing sight of northern Wyoming in the pre-dawn, he sucked on the cigarette, let the silence press in. He thought of his high school years, forced out the door at six in the morning to ride the boundary and be back in time to do his barn chores. And he thought of Alison McIntyre, who had called, left a voice mail, reminded him of that drink they were going to grab when she made it to Aspen.

She was in Aspen, but Gallen hadn't called her back, and he wasn't going to. She was beautiful and smart, and she was into horses. And she could kiss. But he didn't think he could draw someone into his life and put them in a firing line that was intended for him. He still felt terrible at how his own actions had made her a captive of Hamas, and he didn't know if he could accept the risk of that happening again.

Roy had picked up Alison's voicemail, asked him about it, and seeing Gallen's indifference, had called him a pussy and told him, 'Nothing ever did scare you, son, 'cept a girl givin' you the eye.'

Roy hadn't stopped ribbing him yet for allowing Yvonne, a neighbouring eligible divorcee, to slip through his grasp. The truth was he didn't yet have the confidence to take on a full adult relationship. He didn't know if it was too many years of combat or the circumstances of his divorce from Marcia. He just knew he'd been ducking it all, and Alison was no different.

Jessie snorted, shook her bridle, bringing Gallen back to the present. Two hundred yards down the rise, on a short plateau breasting the creek, was a herd of bucking horses, grazing, nibbling at each other, steam rising off their backs like a hot pool. Gallen counted them, and then did it again. All there: twenty-seven.

He sucked on the cigarette, checked the gates he'd opened on his way to the bottom of the three hundred and sixty acres. The ones he could see were still open, all the way to the horse yards around the barn and the run-in field where the nags would spend the winter.

'Get away out, boy,' said Gallen, gripping the reins through his gloves and forcing blood into his freezing hands. Lincoln rose and leapt through the snow, his head held slightly lower than a street dog, his shoulders and head staying steady as his legs and body did all the work.

The animal accelerated down the rise, out to the right of the herd, giving them nowhere to go but into the creek. One horse—a large grey mare—looked at the dog, stamped a front hoof. Beside her, an ugly paint gelding pulled his nose out of the snow and looked back over his shoulder at Lincoln. Neither horse looked scared—they knew the dog, the dog knew them.

'Whoa, boy,' said Gallen, loud enough for his voice to carry. The dog stopped and bellyflopped in the snow, and several horses walked at him until they stood in formation around the grey mare, staring at Lincoln.

'Walk up, boy,' said Gallen, smiling as the dog stealthed across the snow, its haunches barely breaking the level of the drift. 'Whoa.'

The dog bellyflopped again and three more horses arrived in the formation around the grey. Now Lincoln was thirty yards from the grey mare, whose body language was defiant. She stamped the same hoof, snorted in a long plume of steam, eyeballed Lincoln.

Gallen got Lincoln to repeat the advances until he lay ten yards in front of the grey's nose, twenty-four eyeballs staring down on him.

Gallen flicked his cigarette butt, let Jessie walk down the rise as he fixed his old hat harder down on his ears.

The grey stamped again, stared at Lincoln, who stayed solid.

'Okay,' said Gallen. 'Move 'em, boy.'

The dog sprang into action, barking at the grey, throwing his chest from one side to the other as the horse moved her head.

'Move 'em, boy,' said Gallen. 'Move 'em up.' Several bucking horses peeled away from the grey.

'Move 'em,' said Gallen, louder, and Lincoln lunged into the grey's personal space.

Throwing her shaggy head in a display of anger, the grey turned and her herd turned too. Lincoln had won the first round, turning the bucking herd and getting them moving towards the creek and the run-in field.

The thumping of hooves on snow echoed around the creek valley, and the first hawk of the day emerged out of the trees on the other side of the river.

'Get away back,' said Gallen and Lincoln veered to the right, trying to accelerate around the right flank of the herd, keep them from fording at the deep part of the creek. Gallen didn't care about a bunch of bucking horses having to swim, but he wanted Lincoln and Jessie in the shallows where they could stay in control.

Lincoln's tactic worked, moving the herd westwards along the creek to the shallow ford a hundred yards away. Gallen urged Jessie into a trot, the cold air gripping at his ears; he wished he'd worn his ski hat rather than the battered black Bailey.

'Get away out,' said Gallen, using the command to make Lincoln veer left. The animal ran across Jessie's path, transferring his placement so the herd was now between Lincoln and the creek. They reached the shallows, a flat apron of river stones on Gallen's side, turning into a mud chute on the opposite bank after a ford of thirty yards.

The herd loped, steam coming off them in clouds, but Gallen kept Jessie at a trot. It was time to slow the herd and get them through the water.

'Move 'em, boy,' said Gallen, louder now above the hoof beats and the barking. Lincoln sprinted around to head the leading horse, until the herd stopped. Then the dog pulled back, dodged side to side in front of the panting horses as he moved in on them, until the grey mare tossed her head and turned for the water.

Lincoln's barking became manic as he pushed the herd into the ford and got them wading across.

'Move 'em,' said Gallen, trying to encourage the dog as he plunged into the icy cold. Roy had resisted the trend to use Australian cattle dogs on his stock; he preferred some labrador blood in his dogs due to all the water and snow they had to work in. Gallen knew the theory but, still, he felt bad asking a dog to work in that water while he sat dry on a warm horse.

The first of the bucking herd were climbing the mud chute on the opposite bank when Gallen slowed Jessie and let her walk into the creek ford. Lincoln yapped at a straggler who tried to kick him and the horse turned and moved once Lincoln got too close.

At the far side of the ford, the water got deep momentarily and Lincoln paddled to the mud chute, climbed out and started working on the herd again after a quick shake that sprayed Gallen. Jessie dipped into the deeper water, kept her feet and then scrabbled to get onto the mud chute. Leaning forwards down by her neck—keeping his head to one side to avoid a broken nose—he urged her up, but she lost her footing on the bank, lunged to regain her balance, and then slid down sideways into the water.

'Shit,' yelled Gallen, whipping his bank-side boot from the stirrup as Jessie went down on her side, struggling. Keeping hold of the reins, Gallen got one boot onto the mud bank but the other boot jammed in the outside stirrup, pulling him down into the water. As Jessie got her footing in the creek, she stood suddenly, throwing Gallen head first into the water.

Coming up for air, Gallen grabbed his hat. He was drenched and still holding the reins.

'Happy now?' he said to Jessie, who was standing very calm in water up to her shoulders and leaning in for a drink.

Leading the horse up the mud chute, Gallen paused at the edge of the paddock, emptied his boots of water. Fifty yards away, Lincoln stood in front of the herd, who were grazing through the snow cover.

Gallen wiped his face, got back in the saddle and set his mind to a bath. 'Move 'em, boy,' he yelled, and squeezed his heels against Jessie's belly.

The horn sounded as Roy put the oven tray of biscuits on the kitchen counter, half an hour before the sun slipped down behind the Big Horns. Ducking to look through the kitchen window, he dropped the tray of sweet-smelling dough and pushed the tea towel into his back pocket.

'Looks like Kenny,' he said, making for the door.

The white F350 purred on the gravel driveway, steam coming from the tailpipe. A twenty-eight-foot gooseneck trailer sat on the back, horse eyes peering through the side slats.

'Where you want these nags?' said Kenny Winter, slipping out of the front door of the Ford and doing a quick back stretch.

Roy pointed to a gate beside the barn and started walking.

'They travel okay?' said Gallen, shaking Winter's hand.

'Few kicks, and the black mare's a biter,' said Winter, lighting a cigarette. 'But otherwise an easy ten hours down I-90.'

A tallish blond kid, about fourteen or fifteen, climbed out the other side of the big Ford, gave a quick thumb-grip to the brim of his hat. Most people wouldn't notice the gesture but Gallen knew his dad would.

'Who's this?' Roy turned back as the kid stood his full height.

'Name's Ryan, sir,' said the kid. 'Ryan Winter. Guess you're Mr Gallen?'

'You guessed right, son.' Roy beamed as Ryan reached out and shook his hand. Roy Gallen may have looked like a broken-down old redneck but he loved a youngster with manners. He grabbed the kid around the shoulders. 'You know horses, do ya, Ryan?'

'Not as well as they know me,' said the kid, and Roy laughed.

'Come on, tell me what you think of this bucking herd,' he said, walking towards the run-in field with Ryan Winter.

Winter had bought six horses from the auctions at Glenavon. A rodeo contractor was going out of business and all his rough stock herds had gone under the hammer. Winter, who used to work for Roy on the farm, had called from Saskatchewan, telling Roy that some prime horses were selling and did he want some? He did a deal: Kenny brings down some Canadian bucking horses and Roy lets Winter have that roping horse he no longer rides, give his son something to learn on.

Gallen opened the side door of the trailer. The animals didn't look bad.

'Shit,' he said as Winter joined him. 'Nice-lookin' bunch.'

'I know,' said Winter, pulling on gloves. 'Look at this chestnut—rather have him throwing a cowboy than sittin' in a can of dog food.'

They opened the rear door of the trailer and let them into their own run-in field. They'd spend a week getting to know the main herd over the fence, establishing seniority and pecking orders. Some of the new horses would find themselves in the coldest part of the run-in when the winter winds started. But Gallen knew that with more than thirty horses in the herd, Roy could now contract to two rodeos every weekend if he wanted to. The farm was starting to look viable again.

Gallen watched as Roy introduced Ryan to his roping horse, Visa. There'd been many arguments at Sweet Clover about Visa, not only about his age but the true nature of beauty. Visa was a large Roman-nosed jughead with a roan coat that wouldn't shine, no matter the brushing.

'Not much to look at, eh, Ryan?' said Roy, stroking Visa's curved nose. 'But in ropin', it's pretty is as pretty does.'

Ryan scratched Visa between the ears. 'He's pretty to me, Mr Gallen.'

'Sun's over the yardarm?' Winter shoved his gloves in his back pocket as he shut down the trailer.

'Got an ice box full of beer for yer, Kenny,' said Roy, limping bandy-legged to the farmhouse. 'Bunkhouse is ready to go—why not let this boy of yours have the bed near the stove?'

They finished the pot roast beef with torn-up biscuit, soaking up gravy and talking about life up in Saskatchewan, how the land was cheaper and better for cattle. When the farming talk was done, Roy belched and reminded the table that the Bruins and Capitals started in eight minutes.

'Dad, they just got off the road.' Gallen pulled three more cans of Blue Ribbon from the ice box. 'Maybe Ryan's got other things he wants to watch?'

Winter laughed. 'Ryan's a worse hockey nut than Roy.'

'Really?' Roy gave Gallen the eye. 'Just what we need in that team of yours, Gerry. A no-nonsense Canadian boy, stiffen up that defence line.'

'Ryan didn't come all the way to Wyoming to play hockey, Dad,' said Gallen, trying to get off the subject. 'Besides, Billy's got a full roster.'

'No he don't,' said Roy. 'That centre with the Beatles haircut broke his arm on a mountain bike.'

'His name's Jason Peters,' said Gallen. 'And it's a Justin Bieber haircut, not the Beatles.'

'Okay,' said Roy, ruffling Ryan's hair. 'So you sit this one out. But I betcha ten bucks the Bruins wipe the ice with them Washington sissies.'

'Dad,' Ryan looked at Winter, 'guess I can get that ten bucks back to you after all.'

CHAPTER 30

The farrier was about to take five hundred from Gallen for checking the bucking herd and shoeing Jessie and Visa. Rod Dowse had taken most of the morning to check thirty-three animals and, even in a profession where the practitioners were known for complaining constantly about having to work with horses, Rod had set some kind of record.

So when Rod looked away from the five hundred, lifted his hat and scratched his scalp, Gallen knew there was a recalculation on the way.

'I'm thinkin' that's, what, five hours?' said Rod, eyes not meeting Gallen's.

'Don't know about hours, Rod,' said Gallen, lighting a cigarette. 'You said three-forty for the check and twenty per shoe.'

'Did I?' Rod undid his apron chaps, threw them in the back of the old GMC truck. 'That's the hardest five hunnert I ever earned.'

'Try doin' farm labour for Roy,' said Gallen, still holding the cash. 'You'll go back to shoein' for a holiday.'

'Got a smoke?' Rod took the money and grabbed a Marlboro. 'So what's this I hear about a Canadian star we got in the Hawks high school team Saturday night?'

'Who told you that?' said Gallen, annoyed. Winter and his son had stayed on for a few days and Roy had been pushing for Ryan to

212

play for the Sheridan Hawks. 'Fact is, the boy has to be registered, get the insurance an' all. It's not gonna happen.'

'Well,' said Rod, tucking the money in the pocket of a worn denim shirt and nodding towards the farmhouse, 'guess it's official now.'

Following the farrier's gaze, Gallen saw a big red Dodge Ram pull up on the gravel, Billy Higgins slide out and hitch his jeans up under the thermals and canvas jacket.

'Hey, Gerry,' called the Hawks' coach. 'What's this about Ryan Winter? Christ, you know that's Kenny Winter's son?!'

The spare room was like a road map of Gallen's youth: hockey gear bags from when he was ten, from when he started high school and when he made state, and an old blue Bauer bag from when Roy thought he'd be going to USD on a hockey scholarship.

'This'll be the biggest and the newest.' Gallen tapped the Bauer bag. Kenny Winter unzipped it, called for Ryan over his shoulder.

'Try this.' Winter pulled out shoulder pads, shin guards, hockey pants and elbow guards. The old Easton skates that were kept in a small canvas bag were too small for Ryan's feet, and Billy had provided the boy with skates along with a Wyoming Amateur Hockey Association registration.

Ryan took the gear from his dad, shrugged into the shoulder pads and pulled the hockey pants over his hips. They were adjustable and Ryan gave the thumbs-up.

'You know, Ryan,' said Gallen, liking the smell of the gear, 'you don't have to do this. Roy's a bit nutty about hockey.'

'I wanna play, Mr Gallen,' said the kid. 'It ain't no big deal.'

Roy called from downstairs and Ryan left them. 'I'm serious, Kenny. The kid don't have to play.'

'If Ryan don't wanna play,' said Winter, saying his son's name like *Raaan*, 'he won't.'

Lifting one of the bags onto the bed, Winter knocked a pile of clothes and a piece of paper fell out of a jeans pocket. They both stared at it: it was a ticket of some sort, white background with green Arabic script across it.

'That yours?' said Winter, as Gallen picked it up.

'Yeah,' said Gallen, turning the piece of thick paper in his fingers. 'I picked this up in a storage bin, at the mechanic's workshop. Those jeans have been sittin' there since I got back—didn't get round to washing them.'

'The workshop that got bombed?'

'Yes,' said Gallen. 'It fell off one of the bags. I thought it might have been an ID tag, so I grabbed it, but I don't know. What you think it is?'

Winter took it, turned it to the light. The top of the paper carried what looked like official corporate printing and a crest of some sort. Below, someone had dated the paper, written a short sentence and signed it. Over the signature was a stamp.

'I dunno,' said Winter. 'You want me to find out?'

'Sure,' said Gallen. 'You know someone?'

'I'll make a call. You got a scanner and a computer?'

The game was almost four minutes into the first period before Billy Higgins realised that Roy's assessment of the defence was correct: it needed some starch, especially with the big redhead centre from Gillette storming through into Sheridan's defensive zone. Billy walked behind the bench in the Hawks' enclosure, grabbed Ryan Winter by the shoulder, bent down and whispered in his ear. Ryan stood and Higgins called in a defenceman with a bleeding nose.

Gallen watched Winter's son shuffle to the gate in his borrowed skates and his borrowed pads, looking awkward. But as the players exchanged, the stumbling foal took to the ice and powered to his position, moving like a shark, making a provocative fly-by on the big redhead, saying something to him as he swerved past. The crowd could sense a change and the Gillette star turned and mouthed back at Ryan, who was now smiling, tapping his stick.

The face-off spilled out and Gillette took the puck back into centre ice; the big redhead retreated and then found some space down the centre. Calling for the puck, he collected it off his right hip as he accelerated towards the Sheridan goal. As he looked up to offload, the last thing he saw before he was knocked unconscious was Ryan Winter's right shoulder ploughing into his face.

The crowd stood, the Gillette locals screaming for a penalty, the noise lifting the roof as players moved in on the Canadian, but the referee waved the body check away as within the rules.

'Shit, Gerry,' said Billy Higgins, pushing his hat off his forehead. 'You see that?'

'Yeah, I saw that.' Gallen turned to the crowd and caught Kenny Winter smiling.

Dark brown coffee bubbled up into the glass top of the old perc and Gallen took it from the kitchen wood stove, poured two mugs, stirred two sugars into each.

'So, he said eight am, Mountain Standard?'

'That's it,' said Winter, sipping at his coffee. 'My guy is never ten minutes late.'

'Is he thinking in daylight time?' said Gallen. 'Not one of them hillbillies from Arizona?'

'No.' Winter looked at his phone. 'I'll try him.'

Winter hit the speed dial and held the phone to his ear. Outside, Ryan accompanied Roy in the round pen where Visa was being saddled, plumes of steam coming off them in the still of the Wyoming morning. Gallen fetched the plates from the table, took them to the counter. When he turned back, Winter had the look Gallen remembered him for: a cold focus, the assassin lurking just beneath the surface.

'What's up?' said Gallen.

'Voicemail.'

'What's wrong with voicemail?'

'Doesn't kick straight in, so he's not on the phone,' said Winter. 'Phone rang out.'

They stared at each other. Winter's guy was an intelligence contractor to the Pentagon. He didn't miss deadlines to call and his phone didn't ring out to voicemail.

'We get to him on a landline?'

Winter shook his head slowly, chewed his lip. 'What do you think that ticket was, Gerry? I mean, what's your gut?'

Gallen lit a cigarette, threw the pack to Winter. 'It was attached to one of the bags at some point, so I thought it was either an ID tag—like a porter's tag at a hotel—or it was some sort of consignment label. Why, what are you thinking?'

'I'm not a languages expert,' said Winter, lighting a smoke. 'But look at this.' He pulled the ticket from his pocket and flattened it. 'See these hooks with the dots above them?' He pointed to a couple of Arabic characters at the crest level of the ticket.

'Yep.'

'This form of script, I'm pretty darned sure, is the Iraqi Arabic.'

Gallen breathed out in a sigh. 'What are you sayin', Kenny?'

Winter fixed him with a look. 'Perhaps it's what you ain't sayin' to me, Gerry.'

'What's that mean?'

Winter smiled. 'There we were, messin' around in Jordan with Hamas and the FBI. But maybe this goes back to Iraq?'

Gallen looked away.

'Were you gonna tell me?'

'I thought we were done with Jordan,' said Gallen. 'I only found out about Iraq on the flight into JFK.'

'How?'

'Barrowman told me,' said Gallen.

'Told you what?'

'That the al-Haqs wanted something in those bags because they're Baathists.'

'Baathists? What's that, they want to return Iraq to life under Saddam?'

Gallen shrugged. 'That's what Barrowman said. Said the al-Haqs were Saddam's fixers but they were also al-Tikriti.'

'From Saddam's hometown, maybe his clan?'

Gallen nodded, examining the piece of paper. 'The way Barrowman told it, Saddam set up the al-Tikriti around the world with money and influence, looking to the day when he wouldn't be around. Apparently he didn't think much of his sons.'

'So if that crest is something official from Baghdad,' said Winter, 'then you had something that was sent from . . . what? From Saddam to the al-Haqs?'

'But Saddam was killed in 2006.'

Winter nodded. 'Well, whatever it was in those bags, my guy is now shut down.'

'You think he's okay?' said Gallen.

'It's not him I'm worried about,' said Winter. 'This place is probably already under surveillance.'

CHAPTER 31

They loaded Roy and Ryan's bags, took them through the cellar and out the loading door, across a hidden piece of ground to the barn. Then Gallen asked Billy Higgins for a favour. The big man turned up an hour later, drove into the drive shed of the barn and loaded Roy and Ryan into the back of the Dodge.

Gallen took their cell phones. 'This is just a for a few days, okay, Dad?'

'I have a choice? Thought you were out of all that special forces shit?'

'Told you, Dad—I drove a truck.'

Higgins pulled out and Gallen walked back to the house, scoping the trees along the western boundary as he stepped into the mud room. Winter sat at the kitchen table, pistols, clips and cell phones in neat stacks. The landline phone lay upside down in front of him, screwdriver poised over it.

'You killed the internet?' Gallen looked through the window at the trees.

'Done,' said Winter, bringing a finger to his lips. Taking the back off the phone, he checked quickly for bugs and screwed it back together. The handpiece was made of two pieces of moulded plastic joined at a seam. Checking along it for signs of disturbance, he put the phone in front of him.

'Clean.'

Gallen's pulse banged slightly in his forehead and he massaged his temples. 'Satellite?'

'Disconnected,' said Winter, who set about packing the guns and the phones into a holdall. 'We set?'

'Yep.' Gallen hoisted his backpack over one shoulder and headed for the cellar stairs. 'Lock up on your way out.'

Gallen pushed gently upwards on the cellar loading doors, saw Winter's Ford idling beside the water tank, the rear passenger door pressed against scrubby weeds growing out of the tank stand. Easing out of the cellar, Gallen ran in a crouch to the scrub and slipped into the Ford truck, staying low and pulling the door behind him.

As they pulled out of the Sweet Clover drive, Gallen felt Winter turn right and accelerate down the gravel road that would eventually take them into Clearmont.

'See anything?' said Gallen from his hidden position.

'Nope,' said Winter.

They motored for forty seconds, the big diesel growing through the gears, until Gallen could feel the brakes gripping at the end of the lane.

'Right on schedule,' said Winter.

'What is it?'

'Bell man,' said Winter. 'He's sitting on a chair at the junction box, and the van's got them aerials out the top.'

'Shit,' said Gallen. 'We made?'

'Let's see,' said Winter. They waited for traffic and then Winter accelerated, headed east for town.

'Shit,' muttered Winter. 'Dude stood up, checked his clipboard.'

'Checking the rego?'

'My guess,' said Winter. 'Now he's walking to the van.'

'We're made,' said Gallen, getting off the floor of the Ford and climbing into the front seat with Winter.

'I know that, Gerry. The thing is: who did we piss off?'

It was Monday morning in Clearmont, which generally meant Alka-Seltzer and late starts. They passed the Clearmont water tower on their left as they cruised through slush into town, looking for vans that didn't belong, Chev Caprices with government pool tyres and black Lincoln Navigators driven by men in dark suits.

'Down here,' said Gallen, and they peeled to the left into a row of pre-statehood houses that sprang out of the oaks and snow like something on a postcard.

'Here, number forty-eight.' Gallen pointed to a house.

Winter pulled in to the kerb and Gallen got out, looked up and down the street, then walked to the side door of the immaculately presented house.

A woman opened the door to his knock, nodded and let Gallen inside. As she took his jacket, she asked him if he wanted coffee and Gallen said, 'No thank you, ma'am.'

Taking the easy chair offered in the den, Gallen looked around at the books along the walls and the art that clearly hadn't been bought in a Wal-Mart. When his mother used to talk about what was possible outside of Clearmont and Sheridan County, Gallen suspected this was what she was talking about. After all, the owner of the house—Dr Kahn al-Ali—had employed his mother as a receptionist in the old days, when she was still contributing to the mortgage at Sweet Clover and Kahn was the town's doctor.

Kahn entered the room, doddering slightly, unlike the sprightly man Gallen remembered.

'Ah, Gerard,' said the old man, smiling as he shook hands the oriental way—a two-handed clasp. 'How's your mother?'

'She's fine,' said Gallen.

Kahn had come out to Wyoming to escape the Shah's regime in Iran and immediately taken to riding horses and dressing Western; he bought a Chev truck and wore an orange hat in hunting season. It took the town thirty years to get used to an outsider being their doctor, but once they knew him, he became a protected species.

'So, this is a nice surprise, but how can I help you?'

Gallen pulled the piece of paper from his jeans, unfolded it and passed it across. 'Wondered if you could help me with this?'

Dr Kahn pushed a set of half-glasses to the end of his nose and peered down at the paper.

'Well, for a start, Gerard, it's the Iraqi Arabic script—also known as Mesopotamian Arabic.'

'Yeah, sure . . .'

'And you know I'm Iranian? I guess we all look the same?'

Gallen blushed slightly. 'I know, doctor, I was—'

The doctor laughed. 'It's fine, I was just having a joke. I can read it.'

Gallen sat back, feeling his cheeks burning. During the years when Dr Kahn was an outsider, Gallen had to put up with the comments at high school about how Arabs had strange sexual needs and what his mother was putting up with. So he was fighting at school and also being told off by his mother for being a redneck ignoramus whenever he made comments about Arabs.

He fought against racism at school and was told off for it at home.

Dr Kahn turned the paper over, looked at the back and then looked up slowly at Gallen. 'Where did you get this?'

'Found it.'

Standing with difficulty, Kahn moved carefully to the lace-covered windows and peered through. 'The man in that white truck. He is with you?'

'Yes,' said Gallen, hairs rising on the back of his head. 'What is it?'

'I think you should go, Gerard.'

'Look—'

'No, you look, young man,' said Kahn, eyes a mix of anger and fear. 'You do not understand the Middle East, but I do. This is not a world of cowboys and lone rangers and men in white hats and dogs who rescue people.'

'I didn't—'

'These people will chase you and I, and they will torture us and kill our families for this, you understand?'

'Look, doctor,' said Gallen, standing, but the doctor wouldn't be silenced.

'I escaped from Iran with forty minutes to spare, did you know this? My entire life came down to less than one hour of luck.'

'I didn't—'

'My father,' said Kahn, 'killed for publishing a newspaper; my mother, in an asylum from the torture; my sister, disappeared. Me? I got the call that my mule was ready to take me, and I left the university as soon as I got word. Forty minutes later, the SAVAK come for me but can only find my best friend and they take him to the cells, never heard from again. Ever.'

Dr Kahn walked in circles and Gallen heard him sniffling.

'And you know what happened to the thesis my friend was writing for his doctoral program?' said the doctor, smiling at Gallen through tears. 'The tutor who informed on him stole it and published it under his own name. It was translated into English and, the last I heard, that tutor was lecturing in paediatrics at Johns Hopkins.'

The once-proud man shrugged and let himself fall back in his chair, pinched at the bridge of his nose to stop the tears. 'I come out to the last place in the world where the Arab world can ever touch me again; to a place where people gossip about how fast the school bus driver takes the rail underpass. And now . . . this.'

Gallen let the moment pass, even though he'd seen Evelyn Masters take the school bus through that underpass way too fast. 'What makes you think we're both in danger from this piece of paper?'

'This is a receipt from the Central Bank of Iraq, in Baghdad,' said the doctor, wide-eyed. 'It's signed and stamped March the twentieth, 2003.'

It took a few moments for the date to register. 'Okay, so someone gets a receipt from Iraq's Central Bank on the day we invade.'

'Do you know how well connected with Saddam you had to be to withdraw money from his Central Bank?'

Gallen hadn't thought about it like that.

'See this name here?' said the doctor, holding out the paper.

'That's a name?'

'Yes,' said the doctor. 'It is Saeed Saleh Abdullah. In Iraq, the family name is generally referred to as Saleh.'

Gallen reacted to it but he didn't know why. He'd heard that name mentioned, years ago, in a briefing room. What was it? One of the playing cards, the most wanted of Saddam's men? He couldn't recall.

'Saleh,' said Gallen. 'Remind me.'

'The Saleh Abdullahs,' said Kahn, 'one of the power bases behind Saddam. They intermarried with the al-Hasan al-Tikriti clan.'

It meant nothing to Gallen.

'Think about it like the Kennedys marrying into the Bushes,' said the doctor. 'Saddam's CIA was run by Barzan Ibrahim al-Hasan al-Tikriti. He was most wanted by the Pentagon and he was hanged. His head fell off, remember?'

Gallen did remember. The drop was too long and Condoleezza Rice told off the Iraqis for it.

'Well, Barzan's son-in-law was Azzam Saleh Abdullah. Saeed Saleh Abdullah is part of the Saddam family.'

'Saeed Saleh signed the receipt at the Central Bank?' said Gallen. 'So what did he receive?'

'It's a bank, Gerard,' said the doctor. 'It was filled with money. And if you have the receipt then you probably have the money.'

'No, I don't—but I know where the twelve million went.' Gallen stood and looked at the street.

'Twelve million?' said the doctor, confused. 'Saeed Saleh didn't sign for twelve million dollars.'

'No?'

'No, Gerard,' said the doctor, shaking the receipt at him. 'Saleh withdrew one billion dollars from his government's treasury as the bombs started falling.'

Gallen felt a jolt. 'A billion?'

'This is what I'm saying,' said Kahn. 'A billion dollars is a life sentence. You don't know these people, Gerard, but I do.'

CHAPTER 32

A dark Crown Vic turned into the street and parked by the kerb a hundred yards away as Gallen got into the F350 with Winter.

'Get anything?' said Winter as he accelerated down the street.

'It's a receipt from the Iraqi Central Bank in Baghdad,' said Gallen. 'That Crown Vic followin'?'

'Like a goat.' Winter turned right into a side street that would take them around the block and back to the main street of Clearmont. 'So, he say anything else?'

'Shit, Kenny, he's just an old doctor.'

'Don't fuck with me, Gerry.' Winter turned left and accelerated north, aiming for Gillette. 'You're in there a half hour—the fuck he say?'

Gallen breathed through his nostrils, stayed calm. 'The Crown Vic still with us?'

'Yep,' said Winter.

'There goes the cell phone plan.'

They'd planned to drive to Gillette, where there was a communications wholesaler who'd hook them up with cell phones in fifteen minutes, buy them on Kenny Winter's alternative identity. It wasn't hi-tech, but it was the kind of thing that would let them slip off the grid for a few days, make some calls. But with the government car behind them, there'd be spooks all over the comms shop as soon as Winter had bought his phones.

Gallen watched the foothills flashing by, remembered some of his high school antics when booze and cars came together in a bad mix.

'This thing got four-wheel drive?' said Gallen, lighting a smoke and stealing a look in the side mirror. The Crown Vic was two hundred yards back, keeping speed.

'Yep,' said Winter. 'You got a track in mind?'

'In seven minutes, we'll cross the Powder River,' said Gallen. 'First right on the other side. Let's see if you Canadians have what it takes off-road.'

Winter nodded. 'So, the Iranian doctor?'

'He read the thing, and you were right: Iraqi Arabic.'

'What is it?' said Winter, one eye on the mirror.

'The receipt is dated March twenty, 2003.'

'That's . . .'

'Yep,' said Gallen. 'Someone was in a hurry to clean out the treasury before the Americans pulled in.'

'Who?' said Winter.

'The person who signed for it was a dude called Saeed Saleh—he's got a longer clan title, but the thing is he's from one of these families related to Saddam by marriage and other connections around Tikriti. You know Tikriti?'

Winter smiled. 'Famous for spider holes. So an Iraqi heavyweight goes to the Central Bank as the war starts, gets twelve million dollars out and . . .?'

Gallen wanted to break the news gently. 'Well, the thing is, Kenny, it wasn't twelve million dollars.'

'How much?'

'One billion,' said Gallen, seeing farms flash by as Winter cruised at seventy.

There was silence. Then Winter cleared his throat. 'Shit, Gerry.'

'I know,' said Gallen. 'The doctor wasn't happy about our being there.'

'No?'

'No, he said taking one billion dollars from these people isn't a windfall—it's a life sentence.'

*

225

Winter took the bridge over the Powder at sixty-five, pointed at the sign for the side road and pulled the gear lever back to third. The big Ford screamed slightly as it scrubbed speed off with a lower gear and Winter took the truck in a sideways drift into the road. Immediately they were into an undulating country back road over swamps and fords that had been ploughed that morning. It didn't worry Gallen because he knew that the snow ploughs only operated to the first ford and then it was a trap for a sedan with just two wheels driving it.

Winter kept his speed at sixty along the road, cattle munching in the snow and hawks circling in the cold. The first one-lane bridge loomed up and Winter kept the power on, getting some air as they crossed it.

'Shit, this is bayou country,' said Winter, as the terrain on the other side of the bridge opened up. It was a series of swamps and tributaries that fed the Powder, and in summer it was where daytrippers picnicked and teenagers drank beer, chased girls. Gallen grabbed the handgrip above the door as the road went into a series of whoop-dee-doos.

'Watch out for the slight left,' said Gallen, 'and then it's a ford. Should be twenty yards, stone bottom.'

As they dipped into a long left Gallen looked in the side mirror, saw the Crown Vic closing. 'Shit, they're flying!'

Winter hit the pedal and accelerated as the ground fell away to the ford, the water flowing through the snow on either bank. Gallen's fillings bounced as they hit the middle of the creek, the F350 slewing sideways as the dually rear axle landed in the water, Winter keeping the diesel winding.

The truck flew up the far bank of the ford, the transmission squealing for purchase. They were now into an area of more trees, the road growing narrower, more winding, and starting to climb into the foothills.

Gallen glanced into the side mirror again, saw the Crown Vic only twenty yards behind the truck.

'Shit, Kenny, what've they got in there?'

'Dunno,' said Winter. 'Let's see if they can stay with us on the hills.'

Punching the accelerator, Winter threw the truck into a slide as they neared two hairpin bends rising up from the bayou. The big truck leapt and groaned as it tried to take the turn but then launched out the other side as Winter pulled the gear shift to second and pushed his foot to the floor, spraying roadside trees with gravel.

In the mirror Gallen could see the Crown Vic slide almost into the ditch. The second hairpin loomed and Winter charged at it, Gallen pushing his feet into the bulkhead and clinging to the handgrip as they approached it too fast. 'Kenny!'

Winter threw the F350 the wrong way and then corrected. Before Gallen could stop screaming the truck was power-drifting through the corner like a championship rally car.

They made the corner with inches to spare, the ground falling away beneath Gallen's seat. Whipping around to look out the rear window, he saw the Crown Vic travel sideways at speed and slam heavily into the clay wall cut into the hill. The car bounced back onto the road but there was something wrong with its front end. Easing off the power as they raced up the slope, Winter slipped the gear stick back into drive.

'They're gone.'

Gallen looked in the side mirror, saw the pursuing car stopped in the middle of the road, one front wheel at a bad angle.

'You wanna double back?' said Winter. 'Find out who these people are?'

Gallen looked at his friend, saw someone who would always be more comfortable with direct confrontation than him. It was the difference between the recon soldier and the assassin: one silently observed the situation; the other was the situation.

'I'd like to see who they are,' said Gallen. 'But I don't want to kill them.'

'Shit, boss,' smiled Winter. 'You took all the fun out of it.'

There was a small picnic area another minute up the road and Winter pulled over, left the engine running. 'Let them think we're still drivin'.'

Gallen pulled the Heckler & Koch pistol from his backpack, checked for load and safety as Winter extracted a rifle from a canvas bag in the back seat.

'No killing, Kenny.'

'Sure—but look at that glass,' he said, handing Gallen the rifle and pointing to the scope mounted on top. Gallen held it to his eye, looked down the big Leupold and was amazed at not only the magnification but also the clarity.

'Nice,' he said, handing it back.

They dropped into the trees, sliding across snow and scree until they hit the mossy bog. Gallen's feet were wet and cold through his boots by the time they were ready to move across to the Crown Vic, and his thigh was aching. The doctors were right: only rest was going to fix the wound and get him his strength back. And exertion was a sure way to slow the recovery.

After walking through the bog for two minutes, Gallen held up his hand: they could hear the occupants of the car talking, and not in a good way. The burbling of the F350's diesel floated down among the limbers and douglas firs as they kneeled and moved to the crest. Down on the road, about forty yards away, a man dressed in jeans and a leather jacket stood in front of a crippled Crown Vic, shouting into a sat phone while he stuck a finger in the other ear.

'I have no idea what it's called, but these are the coordinates,' said the man.

Gallen ducked down, looked at Winter, who was looking down the Leupold. 'Don't need that, Kenny. It's Daly.'

'I know,' said the Canadian, having some fun. 'But lookie here. Who's this in the front seat?'

'Who?' said Gallen, and Winter handed him the rifle.

Squinting down the scope, he got a massive close-up of Daly, so clear he could see the scrapes down the side of his right temple from the bomb blast. Moving the scope slightly to his right, he picked up the man in the front seat, who was on his own phone. This one was dressed like an outsider—LL Bean outdoorsy wear and a cattle-man's coat of the type you could only buy in LA or New York.

'Remember him?' sniggered Winter.

'Sure do,' said Gallen. He was looking at Barry Amundsen, and he did not look happy.

The drive over the spur brought them out on the 14–16 highway to Gillette, some ways east of where they drove in. Gallen had decided to leave Lang and Daly where they were and keep to their plan. He wanted new phones and he needed to eat. The road dipped down and came up again, and as Winter slowed to take a right for Gillette, they almost drove into a black Little Bird helicopter. Parked and depowered on the shoulder of the highway, its rotors hanging down limply, it looked like a dead insect.

One of the perspex doors opened and Winter stopped the truck. A man got out and walked towards them, a small bandage on his forehead the only reminder of what he'd looked like two weeks earlier on the British Airways 777.

Gallen dropped his window. 'Hey, Jim.'

'Gerry,' said Jim Barrowman, rugged up in a down-filled mountaineer's jacket and Sorel boots. 'Wanna grab a coffee?'

'We're going to Gillette, you wanna meet for lunch?'

'No thanks,' said the FBI man, getting into the cab and blowing on his hands. 'It's cold out there.'

'I guess landing your Little Bird on Highway 14 in the middle of nowhere is hardly a coincidence,' said Gallen, lighting a smoke. ''Less you saw a bunch of pronghorn as you flew over, thought they were rare or something?'

'No coincidence, Gerry,' said Jim, his nose red and running. 'I need some answers about this receipt you sent for an opinion.'

'Shit, that was fast.'

'No jokes, Gerry. Where the fuck did you get that?'

Gallen paused, shot a look to Winter. 'Well, Jim, since you asked so nicely.'

'No, Gerry,' said Barrowman. 'I mean it.'

'It was attached to one of the bags that Daly and I got back to the FBI. It fell off its luggage string and I shoved it in my pocket, didn't think about it until I was helping Kenny's boy into some of my old hockey gear.'

'Where is it?' said Barrowman. 'This is important.'

Gallen handed it over and the FBI man seized it. 'Jesus Christ, Gallen. Where's the document that goes with it?'

'What document?' said Gallen. 'This was lying in the storage box when I picked up a bag. That's all there was.'

Barrowman sat back heavily in the seat, absently touched the dressing on his forehead. 'Remember I told you about the

Baathists? The people just waiting to return Iraq to a Saddam's paradise?'

'Sure.'

'I was high on painkillers and wine, I should never have done that.' He rubbed his chin, making a decision. 'The thing is, Gerry, we need a crew who can operate on contract but without implicating the FBI. I need someone to go back into Jordan, tidy this thing up.'

'Chase Lang can't do this?' said Gallen. 'They've been following us.'

'Would you understand me if I said Chase was just too associated with the Pentagon for my own good?' said Barrowman. 'Besides, you're up to speed on the whole thing. I don't have the time to brief anyone else and you've still got a security clearance.'

Gallen breathed out. Former officers in the US military never lost their security clearance unless specifically disqualified.

'What about Amundsen? The station at the embassy?' said Gallen.

Barrowman looked at his hands. 'I need someone who answers to the FBI.'

'That's not the CIA?' said Winter.

Barrowman deadpanned him. 'I need you on a plane tonight.'

CHAPTER 33

The Gulfstream G-IV corporate jet was one of the quieter ways to travel but Gallen still woke to a faint roar. Pushing back the blanket and raising his head from the reclined leather seat, he looked around the dim cabin with its drawn sunshades and muted wood grain finishes.

'Just passed into Algerian air space,' said a voice. 'Get ready for the rockets.'

Across the aisle, Jim Barrowman sorted papers on the table in front of him and used a laptop one-handed.

Sitting up, Gallen shook out the fatigue. The pain in his leg was taking its toll on his entire system, and the painkillers made him groggy. He could see Winter stretched out and sleeping in the reclined seats at the front of the cabin.

'Coffee just brewed,' said Barrowman, sipping. 'You good for a chat?'

Gallen grabbed a mug of sweet coffee and took the seat opposite Barrowman's. A pile of material sat between them, among it the blueprint he'd retrieved, which was now in a condensed and photo-copied format.

'We closer to understanding this?' said Gallen, picking up the blueprint.

'The techs think it's an underground bunker.'

'You mean like a vault? A billion dollars is a lot of dough to hide.'

Barrowman cleared his throat. 'Maybe I gave you the wrong impression of what I do.'

'You follow the money trails, right?'

'Yes, but my actual division is the WMDD.'

Gallen had never heard of it.

'It's the Weapons of Mass Destruction Directorate,' said Barrowman, yawning. 'A lot of what we do is track money movements and freight manifests, because that's where the trails are, but our broader mission is ensuring that the wrong people don't have the means to buy or build these weapons.'

Gallen rubbed his eyes, not wanting Barrowman to see his surprise or reluctance. 'Well, Jim, I've done a lot of things in my career, but I'm not an expert in nukes or viruses.'

'No,' said Barrowman. 'But you're a decorated special forces captain . . .'

'Former.'

'Okay, former special forces captain, who is working privately and who is not on our banned contractors list.'

'Lucky me.'

'Although someone did have a flag,' said Barrowman, pointing over Gallen's shoulder at Winter. 'You obviously trust him.'

'With your life.' Gallen slurped coffee, assessed the information. 'So I've been buzzing around Jordan, chasing money, but the real thing isn't money?'

'Precisely.'

'What is it?'

Barrowman paused. 'Four weeks ago Iraqi construction workers were renovating a water-treatment reservoir in the northern suburbs of Baghdad. It was one of the underground reservoirs that also doubled as air-raid shelters and bunkers for Saddam and his retinue.'

'Okay,' said Gallen, wishing he could smoke.

'The workers mistakenly punched through a wall that was supposed to be left intact, and found a gallery containing nine loaded shipping pallets.'

'What was on the pallets?'

'About seventy per cent of it was US dollars, in C-notes and thousands. The rest was euros.'

Gallen whistled. His men used to dream of finding a haul like that and devoted hours to imagining what they'd do with it if the captain would look the other way.

'So this was the billion dollars? Where from?'

Barrowman walked to the small kitchenette at the back of the cabin, poured more coffee. 'You remember in the nineties, the UN and the IAEA were monitoring Iraq for nuclear and biological programs?'

'Sure,' said Gallen.

'I was with the UN's Special Commission, the Nuclear Verification Office.'

Gallen smiled. 'Who were you answering to?'

Barrowman smiled back. 'Then I'd have to kill ya.'

They stared at each other. Gallen had spent his professional life dealing with spooks and their shaded biographies. 'What happened? There were no weapons of mass destruction, right?'

Barrowman laughed until he coughed and had to bang his chest. 'Shit, Gerry. That's good.'

'It was all over the news: no weapons of mass destruction in Iraq.'

'Yeah, I read that too.'

'And?'

'After a decade of the Iraqis lying about their uranium-enrichment centrifuges and VX warheads, suddenly there's no weapons of mass destruction in Iraq? Seriously?'

Gallen sipped the coffee. 'I didn't really think about it.'

'No one did,' said Barrowman. 'The UN spent most of the nineties chasing Saddam's WMD infrastructure, until we were kicked out in ninety-eight.'

'What happened?'

'In 2004, the Director of Central Intelligence released a report saying there were no weapons of mass destruction in Iraq,' said Barrowman, facetiously opening his hands. 'Mazel tov—all gone.'

'Those boys from Langley have their ways,' said Gallen. 'But I thought it embarrassed President Bush?'

'Who knows what Bush really thought about it. Thing is, the world drew a line under weapons of mass destruction in Iraq, which meant the questions from the media all became political, not operational.'

'How does this square with the billion dollars in the reservoir?'

'I guess you've now heard of Saeed Saleh?'

'Saddam crony.'

'On the eve of Iraqi Freedom, Saleh takes a couple of trucks down to the Central Bank and has a billion dollars loaded on the back. It was headed for one of Saddam's underground palaces, awaiting the end of the American invasion when the rebirth of the Baath Party could begin.'

'Saddam was planning for renewal before Iraqi Freedom even began?'

'Sure,' said Barrowman. 'Saddam and his Baath Party thought we wanted the oil, but that we'd tire of having to actually run the country.'

'Hah.' Gallen shook his head. Most of his peers from the Marines complained that they'd been trained to take a country, not to govern it.

'Months later, the US Army engineers discovered a sophisticated residential command-and-control centre two hundred feet underground, about a two-hour drive north of Baghdad. We think that's where Saleh was headed with the money, but the convoy was struck by a missile that night and Saleh was killed.'

'So what happened to the billion dollars?'

'We believe the guards and the intel people probably went to the closest dumping point they could find and stashed the money in one of their dual-purpose reservoir galleries.'

Gallen cottoned on. 'And the first thing the Coalition Provisional Authority did was take control of the country's infrastructure.'

'Exactly,' said Barrowman. 'The billion dollars was hidden very well, but the Baathists couldn't get back in there to pick it up. Then, a month ago, a gang of workers find it.'

'Where is it now?'

'Still there,' said Barrowman. 'DIA are running a honey-pot trap.'

'Who did they want to trap?' said Gallen. 'The war was won more than a decade ago.'

'Pentagon wants to flush out the Baath Party revivalists, the heirs to Saddam. So they let the news trickle into the banking and military networks: that the US contractors were abandoning the reservoir upgrades and were going to build an entirely new system.'

'So no more American security on the city reservoirs? That it?'

'Yep,' said Barrowman. 'This was before I became involved. They stripped the site and set it up with infra-red surveillance systems. Waited for the Baathists to come back for their dough.'

'And?' said Gallen.

'A strange thing happened,' said the FBI man, cagey. 'A highly organised team disabled the surveillance, broke into the reservoirs and took the loot.'

'How did they shift a billion dollars?'

'They didn't,' said Barrowman. 'They took twelve million.'

Gallen put down his empty coffee mug too carefully, pulled out a cigarette.

'Yes, I mind, really,' said Barrowman.

Gallen lit the smoke, transfixed by the story. 'They break in for their billion and only take twelve million? That's, what, twelve per cent of one per cent of the dough?'

Barrowman smiled, reached for the Marlboros, lit one for himself. 'You've been a soldier, Gerry. What kind of crew risks their lives to sneak into a US facility and then basically ignore a billion dollars?'

Gallen took a long draw on the smoke, blew it to the ceiling. The entire gig was starting to annoy him. 'I guess a soldier who wasn't motivated by money would do that. Maybe they were motivated by something else?'

'And that's what we're chasing.'

'What's the something else?'

'Have another look at the receipt you found,' said Barrowman, turning the laptop and displaying a blown-up photograph of the back of the Central Bank receipt. 'The first item on the manifest—that's your billion dollars.' Barrowman moved his pen to the second item on the manifest. 'And this next one is where the Directorate comes in. It says Security bin 17, and scribbled beside it is PC-3 Group 5.'

Gallen shrugged. 'What is it?'

'Security bin 17 is a lock box in the vaults of the Central Bank,' said Barrowman. 'PC-3 is short for Petrochemical Project 3—the cover name the Iraqis gave to their nuclear weapons program.'

'And Group 5?'

'The PC-3 programs numbered groups one to four. They were all under the control of the Military Industrialisation Commission. PC-3 Group 5 was a sort of mythical group outside of that commission's control. The weapons inspectors, the Mossad and MI6 always suspected this group existed but couldn't prove it.'

'What did Group 5 do?'

'The others were about R and D. But Group 5 was allegedly a super-secret facility that stored the weapons and prepared them for deployment. Group 5 was political, not military, hence its hiding place in a bank rather than an army base.'

Gallen looked at the receipt on the screen again. 'So the papers in that bag . . .'

'Totally useless,' said Barrowman. 'The nugget was the blueprint.'

'That's PC-3 Group 5?'

'We think so, but without the overlay it's hard to work out what it is or where it's located.'

'You walked up to me at Denver International, asked me about the al-Haqs. Where do they come in?'

'We've been monitoring the al-Haqs for years. During the Saddam regime they shifted money around but their legitimate shipping and transport operations were also used by Saddam to import the components of his nuclear program. The al-Haqs were the cut-outs used when those components needed valid end-user certificates.'

'So the al-Haqs planned all of this?'

'No,' said Barrowman. 'The al-Haqs are profiteers, arms dealers, money launderers. This was planned by the Baath true believers, the sleepers.'

Gallen nodded. 'But we have the blueprint, right? Me and Daly— we delivered them to Amundsen and that big dude.'

'That big dude is David Rogers,' said Barrowman. 'And yes, we have our copy of the blueprint, but the FBI and CIA no longer have a monopoly on that information.'

Gallen leaned forwards. 'What?'

'It was stolen, last night, from the CI-fucking-A. You think I'm in a helicopter in the middle of Bumfuck, Wyoming because I like you?'

'Stolen?' said Gallen. 'I don't understand.'

'Captain David Rogers has disappeared, and with him went the

236

blueprint. Amundsen is climbing the walls, he's running around with that mercenary friend of yours—Daly?'

'Do we know where he's going?' said Gallen, stunned.

'This is a grab from a surveillance system at Marka Airport's helicopter terminal, in Amman,' said Barrowman, touching a button on the laptop and bringing up a grainy black and white picture. It showed two men walking past a toilet sign, the tall black man carrying one of the bags Gallen had retrieved twice already. But it wasn't the distinctive form of David Rogers that made Gallen reach for the laptop. It was the highly groomed character in a white shirt and immaculate dark blazer who had captured Gallen's attention.

His throat dry, he pointed. 'Who's that?'

'His name is Tookie,' said Barrowman. 'Tookie Saleh, the nephew of Saeed Saleh.'

Gallen turned slowly to Barrowman. 'This is the man who stood on the roof when the workshop went up. I told you about him.'

Barrowman's face changed. 'You sure? This man, walking beside Rogers?'

'That's him—this is my third look at him.'

Barrowman slumped back in the seat, rubbed his face.

'Well,' said Gallen, 'who is he?'

'Tookie Saleh is a Baathist extremist,' said Barrowman. 'Blames all the ills of the world on the fall of the Iraq Baath Party.'

'He looks young,' said Gallen, seeing a man who couldn't be past his mid-twenties. 'What sort of power does he have?'

Barrowman looked away. 'His uncle ran Group 5.'

Gallen crushed his cigarette and looked over his shoulder to where Kenny Winter stood like an ice statue in his thermals.

'What's in the Group 5 bunker?' said Winter.

Barrowman cleared his throat. 'I don't know.'

'Let me put it another way,' said Winter, leaning into Barrowman's space. 'What does Tookie Saleh think is in there?'

The FBI man looked at Gallen and back to Winter. 'He probably thinks he has the means to wipe out Israel.'

CHAPTER 34

Gallen recognised the other FBI agent as they walked the air-conditioned hallway of the Marka Airport helicopter terminal. He was Barrowman's offsider, the calmer guy from Denver International. He was sitting on a sofa by a low coffee table, glaring at a laptop screen while a local man talked into his ear.

Looking up as Barrowman swept in, Special Agent Cole stood. 'We got a sighting in al Jufur. It's a tiny town in the middle of the eastern desert.'

'What was the sighting, Matt?'

'Gas station owner saw a Bell helicopter with Iraqi markings land just out of town, then head east, for the border. He called the cops.'

'How long ago?' said Barrowman.

'Ten minutes.'

'Get the chopper ready,' said Barrowman. 'We got food?'

'Sure,' said Cole, nodding his head at several canvas bags arrayed around the lounge area. 'There's something else.'

'What?'

'You know that Agency asshole, Amundsen?'

Barrowman nodded. 'Yep.'

'He's here and making a lot of trouble.'

'What kind of—' started Barrowman, as a loud voice called his name.

They turned and saw an angry-looking Barry Amundsen stalking down the hallway towards them, two associates in his wake.

'Jimbo,' he said, 'we gotta talk.'

Walking past the FBI group, Amundsen reached a door marked Staff only and beckoned.

'I'm kind of busy, Barry,' said Barrowman.

'Okay,' said Amundsen, walking to the FBI team, his sand-coloured suit stained with sweat. 'Since you're too busy, Jim, let me break it down: Agency jurisdiction on this one, Tonto. Read me?'

Amundsen's big flushed face pushed inches from Barrowman's.

'Forgot your Scope again, Barry.'

The two men stared each other down like a couple of stags until Amundsen started laughing and the tension went out of the room.

'You rude bastard, Barrowman,' chuckled Amundsen, slapping for his cigarettes. 'Scope? Oh my God!'

'I could do with a coffee,' said Barrowman, moving towards the staff door, Amundsen in tow. 'Gerry, will you join us?'

They sat around a coffee table in an upstairs pilot lounge, looking through tinted glass at the dusty runways.

'Guess you two know one another?' said Gallen, as he stirred sugar into his coffee.

'From the old days, running around Iraq looking for Saddam's secrets,' said Amundsen, nodding at Barrowman. 'This lunatic was convinced there was a large facility, with operational warheads, sitting out in the desert somewhere.'

'It was a strong hunch.' Barrowman accepted a cigarette from Amundsen.

'It was a strong ticket back to the States is what it was,' said Amundsen. 'Could've been Bush's best buddy.'

Gallen thought about that and looked at Barrowman. 'So, you were in Iraq after the UN weapons inspections? During Iraqi Freedom?'

'That's classified,' said Barrowman, 'and Barry was just about to shut up. We got a sighting in al Jufur, by the way.'

'I heard,' said Amundsen. 'Chopper comes in, lands, and takes off.'

Barrowman slurped coffee. 'A pick-up? Or a set-down?'

'Any ideas, Gerry?' said Amundsen.

'Let's find out,' said Gallen.

The spacious Sikorsky S-92 helicopter banked over the south of Mahattat al Jufur, a collection of about thirty mud-brick buildings on the side of Highway 10 to Iraq.

Special Agent Cole relayed instructions from the gas station owner on the ground, and guided the pilot to a homestead in the desert about three miles north of the town.

'Up there.' Barrowman pointed to the overhead bins.

Standing, Kenny Winter unloaded a walkie-talkie kit bag and two M4 carbine assault rifles from the bin over his head and handed one to Gallen. Reaching in further, he pulled out two Kevlar vests.

'You want one?' he said to Barrowman.

'I won't need one,' said the FBI man. 'Didn't Gerry tell you?'

Gallen smiled as he tested the battery power on the Motorola walkie-talkies. 'Jim's more like project management on this one, Kenny. FBI has us down as security contractors.'

'That about covers it,' said Winter, sitting down and shrugging into the vest as the pilot circled the homestead. It had a livestock fence around it and a set of cattle yards that looked a little puny.

'Your average Wyoming steer would walk straight over those fences,' said Gallen, checking for load and safety on the rifle.

'Saskatchewan cattle would eat 'em.' Winter looked cyborg-like with his dark wraparound shades, throat mic and short blond hair. He pulled down a black cap, looked out the window.

The chopper flared and the motors whirred to let down the landing gear. Dust flew and Barrowman leaned over to Gallen. 'I'll be right behind you. Let me do the talking, okay, Gerry?'

Gallen shrugged his assent without actually committing to it. As a general principle he didn't like to hand over basic duties to someone whose background wasn't clear. He switched on his radio, chose channel 5 and raised a full hand at Winter, who adjusted his own radio.

The chopper landed as they swapped quick radio tests and Winter walked to the front of the cabin, opened the right-hand door, lifted the top part of the door and let the built-in air stairs drop to the ground. Gallen stood at the big Canadian's left shoulder, surveying the ground through the swirling dust from the rotors: thirty yards to the house, outbuildings another thirty yards past the house and two SUV vehicles parked out front.

Gallen cocked the rifle's action, looked down the sights for luck. 'Let's go.'

They crossed the rocky terrain, dirt flying into their faces, and fanned to either side as they approached. The first shot exploded off a rock three feet in front of Gallen as he closed on a red Chev Tahoe between him and the house.

Hitting the deck, he rolled to his side where a small rockery had been built. The second, third and fourth bullets smashed against the rocks near his head, making him duck for his life. Looking to his right, he could see Winter circling for cover behind one of the outbuildings which looked like a machine shed. Behind him, he could hear the rotors continue to depower: why weren't they taking off again? Lifting his head, he saw a slight movement in the front window of the house to his far right. It looked like a newish AK-47.

'Got one shooter at the front window, Blue Dog,' said Gallen. 'How you lookin'? Over.'

More bullets flew, this time at the machine shed, and Gallen saw Winter lean back for safety, his head still. 'Two shooters: one from the window, one advancing, over.'

Gallen put his head up slowly and saw the shooter in the front window moving to another, obviously not happy with the line of sight obstructed by the Tahoe. Waiting for the shooter to slide the window back on its rollers, Gallen popped a single shot into the room. The barrel of the AK flew upwards and Gallen could hear bullets hitting the ceiling as the shooter fell back.

Gallen keyed the mic as he picked up and ran for the Tahoe. 'Front window shooter down.'

'Copy that,' said Winter. 'Dude at the back window has pulled away, Red Bird. I'm guessing he's heading your way, over.'

Gallen hit the Tahoe and felt his leg want to give way. He wasn't fit enough, wasn't strong enough to be back in the field. Lifting his head, he scoped the front the of the single-storey home, couldn't see the new shooter.

A volley of gunfire erupted from the other side of the house, and then a man was screaming.

'Leg shot,' said Winter on the radio. 'Dude took it in the bone, over.'

'I'm going in,' said Gallen, fading to his right, away from the cover of the SUV, and ranging around the side of the house where it was shaded from the desert sun. Checking his clip, he gasped for breath, his throat rasping as sweat poured down his neck and under his vest.

He got to the far corner of the house and stopped, looked around. The shooter with the shot leg lay writhing in the dust beside a water tank. Winter stood over him. He looked at Gallen. 'I'll take this entry, boss,' he said, and moved to the back porch.

Gallen ran back along the side of the house and around to the front. Where was the support from Barrowman, Amundsen and Cole?

Ducking under the front windows, Gallen reached the front door and hid behind the jamb. The door was ajar and he pushed it open. A hallway opened up, blood smeared down white lino towards the back of the house.

'Red Bird, through here,' came Winter's deep, slow voice, and Gallen followed it.

'You okay, Blue Dog?' Gallen kept a shoulder on his M4 as he moved carefully through the house.

'Yep,' said Winter.

Gallen walked across a carpet covered in plaster dust. Nobody. Then the first living room gave way to the second and Gallen kept his rifle at his eye, scoped the room back and forth as the scene unfolded: Winter's gun was on the ground and he gestured with his head as Gallen looked at him. Shifting his gaze out the window and to the helicopter, he saw the FBI and CIA teams being led to the house, hands on their heads, armed thugs following.

Looking back, Gallen was about to ask Winter *what the fuck*, when he realised a large shape had just stepped out of the shadows.

'Hello, Gerry,' said Baba el-Masri. 'I'm starting to think you are following me.'

Gallen was acutely aware of the thug who sat behind him in the Chev Tahoe. One bullet from the chromed Desert Eagle he carried would go straight through Gallen's seat and sever his spine. Winter had been lumped with Amundsen and Barrowman—it didn't look good for any of them.

'So, now you are friends with the FBI and the CIA?' said Baba, accelerating away from the house in the air-conditioned SUV. 'A step up from Spikey, yes?'

'It's a contract, Baba. It don't mean nothing.'

'Where are they going?' said Baba as they reached sixty mph across rough roads.

'Into Iraq,' said Gallen, not wanting to ruin Barrowman's gig. 'The al-Haqs up to no good.'

'Ah, yes, yes,' said Baba, absent-minded. 'The al-Haq brothers are always in trouble.'

Baba slowed the Chev as they crossed a cattle grid, turned left and headed for a cottage beside a dipping station.

'Let's look.' Baba got out of the Chev and walked to the cottage. Gallen took a deep breath, wondering if this was it: an execution.

Baba opened the front door of the cottage with a key. 'Enter,' he said, holding the door open.

Walking into the cool of the air-con, Gallen looked around. The sparsely furnished living room looked modern but it was clearly a prison. A door into a bedroom was open and he could see two feet on the bed.

'You going to tell me what this is?' said Gallen. 'Where are we?'

'I told you that Ariq al-Haq means money to me?' said Baba.

'Sure,' said Gallen.

'For many years I have kept my eye on a man the al-Haqs wanted,' said Baba. 'One week ago they tell me that they are ready to pick him up, and they want to do this outside of the city.'

Baba lit a smoke, offered one to Gallen. He could sense Baba's bodyguard keeping his distance and staying at his five o'clock: a professional.

'So I tell al-Haq that I can keep this man at my farm, that I have a facility that is good for this work,' said Baba, holding his hands out and looking around at the cottage. 'But then, this morning, they come to the house in their helicopter, and they say where is the professor?'

'I tell them he's nearby, and I ask them if they want tea. "No," they say, "we have to get to Badush."'

'Badush?' said Gallen. 'That up northern Iraq?'

'Yes,' said Baba. 'In the Mosul region, near Turkey.'

'So?'

'So, I say that I don't know anything about no Badush, and al-Haq tells me it's none of my concern. And I tell him that I keep the professor on the ice for all these years and then I deliver him, and now I learn he's going back to Iraq?'

'Back?' said Gallen, seeing the feet on the bed move.

'Well, yes,' said Baba, confused. 'He's an Iraqi professor, a physicist. Quite famous.'

Gallen was feeling impatient: if they were going to kill him he could do without the speech. 'So he's still here?'

'Sure,' said Baba, pointing at the room. 'I decided to retain him. I told them, if you're going to take this man back to Iraq it can only be for bad things, and bad things for Jordan.'

'Why?' said Gallen.

The feet in the bedroom descended off the bed.

'Because he designed the Iraqi bomb,' said Baba. 'He's a nuclear genius.'

A middle-aged man in chinos and a polo shirt emerged into the living room, yawning.

Gallen's mouth dropped open.

'Meet Professor Tahar,' said Baba with a flourish.

The man smiled. 'Hello, Mr Gallen.'

'Shit,' said Gallen. 'Zaki—is that you?'

CHAPTER 35

There is a very American way of saying *what?!*, which suggests the person you are speaking to is slightly mad. Gallen cringed as Barry Amundsen finally said it in a way that Baba el-Masri was going to find offensive.

'What Barry is trying to say,' said Gallen, leaping into the negotiation, 'is that he can't really give you a billion dollars. It's not his.'

'That's precisely what I'm frigging saying,' said Amundsen, hand slapping flat on the dining table they were seated around, and looking to Barrowman for support. 'I can't even confirm there's a billion dollars anywhere in Iraq, Baba. That's just crazy rumours, okay?'

'That's a Sikorsky S-92 helicopter,' said Baba, nodding with approval. 'That'll get us to Baghdad and back.'

'No, no, no, no.' Amundsen shook his head and crossed his forearms in an NFL referee gesture. 'We're not going to Baghdad with you, Baba. We're in the middle of something here.'

'Well, I need some recompense for my costs in securing the professor,' said Baba. 'This is a difficult economy . . .'

'Okay, okay,' said Amundsen, flustered. When he'd seen the professor, his eyes had popped and Gallen assumed he wanted to be

245

in the air, chasing al-Haq and Saleh. 'If you hand back my phone, I can make a call, see if we can cut you a cheque.'

'No,' said Baba thoughtfully. 'I know the CIA phone, you see. Right now your section knows where you are and if you call someone there, you can give them a code, set all the hounds running.'

Amundsen looked at his watch. 'I can call a civilian—'

'Not this Daly? The one working with you?' said Baba. 'He is DIA—same as CIA, only with manners.'

Amundsen gave a fake laugh, held up his hands in mock surrender while sharing a smile with Barrowman. Gallen had already witnessed what Baba looked like when he lost his sense of humour and he didn't want Amundsen making it like that.

'You know something, Baba?' said Gallen, offering him a Marlboro and a light. 'You might get more mileage out of helping the United States at this crucial time, thought about that?'

'How would I do that?' Baba sucked on the smoke and ignored Amundsen, who was beside himself with impatience.

'Well, you've come halfway by keeping the professor away from the al-Haqs. You didn't want them getting up to no good with the nukes, right?'

'Sure,' shrugged Baba. 'The Iraqi wants to bomb the Jew with the nuke, guess whose country that flies over?'

'My guess is, Baba, that Amundsen won't cut you a cheque, but he might cut you a deal . . .'

'Now just wait a minute,' said Amundsen, trying to step back into the conversation, but Baba waved him away.

'Tell me a deal.' Baba drew deeply on the cigarette.

'You have a construction company?'

'Yes, Alpha Constructions,' said Baba. 'All legal.'

'One month ago, contractors to the CPA in Baghdad mistakenly smashed through a reservoir wall,' said Gallen. 'The wall is still broken, that right, Jim?'

'Far as I know,' said Barrowman, not looking enthused.

'So the CPA is going to use a contractor to fix it, and maybe Alpha wins the contract.'

'Why would I want a contract in Baghdad?' said Baba.

Amundsen fixed Gallen with a homicidal look as Barrowman groaned and rubbed his face with both hands.

The Sikorsky was set up with side-by-side seats down the port side, three seats across the rear bulkhead—just like a school bus—and a row of single seats up the starboard side. The professor sat in the middle rear seat, Barrowman to one side of him.

Barry Amundsen had elected to drive back to Amman, nervous about the impact of Zaki's discovery and furious about Gallen's deal with el-Masri.

Barrowman scribbled notes, showed Zaki his charts, papers and anything else he was carrying. They were headed north-east, across the al-Hamad desert—famed for its Bedouins and smuggling routes—along the Syrian border, headed for Mosul in the north of Iraq.

'You think Jim is gonna forgive you for that?' said Winter, leaning over Gallen and looking out at the desert. 'That boy Cole didn't look like he was in the mood to be held as collateral by Baba.'

'Baba will look after him,' said Gallen, 'if he wants a shot at all that money.'

'What's goin' on back there?' Winter nodded at the back seat.

'Zaki's helping them with their blueprint,' said Gallen, not convinced. 'But he was a nuclear physicist and a weapons engineer. I'm not sure he knows where the facility is exactly.'

'Well,' said the Canadian, 'if he don't know where the facility is, then what did al-Haq and Saleh want with him?'

They looked at one another, until Winter cocked a eyebrow. There was one reason why they'd need him: they knew where the nukes were and wanted someone to help deploy them.

'Anyway, I wanted to talk about something without these dicks and spooks hearing it,' said Winter. 'You seen this?'

Gallen followed Winter's finger, which pointed out the other side of the cabin. 'What am I lookin' at?'

'Look to the helo's seven o'clock.'

Gallen kneeled and pushed his face up against the safety glass, and angled to his left to see what was almost behind the Sikorsky. 'Don't see nothing.'

'Saw a flash, is all,' said Winter, lowering his voice. 'Couldn't work out if it was in the air or on the ground.'

Gallen craned to his left, taking in an azure sky that became strangely dark as it hit the endless desert horizon. 'Still nothing.'

'Must have imagined it,' said Winter, taking a seat. 'So, what are we looking for?'

Gallen thought about it. 'An underground warehouse filled with nuclear warheads.'

Winter sneered. 'Iraq's the size of France. That's the best they got?'

'Baba told me that al-Haq and Saleh were heading for Badush, near Mosul. It's in the north, but that's still a huge area.'

'Don't we have a copy of the blueprint?'

'Yes,' said Gallen. 'But it was unmarked—all it had was a drawing. It's missing a detail overlay, something you lay on it so it makes sense.'

Winter nodded. 'So Saleh has the overlay? They've been waiting all these years to find the blueprint?'

Gallen frowned. 'I don't know. Tookie Saleh was only sixteen or seventeen when Baghdad was bombed: maybe he was given the overlay by his uncle? Now David Rogers brings the blueprint, and away he goes.'

'You put the Baathist revival in the hands of a teenager?' chuckled Winter. 'Wouldn't ask my boy to do that.'

'Be too many girls, too much hockey for that,' said Gallen.

'Too much rye,' said Winter, squinting and pointing out Gallen's window. 'There!'

Turning to his left, Gallen stared into the perfect blue and tried to focus. 'Where?'

'Your ten o'clock.'

Looking to the rear of the helicopter, Gallen saw a faint dark shape almost hidden against the dark of the horizon, about twenty miles away. 'Going about the same speed as us—same altitude. Another helo?'

'I didn't see it long enough to make that call,' said Winter. 'If you're seein' it clear, then it's closing.'

'In my backpack, Kenny,' said Gallen. 'Grab my binoculars, will ya?'

Winter handed them over and Gallen pressed against the glass, tried to focus the binos on the aircraft as it slipped in behind the Sikorsky again.

'At our six,' said Gallen, handing back the binos. 'What's your call?'

'I'm gonna grab those rifles.'

Gallen nodded, fatigue buzzing behind his eyeballs. 'I'll have a chat with the pilot.'

Ducking up the small steps at the front of the cabin area, Gallen looked over his shoulder before pushing the flight deck door. Barrowman caught his eye as he pushed into the cockpit.

A middle-aged American looked up then turned back to the tawny rocks and sand that blurred past beneath the perspex bubble under his foot controls. 'I help you, sir?'

'Gerry Gallen, I'm with Barrowman,' said Gallen, trying to get a line of sight to the rear of the helicopter. 'You seeing anything on your screen?'

'Which screen?'

'Radar,' said Gallen, looking down at the layout of the flight controls.

The pilot touched a screen that had a dark dot in the middle. 'Screen covers about seventy miles.'

'That one there,' said Gallen, pointing to a dark pulsating shape almost following the Sikorsky. 'What's that?'

'Syrian army or air force,' said the pilot. 'We're flying along the border, they're probably just keeping an eye on us.'

'How d'you know they're military?'

'I interrogated them for ID, and there was no response,' said the pilot. 'If they don't respond to a friend-or-foe interrogation, then they're military, and not our military.'

'They made contact?'

'No,' said the pilot. 'That's not unusual for this part of the world.'

Gallen didn't like it. 'They closing?'

'Yes,' said the pilot, relaxed. 'We may have crossed the border, it's hard to tell out here. I'll bank to the south, get away from Syrian turf, if you like?'

'We can't waste time,' said Jim Barrowman, giving Gallen a start. 'We can't go the long way around, Danny.'

'Okay,' said the pilot. 'Just explaining an IFF to your buddy here.'

'Thanks, Danny,' said the FBI man. 'I'll explain it to him.'

Gallen returned to his seat, annoyed with Barrowman, who followed on his heels.

'We're being followed by military,' said Gallen as he twisted into his seat. 'Ain't Syrians Baathists too?'

'Forget it,' said Barrowman. 'We have to get to Badush.'

'Army can do it,' said Gallen. 'We've got twenty thousand soldiers in Iraq.'

Barrowman sighed. 'You haven't noticed a certain secrecy to this whole thing, Gallen? This isn't the kind of mission we want army guys photographing, uploading to Facebook.'

'Soldiers ain't that bad, Jim,' said Gallen. 'Secret's still a secret.'

'Soldiers like you were trained for discretion,' said Barrowman. 'Not every US soldier is careful with their iPhone.'

'Just sayin'.'

Barrowman held up his hand. 'Our government wants to pull out of this part of the world, okay? That isn't gonna happen when Fox News is reporting there's WMDs in Iraq after all—whole dumps of nukes just waiting for Saddam's heirs to fire them up.'

'You say whole dumps?' said Gallen. 'Shit, Jim, what's going on here?'

'Zaki is not exactly small talk,' said Barrowman, rubbing his unshaven face. 'Jesus Christ, he's just taken us through the arsenal and it's not pretty.'

'Arsenal?' said Gallen, surprised. 'That's not a few hidden warheads, Jim.'

'No it's not.'

'So what we talkin' about?' said Winter.

'What we're talking about is classified,' said Barrowman. 'Let's just say we have to get there before Tookie Saleh.'

'Don't matter how many nukes they got,' said Winter. 'If they got nothing to fire them with, they'll just blow themselves up.'

'That's the problem.' Barrowman chewed his lip.

'What?' said Gallen.

'Iraq's Al-Samoud II missile was declared illegal by the UN in

March 2003. UNMOVIC destroyed just seventy-two of them, and three launchers.'

'So?' said Gallen.

'So, if Zaki's right, we missed a lot of Salmoud IIs and their launchers.'

'What's the range of these things?' said Gallen.

'Good enough that they had to be destroyed in the first place.'

They heard what sounded like a metallic slap on the roof of the Sikorsky. Barrowman looked up briefly, then started to talk again.

'Shit!' yelled Kenny Winter, leaping across Gallen into the aisle, where he pushed past Barrowman and grabbed an assault rifle from the opposite seat.

Looking to his left, Gallen saw the black helicopter pull level with the port side of the Sikorsky, a minigun turning menacingly beneath its fuselage, its barrel aligning with Gallen's seat.

As Gallen launched sideways into the aisle, Winter was already braced, rifle at his shoulder, aiming at the black helo through the window.

The blast of the M4 roared in the confined cabin, deafening Gallen as he reached for the other M4. Brass spewed from Winter's rifle and cordite filled the air as glass exploded and the Sikorsky banked over to starboard, the pilot taking evasive action as they took incoming from the black helicopter's minigun, its bullets slapping the airframe like a hammer.

Gallen fell against the starboard-side window as the pilot took them deep into a dive, air now racing into the cabin in a screech as they bottomed out and flew upwards at forty-five degrees. As they levelled out again, Gallen joined Winter on the port side, aiming though shattered windows, looking for the black helicopter.

Barrowman yelled and Gallen turned in time to see a waterfall of sparks fall on the FBI man and a thick plume of smoke billow from the ceiling.

'Jim,' said Gallen, reaching for him. Another round of bullets scythed through the fuselage, sending insulation and pieces of metal flying as the black helicopter flew over the Sikorsky at high speed.

Winter switched to the starboard side of the helicopter and let off two bursts of auto gunfire into the blue. Gallen got a proper grip on

Barrowman and pulled him out of the flames that were now pouring from the ceiling.

'Leave him,' said Gallen as the FBI man struggled to return for Zaki, now obscured by the black smoke and flames.

'Watch it,' yelled Winter from behind him, and before Gallen could turn, the port side of the Sikorsky started lifting. Grabbing onto a seat back while keeping Barrowman balanced, Gallen retained his feet as the Sikorsky's port side moved upwards with a jerk. And then the port side was trying to become the starboard side.

A barrel roll, thought Gallen, as his head slammed into the ceiling.

CHAPTER 36

The first landing threw Gallen to the floor of the aisle and sent him bouncing and sliding towards the cockpit steps. As the airframe took off into the air and twisted to the port side, Gallen grabbed a seat leg and swung a hand over the armrest.

When the chopper landed for the second time he took the full force in his chest and right pectoral as the aircraft skidded at a hundred miles an hour through the rocks and sand of the Syrian desert.

The helicopter came to a rest inside of five seconds, the airframe groaning and grinding as it was engulfed by flames. Letting go of the armrest, Gallen fell back on Barrowman, who was unconscious. Pushing onto his knees, Gallen felt his shoulder joint grab with pain as he reached for the FBI man. He prayed it was a torn muscle, not a broken collarbone.

'Jim, wake up,' he said, slapping Barrowman hard. 'Wake up, Jim. Gotta get you outta here.'

Holding him by the collar, Gallen tensed his knees and pulled back, dragging Barrowman across the seat legs, the airframe having settled forty-five degrees to the ground. His foot slipped and he fell through the legs, his knee protesting in agony as all the weight was taken on the interior cruciate.

'Fuck,' he groaned, breathing deep and closing his eyes, making himself stay conscious even as he felt drool pouring off his bottom lip. 'Holy shit.'

The flames at the back of the cabin surged and the familiar roar of an accelerant-fuelled fire shook the space.

'Come on, Jim,' he urged, replacing his right foot on the seat leg and moving backwards with greater caution, his eyes not leaving the flames.

A scream erupted as he got to the small vestibule at the front of the Sikorsky's cabin. Kenny Winter emerged from the black smoke, stumbling into the sloping aisle and blindly feeling his way towards Gallen, his eyes gummed up with kerosene soot.

'Kenny!' yelled Gallen, giving Winter something to aim for. 'This way. Over here, Kenny. You can do it.'

The Canadian scrambled to the vestibule, where Gallen pulled up on the door-release handle, pushed up the top half of the door to its position and kicked down the air stairs.

Air flooded into the smoke chamber as a bang sounded and the grey cloud of the fire bottles filled the cabin. Because of the angle of the airframe, the air stairs were horizontal and Gallen left Winter and Barrowman in the vestibule as he stepped out, looking for the black helo. The skies were clear but he could hear a faint thromp of turboshaft engines above the hiss of the extinguished fires.

Moving back along the stairs, he found Barrowman now conscious but Winter still unable to see. Gallen led them along the stairs and at the end told Winter there was a fifteen foot drop to rocks and sand.

'Knees soft for two seconds,' said Gallen, 'then roll with the impact. Jim, can you get him to that berm?'

Barrowman nodded as Gallen pointed at a mound of rocks forty feet from the chopper. 'Where are you going?'

'Rifles,' said Gallen. 'Now go.'

Moving back into the cabin, Gallen smelled kerosene and burnt halon—the agent used in aviation fire bottles. Pulling a tea towel from the vestibule kitchenette, he wrapped it around his face and tied off before plunging into the ruined cabin. He could see Zaki, charred and lying sideways on his seat. He found the two M4 rifles:

one jammed between two seats, the other barrel-first in the rocks that sprang through the portal.

He grabbed them and slung them across his shoulder, his thigh aching with the bending and the strain of moving along the angled cabin. The thromping of turboshafts grew louder and, looking out through the skyward-facing windows of the starboard side, he saw the black helicopter racing in a fast arc around the stricken Sikorsky.

Clambering as fast as he could towards the vestibule, he checked in the overhead bins for ammo. The first bin held a red life raft bag and a desert survival kit. In the next bin he found a black cordura bag filled with spare rifle clips and boxes of ammo. As he reached for it, he found a bright green medic's bag sitting behind it, and took that too.

Hurrying clumsily with his new load, he made it to the vestibule and decided to check on the pilot. As he stuck his head up the cockpit stairs, he saw immediately why they'd so drastically lost control and rolled into the ground: Danny, the pilot, had only half of his head and the front half of the Sikorsky had been shot up by the minigun, rendering the foot pedals and controls useless. It looked like a threshing machine had stormed through the cockpit.

Pulling back, Gallen raced for the air stairs and, hobbling along them, leapt to the ground, rolling in a paratroop landing and gaining his feet again, moving for the safety of the berm.

'Watch it, Gerry,' said Barrowman from behind the berm. 'They're coming in.'

Limping to the mound, Gallen dived between the scrub and slid to the bottom of a small crater where Winter was blinking his eyes like a madman, trying to get the tears to take the soot out of his eyeballs.

'You okay, Kenny?' Gallen dropped the bags and slipped the M4s off his shoulder, handing one to Barrowman.

'I'll be right in a coupla minutes,' said the big Canadian, kneeling over so he was looking into the sand. 'Kill those pricks for me, will ya?'

Joining Barrowman in the lee of the berm, Gallen released the clip on his M4 and checked the slot. He saw nineteen rounds and jammed the clip back into the rifle as the black attack chopper slowed and flared over the Sikorsky.

'You fired one of these?' Gallen shouldered the rifle and aligned his aiming eye.

'On a range, three or four times,' said Barrowman.

'Make sure you get a good shoulder or you're gonna waste rounds.'

'Got it.' Barrowman settled the stock into his right shoulder.

'Aim for the pilot,' said Gallen. 'Fire.'

They opened up on the hovering helicopter, its nose lifting so it couldn't aim the minigun. The plexiglass of the cockpit starred with their rounds, and the pilot pulled back, the natural reaction of all rotorcraft pilots.

'Okay, they're coming back with the minigun.' Gallen watched the chopper pull away, revealing itself as a Little Bird, the chosen ride of the US Army's special forces community. As the Little Bird swung around in a new arc, Gallen saw a shooter in plainclothes, harnessed in the open side door, training a marksman's rifle on him.

'Shit,' he yelped as the rifle coughed, putting three rounds into the sand mound in front of Gallen. Spitting grit as held his head down, Gallen looked to his left and saw the Little Bird swinging to a better position where the three of them were more exposed. Raising the M4 again, Gallen took a kneeling marksman pose and shot at the pilot. It wasn't the best shot to take—if you had the time, your best shot on a helo was at the tail rotor, since even one lucky shot could disable the aircraft and then things evened up. But Gallen's adrenaline was surging, and he needed to push the pilot away from aiming that minigun, so he poured more rounds at the plexiglass. The plexiglass door panel shattered into pieces, and the pilot pulled away again, turning and flying as if in a retreat. Gallen knew better: the minigun was an electrically powered Gatling-style weapon that could fire up to six thousand rounds per minute of 7.62 NATO cartridges. Its effective range was one thousand metres, while the M4—essentially a shortened M16—was effective over one hundred metres, but used mostly over fifty.

The Little Bird pilot was standing off where he couldn't be harassed by Gallen's M4.

'What's he doing?' Barrowman panted with fear. 'He leaving?'

'No,' said Gallen. 'That gun under the fuselage?'

'The black, spinning thing?'

'Yeah,' said Gallen, watching the Little Bird bank at five hundred metres. 'That can be dialled up to one hundred rounds per second, and if the pilot wants to, he could cut through this berm in about four seconds.'

'What're we gonna do?' said Barrowman. 'Look—he's coming round again.'

'We're gonna load up, stay low, wait for our chance,' said Gallen, sliding down the depression behind the mound to where Winter, his eyes red but open, was now sitting up and pulling the third assault rifle from the black bag.

Barrowman slid down to join them as Gallen opened the gun bag, pulled out two fresh clips. 'Stay calm, wait for them to get close, and then drill 'em.'

Barrowman's hands shook as he slammed the new clip home. 'Don't know if I can do this, Gerry.'

'Guess what?' said Gallen. 'You already are.'

Finding several pairs of Oakley desert goggles in the bag, Gallen distributed them. 'You'll need these.' He handed them to Barrowman.

The sound started with a low howl and built into a banshee screech as the minigun wound up to its operating cycle, and then the air tore open as the pilot hit the fire button. The scream of lead coming through the air at a hundred rounds per second was as frightening a sound as Gallen had ever heard—a noise so disturbing to the human sensory system that US Marines were trained to become accustomed to the sound of even friendly fire, given how many soldiers panicked when they first heard it.

'Shit!' screamed Barrowman, hands over his ears as Gallen swung an arm over him, pressing him into the dirt while stones and sand exploded, filling the air with a maelstrom of grit and dirt.

'The fuck!' yelled the FBI man, grinding his face into the dirt as the noise increased and the dirt and rocks flew in an anguished swirl, the bullets starting to exit through the near side of the berm.

'Wait,' screamed Gallen, pushing the M4 into Barrowman, making him take it. 'Wait for it.'

A break in the onslaught came after ten seconds, the air settling with dropping dirt and rock particles, making Gallen gag.

'We ready?' he said.

'Lookie here,' said Winter, and Gallen turned. The Canadian was holding a modified M4 carbine with a grenade launcher under the main barrel. 'Let's see if that Little Bird likes grenade burger.'

Barrowman was hyperventilating, in shock, as the thromp of the turboshaft loomed overhead and the Little Bird came into view.

'Now!' said Gallen, and they opened up on the attack bird, pouring as many rounds as they could into the predator. Barrowman yelled at the aircraft and Gallen hit the side-door marksman in the forearm—he could see his hand fly away from the rifle and his face grimace. The Little Bird pulled away again, showing more of its belly as they shot at it. As it peeled away, Winter kneeled and very deliberately aimed up. The grenade shot whistled through the air, leaving a faint grey trail. At first it looked as though Winter would score a direct hit on the exposed belly but it lost upward trajectory too soon and flattened out, hitting the right landing skid at its forward upright strut.

'Got it!' said Barrowman as the grenade exploded, blowing the right skid off the Little Bird and making the helicopter veer and shake in the sky.

They stood slowly as the attack helicopter tried to regain its equilibrium, seeming to fly sideways for half a mile. Then it was gone, accelerating towards the western horizon of the al-Hamad.

'Nice shootin', Kenny,' said Gallen, choking on rock pieces and staring after the retreating chopper.

'Shit,' gulped Barrowman. 'Think they're gone? I mean, for good?'

'I think they're just startin',' said Gallen. 'Let's get moving.'

CHAPTER 37

They buried the dead while Winter tried to get the radio working. Barrowman and Gallen lined up Zaki and Danny the pilot and put them in shallow graves.

'I guess it's a cross for Danny,' said Gallen. 'Just a plain stone for Zaki?'

'Who said he was Muslim?' said Barrowman. 'Lots of Christians and Jews in the Iraqi academic world.'

'I'll leave it as a single spoon, then, rather than two fashioned into a cross,' said Gallen.

They were both sweating as they sat in the shade created by the fire blanket they'd rigged. It was three pm, just past the hottest part of the day in the desert, and Gallen was dreading some of the decisions that had to be made.

They'd found four five-litre jugs of water in the Sikorsky kitchen area: they were not quite enough for three men in the desert and too heavy to carry without exertion.

'Kenny,' said Gallen, calling up into the cockpit stairs. 'Time for your water ration.'

Winter joined them. They opened a packet of chocolate-chip cookies and Barrowman poured three plastic cups of water.

'Radio's screwed,' said Winter. 'Took a direct round and a connection's been severed. I can get power from the batteries, but I can't select a channel.'

Gallen nodded, looked at Barrowman. 'What's the ration status, Jim?'

'Four jugs of water which gives us about twenty litres, less what we just drank,' said Barrowman. 'I've found three bags of cookies, a can of coffee, a bunch of coffee creamers and ten muffins sealed in their own cellophane bags. Oh, and a dozen apples and oranges.'

Gallen drank the last of his water. 'I rounded up all the navigational material I could find,' he said, unfolding a map of the al-Hamad. 'Danny carried physical maps and a divider and slide rule with him in his satchel, but we'll have to count back to get a position.'

'Know the cruise speed of this helo?' said Winter.

'The manual in the cockpit says two hundred and eighty kilometres an hour,' said Gallen. 'There was only one pilot and five passengers so I'm assuming we were travelling at recommended cruise.'

The others nodded.

'It was ten to midday when we left al Jufur, and I believe we came down at about a quarter to two in the afternoon.'

'So flying time of about two hours?' said Barrowman.

'Heading roughly north-east,' said Gallen. 'I set the dividers to two hundred and eighty kilometres,' he said, walking them across the map to the north-east of al Jufur.

'Shit,' said Winter, looking down on where the dividers terminated at their second stride. 'There's nothing there.'

'There's sand and sunshine,' said Gallen, drawing a small circle with the pilot's retractable pencil. 'If Danny was correct, and we were flying along the Syrian border, then we're right here. About three hundred klicks from Palmyra, about two hundred from Rutba and two hundred kilometres from Al Qa'im.'

Winter and Barrowman drew in closer, looked down on the map.

'So we have some decisions to make,' said Gallen, leaning back on the fuselage. 'There's an emergency transponder on this aircraft and I have no doubt we'll be picked up by this time tomorrow if we just stay put.'

'Then let's do that,' said Barrowman, a little too quickly.

260

Gallen shook his head. 'Our friends in the black helo are gonna come back, finish what they didn't get round to the first time.'

'Gerry's sayin' we have the choice,' said Winter. 'Stay and fight. Or walk.'

'Walk?!' said the FBI man, an edge creeping into his voice. 'To where?'

Winter shrugged, looked at Gallen.

'Well?' said Barrowman.

'This ain't Washington, Jim,' said Gallen. 'You don't show a badge and the bad guys shit their pants. Kenny's right—the choice ain't between good and bad, it's between might die of dehydration and will probably die of lead poisoning. This won't end well.'

Barrowman's larynx bobbed. 'And that's it? Two special forces soldiers sit around in the desert, wait to die?'

'Gives us time to find Jesus,' said Winter, biting a cigarette and offering one to Gallen. 'He's around here someplace.'

'Oh man.' Barrowman held his head.

A massive lappet-face vulture circled two hundred feet above them. Gallen thought of something and, standing, he brushed off the sand. 'Kenny, these birds have a cargo hold?'

'Don't know,' said Winter.

'Under the tail,' said Barrowman, standing.

They found a lever in the vestibule area. Gallen pulled it down and a whining sound started, which lowered the rear door under the tail. It only opened a few feet because of the angle of the crash, but it was enough for Gallen to climb inside.

'See what's in these,' he said, throwing out the bags and suitcases that were held upright behind webbing in the hold.

Clambering back out, he found clothes and testing kits all over the sand.

'That's mine,' said Barrowman, pointing at a Zero case. 'But these ones belong to Amundsen—he must have forgotten to take them when he left for Amman.'

Gallen didn't know what he was looking for, but when the CIA travelled they often carried interesting equipment.

Winter went through a small wheelie bag filled with clothes and then opened a laptop case. 'Lookie.'

The laptop was in a case that opened, the lid of which contained what looked like a portable telephone exchange.

'What is it?' said Barrowman.

'Satellite uplink,' said Gallen, almost to himself. 'CIA talks to itself and sends photos, files and other data back to Langley via these things. Totally encrypted.'

'Sounds like you know what you're doing?' said Barrowman.

'I've used them,' said Gallen. 'It's what I did. But the problem is they're protected from unauthorised use—you don't want Joe Bedouin picking up something like this and setting off Gulf War Three, right?'

Retreating to the shade, Winter tried to start the uplink while Gallen pored over the map. There were small dotted lines in the shape of well heads at various points, but it was not clearly defined what they were.

'They oases?' said Barrowman.

'Could be, but the dotted lines ain't a good sign,' said Gallen. 'The mapmakers weren't exactly committing to there being water in there.'

'So, we going to die out here?' said Barrowman quietly. 'That really it?'

Gallen looked at him. So much had happened since he first met this man at Denver International: he'd sat there being harassed by Barrowman when it was a cop's world; and now it was Gallen's world, and the more that occurred to him, the more he wondered what had become of his life that the proximity of death could be considered his domain. 'Comes to everyone, Jim.'

'Shit,' said Barrowman, standing in a huff. 'I hired you because of your record, because of the Silver Star and the five combat tours, Gerry. You were a captain who never sat behind a desk, who led teams through the worst places on earth and lived to talk about it.'

'Conserve your energy, Jim,' said Gallen.

'What's the point? Shit, I even took on an assassin—you know what the Bureau thinks of employing assassins?'

Winter looked up, the uplink case on his lap. 'Thing powers up, but it needs a password to connect with the satellite.'

Barrowman kicked a rock at the helicopter and walked into the sun. 'This is nuts. Fucking nuts.'

Moving over, Gallen sat alongside Winter. 'Nothing?'

Winter pointed his fingertips at the screen of the laptop. 'The computer won't let me in.'

'What if we just push this?' said Gallen, turning on the machinery in the lid of the case. Lights came on that showed 'UHF/VHF' but Winter couldn't find a way through the password-protected panel on the screen.

'We need a plan, keep Jim busy,' said Winter. 'And the only plan I can think of involves killing folks.'

'Tell me,' said Gallen.

'When the bad guys come back maybe they see two sets of footprints, heading off into the desert?'

'And number three lies in wait, kills them when they land?'

'I like that idea, boss,' smiled Winter. 'I officially volunteer.'

'What if they follow the footsteps, kill me and Jim, then fly away?'

'I think they want to search the chopper, don't you?'

Gallen nodded. 'Yep, I reckon.'

'So, let's do it the Comanche way.'

'Bad guys land, thinking there's no one at the helo?'

'Yep,' said Winter. 'And then *whammo*.'

'Lemme think about it.'

Feeling a buzz on his butt Gallen jumped up, worried he'd been sitting on a scorpion, but brushing at the seat of his pants, he realised it was his iPhone. Pulling it out of his back pocket, he held his hand up to shade it from the sun and looked at the screen.

'The fuck?' said Winter, standing too. 'Your phone's goin'?'

'I . . .' said Gallen, confused. Tapping on the glowing icon for the Tactical NAV app, he watched the message come up.

'Holy shit,' said Gallen remembering how he'd sent a map reference link from the app two weeks ago in Amman. 'It's a reply from Mike Ford, wanting to know if I need a hand.'

After two and a half hours of walking east across the flat barrenness of the al-Hamad, Gallen sat down with Barrowman and they drank.

'Shit, Gerry,' said the FBI man. 'I don't know about this.'

'If anyone's qualified to get us out of this shit, it's Kenny Winter. He's an *assassin*, remember?'

'I'm sorry,' said Barrowman, throat bobbing with the water intake. 'Has he done this sort of thing before?'

Gallen sipped at his water. 'Who? Kenny?'

'Yeah, I mean, I didn't feel very good, you know, burying him.'

'He has air,' said Gallen. 'He won't die, and at least it'll stop him playing with himself.'

'Jesus, Gerry,' said Barrowman, shaking his head. 'How can you joke about this stuff? We're in the middle of a desert, and we just buried your friend alive beside a crashed helicopter. It's actually not that funny.'

'You're right,' said Gallen.

'So, he's done this before?'

'Nah,' said Gallen. 'He's a fan of the old Westerns. You know, the ones with the Comanche warrior tricks. I think he saw this one when he was a kid. Probably a Jack Lord B-movie.'

'Jack Lord? That was *Hawaii Five-O*.'

Gallen laughed. 'You wanna hang with soldiers, Jim, you gotta learn your Westerns.'

'I got some things to learn, sure,' said Barrowman.

'Since we're out here, you wanna tell me what we've been chasing?'

Barrowman drank his water, thoughtful. 'Well, most of the answers lay with Zaki.'

'You get nothing out of him?'

'Yep, Gerry,' said Barrowman. 'We did.'

'So?'

'It's embarrassing,' said Barrowman. 'Zaki told us there were three phases of the Iraqi nuclear weapon program: creating highly enriched uranium from local reactors; weaponising the HEU with an implosion trigger; and a delivery system.'

'Why is that embarrassing?'

'Because the CIA wrote in their 2004 report that this program had failed—cleaned out, shut down, never happened.'

'How did we get it so wrong?' said Gallen.

'I think we focused too hard on the official Saddam regime, not the hidden parts.'

'How?'

'Remember I told you the Iraqi nuclear program was called PC-3, which was divided into four official groups concerned with R and D?'

'And there was a Group 5, which was going to deploy these things, but it was totally hidden.'

'Exactly,' said Barrowman, his eyes following what was now a group of three circling vultures. 'Zaki said Group 5 was run by a member of Saddam's cabinet, not by the Military Industrialisation Commission. So when Saddam shut down the four official PC-3 projects to appease the weapons inspectors, the fifth group kept operating.'

'How did they hide Group 5?' said Gallen.

'It was officially relocated into the University of Baghdad. But they all worked secretly at the Operation Barq facility.'

'Barq?' said Gallen.

'It means lightning. Operation Lightning.'

'With highly enriched uranium, weaponisation and a missile?' said Gallen.

'Yes,' said Barrowman. 'Operation Barq was a very large underground facility, which Zaki says is around the Badush area. The regime used to fly the scientists in and out at night. He couldn't tell us exactly where it was.'

'You're the money-trail guy,' said Gallen. 'Saddam had to be throwing a lot of money at this thing?'

'Good question. I asked Zaki and he said the gossip among the scientists was that it was funded through al-Haq fronts in Jordan, Singapore and Germany.'

'Nice.'

'Yes,' said Barrowman. 'There was also the issue of cash: the scientists kept their university salaries and were paid bonuses in kind: renovations to their houses, rent paid on their behalf, cars given to them, school fees paid.'

'Who did that come from?'

Barrowman smiled. 'Saeed Saleh. This fellow, Tookie, has inherited more than just Baathist extremism. He's got an entire finance and banking network.'

The thromp started as the sun sat on the horizon, when Gallen and Barrowman had been walking for another half hour.

Turning, Gallen held his binoculars to his eyes and watched the small shape on the horizon, made obvious by the spotlight under its nose.

'This is it, Jim,' said Gallen. 'Get your rifle ready.'

The shape became larger and Gallen watched it, knowing that if the helicopter followed them to this point, they'd be dead: there were no mounds or berms out on the desert. There was nowhere to hide from the minigun.

The Little Bird followed their footsteps, its light getting closer, until the bird turned in a bank and headed back for the Sikorsky. Gallen felt Barrowman's breath expel.

'Now what?' asked Barrowman.

'We wait,' said Gallen. 'If it works, he'll fire three shots.'

'If it doesn't work?'

'He'll fire a lot more than three.'

Barrowman sighed in a way that Gallen didn't like. 'I can't believe we're trying something from a cowboy movie.'

'I guess we're even,' said Gallen, lighting a cigarette. ''Cos I can't believe we're out here chasing Saddam's nukes.'

CHAPTER 38

The thromp of the turbo shafts didn't abate, it got louder as the Little Bird disappeared.

'What's going on?' said Barrowman. 'Why's it getting louder?'

Turning, Gallen looked up and saw a second helicopter coming in from the dusk in the east. There was nowhere to hide and nowhere to run, so they stood stupidly as the blue-grey Huey banked in a wide circle and sped around them. Gallen couldn't see any armaments on the airframe but that didn't mean there weren't any shooters inside.

The old Huey flared, its rotors throwing up dust and rocks as it eased its weight onto the skids. Holding his forearm over his face to protect his eyes, Gallen saw a man lean out of the starboard pilot door, jump to the ground and start walking.

'Who's that?' said Barrowman, but Gallen had already lowered his rifle. The bandy walk was more suited to a bull rider, but he recognised the man as a former Australian navy commando.

'Mike, that you?'

The man took off his flight helmet as he approached. 'Gerry,' said Mike Ford, all smiles. 'You pick some strange places for a meeting, mate.'

*

They'd only been in the air for thirty seconds when Gallen realised he'd been waiting for a three-shot signal from Winter. With the noise of the Huey, there was no way they'd hear it now.

'Approach it carefully,' said Gallen into the intercom mic as they flew for the downed Sikorsky. Late afternoon and dusk came together very quickly in the al-Hamad and the sun had disappeared, leaving a pale purple hue against the western horizon, making it look as though they were flying into darkness.

'You said the bad guys were in a Little Bird with a minigun?' said Ford from the co-pilot seat. 'Who are they? Sounds like an American rig.'

Gallen shrugged. The faint shape of the downed Sikorsky sat in the gloom of early evening, a floodlight from the parked Little Bird illuminating the wreck.

'Take it easy, Mike,' said Gallen into his mic. 'Don't want to put Kenny in danger.'

Moving to the left side of the rattling old aircraft, Gallen cocked his M4 and keyed his mic. 'Pilot, gimme port.'

The pilot banked slightly to the right and approached so Gallen would have a clear line of sight from his port side of the Huey. Sliding the door back, he looked down on the scene, aiming up and looking for movement. There was none. One body lay between the parked Little Bird and the Sikorsky, its prone form virtually face down in the hole where Barrowman and Gallen had buried the Canadian four hours earlier. The clothes were wrong for Winter.

'Got one bad guy down,' said Gallen into the mic.

'Roger that,' said Ford above the roar of the two motors.

The pilot held his banking turn, giving Gallen a clean shot at anyone around the Sikorsky, but there was no sign of life. As they got to the west of the Little Bird, Gallen saw something in the pilot's seat. Reaching to the ceiling he pulled down a searchlight on a retractable arm, flicked the switch. The scene lit up: the pilot's throat was slit, his head lolling to one side, a once-white shirt now dark red.

'Kenny's been here,' said Gallen. 'Put me down.'

'Let me go, Gerry,' said Ford. 'I'm fresh.'

The Huey touched down and Ford, dressed in blue coveralls with a black Kevlar vest over the top, slipped from the co-pilot's seat and slapped on the door, giving the pilot the signal to lift into the air.

'Starting with the Little Bird,' said Ford into his headset, breathless as he jogged across the ground.

They watched him from a hundred feet in the air, Gallen giving the Aussie support with the Xenon light. For most of his recon career he'd fantasised about being the guy in the gunship door, lighting up the terrain with his searchlight. It felt powerful but his gut churned with worry about Winter.

'Little Bird has one occupant,' said Ford. 'Deceased. Moving to the other ship.'

The Huey circled, Gallen keeping the Xenon trained on the ground in front of Ford. They watched him stop at the male figure in the sand. 'Male, deceased,' said Ford. 'Mid-thirties, unarmed. Looks American. Moving into the downed helo.'

Gallen swapped a quick look with Barrowman, and turned back to see Mike Ford climbing onto the extended air stair and disappearing into the Sikorsky.

'The helo is empty,' said Ford, reappearing twenty seconds later. 'We expecting anyone else?'

Gallen thought about it. 'Expecting one other bad guy . . . and Kenny.' Leaning forwards, he got the pilot's attention. 'Can we bank the other way? I want to search terrain around the helo.'

The night had descended except for a thin line of pale orange along the western fringe. The Huey dipped onto its other side and made a long banking turn around the Little Bird, in the opposite direction, allowing Gallen to strafe the surrounding desert with the searchlight.

The light swept across the endless space in an eerie effect. It was like using a powerful flashlight underwater.

Gallen was about to ask the pilot to land and pick up Ford when something moved across the Xenon beam.

'Your three o'clock,' said Gallen. 'Mike, can you give us a coupla minutes?'

'You got it,' said Ford.

The pilot straightened the ship and turned on his own searchlight located under the nose. They illuminated the ground in front of and beneath them. Running through the light were two men moving away from the Huey.

'That's our guys,' said Gallen, leaning into the cockpit. 'Come up on their right.'

The pilot brought the Huey alongside the first man, an athletic mover who carried an assault rifle and wore the kind of clothes designed to look casual but which were military. He looked at Gallen and instantly threw up his arm to deflect the light.

'Shit,' said Gallen, turning to Barrowman. 'It's Rogers.'

Barrowman joined him at the Huey port door, looked down. David Rogers had stopped, turned his face away, and lifted the assault rifle towards the ship. Gallen aimed up, got a shot off at the Pentagon spook, making a burst of dirt fly out of the ground beside his foot. Rogers ducked reflexively and then shot at the Huey, firing wildly, the Xenon obviously still burning in his retinae. Two shots tinkled against the airframe and then Rogers was looking at his rifle, throwing it away in disgust.

Gallen was about to ask the pilot to bring it down but then saw another figure walk into the circle of light. Kenny Winter, staggering slightly from exertion, mouth hanging open, blood down his T-shirt.

'No, Kenny,' said Gallen as the Canadian walked up to the big form of David Rogers. They circled each other, arms out like wrestlers waiting for the clinch.

'Shit, don't do it, Kenny,' said Gallen, loud enough that he surprised himself. He knew who Winter was and what he'd done, but now he'd met Ryan it was different. Fighting could be left to younger men.

'Take us down.'

The Huey descended as Rogers went for Winter's wrist. Rather than pull back, Winter threw his right hand forwards, taking Rogers by surprise and allowing the Canadian to hit his opponent in the face. Flinching slightly and turning his head, Rogers stumbled and Winter was onto him, hitting the DIA man in the chest with his shoulder and toppling him.

Rogers managed to stop falling backwards directly, twisting slightly as Winter took to the ground so that Winter hit the dirt with his right shoulder, and Rogers was able to use the momentum to gain the top position.

The Huey touched the ground and Gallen jumped out as Rogers threw his right leg over Winter's hips and punched the Canadian hard in the face. Winter's head jolted back and his hands reached for Rogers' face.

'No, Kenny,' said Gallen, running to the altercation, rifle cocked. 'You don't need to—' Rifle shots cracked from the darkness. Turning back to the Huey, he saw Barrowman, staring from the helo.

Winter got a grip into Rogers' eye sockets, and the big American's fists uncurled as his hands went to save his face.

Gallen kneeled. 'Light!' he yelled over the Huey's rotors and turbo shafts.

Barrowman grabbed the hand-held searchlight from the Huey's port door, and strafed the surrounding darkness. The arcs stopped as the light fell on a man with an assault rifle. Gallen fired three rounds, and the man fled. 'Jim—get that guy,' said Gallen, turning back to Winter's fight.

The Huey lifted off with a blast of dust as Gallen got to Winter, who had turned the tables and was kneeling over David Rogers, his left hand around the man's throat and a right fist poised to strike.

'Okay, Kenny,' said Gallen, panting as the noise of the ship decreased. 'I got 'im, buddy.'

Winter looked over, paused. As he did so, Rogers' hands grabbed the back of Winter's neck, pulling the Canadian's face down fast into an upward head-butt. Stunned, Winter rolled off as Rogers—his eyes puffed and his cheeks bloodied—pounced on Winter, punching him in the carotid artery on the side of the neck. Winter's head and neck went limp momentarily as Rogers leaned in to put on a choke hold.

'Hold it,' said Gallen, standing over the American, his M4 inches from Rogers' face. This time Rogers paused, and as he did, a massive prairie-boy paw slapped into his face, the index and second fingers sinking into his eye sockets to the second knuckles.

Rogers let out a muffled scream and his hands rose immediately to stop the gouging. Winter swung his arm in a fast arc, slamming the back of Rogers' head into the dirt. The American went limp.

Winter stood, panting, blood running out of a split left eyebrow, his top lip busted and his gums bleeding above his front teeth.

Gallen walked over to David Rogers, who groaned, his eyes flickering as the brain tried to regain consciousness.

'Dude can fight,' said Winter, spitting something off his bottom lip.

Out of the darkness, Mike Ford jogged into the circle, which was now in darkness.

'Kenny?' said the Aussie, coming in closer. The faint orange line on the horizon had faded to dark blue. 'That you?'

'Nice timin', Mike,' said Winter. 'You just missed it.'

'Hah,' said Ford, laughing. 'You're a mad bastard, Winter. Still beating people up?'

'Only if the pay's right.'

The Huey hovered two hundred yards away, its searchlight holding on a man who raised his rifle. Shots rang out, spits of rock bounced up around him, and he dropped the weapon.

'The FBI gets its man,' said Winter.

'Gotta smoke?' said Ford, looking at Gallen and Winter.

'Gotta cold beer, Mike?' said Winter. 'Swap ya.'

CHAPTER 39

The darkness slowly diminished as he was borne up, faster and faster, the light coming at him like a train, and then . . . Gallen woke with a start, the bedside phone buzzing like an insect. Reaching out of the tangle of white sheets, he grabbed the handset, croaked a greeting that didn't come out properly.

It was Barrowman, wanting him to be on deck in thirty minutes.

'The fuck's the time?' said Gallen, looking around the darkened room on the third floor of one of the US embassy apartment buildings. The heavy drapes were pulled and he couldn't see his G-Shock.

'Five to seven,' said Barrowman. 'Meet you for breakfast at seven-thirty. There's a cafe downstairs.'

'Yep,' said Gallen, sitting up and rubbing his short hair.

'And, Gerry, just you, okay?'

Barrowman looked fairly chipper for a man who'd been scared shitless twelve hours earlier, thought Gallen, sitting and ordering a pot of coffee and a basket of biscuit.

'They don't do that here,' said Barrowman, open-necked shirt, sports coat and Ray-Ban aviators. 'Actually, no one eats biscuit, are you aware of that?'

Gallen settled for eggs over easy, bacon, hash browns and toast. 'That allowed?' said Gallen, as the Iraqi waitress walked away.

'We need to get focused,' said Barrowman. 'I have an eight-fifteen with Arnie Dorfmeir, the Bureau's station chief in Iraq. I'd like this to go well—he's one of the most powerful Bureau guys outside of Washington.'

'So what's he doin' in Baghdad?' said Gallen, regretting it immediately.

'This is our biggest embassy, Gerry,' said Barrowman, lowering his intensity slightly as the waitress delivered Gallen's coffee. 'More than one hundred acres, twenty-five buildings. If you're the Bureau's guy in Baghdad, you run the largest counter-terror and counter-insurgency policing operation in the world, okay? Right now, Arnie is your employer, and he is not someone you wanna play footsie with.'

'Okay,' said Gallen, pouring himself a coffee, looking for real sugar, not the synthetic crap. 'So I play nice with Arnie. What do you need from me?'

'We're in a delicate situation, what with Rogers in custody and the Agency's report on WMD perhaps not panning out.'

Gallen looked at him. 'Don't ask me to be political, Jim, 'cos that may not be to your advantage.'

Barrowman held up his hands. 'Nothing cute, just don't do anything that gets you thrown off the gig.'

'Shouldn't we be moving north?'

'Daly's covering the Mosul situation for now,' said Barrowman. 'But Arnie wants to talk before making a decision.'

'A decision?'

'We don't have a gig if Arnie is uncomfortable,' said the FBI man. 'So please, Gerry: make him comfortable?'

The FBI's Iraq station was housed in a sprawling building on the US embassy campus, decorated in what could be called bunker-chic. It was squat and heavily reliant on concrete and the meeting room they sat in looked out through blast-proof tinted glass onto the Tigris River.

Arnie Dorfmeir was early forties, of medium build, and had very intense eyes. He wore a waistcoat with his grey suit and peered over half-glasses that balanced on the end of his nose. He looked half-cop, half-lawyer, which Barrowman assured Gallen he was, having risen up through the prosecutions side of the Bureau.

'So, Mr Gallen,' Dorfmeir said, opening the first folder. 'Former captain, Force Recon, combat tours of Mindanao and Afghanistan. Silver Star, several other citations, honourable discharge. Says here you were approached three times for a promotion to DIA, and you turned it down?'

'It's such a nice sheet,' said Gallen with a smile. 'Then it turns all catty.'

Dorfmeir laughed, threw the file on the table between them and rubbed his face. 'Okay, so I have no concerns with you and this Royal Australian Navy commando—Ford, is it?'

'Mike Ford,' said Gallen. 'He's a good operator.'

'But, listen—Kenny Winter? He's a problem.'

'A problem, sir?' said Gallen.

'Interpol flag—Winter is on our list of wanteds.'

'Really?' said Gallen.

Dorfmeir opened another file. 'Sri Lankan police have a warrant for David Ellis. Five counts of murder.'

'Murder?'

'Yes, it seems he killed four people in a Colombo hotel in oh-eight, and then having taken care of the bodyguards, used a shaped charge on a hotel door, blew it off its hinges and then killed a transport magnate who was hiding inside. His name was Nitish Fernandez, better known as Dippy.'

'I see.'

'I gather from your lack of surprise that you know Mr Winter has operated as David Ellis?'

'I have no comment, sir.'

Dorfmeir stared at Gallen and then at Barrowman. 'Special Agent Barrowman has brought me up to date and I want a squad on a plane for the north as soon as possible. But I need you to help us first.'

'Help . . . you?' said Gallen, careful. 'How would I do that?'

Dorfmeir smiled and Gallen could feel Barrowman tensing.

The cells in the FBI station were clinical and clean, and were run by people in US Marshals shirts. In the antechamber that preceded the cell block, Gallen was shown into an interview room where David Rogers sat in orange coveralls, his wrists chained to a U-bolt in the concrete floor.

'David?' Gallen took a seat opposite Rogers. The Marshal closed the door as she left.

'The fuck you want, Gallen?' said the DIA man. His face looked as though an art student had made their first attempt at cubism. His eye sockets were puffed and torn, his eyeballs were red and he was missing his left incisor.

'To talk.'

'You wanna talk?' said Rogers, leaning forwards in a threat. 'Go pay a hooker. I ain't talkin' to no jarhead jackass.'

'You tried to kill me and my crew, David,' said Gallen, taking a cigarette from the breast pocket of his denim shirt. 'Wanna tell me why?'

'The fuck you think?' said Rogers, angry but his heart not in it. 'And this is a US government building, dude. Smoking ain't cool.'

Gallen lit his Marlboro, slid the pack and the disposable lighter to Rogers.

'Shee-it,' said Rogers, smiling as he nibbled a smoke out of the pack and lit up. 'This the good cop routine?'

'Ain't a cop, David,' said Gallen. 'I'm a farmer.'

Rogers laughed at the ceiling, looked back at Gallen. 'Yeah—you're a farmer like Beyoncé's a choir girl.'

'Beyoncé is a choir girl,' said Gallen, drawing on his smoke. 'Saw that in a magazine.'

Rogers looked down at his smoke. 'That boy of yours can fight.'

'Said the same about you.'

'That's Kenny Winter, right?'

'That's him.'

'Boy's got hands like a barn door,' said Rogers. 'Where you get hands like that?'

'Hauling water, baling hay, fencin'.'

Rogers smiled, nodding. 'You know how it is, Gerry. I can't talk to you.'

'You get seconded into a joint Agency–Bureau operation—as the Pentagon's guy—and suddenly you're running round with Tookie Saleh? The fuck's that about?'

Rogers looked away. 'You've been where I've been, Gerry.'

'Shooting an FBI aircraft out of the sky?' said Gallen. 'I never went there, David. Sorry.'

'You know what I mean.'

Gallen looked at Rogers, a small light dawning in the back of his mind. In his world, once you'd been indoctrinated by the spooks and the briefers, they owned you. No excuses, no ifs, buts or maybes: you rode to their orders and if you got caught, you shut your mouth like a good little trooper. What was Rogers telling him?

'Okay,' said Gallen carefully. 'You know my background. What's yours, that you know what we share?'

'Army, Bragg, SOCOM, then this place—usual shit,' shrugged Rogers.

'Then DIA?'

'Turned thirty-one, had a child on the way, they offered me an intel billet and two bars,' said Rogers, referring to the captain's insignia. 'Seemed like a good move. My wife of the time thought it would get me outta the field.'

'What was your specialty?' said Gallen, knowing that special forces soldiers were drawn into the Defense Intelligence Agency because of an expertise.

'I'm not at liberty.'

'I'm assuming it's nuclear munitions,' said Gallen.

'Assume what you want,' said Rogers. 'That's all classified.'

'While we sit here, David, we got Saleh getting his hands on a bunch of buried nukes and starting World War Three. He's already got a head start on—'

'No he don't.' Rogers shook his head.

'Sorry?'

'Tookie ain't got a head start,' said Rogers, his eyes refocusing. 'Shit, Gerry. You got the overlay, right? For the Badush blueprint?'

'The blueprint?' said Gallen.

The door swung inwards and two men swept into the room, one of them pushing a Marshal at Rogers.

'Stand down, Marine,' said a white guy in a black suit and black tie, stepping into Gallen's personal space.

'The fuck are you?' said Gallen.

'Don't concern yourself,' said the man. 'I'm here at the orders of the Secretary of Defense.'

The Marshal unlocked Rogers, who stood, rubbing his wrists.

'I don't care where you got your orders, Men in Black,' said Gallen. 'He's being held on charges of espionage and aiding the commission of a terror act. It's fairly serious, you might like to look it up?'

'I don't have to look up a damned thing, Gallen,' said the man, trying to hinder Gallen as he stood. 'The paperwork's in, this interview is over.'

The man turned to Rogers, gestured for him to go, then turned for the door himself. 'You got a little lost, didn't you, Gallen?'

'Ain't lost, pal,' said Gallen, just itching to give this dude a slap.

'You used to be a soldier,' said the man, leaving. 'Now you're some cop's bitch?'

Gallen wandered into the corridor, watched the Man in Black pushing Rogers down the hall. Barrowman emerged from the observation room, stood beside Gallen.

'You hear that?' said Gallen. 'I mean about Badush?'

'Yeah,' said Barrowman, keying his cell phone. 'I heard that about the overlay too. Maybe we got more time than I thought.'

CHAPTER 40

Mosul Airport loomed pale brown through the Mesopotamian haze as the King Air 200 lined up for its final approach.

'This asset of yours?' said Gallen, still trying to get answers from Barrowman. 'Why are we trusting him?'

'He made some big calls, back in the INVO days,' said Barrowman, allowing Mike Ford to tweak the rear fasteners on his Kevlar vest. 'They were the right calls.'

'Bet Rogers has a similar sheet.' Gallen looked across the aisle at the FBI man.

'Rogers wasn't my guy,' said Barrowman. 'He's Pentagon, just like Daly. On a multi-party operation like this, I'm told who I work with.'

'You ordered to work with me?'

Barrowman smiled. 'You were needs-basis, time-sensitive.'

'I was bottom of the bucket?'

'No offence,' said Barrowman. 'It suited me to have a private operator with no official connections to the Pentagon.'

Gallen nodded. 'So you knew the military side of this wasn't quite right?'

'I knew the Pentagon and FBI have different goals, lots of unshared history.'

'You sound like a politician, Jim,' said Gallen, watching the small farms pass under the King Air as they descended. 'You knew nothing about Rogers' role?'

'Nothing I could stand on.'

'The fuck does that mean?' said Gallen, annoyed.

'It means you get assigned, you're told the mission, and who you work with is not about your personal feelings, Gerry,' said Barrowman. 'I thought with your background you'd understand that.'

'So you had a feeling about him?'

'He was dropped in late, and his intel was Saleh-focused, it wasn't about the al-Haqs, in my opinion.'

'So?' said Gallen.

'So, if you come from the al-Haq angle, you're talking about money trails, Singapore bank accounts, Delaware fronts, end-user certificates and lots of Jordanian incorporations. But if you have insights into Saeed Saleh and his family, you're talking about things you'd only know if—perhaps—you saw things from a Saddam perspective.'

'You mean, Saeed Saleh was a spy for the US?' said Gallen.

'Doesn't always work that way around, Gerry,' said Barrowman.

'Who's Rogers working for?'

Barrowman shrugged. 'You tell me.'

'I asked what his speciality was when he was plucked out of SOCOM and promoted into DIA.'

'I heard. What were you getting at?'

'Defense Intelligence Agency needs people who specialise—in languages, banking, sigint, encryption, nukes and what have you. He said his was classified.'

Barrowman nodded. 'I need you to meet Bazi and get focused. If Tookie Saleh is around this area, then people are going to start shutting their mouths, getting scared. We need to stay ahead of that.'

A young man was waiting outside the main terminal building when Gallen, Barrowman, Winter and Ford emerged into the heat and dust of the Kurdish city.

'I'm Loran,' said the kid. 'Bazi is this way.'

Loran led them to a white Toyota people mover in the middle of the car park.

'Wait here,' said Barrowman. 'Shouldn't take long.'

The young man frisked Barrowman very quickly, took his Glock and ushered the FBI man into the side door of the van.

Gallen bummed a smoke from Ford, accepted the light. 'Thought you were in Honolulu?'

'I was,' said Ford, smiling under the dark wraparound shades. 'The salvage company took a gig in Umm Qasr, clearing ordnance out of a waterway.'

'They okay about you being here?'

'Don't know,' said Ford as he opened a water bottle. 'The joys of management, mate.'

'They got a crew in from Hawaii?' said Winter. 'Couldn't find any divers in Europe?'

Ford chuckled, flicked at his smoke. 'There's a lot of clean-up work right now that the Pentagon's keeping away from the Frogs and Krauts.'

'Why?' said Winter.

'There's a ton of unexploded ordnance from the Iraqi side that's filled with Yankee goodies. Pentagon doesn't want the NATO partners seeing it.'

Gallen looked at the Aussie. 'For instance?'

'For instance, the Europeans were having great fun finding the cache of night-vision goggles made in Texas, or the C-and-C systems in the western desert that were built in California for the US Navy.'

'You're kidding me,' said Winter.

'Now we're pulling this stuff up from the shipping lanes, but the DIA boys are straight in there, taking it away,' said Ford.

'What is it?' said Gallen. 'What's DIA hiding?'

'This is on the QT, okay?' said Ford. 'I signed their cone of silence forms.'

'Loose lips,' said Gallen.

Ford looked around. 'This FBI dick cool?'

'No, so talk while he's having his orgy.'

'I was drinking with a US Navy captain in UQ—he was telling me they'd pulled a Scud out of the main shipping channel two weeks ago. It'd been fired at Allied shipping during Iraqi Freedom.'

'Lucky for crap Iraqi technology,' said Winter.

'That's the thing, Kenny,' said Ford. 'This captain bloke's telling me it wasn't Iraqi technology at all.'

'No?'

Ford laughed. 'These Scuds have Goodyear guidance arrays in them, mate!'

'What's that?' said Winter, aware that the Australian was a comms specialist.

'It's the guidance system in all the best American cruise missiles and ICBMs,' said Ford. 'It's gyroscopic inertia technology which creates radar pictures of where it's been aimed, while its flying. Totally classified. And it's installed in a Scud. A frigging Scud missile.'

There was silence. Winter stared at Gallen.

'What have I walked into?' said Ford, cottoning. 'Come on, guys, what's wrong?'

Gallen's ears roared. Saddam operating a secret nuclear missile program was one thing, but if it included US technology, the scenario had become more complicated and potentially catastrophic. 'Kenny, can I borrow your phone?'

Winter handed it over. 'What're we dealin' with here, boss?'

'I don't know why I didn't do this two days ago,' said Gallen, punching in a number for international directory. 'I need a number for Timeless Solutions in Jakarta,' said Gallen, sucking on the cigarette and looking at the white van, seething. 'Yes, the Indonesian Jakarta. And yes, connect me, please.'

Gallen walked in circles in the car park as the phone was answered at Timeless Solutions.

'Gerry Gallen for Pete Morton,' said Gallen. 'It's urgent.'

An American voice picked up. 'Gerry, how's Mosul Airport? Warm, but not too much, right?'

'Okay, you know where I am,' said Gallen, looking around the car park, wondering if Daly and Lang were also picking up the call. 'I need a quick check on a dude who wants to work with me. He's Defense Intelligence Agency, but I can't make sense of his MOS.'

'Name,' said Morton, a former recon captain who'd gone into the intelligence game and now operated corporate fronts, doing deniable things for governments.

'Rogers,' said Gallen. 'David Rogers, rose to captain in the army.'

Gallen listened to the keystrokes. Like most intelligence operators, Morton had become more expert with a keyboard than a gun.

'Won't let me in,' said Morton. 'He's obviously heavy, so let me try something else.'

'What?' said Gallen, nervous about being tracked so quickly on the cell phone.

'I've got a back entrance into DoD. I use the Tricare database.' Morton was referring to the Department of Defense health insurance fund.

'I need it fast, Pete,' said Gallen. 'I'm standing in a car park.'

'Okay,' said Morton. 'Tricare has Captain Rogers as an 89A with an ASI of F1.'

Gallen knew the last bit because he'd held the same Additional Skills Identifier when he was in the Marines. An F1 designation meant you'd qualified at Fort Bragg in special forces intelligence; it meant you got to sit in the big tent, listening to assholes talk about strategic objectives. Then you were the one who wandered into the hills, your men complaining about having to sleep in the snow. But he had no idea what the 89A designation meant.

'What's that MOS, Pete?' said Gallen.

'Just looking it up,' said Morton. 'Here it is. Okay, so looks like our man is a specialist in ammunition stock control and accounting.'

'What?' said Gallen, too loud. 'The fuck is that?'

'You know,' said Morton. 'Make sure that when the manifest says there's twenty nukes on base, there's not nineteen. Head shed gets particular about that stuff.'

'Nukes?' said Gallen, pulse banging in his temples. 'What's nukes got to do with it?'

'That's what they do, Gerry,' said Morton. 'And besides, there's a medical note on his Tricare file.'

'What does it say?'

'The insurer requires six-monthly radiation checks,' said Morton.

'Oh, shit,' said Gallen.

'Yeah,' said Morton. 'Fuck that for a game of soldiers.'

*

The Nissan Patrol followed the white Toyota along the Iraqi Highway 1 north-west out of Mosul, Winter at the wheel. The atmosphere was tense, Gallen sitting in the front passenger seat, M4 carbine between his legs, Barrowman and Ford in the back.

'I didn't tell you because it shouldn't have made any difference,' said Barrowman. 'We've been chasing down a network for years. Rogers is a symptom, not the cause.'

'I need to know,' said Gallen, turning and looking at Barrowman. 'Why is there Goodyear guidance systems in a Scud missile? The fuck is that about?'

Barrowman flushed slightly. 'That's embarrassing is what that's about.'

'So?'

Barrowman cleared his throat. 'You remember when the Berlin Wall came down and the Cold War ended?'

'Sure,' said Gallen. He was in his last year of high school, had got his offer from the University of South Dakota. A hockey scholarship . . . and all the while, he was waiting to graduate so he could join the Marines.

'The Pentagon decided to scrap a highly effective medium-range missile series called the Pershings.'

'I remember them,' said Winter. 'Kept Europe safe.'

'We scrapped them, burned them out with their own propellant systems down at Longhorn, in Texas.'

'So what was the problem?' said Gallen, flicking his smoke out the window, checking the sky for gunships.

'Pentagon accountants realised these Pershings contained hundreds of millions of dollars worth of guidance systems from a company called Goodyear Aerospace.'

'The arrays?' said Ford.

'Yeah,' said Barrowman. 'When a missile leaves the atmosphere, the arrays can fix on the target and guide the missile by manipulating its vanes as it picks up speed on the downward trajectory.'

'So they save these Goodyears?' said Gallen.

'Stockpiled them for reuse.'

'So?' said Winter.

'They also saved the warheads. These were the W85 warheads, the ones that could flatten Kiev with a single missile strike.'

'Lots of power?' said Winter.

'So much that the Pentagon decided to reuse them in the B61 gravity bomb—it's a throwback to Little Boy, except more than twice the power.'

'Where does Rogers come in?' said Gallen.

'The gravity bombs were deployed in a strange way—analysts of the time didn't understand it, and I still don't get it.'

'What?' said Gallen.

'They were deployed at Incirlik Air Base, in southern Turkey,' said Barrowman. 'They were a gift from President Clinton, who knew the Turks were worried about US attempts to bring Iran back into the fold. The B61 bombs were their insurance policy, their big stick to shake if Tehran ever got close to a nuke.'

'They still there?' said Winter, spitting out the window as farm land flashed past.

'We don't know,' said Barrowman.

'You don't know what?' said Gallen.

'The deployment was split into two: at one facility at the air base, you have forty B61s for use by the Turkish military. There's also fifty of these nukes for use by the US Air Force.'

'So there's ninety of them?' said Gallen.

Barrowman shrugged. 'In ninety-nine, when the UNSCOM weapons inspectors had been kicked out of Iraq, Saddam's political adviser had a great plan. He thought that instead of trying to build a nuclear weapons program, perhaps Iraq could acquire someone else's.'

'What happened?'

'The political adviser was Saeed Saleh. He kept alive Group 5 from the dismantled PC-3 program, and started a series of clandestine discussions with a hardline group in the Pentagon. They found common ground.'

'What?' said Gallen, surprised.

'With Iraq disarmed, there were people in the Joint Chiefs who wanted to ensure that Iran didn't upset the balance of power.'

'So the Iraqis got the nuclear bombs?' said Winter.

'How did they get the B61 bombs off an air force base, out of Turkey, and into Iraq?' said Gallen. 'Shit, Jim—this is too much.'

'They needed a true believer, someone who would march to their orders, work with the Iraqis.'

'And?'

'And a person who was a nuclear weapons verifier.'

'Someone with an 89A MOS,' said Gallen, almost to himself.

'They found David Rogers,' said Barrowman. 'And the funny thing is, the air force manifests still show there's fifty nukes at Incirlik Air Base.'

'How wrong are they?' said Winter.

'We believe they're out by a half,' said Barrowman. 'This cache could flatten every major city in the Middle East in one afternoon.'

CHAPTER 41

The white Toyota people mover stopped on a rise that overlooked a tiny village. Gallen emerged from the Patrol and walked behind Barrowman to the Toyota, where a middle-aged local man with a camel face lit a cigarette.

'Bazi,' said Barrowman, with a distinct lack of intimacy, 'this is Gerry, a security contractor who's working with me.'

Bazi nodded, avoided eye contact and ignored Gallen's outstretched hand.

'I show you, yes, Jim?' said Bazi. 'And then you go, I am no more to say, okay?'

'Sure, Bazi,' said Barrowman, fishing a Bears cap from his jacket pocket, pulling it down against the afternoon sun.

They followed Bazi down to the village, a walk of a hundred and fifty yards across dust and rocks, past flocks of sheep and goats.

'See any pasture?' said Winter, at Gallen's shoulder. 'What're they grazin' out here? Two head per acre?'

Gallen looked around, seeing bare ground with a few shrubs growing out of the rocks. As he did a casual count of the stock, he saw something in the distance: a series of large concrete ramparts rising above the horizon formed by a small saddle.

'What's that?' said Gallen.

'Badush Dam,' said Ford, raising his map.

Gallen had asked Winter and Ford to stow the rifles, so they entered the village with pistols under their shirts, but no display of gun power. The main street was bare and featured roadside shops that were hard to tell apart from the dwellings. Women crouched on front doorsteps making bread and cooking; kids ran around with their dogs; battered Toyota pick-ups puttered down the street, the locals not even interested in the foreigners.

There was a red Toyota van parked outside a shop that looked like a post office. Barrowman asked Gallen to keep his people outside, then Gallen and Barrowman followed Bazi into the store, took a seat in the darkness.

'Coffee?' said Bazi, pointing at Gallen.

'Sure,' said Gallen, lighting a smoke and looking around. There were boxes and crates stacked around the room, a small kitchenette along one wall and a series of weathered posters that displayed package sizes and weights along with pictures of how to properly package something fragile.

'The fuck is this place?' said Gallen.

'He's a local businessman, used to be the postmaster,' said Barrowman. 'Bazi has something to show us.'

A man in his forties came to the table, put a pot of coffee and four cups down, then took a seat. Gallen watched him pour the coffees, and noticed there was no introduction.

For twenty minutes, they sat around a table while Bazi had a conversation with the owner. It appeared to be going nowhere. When it became animated, as only conversations between Arabs could become animated, Gallen noticed two sets of eyes peering around a doorway. He smiled, gave a small thumbs-up. A face appeared, that of a boy, perhaps fifteen. He smiled and Gallen gave him a wink.

Another face appeared, this one younger, perhaps ten or eleven.

The boys, intrigued, walked into the store, pretending to be doing something useful, but really just interested in the visitors.

The owner caught Gallen's eye and swivelled, sending a blast of invective at the two boys. They ran back to their doorway, and continued to spy.

Bazi leaned into Gallen. 'Our host say he's sorry for the rudeness of his sons.'

'Tell him they're fine,' laughed Gallen as the kids pulled faces at him.

As they hit the street again, Ford dragged Gallen to Winter. 'Got a chopper, boss,' said Winter, scanning the clear blue skies. 'Little Bird with a serious rig under the fuselage.'

'US?' said Gallen.

'Not many Iraqi Little Birds,' said Winter. 'Mike, you seen any?'

Ford made a face. 'They're Pentagon and Agency, far as I know.'

They moved onto the dirt street, Gallen asking Barrowman to stay closer to the shop awnings, maybe walk back to the vehicles via the back alleys.

'Actually, Bazi has to take care of some business,' said Barrowman. 'We'll wait for him at the Patrol.'

Winter pulled some bottles of water from the Patrol and they lit their smokes. Gallen grabbed his binoculars from his backpack and glassed Badush Dam. Its giant concrete bollards were visible from his angle: there were four of them, spanning what looked like about two hundred yards, east–west. In his special forces days, such estimates were drilled into them: if you couldn't photograph it, you sketched it, and if you sketched it, you included a scale; if you didn't know the scale, you used your damned brain. Gallen always remembered that last bit, because in the Basic Recon Course there was an instructor who referred to candidates' brains as their 'pea-sized'.

Gallen handed the glasses to Ford, who'd been plotting their whereabouts with the Tactical NAV app on his iPhone.

'Okay,' said Ford, looking through the Nikons. 'I make it four klicks to the dam, and dam's about two hundred, two-twenty metres bearing east–west.'

'Gotcha,' said Gallen. 'So what's with the map? This village don't exist?'

Ford passed his iPhone to Gallen, locked at the digital map-ref for their location along with an aerial photograph. 'That's the cords, right there.'

Gallen looked at the map reference, with its satellite picture. There was pictorial evidence of the tiny settlement they'd just visited. But there was no mention of it on the USGS map.

Barrowman sat in the front passenger seat of the Patrol, yelling into a cell phone, voice raised against the bad connection. 'No, it's Special Agent Barrowman,' he yelled. 'I need the intelligence section in Quantico. Who's this?'

The FBI man gave up, walked to the front of the 4x4 to join the soldiers.

'Seen this?' said Gallen, passing him Ford's iPhone. 'There's a small town here.'

Ford shook the USGS map. 'US government says it doesn't exist.'

Barrowman cleared his throat. 'I think it started life as a worker's camp, for work on the dam. Maybe it's never been gazetted, or whatever they do up here.'

A sudden sound made Winter pick up his rifle, put up a finger for silence. Retreating behind the hood of the Patrol, they waited to hear the sound again, looked across the terrain. It sounded like a girl or someone in pain. Winter crept to the back of the Patrol with Ford, moving together like a centipede.

Gallen lifted his head over the level of the hood, looked across the ground to a line of scrub eighty yards away. The noise came again, and then a movement, a blur of bodies, away from the bushes.

Gallen caught Winter's eye, gave him the nod, and the Canadian and Aussie moved from their cover, across the naked ground to the bushes. Telling Barrowman to stay put, Gallen checked his Heckler & Koch and circled the opposite way, from the hood of the Patrol.

Pausing at the scrub, Gallen kneeled. He was now thirty yards north of Winter and Ford, who pushed the scrub back carefully, looking for a clear entry. A low thromp sounded and Gallen turned his head: a single black helicopter flew northwards over the dam area, the sound of it bouncing off the water, amplifying the noise.

Winter gave the thumbs-up to enter the scrub, and Gallen moved into the area at the same time as Ford. The ground fell away, through more scrub, and Gallen trod carefully, his pistol held in front of him in cup-and-saucer grip, ready for any surprises. To his right, he heard the sound again, and this time it came through clearer as a child's laugh. There was a crash of branches and the fall of adult feet, and Gallen saw a blur of action through the scrub. Winter and Ford on the move.

Gallen sped down the slope, staying vigilant but trying to move across to where Winter was running. Almost falling into a dry gully, Gallen realised he was in a clearing. To his right stood Winter, a sweat stain down the middle of his dark military shirt. Ford was on his knees, frisking someone.

Jogging up the gully towards his men, bouncing off the rocks, Gallen got the idea that this wasn't just a dry river bed: it seemed like some kind of refuse pile, tailings from a mine perhaps.

Winter and Ford were on a flat concrete platform when Gallen arrived, panting. Winter's rifle was now at his side and Ford was looking sheepish. Standing there were the two boys Gallen had seen at the old post office. They beamed as Gallen gasped for breath.

'Hey, fellas,' said Gallen. 'Thought you was someone else.'

'Sorry 'bout that, boss,' said Winter. 'My nerves playin' up.'

Gallen nodded, since his were too. Once you'd done a combat tour in this part of the world, you didn't let anything go; couldn't give anyone the benefit of the doubt. If someone was spying on you from the bushes, you got to the bottom of that real quick. Gallen looked around. 'Kenny, you see that helo?'

'Heard it, sure,' said Winter.

Gallen nodded. 'How about getting up to the Patrol, hiding it somewhere? Hide Barrowman while you're at it.'

'Can do, boss,' said Winter, stowing his rifle and moving back into the scrub.

'So, boys,' Gallen said, looking down. In his experience it was worth getting children and mothers onside in a combat zone, especially where you lacked language skills and cultural relevance. 'You go for the Giants, right?' he said, pointing at the older boy's NY Giants shirt.

'Giant are champion,' said the kid.

'Sure they are,' said Gallen, biting a smoke out of his pack. 'So why they let Kareem McKenzie go? I loved that guy.'

The boy shrugged and Gallen offered him his water bottle, looking over the boy's shoulder. The source of the rubble in the gully became clear. There was a collapsed pile of dirt, clay and concrete which was in the process of being grown over. The concrete pad they were standing on was obviously once part of the ruined structure. Looking further around the demolition zone, Gallen could see deep bulldozer tracks, now dried in the sun and overgrown with weeds and scrubby trees.

'Used to be something here,' said Gallen, offering a smoke to Ford. 'Been demolished.'

'I know,' said Ford. 'We ran down an old driveway to get here.'

Gallen faced the boy. 'What is this?'

'Police house,' said the boy, sweeping his arm backwards at the rubble.

'Why is it . . .?' Gallen made a gesture with his hands suggesting it had been blown up.

The boy shrugged. 'War come.'

'The war come,' said Gallen, 'so police house *boom*? From Yankee bomb?'

The boy looked at his little brother. 'Maybe not from Yankee.'

'No?' said Gallen.

The boy shook his head. 'Maybe not police house.'

Gallen nodded, looked at Ford, whose eyebrow was rising. He looked at the kid.

'So, not police house?'

'Maybe for dam,' said the boy, pointing towards the Badush Dam. 'I show.'

'No, no, it's okay,' said Gallen, trying to stop the kid. 'I know where the dam is.'

'Wait, boss.' Ford held out his hand. 'He's going to show us something else.'

The boy made a come-on sign with his hand to Ford, and the pair led the way towards the rubble pile. Gallen walked with the smaller boy, wondering what was happening. The helo sound got louder and Gallen wanted to be back with Winter and Barrowman.

Ducking under small trees and dancing over bracken, Gallen followed the two boys across the rubble until they were walking along a slit trench.

'Where we goin', Mike?'

'Don't know, boss,' said Ford, as the trench floor got lower. The boy in front of Gallen ducked and crawled sideways. Looking around, sure it was a bad idea, Gallen followed into the crawl space. After a crawl across dried clay that lasted for thirty seconds, they came out in a concrete bunker, the first signs of light coming from a stick with a rag around it lit by the older boy.

'What's your name?' said Gallen, looking around the space.

'Asaf,' said the older boy. 'You want see?'

'Sure,' said Gallen.

They walked down a tunnel for five minutes, the angle taking them deeper, the atmosphere becoming colder. The structure was high enough to allow trucks through it, and perhaps wide enough for two trucks to pass.

'What you think this is?' said Gallen, turning to Ford, his eyes wide in the dim glow of Asaf's burning rag.

'It's a freight entrance,' said Ford.

'For what?'

'Kid said the dam,' said Ford. 'It seems to be running in that direction.'

'So Saddam's people build a dam, and hide the freight entrance to it under a police station?'

'And then they demolish the police station and fill in the freight road,' said Ford. 'I don't get it.'

Gallen turned to follow Asaf and almost walked into his back. In front of them was a wall of clay and concrete rubble.

'What's this?' said Gallen.

Asaf shrugged. 'War start.'

Gallen looked up at the demolition job that had forever sealed the freight road into the Badush Dam by dropping the roof of the tunnel. He was getting a very bad feeling about this place.

'I bet the war started.' He kicked at the loose concrete. 'But what was Saddam trying to finish?'

CHAPTER 42

The clamour started as Gallen and Ford broke through the scrub at the top of the slope and looked around for Winter and the Patrol. The 4x4 was not on the cleared space on the rise, but they could hear the sound of machine gun fire coming from the village with no name.

'Minigun,' said Ford, checking his M4. 'I'd know that sound anywhere.'

Ducking back into the scrub, they searched the sky, back to back, looking for the threat. There was a small saddle between their position and the village, it seemed to be where the sound of the rotor blades and gunfire was coming from. As he was about to suggest that they break cover, move closer to the village, a bunch of goats sprinted across the bare saddle, running away from the village.

'What's this?' said Gallen, and then he was standing. Following the goats were two boys, running for their lives.

'What the fuck?' said Ford, moving in front of Gallen. 'That's Asaf!'

Gallen brought up his Nikons, let them auto-focus. 'Running from somethin',' said Gallen. 'They looked terrified. But we can't go down there.'

'No?' said Ford.

'No, Mike. We have to link up with Winter and Barrowman.'
Gallen brought the Nikons to his eyes again. 'Besides, they'll make it
to the tunnel.'

'I don't think so,' said Ford, standing. Gallen took his eyes off the
binoculars and watched the Little Bird crest the saddle and swoop
down on the boys.

'Screw this,' said the Australian, shifting to a slightly flatter area,
kneeling in a marksman's stance.

Gallen went to grab him, but decided against it. They were going
to give away their position at some point regardless, so why not do
it for a couple of kids?

The Little Bird came in fast, but Asaf dived behind a large rock
about fifty yards short of the tunnel entrance, dragged his brother in
with him. The helo overran the rock and banked in a long arc, almost
over Gallen.

'Gotcha,' mumbled Ford, and he pumped five bursts of three-shot
fire into the open side door of the Little Bird. The man looking down
on them expressed surprised for one second through his clear goggles
before his head jerked back and he slumped in his harness.

'Shit,' said Gallen, pointing at the tunnel complex. 'We're
blown.'

Making their way down the embankment, Gallen kept one eye
on his footing and another on the Little Bird, which was locked in
a lazy banked arc, the two pilots probably trying for a reading on
where the incoming was coming from.

'Let's go,' said Gallen as he reached the old freight road to the
false police station.

'Where?' said Ford.

'Tunnel,' said Gallen.

'See you there,' said Ford, veering off into the scrub. 'I'm getting
those kids.'

Gallen tried to stop, slid and almost fell over, the strain triggering
another tear in his wound. Limping towards the scrub, he tried to
take control. 'Mike!'

But the Aussie continued to crash through the scrub.

'Mike!' he yelled.

'See you at the tunnel, boss,' said the navy commando.

Swearing to himself, Gallen followed him into the scrub.

The Little Bird came around for another shot as Gallen crossed the dry creek bed. The gunship was now travelling slower, and had ignored the boys for a few seconds. They were on a sweep for gunmen, and Gallen could see the minigun swivelling beneath the fuselage in anticipation of the pilot squeezing the trigger on his cyclic.

Ducking beside an overhang, Gallen waited for them to fly over, but the helo slowed further, almost hovering, so close that Gallen could feel the down draught and smell the kerosene fumes. It moved out of sight and Gallen ran again, for where the boys should be. As he crested a small rise, he almost ran into Asaf, who was panicked, panting with fear.

'Help, mister,' he said, and then his little brother was hiding behind Gallen too. It was his worst nightmare: war was an adult business—children and battle didn't mix.

Leading them back to the rock overhang, Gallen kept his eyes on the sky, waiting for the gunship to come back. Now it seemed to be hovering just over the saddle, waiting for a sighting. Telling the boys to stay put, he ran over the crest, M4 ready, as the screaming sound of the minigun opened up at a part of the gully where the trees were larger and hung over the dry creek bed.

'Mike,' yelled Gallen, scrabbling down the slope as the helo flared outwards and in a tight circle, pounding a part of the gully with a long volley of fire that lit up the air with the comet-like flash of tracer rounds. 'Shit,' he said. He assumed they had Ford trapped. Kneeling, he measured up a shot that he thought could only be eighty yards, but with the shortened barrel of the M4 he wouldn't have a lot of accuracy.

The door gunner was dead, still hanging in his harness, but the pilots were harder to see, and with the sun reflecting off the cockpit glass, Gallen decided to put his remaining rounds into the Little Bird's fuel tanks and engine bay.

Switching the weapon to single shot, Gallen calmed his breathing and looked down the sights. As he did he saw movement from the gully. Easing the rifle from his face, he looked down and saw Mike Ford scrambling up the slope.

'Mike,' said Gallen, waving at him. 'We're up here.'

Ford's face scanned the bush and, settling on Gallen, started climbing towards him. Ford was twenty feet away when the Little Bird dipped its rotors and banked.

'Oh, fuck,' said Gallen, as the helo aimed at him. Ducking into the thicker scrub, he aimed his M4 at the helo but it raced over both of them and headed for the tunnel entrance.

'Where they going?' said Ford, breathless as he got to Gallen.

'Don't know,' said Gallen, pointing. 'Got the boys stashed behind that rock.'

'No you haven't,' said Ford. 'Look.'

Following his finger, Gallen turned and saw what had made Ford's face drop. The boys had broken from the rock overhang and had made a run for the slit trench. The pilots in the Little Bird had seen them, and were giving chase, the boys scrabbling like lunatics across the broken lumps of concrete.

Ford took a standing marksman stance, shot at the back of the helo until his breech clicked empty. 'Shit,' he said, throwing the M4 aside and pulling out a Beretta pistol as he started running.

Gallen limped along behind the Aussie, knowing he couldn't keep up and knowing it was hopeless. The first shots from the minigun came in a two-second burst, but Gallen couldn't see if the boys had made the trench. The concrete and rocks of the rubble pile flew up like confetti from the hundred rounds per second, some of the concrete being hit so hard that a pall of grey dust arose over the slit trench.

Then it stopped, and the aircraft swivelled on its axis, pointing back to the clearing where the Nissan Patrol had reappeared.

'Look, boss,' said Ford, and Gallen saw it too. A large blond man in a pair of jeans and dark shirt stood on the roof of the Patrol, something sitting on his shoulder.

'Fuck,' said Ford, a smile on his face. 'Mad bastard's got an RPG.'

As he said it a light grey smoke trail wormed through the still air, terminating at the engine bay behind the Little Bird cabin. The gunship didn't erupt like they do in the movies: the grenade expanded, blowing out the fuselage panels and cutting loose one of the five rotors, which let go with such force that it sailed half a mile through the air. The engine complained loudly as it broke, the whistling of the turbo carrying on long after the helo gained terminal speed into the gully below. When the Little Bird hit the dry creek bed, it broke again, bounced and spewed jet fuel into the air, making the valley smell like a commercial airport.

Looking around, Gallen saw that Ford had already taken off, chasing after the boys. 'Come on, boss,' said the Aussie. 'There'll be more of those.'

Gallen followed, his thigh complaining at every step. He forced himself over broken ground and up towards the slit trench that marked the secret entrance to the tunnel.

Looking over the edge of the trench, Gallen dreaded what he'd see. He wasn't sure he could handle the sight of an injured child. Then he let out the breath he was holding. Ford was helping the younger of the boys out of the hole.

'He's lucky,' said Ford, passing the kid up to Gallen. 'Took a sliver of concrete in the eye, but he'll live.'

There was a rudimentary medic's kit in the town, and it was brought down to the old post office for Ford to use on the kid. He worked through the late afternoon and into the evening, patching up the eye and ensuring it wouldn't infect.

'Bazi,' said Ford, as he washed up, 'tell your friend his son is going to be healthy, but he has to wash that eye out with saline twice a day, okay?'

Bazi relayed this to the postmaster, then nodded at Ford.

'I'm leaving one bottle, but he'll have to get another big bottle from the hospital.'

Bazi conveyed the message and got into a longer discussion with the postmaster, who picked up his son, kissed him on the bandaged head and carried him down a hallway.

'Pawan wants to speak with you,' said Bazi.

Ford looked at Gallen, who nodded. Pawan returned to the room, handed a cardboard tube to Ford, nodded at the Aussie to open it.

Bazi spoke with Pawan, then turned to Ford. 'He says a long time ago, the adviser to Saddam—the dog Saleh—was travelling to Badush Dam once a week. The Kurdish freedom fighters tried to bomb him on the road into the workers' camp, and although they failed, someone picked up this tube and other papers from the destroyed car.'

Ford took the lid off the tube and drew out a roll of paper.

'Pawan says that if you're interested in the dam and the tunnels, then you might be interested in this,' said Bazi. 'He says it is yours: a gift for looking after his son.'

Ford smiled, bowed slightly to Pawan, and then unfurled the roll. It was a heavy tracing paper of the kind used by draughtsmen. Barrowman hurried to his side, and Gallen stood behind Ford's chair. The paper was covered in diagrams and explanations in Arabic that meant nothing.

'This is amazing,' said Barrowman, reaching for the sheet of paper.

'What is it?' said Winter.

'It's the overlay to the blueprint,' said Barrowman. 'It's the key to the Baathists' arsenal.'

CHAPTER 43

As Gallen rolled up the overlay and put it back in the tube, a hurried knock came at Pawan's door. A young man stormed in, jabbered something hysterical at Pawan, and ran out again.

'The federal police are on their way,' said Bazi, looking worried.

'You want us to report the downed helicopter?' said Barrowman. 'Might take some pressure off you.'

Bazi shook his head too hard. 'No, you not understand: federal police work for the Americans. They are here to kidnap someone, maybe take the ransom to catch the shooters?'

Gallen looked at Pawan. 'Thanks for your hospitality, sir.'

Calling the rest of the men onto the front porch, Gallen looked down the street to where two white Nissan Patrols were stopped outside someone's house. The yelling that carried across the still evening air was in a language that Gallen did not understand, but he got the distinct impression it included the sentense: *The Americans who shot the helicopter are up the street!*

Pawan joined them as citizens emerged onto the street to see what the commotion was about. He looked Gallen in the eye, and jingled his keys.

'Get in Pawan's van,' said Bazi. 'And stay down.'

Sliding the door back as Pawan got into the driver's seat, Gallen found an open area strewn with large canvas mail bags. He slid under one as Barrowman, Ford and Winter joined him. The van fired to life and before Ford could slide the side door shut, they were accelerating up the dirt street.

Dim lights flashed by, and then Pawan made a sharp right-hand turn and accelerated in a way that would have seemed extreme in Casper, but which might be normal in northern Iraq. The van gained speed, and Gallen saw Winter's head poke out from under the mail bags.

'Where we going?' said Winter, and Pawan yelled from the front seat, 'Down, down!'

The van struggled for traction on the dirt as Pawan changed down from third to second and hit the brakes. Then he was swearing and the van was sliding to a halt. Through thin fabric Gallen could see red and blue lights flashing and cops telling Pawan to do something. The door opened and Pawan's voice was now coming from outside.

Prodding Winter in the back, and then Ford, Gallen eased his P9 from his waistband. The side windows of the van were panelled over so Gallen waited for the side door to slide back or the rear loading door to be raised. Either way, he thought he could make out no more than two cop voices and the lights didn't look saturated enough for there to be more than one vehicle. Winter raised his head, checked his Beretta, gave Gallen a wink. Ford duck-walked to the rear door, as Gallen aimed at the side entry. They waited in the dark, the lights casting a strange disco effect, as Pawan's voice carried through the van. Who knew one man could talk so much?

Gallen's heart raced: he knew they'd be able to take down these cops, but they'd have to shoot to do it and then they'd be fugitives in a foreign country.

Pawan's voice grew louder, and then he was leaning back into the driver's area of the van, grabbing a packet of cigarettes. The men talked while Gallen's guts churned, and then they could smell cigarettes being smoked.

'You want this to end,' whispered Winter, fingers wrapping and unwrapping around the stock of his pistol, 'just let me know.'

Gallen nodded, kept his ear to the sliding door and his Heckler & Koch raised. Sweat ran down his face as the police finished their cigarettes. A light filled the rear window of the postal van and they ducked instinctively. The cops' voices carried down the side of the van as they moved to question the next vehicle, one of the cops slamming his open hand on Pawan's van as he walked past.

As Pawan took the driver's seat again, a cop stood at the rear window. Gallen froze. The cop looked him in the eye, craned his neck and moved closer to the rear window of the postal van.

'Gimme the word, boss,' whispered Winter, coiled in the darkness.

Gallen tried to whisper but could only croak. 'Wait.'

The cop's face almost touched the glass and Gallen could smell the gun oil of Winter's pistol, raised and primed to shoot.

His pulse roared in his temples, he held his breath and the cop's hands rose to his face, touched at his beard. And then the cop was preening, turning his face slightly and lovingly stroking his facial hair.

Pawan put the van in gear and said his farewells to the other cop, while Gallen sagged in the back, his heart palpitating. 'Shit.'

Winter's breath whistled out of him in a long hiss of relaxation. 'Mirror glass,' said the Canadian as they accelerated out of the town. 'Almost the last thing that dude ever saw.'

Gallen took a shower and emerged into his fourth floor room at the Nineveh International Hotel, which looked out over the lights of Mosul. Glancing at his G-Shock, he saw it had turned nine-thirty pm. Pulling on his jeans and a new sweatshirt he'd bought from a store across the road, he padded into the hallway and knocked at the room three doors down.

'You're late,' said Barrowman, drying his hair as he walked towards a table in the middle of his large suite.

'I was sulking about the smaller room,' he said.

'Beer, boss?' said Winter, leaning into Barrowman's fridge.

'Any Miller?' said Gallen, taking a seat at the round table.

'Heineken, Carlsberg, Stella,' said Winter. 'Euro shit.'

'Heinie,' said Gallen.

'Rum and Coke,' said Ford, who'd had a shave for the first time that Gallen had ever witnessed.

'No one drinks rum and Coke,' said the Canadian. 'Can do a Jim Beam?'

'Can we just get started?' said Barrowman, looking stressed. 'Sorry, but I need to have a plan.'

Winter joined them, putting the drinks and a bowl of peanuts on the table.

'I used the hotel business centre and blew this up to its original size.' Barrowman pointed at the dark blueprint he'd recreated from four quarters of photocopy paper. 'It's now the right size for the overlay.'

Spread across the top of the photocopies, the overlay and blueprint together looked like a complete document.

'I asked the concierge and he translated some of the notes on the overlay, but it's actually quite simple,' said Barrowman. 'It seems that Operation Lightning was centred on a storage facility hidden beneath Badush Dam.'

'What?' said Gallen. 'Under the powerhouse?'

Barrowman shook his head. 'Look at the blueprint. Remember when you first saw it you thought those lines at the top depicted clouds?'

'Sure,' said Gallen, looking again at the wavy lines across the top of the page.

'Well, that's water—the dam water.'

Gallen took it in. 'That means the secret storage facility is . . .' Gallen turned the blueprint to get his bearings. 'It's built into the eastern bank. Several hundred feet down.'

'That's what the blueprint shows,' said Barrowman.

'Shit,' said Winter. 'I thought it'd be in one of these buildings up here.' He pointed at the office blocks that sat on top of the dam.

'When you think about it, the facility had to be well hidden enough to pass the UNSCOM inspections and then the CIA's 'No WMD' report in oh-four,' said Barrowman. 'I've been on the phone to my guy in Baghdad and we stitched together a timeline.'

Gallen sipped at the Heineken, not really in the mood for beer. 'When was it built?'

'The Iraqis started building Badush in the early nineties to catch the spill from the much larger Mosul Dam further up the Tigris.

But around ninety-eight, Saeed Saleh acquired twenty-five B61 nukes from the US air base in Turkey, and he needed a place to hide them.'

'UNSCOM was around in ninety-eight,' said Ford. 'Not a great time to be bringing nukes into Iraq.'

'Exactly,' said Barrowman. 'So Saleh orders a halt to work on Badush Dam, citing escaping gases in the foundations and what have you. All the workers are laid off, and then interesting work starts up while the dam is not being built.'

'For instance?' said Gallen.

'This police station,' said Barrowman, placing his finger on the blueprint. 'It's two miles away, but it was most likely a front for the tunnel that led down into the bowels of the dam.'

Barrowman's finger ran along the tunnel to the main gallery.

'Then?' said Winter.

Barrowman leaned back. 'They build it, in secret, although the dam was never finished as a working hydro facility. As it became more obvious that the United States would invade, Saleh's contacts in the Pentagon are in his ear.'

'They know the CIA is going to do a big report on WMDs?' said Gallen.

'Yes,' said Barrowman. 'And they want the report to be clean. They don't want a report from the DCI saying that Saddam has a stockpile of nuclear weapons that he took from Incirlik Air Base.'

'The nukes weren't stolen from Turkey, they were illegally gifted from the US,' said Gallen, appalled.

'That's about it.'

'So these Americans tell Saleh to shut down the facility?' said Gallen.

'They say that,' said Barrowman, nodding. 'And they say to make it so no one ever finds this stuff.'

'So that's why we find the demolished police station and the collapsed tunnel?' said Gallen.

'I think that's it,' said Barrowman.

Gallen chewed his lip. 'So what do we do? And what are al-Haq and Tookie Saleh going to do with these things? The place is sealed.'

'I've been going over this,' said Barrowman, grabbing a black hotel pen and pointing to a section on the blueprint. 'Mike, you're the navy commando—what is this?'

Mike Ford leaned over on his elbows, so his head was above the cross-sections that Barrowman was pointing to on the overlay. The line drawing showed a sort of S-bend at the base of the secret facility, about two hundred feet below the water's surface.

Ford leaned back, breathed out and looked at the ceiling. 'Can only be one thing.'

'I thought so,' said Barrowman.

'What's he talking about, Mike?' said Gallen.

'The facility isn't sealed,' said the Aussie, sipping at his drink. 'That's an emergency air lock.'

'Air lock?' said Winter. 'For what?'

'For divers, mate,' said Ford with a big smile. 'Looks like we're gonna get wet.'

The phone buzzed once and then the light flashed. Opening his eyes from where he was dozing on the hotel bed, Gallen turned and grabbed the handpiece. 'Yep?'

'Hey, Gerry,' said the American voice. 'Wanna talk?'

Gallen sat up, shook his head. It was Chase Lang. 'Well, Chase. What would we talk about?'

'Thought you was working for me, Gerry?'

'I was,' said Gallen, on alert. Lifting his G-Shock from the bedside table he read the time: 11.12 pm. 'But then me and Daly, we got the bags back to the FBI . . .'

'I signed you up for a month,' said Lang, chuckling lightly. 'That was twenty-one days ago, Gerry.'

'That long?' said Gallen, rubbing his temples, wondering what he was going to do about Chase Lang. 'Thought you said I was signed for a month but all you wanted was the bags, that the gig'd be over in a coupla days?'

'Seen your banks account lately?'

Gallen sighed. He hadn't.

'Meet me for a drink, Gerry,' said Chase Lang, that smooth confidence never deserting him.

'I can't,' said Gallen. 'I'm in FBI lock-down.'

'Yeah, I know,' said Lang.

'Know what?'

Lang laughed. 'Just bumped into Conrad Lunske down here in the lobby. He's an old buddy of Joe's.'

'Daly's here?' said Gallen, a cold sweat on his forehead.

'Shit, yeah!' said Lang. 'Just bought me a beer. We're in the Dilja bar, come on down.'

'I can't,' said Gallen, dreading the imminent calling in of the IOU.

'You know I'd never call in a favour on you, Gerry,' said Lang, smooth as a car salesman. 'I woulda signed you up with that CPA order seventeen just 'cos you served, 'cos I respect the Force Recon boys, 'cos no one asks for the shit duty, Gerry, am I right?'

Gallen hung up, swore at himself fifty times as he pulled on his jeans.

At the back of the Dilja bar, Gallen saw Daly perched on the outside edge of a rounded booth. As he approached, the booth opened up and Gallen stood still, looked down on the table. He was expecting Daly and Lang, but not the man sitting in the corner, jean jacket and bolo tie.

'Okay, so this ain't Lunske,' said Gallen, looking around the other booths to see who was looking at him. 'Not even close.'

Lang smiled. 'You having a drink?'

'Coffee,' said Gallen, making Daly move over so he could sit.

Chase called over a waitress and got the order in. 'Thanks for coming down, Gerry. This is Doug, one of my guys at Defense.'

'Thanks for this, Gerry,' said Doug, early fifties, with a physical hardness about him.

'I'm here for Chase,' said Gallen, annoyed at being tricked. 'I don't owe you.'

'No,' said Doug. 'But you owe your country.'

'The fuck you talkin' to like that?' said Gallen, standing. 'I don't owe my country a goddammed thing. I *served*, dude. It's a small distinction.'

Lang raised one hand. 'Doug don't mean nothing by that. If you weren't there, it's hard to know, right, fellas?' Lang nodded at Gallen and Daly, getting their assent.

'You've had a big day, Gerry,' said Lang. 'Doug has been working with us on a few matters that we'd like to bring you up to date on.'

Gallen controlled his breathing, felt the P9 pistol warm against the skin of his stomach. 'With the updating, let's start with a Little Bird gunship.'

Lang shrugged. 'Heard one was downed outside of Mosul today.'

'You tellin' me you had nothing to do with that?'

'With what?' said Lang, looking from Daly to Doug. 'With the helo going down?'

'Looked about the same as the one shot us down in the al-Hamad,' said Gallen, hand poised over the stock of the pistol. 'Tore us up with a minigun, out on the Syrian border.'

'You sayin' I had you shot down?' said Lang. 'That it?'

'That wasn't you?'

'What was the rig?'

Gallen paused. 'Black Little Bird, single minigun under the pilot. Door gunner in the back, bad shooter.'

'Okay, for a start, I don't run Little Birds,' said Lang, holding up his thumb. 'I can lease you Kiowas and Apaches out of a company I have in Bahrain, but no MH-6s.'

'Okay,' said Gallen.

'Secondly, Gerry,' said Lang, holding up his index finger, 'when you needed dough to buy back that doctor from Baba? I gave you the money.'

Gallen looked away.

'And third, I like you, fool! You're honest, you're a combat vet, you're former special forces. I need people like you. Besides, you're American! The fuck am I trying to kill you?'

They stared at each other. Soldier stares, until Daly waved a hand between them, tried to joke it out. 'Okay, lovers. Enough of the bickerin'.'

'So why am I here?' Gallen leaned back as the waitress delivered his pot of coffee.

'Doug needs a chat,' said Daly.

Gallen poured his coffee, shook down a stick of sugar. 'That's nice for Doug. Maybe I need some answers.'

Doug opened his hands, raised an eyebrow, like a man who'd been born smug. 'I'll see what I can do.'

'Where's David Rogers right now?'

'He's off the scene,' said Doug.

'Why?'

Doug shrugged. 'Got caught by the cops. It's over for him—you know how that goes, Gerry. Can't work once you're in the police system.'

Gallen inhaled deeply, breathed out slow. 'Okay, so what's your story, Doug?'

'Jim Barrowman and I,' said Doug, 'we both spent time in weapons inspections. Jim was with UNSCOM and I was an investigator for the DCI's report.'

'Okay,' said Gallen.

'But time moves on, Gerry, and although Jim is a good operator, he doesn't see the end game the way the United States government sees it.'

'You mean, the way the Pentagon sees it?'

'Okay,' said Doug, leaning back. 'If we're being technical, let's say there're powerful elements in the Joint Chiefs who don't want this to end with an arrest or a court trial.'

'They don't want the cops running it?' said Gallen. 'That it?'

'They see this as a mess that the armed forces got itself into and perhaps it's a mess we should be fixing in house, without frightening the horses.'

'Which mess?' said Gallen.

Doug laughed. 'Listen, Gerry. I wasn't there when the deal was done with Saddam, although I'd still rather have Saddam armed with nukes than the Iranians.'

'Thanks for your opinion, Doug,' said Gallen. 'It's always nice to know that someone is doing the thinking for the rest of us.'

'Point is, Gerry, we have a situation that needs to be reversed, and it can't be reversed if an FBI dick wants to be on the front page leading someone into the cells. See what I'm saying?'

'You want this under the rug?'

Doug shook his head slow. 'The United States is about to pull out of Iraq, leaving it to its own devices. We spent a decade here, Gerry, and we never scratched the surface. The last thing we can do is leave during a scandal where the US military is implicated in arming Saddam with nuclear weapons.'

'So the Pentagon cares, all of a sudden?'

'A decision was made when UNSCOM was going to shut down Saddam,' said Doug. 'That was then, Gerry. The Joint Chiefs were worried about the Iranians and I think history will prove them right. Only a strong—nuclear-capable—Saddam was going to keep Iran in check.'

'But this is now?'

'That facility was supposed to be sealed and forgotten,' said Doug. 'But it's been discovered and now we need to act, without the Iraqis reading about this on their front pages for the next year. It will destabilise a country already on the edge. We can't take a decade of war and rebuilding and flush it down the john.'

'What about the al-Haqs?' said Gallen. 'And this Tookie Saleh dude?'

'What do you know about them?' said Doug.

Gallen paused, wondering what that was about. 'I wouldn't worry about what I know, Doug. I'd worry about a bunch of Baathists who see themselves as the alternative government, because that's what Iraqis might be looking for right now.'

There was silence around the table, long enough that Gallen thought he might have said the wrong thing.

'Well, I didn't know soldiers were so interested in politics,' said Doug.

'I'm not,' said Gallen. 'I'm a trained observer.'

Doug nodded. 'Okay, the re-emergence of Tookie Saleh is unexpected and could be dangerous. But we think we have him contained.'

'Contained?' said Gallen. 'What does that mean? He tried to bomb us into oblivion three weeks ago.'

'He's in Syria,' said Doug. 'He's contained.'

Gallen drank his coffee, wanting to be out of there. 'So where do I come in?'

'At the point of completion,' said Doug, waving his hand at Daly and Lang, 'perhaps call us in.'

'Call you in?' said Gallen, smiling.

'Not talking about any rough stuff, Gerry,' said Doug. 'Just that, if he don't have the evidence, then he doesn't have a story for CNN, see what I'm sayin'?'

Gallen didn't like it. 'So I tell Jim he can find the Badush nukes, but it will have to be kept secret?'

Doug looked at Lang.

'The issue goes a little deeper than Jim Barrowman,' said Lang, scratching at the label on his beer bottle. 'See, a very powerful person assigned Jim to this mission.'

'So?' Gallen readied to leave.

'So,' said Doug, 'Jim Barrowman is answering to the President of the United States.'

CHAPTER 44

Gallen tried Winter's room first then, getting no response, went next door to Ford's. Winter sat smoking in front of the TV's morning news while Mike Ford checked his diving gear lying across the floor.

'What're you looking for?' said Gallen, pulling an orange juice from the minibar and taking a seat at a writing table.

'Just checking the gear,' said Ford. 'Delivered by the FBI in the small hours. I'm sure it's okay but, you know, training dies hard.'

'Two-hundred-foot dive,' said Gallen. 'Remind me—that dangerous?'

'Yep,' said Ford, 'if you ignore what I tell ya.'

'What should I remember?'

Ford looked up. 'At anything beyond one hundred and eighty feet, oxygen narcosis is fairly usual.'

'Okay,' said Gallen.

'But we're not hangin around on this dive,' said Ford. 'We'll be getting to two hundred and going into an air lock, so we'll dive on air. You just follow me.'

'Shit,' said Winter, pointing at the news. 'This country ain't ready for independence. Lookit this shit.'

Gallen watched a BBC report about a souk bomb in the south of Baghdad: no indication of an attack on the US or the Western allies, simply a destabilising act of terror.

'How are the Americans going to walk away from all this?' said Winter. 'I mean, really?'

Gallen didn't answer. 'We're hitting the road at eight, so we have half an hour for breakfast. Anyone hungry?'

The ride out to Badush was fast and uneventful, the dark Land Cruiser that belonged to the FBI personal security detail taking the lead, Barrowman's team following in a Mitsubishi SUV. Behind Gallen's vehicle was a nondescript forty-ton truck which also towed an IRB powerboat on a trailer.

Gallen went over the events in his head: he'd taken the meeting with Lang because even if he could get through this gig with his health intact, he'd always have to contend with Chase Lang in civvie life. It wasn't fair but it was the way of these things: special forces people who went private were signing up to a life that was beholden to powerbrokers such as Chase Lang.

But the Doug connection was worrying. And the way he'd left the conversation—that he'd call it in when they found the nukes—was something he didn't want said about him. It was against all his training and his upbringing.

And there was one thing that gnawed at Gallen harder than anything else. Who had sent the Little Bird?

There was a dirt track off the main road just before the highway went across Badush Dam. Taking a right, they followed the FBI security Land Cruiser through the stands of trees and scrub, the dirt pale and almost sandy. Stopping at a concrete-topped levy on the eastern dam wall, they got out, grabbed the scuba gear bags and walked to the water's edge, where the dam wall disappeared into the dark.

Gallen looked left and right, saw the recreational users of the dam, most of whom were camped two hundred yards away where a fake beach had been constructed. It was a perfect lake and along with the picnickers on the embankment lawns there were fishing craft, family run-arounds and waterskiing boats.

'Don't have the place to ourselves,' said Winter, lighting a smoke and bringing the big Nikon binoculars to his eyes. 'Never like that.' The Canadian scanned the lake in grids, muttering his observations as Gallen watched on. 'Got a cabin powerboat with fishing rods over the side,' said Winter, eyes on the glasses. 'Your two o'clock, boss.'

Gallen squinted across the glare of the lake in the morning light. Among the smaller craft, he saw the powerboat, saw some rods. 'What's wrong?'

'Since when do the fish live on the bank?' he said, passing the Nikons to Gallen.

He saw it immediately. There was no one on the aft deck of the boat, no one tending to the rods. But there were three men on the flying bridge, one of them looking down a pair of binoculars straight at Gallen and Winter.

'Shit,' said Gallen, handing back the glasses. 'Keep an eye on them, Kenny.'

Turning, Gallen could see the retrieval people readying the IRB on the trailer. Barrowman was with them. One of the special agents handed him a bag and he walked towards the dam wall.

'We going out on the boat?' said Gallen, pointing at the FBI craft.

'No,' said Barrowman, throwing his bag on the grass and unbuttoning his shirt. 'That's for phase two, if we find any of these things.'

'You're getting undressed?' said Ford, kneeling to the scuba bags.

'Sure,' said Barrowman.

'The dive part will be Gerry and me,' said Ford, standing, hands on hips.

'I'm coming too,' said Barrowman. 'I'm going to see this through.'

Ford shook his head. 'You ever dived?'

'Sure,' said Barrowman.

'I mean, with the navy, Marines?'

'No,' said Barrowman, getting down to his underwear. 'I did a course.'

'Where, in the Philippines?' said Ford, almost snorting.

'Maldives, actually,' said Barrowman.

'What depth?'

Barrowman shook out a wet suit. 'Don't remember.'

'Don't remember?' said Ford. 'So this was in the hotel swimming pool, right?'

'That's where they taught us,' said Barrowman. 'Then we went in the ocean.'

Gallen interrupted. 'I think what Mike's saying, Jim, is that a two-hundred-foot dive, in total darkness, is not something you get an amateur to do, no matter how gifted.'

Winter coughed with laughter, turning away to the water, where he swung an anchor as far as he could into the water, watched the orange nylon line spool out.

'Thanks, Gerry,' said Barrowman. 'I can look after myself.'

'We don't look out for ourselves, because we don't dive by ourselves,' said Ford. 'You freak out or get narcosis down there and you put me and Gerry in danger too.'

'We're wasting time.' Barrowman forced his feet into the wetsuit leggings. 'Suit up.'

The light disappeared at forty feet and they were in pitch black at sixty. Gallen kept his breathing regular and tested the radio comms with Winter.

'Blue Dog this is Red Bird, you copy? Over.'

'Roger to that, Red Bird. Gotcha loud and clear, over.'

'Green Fish, this is Red Bird, you copying this? Over.'

Ford replied instantly, the voice quality fairly good. 'My flashlight's going on now—keep Jim up close to me. Over.'

'Roger that, Green Fish,' said Gallen, seeing the flashlight go on. He hit the switch on the side of his helmet, turning on his own. 'You hear that, Black Fox?'

'Gotcha, Gerry,' said Barrowman, switching on his light. 'Sorry, Red Bird. Over.'

Gallen's chest was hooked onto the guide rope that Winter had dropped down the side and he was happy with their progress. The military way would have been to send a scout team down first to establish exactly where the air lock was located. But at two hundred feet, even the best divers would take their time with decompression stops and would baulk at a fast turn around for another two-hundred-foot dive. The nitrogen could build up in the tissues and so Gallen had suggested they dive together, get it done. He'd been trying to hide his impatience with the gig, but the truth was he wanted to be back on the farm, back with the cattle and back enjoying a date with Alison McIntyre. The meeting the night before with Chase Lang and Doug the spook had been too much—he now knew that if he was ever going to leave the life behind he'd have to avoid ever contacting them again, and give them no excuse to contact him.

He'd have to pay his IOUs, and move on.

'One hundred feet,' said Ford's voice, echoing in Gallen's helmet. 'Keep it smooth, no holding your breath.'

'Roger that,' said Gallen.

'I got it,' said Barrowman.

The coldness wrapped itself around Gallen's throat, his breathing becoming slightly laboured against the increasing pressure. The dam wall was covered in rocks the size of basketballs and fish darted in and out of the crevices as they swam down it. The sound from the regulator rasped like a dry saw and Gallen experienced tiny things with hyper-awareness, such as the warmth around his mask right on the point of maximum coldness. He could feel the warmth of his back where the scuba rig was fitted, in contrast to his cold ass.

They continued to descend, the water becoming so dark that Gallen could barely see the spill of light from Ford's flashlight. He could feel the occasional swirl of turbulence from Barrowman's fin, but the sensory deprivation was starting to mess with his orientation. Making himself breathe normally, Gallen grabbed the nylon guide rope and pulled himself down, hoping it would be over soon.

'One hundred and . . .'

It was Ford's voice, but the radio had lost it halfway through transmission.

'Green Fish, Green Fish,' said Gallen into mouthpiece. 'This is Red Bird, confirm comms; repeat: confirm comms. Over.'

The line crackled, with snippets of voice breaking through. The light was no longer visible and Gallen realised they'd slowed to snail's pace. Accelerating until he could grab Barrowman's ankle, he hauled himself over the FBI man and unhooked his own flashlight from his chest webbing. Struggling to get his fingers working in the cold, Gallen found the on/off button and spilled light onto Barrowman.

'Shit,' he yelled into his mask. Barrowman's face was in a rictus of panic, his body inert. At least bubbles still escaped from behind his head—he was still breathing.

'Fuck,' said Gallen, tapping the flashlight on Barrowman's face plate and then shaking him by the shoulders. He was having some kind of toxicity reaction.

'Mike,' said Gallen, as loud as he could into the mouthpiece. 'Help us.'

Ford had obviously gone ahead, not knowing how slow Barrowman was going.

'Blue Dog, this is Red Bird, do you copy?'

A voice crackled back. Gallen didn't understand it: the radio sets were military issue, highly effective in all conditions. The only thing he could think of was interference. Who was in the water with them? Which of those boats was running jammers or intercepts?

Grabbing Barrowman by the chest webbing, Gallen pulled on the guide rope one-handed, trying to get the cop to the air lock as fast as he could. He pulled Barrowman down for half a minute before the FBI man started to struggle. Small movements at first, that Gallen shrugged off. Then the struggles became more violent and Gallen had to stop, shine the light into Barrowman's face. His eyes were wide and his mouth was slipping off his regulator. If he kept struggling, his mask was going to leave his face. And another problem: Barrowman was starting to grab at Gallen's face; if he lost his mask, they'd be as good as dead down this far.

Grabbing Barrowman's wrists, Gallen fought with him and sensed movement at his right shoulder. Turning his light, he saw Ford's face.

'Gotcha, Gerry,' said Ford, the comms working close in. 'Take one arm each, let's pull him down.'

'Okay,' said Gallen, trying to slow his panting.

They dragged on the FBI man, fighting his struggles and each using one hand to pull themselves deeper on the rope. The inadequate light danced in the blackness, their voices encouraging and reassuring one another.

'Okay,' said Ford after five minutes, his voice also betraying signs of exertion. 'We've hit two hundred and two feet.'

Jamming his heels on the rocks, Gallen turned and looked for an air lock.

'Stay with him,' said Ford. 'I'll walk the wall.'

Hitching himself to Gallen with a fine yellow twine, Ford set off.

Sitting in the dark, trying to keep Barrowman from attacking him, Gallen wondered about how he'd got to be sitting at the bottom of Badush Dam, looking for nukes. It hardly seemed right and he vowed that his military life was over. It couldn't go on—he'd left the Marines for all the right reasons and now it was time to step back, let another wave of youngsters come through.

As he waited, he thought he saw a light, then realised his mind must be playing tricks; Ford had gone the other way. He turned back to see Ford's helmet light blinking out of the darkness.

'Not that way,' said Ford. 'I'll try the other side.'

'I'm coming with you,' said Gallen. 'I can't hold him alone.'

They crabbed across the dam wall for twenty seconds before Gallen ran into the back of Ford. Looking down, aiming his helmet light, Gallen could see a gap in the rocks bordered by reinforced concrete. It was about twelve feet high and twenty feet long, giving the appearance of an underwater letter box slot.

Gallen only lost his concentration for a few seconds but it was enough for Barrowman's swinging arms to grab hold of his mask and tear it sideways, ripping the regulator out of his mouth. Ice cold water raced into his face and air poured out of his mouth as he reflexively gasped and took in a lungful of water.

Scrambling for the air lock, assisted by Ford, Gallen grabbed at his regulator but couldn't swim and put his breathing apparatus back into place at the same time. His lungs ached, his whole body convulsed as he went into the lock and tried to swim upwards, remembering the blueprint.

He hit concrete, his helmet whacking it like a hammer. Panicking for oxygen, Gallen fumbled for his mouthpiece and jammed it into his mouth, doing his best to take a tiny 'sip' of air, and then taking the mouthpiece away and coughing the water out of his lungs. It only worked if you could control the subsequent intake of breath—Gallen couldn't, his body was too panicked. He took another lungful as he convulsed, swam further into the lock, his light pathetic in such darkness.

Feeling his way along the ceiling, he finally felt it give way and swam upwards for five seconds until his face broke the surface where he gasped, coughed and vomited as he trod water. He couldn't see properly for the tears clogging his eyes and the convulsions from his lungs and his stomach.

Looking around to distract himself as he tried to slow his gasping, his light fixed on a concrete ledge three feet away. He swam to the ledge and held on to it, unable to pull himself up with the weight on his back.

Lights broke the surface, and Ford pushed Barrowman towards Gallen. Grabbing the struggling FBI man, Gallen pulled him to the ledge and held him out of the water.

'It's okay,' said Gallen. 'There's no more water.'

Barrowman fought some more before calming as Gallen forced his hands onto the ledge. Beside him Ford pulled himself onto the ledge, then dragged up the gear bag he'd dived with.

Gallen's arms were close to falling off as he kept hold of Barrowman. Having pulled off his kit, Ford reached down and pulled up Barrowman by the scuba straps, dragged him onto dry concrete, before coming back to help Gallen.

Shrugging off his scuba gear, Gallen vomited again. When he'd finally caught his breath, he turned to Ford, who was unpacking.

'What'll we do with Barrowman?'

'He's fine,' said Ford, pulling light bars out of the mesh bag and breaking them. The cavern lit up with a green glow and Gallen could see that if he'd been a few feet to the right he'd have had a set of steps to mount.

'What happened?' said Gallen, checking on his pistol.

'Narcosis from a carbon dioxide build-up is my guess,' said Ford, extracting flashlights, a tool kit and his own pistol from the mesh bag. 'We got comms with Kenny yet?'

'No,' said Gallen, ensuring the mic was still on his throat. 'I'll try again. Blue Dog, this is Red Bird, copy? Over.'

The static crackled loud in Gallen's ear, and he turned it off. 'You give it a try,' he said, moving to Barrowman. Unstrapping his scuba gear, Gallen allowed the groaning cop to roll over and recover.

'He'll come round in about five minutes,' said Ford. 'And he'll have a headache like the worst hangover of his life.'

'Let's see his blueprint,' said Gallen, looking around. 'We can orientate ourselves while Jim's out to lunch.'

Sealed in a black diver's bag, Gallen found Barrowman's pistol and the blueprint. There was a small black sealed bag that felt quite heavy. Opening it quickly he found a radio handset and a plastic box that had been padlocked at the handle. Gallen knew the box was familiar but its contents wouldn't come to him.

Spreading the blueprint in the glow cast by the light bars, they found their position. 'We're here,' said Ford, planting a finger. 'So behind us should be a set of stairs that lead into a main gallery—the gallery once connected to the police station.'

Barrowman groaned.

'Let's have a look,' said Gallen. 'I want this over.'

Taking a light bar each, they left the third beside Barrowman and set off up the concrete stairs. At the top, the gallery opened up: it was wide—about thirty yards across—with a low ceiling, not unlike an underground parking garage.

By the light of the bars, they could see twenty or so large steel crates, each of them about six feet square and stamped with a series of numbers. Gallen walked to the nearest, read the inscriptions: there was a long list of white numbers stencilled onto the dark steel in white paint, but the label at the top of the box was quite clear: B61. The radiation signal was even clearer.

'This is it,' said Gallen. Wandering closer, he saw a stash of smaller steel crates behind the nukes. Ford crouched and held his light bar to the first one. It was marked *Goodyear Aerospace Active Radar Guidance System*.

'Shit,' said Gallen. 'There's, what, forty or fifty of these damned things? This is the money right here—the ability to guide a missile to where you want it to go.'

'There's no way we can shift all this through the air lock,' said Ford. 'What was Barrowman thinking?'

'I was thinking what Chase Lang was thinking,' said Barrowman from behind Gallen's shoulder.

Gallen was about to ask him how he was feeling then stopped as he saw the Glock aimed at his stomach.

'Pistols on the ground, both of you,' said Barrowman.

'You insane, Jim?' said Ford.

'Maybe,' said Jim Barrowman, levelling the Glock at Ford's forehead. 'But I have the gun.'

CHAPTER 45

Barrowman forced them at gunpoint into an empty B61 crate and shut the security door on it, pulling down a lever that locked them in like prisoners.

'This is a little dramatic, isn't it, Jim?' said Gallen through one of the gaps in the steel grille. 'I mean, you were a mess on the way down here. How are you going to swim out again?'

'I'll live,' said the FBI man, on his knee organising something from his bag.

'That's two hundred feet to the surface, Jim,' said Ford. 'If you got the narcosis on the way down, you'd better watch out on the way back up.'

'Maybe I'm not swimming out of here,' he said, laying on the ground ten army-olive packages, each as long as a child's ruler and as thick as a hockey puck. Gallen knew them as US Army high-explosive charges.

'What you got there, Jim?' said Gallen, wanting to keep the man talking. 'Looks like a bunch of one-twelves. What's a civvie boy like you doin' with something like that?'

Next, Barrowman lay a small steel component that looked like a mini yoyo beside each 112 charge.

Ford got in on the act. 'Those one-twelves are very high in RDX, Jim. That's very dangerous material you got right there. And those detonators? Don't get them too close to the explosive, okay?'

In front of his line-up Barrowman placed a small black box from which he extracted an aerial.

'Shit,' muttered Ford. 'Wireless detonation.'

Barrowman put the 112 charges into the main pocket of his black bag, and put the detonators into a smaller pocket. Then he slung the bag over his neck by the handles so it fell on his chest. Barrowman looked at his watch and walked to one of the B61 crates, climbed it and stood on the top. The crate—at six feet tall—meant Barrowman had to bend over to avoid hitting his head on the concrete ceiling.

'What the hell's he doin'?' said Gallen.

Barrowman took a 112 charge from the bag and pushed it sideways into a small gap between the top of each upright concrete pillar and the ceiling. He pushed hard and the malleable stick squeezed into the gap and stayed where it was put. The 112 charge was covered in an olive-green plastic, and Barrowman snipped the end of the charge with a small pair of scissors. Then he reached into his other pocket, pulled out a detonator and pushed it into the exposed end of the 112 charge.

Climbing back down to the concrete floor, Barrowman dusted off his palms and turned to Gallen and Ford. 'You guys are the experts at this stuff. How'm I looking?'

Gallen shook his head. 'Jim, what are you doing? You're gonna blow this place?'

'Why the surprise, Gerry?' said Barrowman, walking to the next crate that stood beside a column. 'This is what Chase Lang wanted, and you promised to call him in when we'd found all this, remember?'

'You see a phone on me?' said Gallen. 'I owe Chase Lang—owe him my life. I had to take that meeting.'

Barrowman pushed his next stick of 112 into the crevice, adding a detonator in the end. 'Why would Chase want to blow this up?'

'He told me you wanted to go to the media with it. He said publicity about Saddam's nukes, right when Iraq has to stand on its own feet, is the worst thing that could happen. You add in the fact that they were supplied by the US and you have a volatile situation.'

'Really?' said Barrowman, going to the next crate, climbing it and having to raise his voice. 'You telling me that a few reports on BBC World Service is more damaging than a bunch of US soldiers giving US nukes to Saddam?'

'Well,' said Gallen.

'Well, well, well,' said Barrowman, a snide mimic. 'Obviously when I told you this story, my disgust didn't register, Gerry. But a bunch of people from your secret brotherhood stole nuclear weapons from their own country's air base and gave them to Saddam Hussein. Oh, and they threw in a few cases of Goodyear missile guidance systems, with the radar-area correlation chips and terminal-guided arrays. Just what Israel needed in the neighbourhood: a missile that actually works.'

'Yeah, I know,' said Gallen.

'No, you don't know, Gerry, or you wouldn't be offering to help a psycho like Chase Lang.' Barrowman was shouting now. 'You allow just one of these warheads into the hands of the North Koreans, with one single Goodyear guidance system, and within a few months they'll be able to flatten Beijing or Tokyo. You need to know this, Gerry.'

Gallen swallowed to moisten his dry throat. 'How'd you know I was talking to Chase?'

Barrowman climbed a crate beside Gallen and Ford's. 'One of my personal security guys was sitting in the next booth, having a snack.'

Gallen shrugged. 'I'm sorry, Jim. I wasn't going to phone it in.'

'Then what were you going to do, Gerry? You'd already said yes to Lang.' Barrowman returned to his black box with the aerial. He switched it on and Gallen could see a red light on the console. The FBI man input a code and two green lights started flashing.

'He's armed it,' said Ford into Gallen's ear. 'This is not good.'

Barrowman looked at his watch. 'Don't worry, fellas, you're not going to die—I just can't have you messing with the plan. But I hope you'll be nice for our guests.'

'Guests?' said Ford.

Barrowman looked at them and smiled. 'Almost royalty around these parts.'

The lights flashed in strange shapes as people approached up the stairs from the air lock, and then two men walked into the gallery. Gallen couldn't see them properly from his angle, but he could see Barrowman holding the black box in front of him.

'Gentlemen,' he said. 'As promised, twenty-five B61 nuclear devices, formerly known as the W85 warhead.'

'I have brought my engineer,' said a male Arab. 'Do you mind?'

'Be my guest,' said Barrowman, like a storekeeper. 'But there's not much to see. These babies are good for forty kilotons, not bad when you remember that Little Boy was fifteen.'

Gallen could see movement through the gloom: someone walking to a crate with a flashlight, opening it and getting to work. Another person put a laptop on a table, opened it.

'And this box with the flashing lights?' said the man's voice. 'What is this?'

'Insurance policy, Tookie,' said Barrowman. 'This place is mined with RDX charges. Anything happens, I push the button and we all drown.'

'Tookie?' whispered Gallen to Ford. 'You hear him say Tookie?'

'Tookie Saleh is here?' said Ford. 'Holy shit.'

'The fuck is Barrowman doin' with him?'

Mumbles wafted across the crates as the FBI man disappeared with Tookie, who seemed to be showing him something. Then Barrowman walked back to where Gallen could see him and knelt down, picked up his radio handset.

'Stand by to check bank account,' he said into the handpiece.

'What's he doing?' said Ford, chuckling. 'He's selling these things to Saleh?'

The engineer made three random checks of the B61 nukes, not coming to Gallen's cage. Then he made a cursory check of two of the boxes containing the Goodyear guidance systems.

'It's all here,' said Tookie Saleh, who Gallen noticed was dressed in expensive street clothes, suggesting he didn't swim into the lock. 'Although I find it disturbing that we have to buy back the thing that was a gift to us in the first place.'

'Consider it a finder's fee,' said Barrowman.

'And if I transfer this money,' said Saleh. 'What guarantee do I have that you don't blow this place anyway?'

Gallen froze as a third Arab crept in front of their crate, pistol held professionally. He stopped behind the crate in front of Gallen's, and took aim around the corner. Gallen was almost looking down the sights—it was a shot of about ten yards to hit Barrowman: an easy shot for a pro.

'You see, Jim,' said Saleh, 'my uncle negotiated this cache of armaments from the Bush government, so I don't see why you should be paid for anything except your time.'

'Well that's too bad—' started Barrowman, but the third man shot him. The first shot hit him high on the left arm, the second shot grazed his chest, and he fell backwards behind a steel crate.

'Get him,' cried Saleh, and the third man ran after Barrowman. Shots came back at the third man, and suddenly he was hopping, holding his shin.

The engineer gave chase, armed with an assault rifle, and Gallen saw Tookie Saleh walk to the discarded detonator switch, pick it up and turn it off. Then he followed the engineer as the third man passed out.

'We have to get out of here,' said Ford, hand reaching through the gap and up to the safety lever. 'That detonator could be live.'

'He turned it off, didn't he?' said Gallen, reaching through his side to see if there was any way out of the crate.

'He turned off the box,' said Ford, 'but we have no idea what fuse is in those detonators. Some are timers. If Jim had no intention of handing over those nukes to Tookie, then he may have had the detonators on timer.'

Gallen looked around the crate: the roof was welded onto the sides and the sides were welded to the base. It was a solid transportation case.

Spooling up the thin yellow twines that he'd attached to himself underwater, Ford fashioned a rope loop, leaned out the gap in the roof of the crate and tried to throw the loop over the downward-facing lever, which they knew could be pulled up because they could see the levers on the other crates. But the loop wouldn't hold over the lever—every time they got it on, it would slide up to the fulcrum point.

'We need to get a hold of that lever,' said Ford. He pointed to the unconscious man. 'What's that shooter got on him?'

The man who'd shot Barrowman lay unconscious about twenty feet from their tiny prison, his pistol near his foot. Ford fashioned another loop, put his arms outside the crate and swung it, tried to throw the rope over the pistol.

The shooter groaned, drool pouring from his mouth. Shots came from somewhere deep in the complex.

'You know anything about lassoing?' said Ford.

'It's called roping,' said Gallen, taking the yellow twine from him. 'And yeah, I know a bit about it.'

Pulling the twine back into the crate, Gallen spooled it up, winding and unwinding it until the grain of the twine was uniform with no twists. Then he knotted a honda at one end of the rope, and made a loop he could throw.

'Can we hurry?' said Ford. 'The bloke's moving.'

'Gotta get this part right,' said Gallen. 'Take care of your rope and your rope'll take care of you.'

'Take care of the pistol, Gerry,' said Ford.

Gallen leaned out the gap in the crate and tried to get the loop swinging above his head. His hand knocked the crate and he dropped the rope.

Spooling it back up, he made another loop with it, unwinding the twine from its previous swing. Gunshots sounded somewhere in the facility.

'Can you just stop that fancy shit?' said Ford in a growled whisper. 'Get the damned pistol.'

Gallen tried again, this time getting his shoulder further out of the crate so he could get a swinging action on the loop. Then, as his wrist came around the third time, he used the momentum of the rope and let go, directing his finger at the pistol. The rope's loop spun in the air in a perfect circle and landed around the pistol.

The shooter groaned and moved, his eyelids fluttering.

'Careful,' said Ford.

Gallen slowly pulled at the rope, dragging it across the concrete floor, letting the loop run to the edge of the gun's muzzle. Then he stopped and pulled at the rope with tiny motions.

'The rope got it?' said Gallen. 'Can you see it, Mike?'

Ford stood on tiptoes, trying for a better angle. 'Yep, you got it, mate.'

'Ready for a pull?'

'Try it,' said Ford.

The shooter let out a long moan and sat up, looked down at his shattered shin. He went to touch the bullet wound and thought better of it.

'Better do it, Gerry,' said Ford.

Gallen whipped at the rope, pulling the pistol in a clattering slide across to the crate.

Dropping to the floor of the crate, Ford extended his hand as far as he could and came up five inches short.

'Lemme try,' said Gallen, getting down and trying the same thing. He came up three inches short.

'Gerry, watch it,' said Ford.

Gallen looked up, saw the shooter looking straight at him. 'Fuck,' said Gallen. The shooter stood to walk and almost collapsed, in agony by the gutteral sounds coming from him.

'Quick, Gerry, the rope trick, mate.'

This time Gallen forgot about the ritual of preparing a rope, just dropped it over the pistol and pulled back. The rope slipped off the handle as the shooter yelled for his comrades and started crawling for his gun, blood smearing across the concrete as he moaned in agony.

'He's coming, Gerry,' said Ford, lying flat on the floor and straining for the pistol.

Now the shooter was trying to run, they could see his eyes, see his pain. As he dived for his pistol, Gallen grabbed at the gun, moving it enough for Ford to get his hand on it. As the shooter came in hands first, Ford shot him in the face.

Panting with fear and exertion, they waited as the shot echoed around the large chamber, the light now dim as the light bars faded, the only solid source of light coming from Tookie Saleh's laptop which was still sitting on the table. Then they heard it: two Arab men yelling out for their third guy.

'Shit,' said Gallen, as running steps came closer.

'His belt,' said Ford, handing the pistol to Gallen and then reaching out and pulling the man to them. The Australian's fingers ran over the large belt, undoing it and then pulling it through the jeans loops, until he had it in his hands.

Feeding the belt buckle through the gap in the roof, Ford directed it until the heavy buckle dangled down over the release lever. The footfalls were now in the main gallery, and they had slowed: two men stealthing.

One of them called out the shooter's name as Ford edged the buckle further down. From his vantage point, Gallen could just see the buckle.

'Lower, Mike,' he hissed.

'That's it,' whispered Ford. 'That's as far as it goes.'

Gallen checked the pistol as quietly as he could. It was a fifteen-shot Beretta with eleven rounds in the clip and one in the spout. Easing the clip back in, he pulled back on the action, cocking it.

Ford jiggled the belt buckle up and down with his fingertips, faster and faster, trying to make the buckle fly out and over the end of the handle. A shadow moved from behind a crate thirty feet away, and Gallen aimed.

'Do it, Mike,' said Gallen, waiting.

The jiggling changed tone—the buckle was latched.

'I got it,' said Ford, putting weight on the belt.

Gallen watched the shadow move and fired. The first shot dropped the shadow as Ford pulled down on the belt with all his weight and lifted up the lever. They spilled out, Gallen in cup-and-saucer mode. Ford stayed in behind him as they ran to the fallen shadow.

Ford kneeled over the still-breathing man, the engineer who'd checked the nukes, and took his pistol: a Ruger 9mm.

Crouching and listening, they heard the scratchings of a man running. 'The stairs,' said Ford. 'He's going to the air lock.'

Running across the gallery, taking care now that there was almost no light, they made it to the stairs and descended cautiously, just in time to see a large shape sink into the inky water.

'That's a mini submersible,' said Ford, running at it. In the dying glow of the light bars, they could see the locking wheel still

328

turning in the turret as it slipped beneath the surface, Tookie Saleh with it.

Gallen panted, nerves frayed, his thigh on fire. He gulped and looked around as they ran out of light.

'Shit, Mike,' he said, wiping his forehead with the back of his hand and feeling dizzy in the dead air. 'I don't think I can do the ascent, not right now.'

'No kidding you can't,' said the Aussie, spitting. 'Bastards took our friggin' tanks.'

They sat in the gallery, leaning against a crate, drinking from the water bottle they'd found in Tookie Saleh's laptop bag. Ford played with the laptop, Gallen looking on.

'Lots of spreadsheets and banking receipts,' said Ford. 'Who knew so many companies were called Nominees or Associates?'

'Who's he been paying lately? What's that one there?'

'That's . . . shit, this can't be right. Tookie paid eighteen million dollars to an account called Protection Nominees Inc. just this morning. It's a Singapore bank account.'

'He was busy,' said Gallen. 'And there's more.'

'There's quite a few payments to Protection Nominees over the weeks, but none like that,' said Ford. 'Where does a man with no obvious source of revenue get eighteen million dollars?'

Gallen shrugged. 'He's Saeed Saleh's nephew. Maybe he knows where the Saddam fortune is buried?'

Ford shut the computer. 'You feeling okay for a walk?'

'Gimme a hand,' said Gallen, allowing Ford to drag him to his feet. 'Damned gunshot wound just won't let go.' Walking around in circles he warmed up the leg, but what he really needed was painkillers.

'I say we find Jimbo,' said Ford.

'Why?' said Gallen.

'Maybe he knew a way out of here,' Ford suggested, feeling his way in the darkness and seizing on Barrowman's bag.

Gallen opened the laptop again and its light spilled onto Barrowman's blueprint with the overlay cellotaped to it. 'If he found a way, it should be on here, right?'

They traced their fingers over the blueprint, Gallen hitting the touch pad when the light automatically dimmed.

'Can't see anything, unless this thing . . .' said Ford, his finger landing on what looked like a thin line running vertically down the page, intersecting with an annexe of the gallery a short way up the tunnel.

'You think that's a shaft of some sort?' said Gallen.

'Let's find out.'

The ladder was set into the wall of the tunnel. Barrowman's body lay at its foot in a pool of dark blood. When Ford aimed the laptop screen upwards, they could see a square hole disappearing into the black, a rail of some sort running up the back of it.

'Freight elevator?' said Gallen.

'That's probably how they were going to shift the nukes,' said Ford.

Gallen stowed the laptop in its bag and slung it over his back. Too many years in recon had made a habit out of collecting collateral. With the light gone from the laptop, Ford pulled out the flashlight with decent battery power and turned it on. As he swung the Maglite to the vertical shaft, the beam passed over something.

'What's that?' he muttered.

Walking to it, he picked it up and brought it back, handed it to Gallen. 'Jim's radio.'

'If I key this, I get the last frequency he used, right?'

'Sure,' said Ford.

Gallen keyed the radio. 'Red Bird to base, you copy? Over.'

He got static as an answer. Gallen tried it again and this time a voice came over the air. 'Copy that Red Bird. Please identify, over.'

Gallen let the transmit trigger out and realised he knew the voice.

'That Special Agent Cole?' said Gallen into the radio.

'Who's this?' came the reply.

Gallen let the handset go idle. 'He must have called Cole, his FBI colleague, to confirm the Saleh payment had gone through.'

'So who've we really been working for?'

Gallen thought about it. 'Maybe that's why they're using private contractors,' he said. 'Maybe they thought we were expendable?'

'Not this little black duck,' said Ford, reaching for the ladder rungs.

'Hang on,' said Gallen, passing him the radio. 'Can you find Kenny's frequency? We can warn him.'

Ford played with the channel selectors until he had what he thought was Winter's band. 'There,' he said, passing the radio back.

'Blue Dog, this is Red Bird, you copy? Over.'

There was dead air for several seconds and then static broke out of the speaker. 'Red Bird, this is Blue Dog, copying you. What's your location?'

'You got ears? Over.'

'I'll find a better place, out of the wind,' said Winter. A few seconds later he said, 'Clear.'

'Kenny, we're climbing out an elevator shaft in this tunnel.'

'Where?'

'We think it comes out about a third of the way between the dam and the demolished police station.'

'Who's we?'

'Barrowman turned bad, Kenny. He locked us up, tried to sell the nukes to the Baathists. Also, watch out for Tookie Saleh and one associate. They left here in a submersible. Where are you?'

'On the lake,' said Winter. 'I'm on the FBI boat with the FBI security detail.'

'Everything okay?'

'Yeah, but they're worried because they haven't heard from Jim.'

'Who's worried?'

'That dude Cole.'

'Watch him, Kenny.'

'What?' said Winter. 'Please repeat.'

'Cole is with Barrowman,' said Gallen. And then the connection went dead.

CHAPTER 46

'You hear that?' said Ford, holding up his finger for quiet. He walked to the base of the shaft, looked up. A scraping, thumping sound echoed down. Gallen heard it too.

At the top of the shaft, daylight broke through, although it was interrupted by something moving. Then a whirring and banging started and Ford looked at Gallen. 'They're lowering the elevator.'

Moving back along the tunnel wall, they found a store of oil barrels and hid in the darkness as the sound became louder, the bark of Arab voices echoing above the slamming of steel on concrete. The elevator cage hit the bottom and a man dressed in dark military fatigues pulled the cantilevered grille back. Five men armed with assault rifles spilled into the tunnel, scoping the area with flashlights along the top of their weapons.

Squeezing further behind the barrels, Gallen watched the sixth and seventh men push a portable floodlight on wheels out into the tunnel and turn in the direction of the storage gallery. Two men pushed another floodlight into the tunnel and set it up opposite the elevator. The elevator door closed and it started its ascent.

One of the soldiers started the generator and as it powered up, they unfurled the lamps until four large lights filled the tunnel with light.

'Who's doing this?' whispered Ford. 'They about to shift the nukes?'

Gallen thought back, wondered where these soldiers had got the jump on them. It could only have come from Barrowman.

The other portable floodlight machine started up, its lights spilling into the tunnel.

'We'll have to sort this,' said Ford. 'We can't let this go.'

'I agree,' said Gallen, as the elevator lowered again. 'These dudes are organised. This ain't amateur.'

The elevator hit the ground, another five soldiers piled out, followed by a skid steer, which revved into the tunnel, turned right and motored for the gallery.

'We won't be getting out that way,' said Gallen, pointing his pistol at the elevator. 'If they have ten triggers down here, they'll have a lot more topside.'

The skid steer revved and beeped as it reversed, and then it reappeared, carrying one of the B61 transport crates in front of it.

'This is not good,' said Gallen.

The skid steer lined up and drove into the elevator, an expert using the double-handle controls. The crate was dropped in the elevator and the skid steer reversed out. The soldier inside the elevator barked into his radio handset and the elevator started its upward ride.

'They'll have the whole lot out of here inside the hour,' said Ford.

Gallen remembered something. 'Lemme have that radio,' he said, trying to recall the frequency given to him by Chase Lang. He found the setting and tried the radio but it was having the same problems as he'd had with Winter.

'Think it's being jammed,' said Ford.

'Shit,' said Gallen, wanting to smash the thing but thinking better of it. 'We have one way out of here, Mike, and that's up that shaft.'

'We could take the ladder up the side, but they'd see us and kill us,' said Ford.

'We could take down a few and take a ride up the elevator . . .'

'But they'd kill us at the top,' said Ford.

'Or,' said Gallen, 'we could wait here until they've done the loading and then make our calls.'

'What if the place is mined?' said Ford. 'What if they don't turn off the jammers? We can't call out and they might seal the top of that shaft. I don't like the waiting option.'

'What else, then?' said Gallen, the elevator making another journey down as the skid steer waited for it with a B61 crate.

'You won't like it, Gerry,' said Ford, his voice a rasping whisper. 'But hear me out, okay?'

'What is it?' said Gallen, ducking behind the barrels as a soldier looked up the tunnel in their direction.

'We swim out,' said Ford.

Silence sat between them like the Grand Canyon.

'Swim?' said Gallen, after a pause. 'As in, the water?'

'Out through the air lock, up to the surface,' said Ford. 'We won't be emerging to a bunch of gun barrels. We might stand a chance.'

Gallen rubbed his face, the fatigue and stress too much. 'The fuck you talkin' about? That's two hundred feet, with no tanks?'

'You did that, Gerry, to get your helmet,' said Ford, referring to the brass dive helmet that US Marines wore on their dress uniform when they'd passed the Combatant Diver course in Florida. Most recon Marines wore a helmet and wings on their dress uniform, signifying paratrooper and combat diver training: it was a status thing. But Gallen remembered the dive course in Panama City as a blur of fear and anxiety, the worst of it being the nocturnal dives which gave him nightmares for months afterwards.

'Yeah, Mike,' said Gallen, trying to relax his throat. 'I got my helmet, but it don't mean I go looking for two-hundred-foot free-dives.'

'I'll look after you in the water, Gerry,' said the Aussie, 'if you can get us past these goons.'

The elevator made its third upward ride as the skid steer turned for the gallery. One soldier was left guarding the elevator shaft. Slinging his rifle over his shoulder so it was worn across his chest, the soldier grabbed a cigarette, lit it and yelled something towards the gallery. A second soldier answered, and as the first soldier went for another drag on the smoke, Gallen hit him behind the right ear with the stock of his pistol.

334

Before the guard hit the concrete, Ford was onto him, tearing the rifle off his shoulders and the pistol from his belt.

Jogging down the tunnel towards the gallery, the B61 crates made a good hide as they approached the storage area.

The skid steer beeped to signal its reverse and a soldier walked backwards, gesturing for it to come straight back. Gallen kept his momentum going, swerving out of the shadows, hitting the soldier with a shoulder charge. Caught unawares, the soldier dropped to the ground. As Gallen ripped a fast right-hand punch to the man's throat, Ford moved into the centre of the gallery, shooting as he walked. By the time Gallen gained his feet with the guard's MT series Colt carbine, Ford had killed two bad guys and the rest of them were firing back.

Ducking behind a crate, Gallen checked the small clip in the Colt: eight rounds left. He swapped hand signs with Ford, who had found his own hide. Ford would hold the ground, so Gallen could swing around and flank the soldiers.

As Gallen moved to his left, a soldier who had the same idea came at him. Gallen dropped him with one shot, put another shot into the guy's head as he jogged past. Ford started up again as Gallen swung his body into the aisle made by the other crates, saw a boot disappear behind one of them.

He had stopped to catch his breath, waiting to see where the next footfalls were coming from, when he heard the clunk of a grenade landing beside his foot. It bounced into the crate opposite him, coming to a rest five feet away. Without thinking, Gallen picked up the grenade and threw it back over the crates.

'Fire in the hole, Mike,' he yelled.

It exploded before hitting the ground, the concussion ripping into unsuspecting ear tissues in the confined space. Dropping his hands from his ears, Gallen took two grenades from the dead soldier's chest webbing. 'Going again, Mike,' he yelled, as someone screamed in agony. He tore the pin out of the first grenade and threw it, further this time, then primed the second grenade and did the same thing.

The blasts loosened concrete from the ceilings and sent paint floating from the crates like dust.

'Clear, Mike,' he yelled and ran into the mayhem of dust and smoke, going from crate to crate.

'Over here,' said Ford, and Gallen moved to a collection of three bodies: two were dead already, the one who was moaning was five minutes away judging by the flap of stomach hanging from him.

'This way,' said Ford, running into the smoke.

A barrel poked around the corner and shot on full auto without the shooter even looking. Ford and Gallen pressed back against a crate and rushed the position.

As Gallen turned he was in time to watch Ford drill two soldiers, one of whom had put his hands up.

Behind them, the elevator clanked to a halt in the tunnel, and an Arab voice yelled out. Gallen and Ford waited, trying to swallow their heavy breathing. Then they heard it: a blast of static on a radio and the soldier talking loudly into it.

'Time to go,' said Ford, and Gallen's stomach almost dropped out of his body.

'They took the tank rigs,' said Ford, handing him a mask, 'but they didn't take the fins and masks.'

'Lucky us,' said Gallen.

'Okay,' said Ford, sitting and pulling on his fins. 'Time for basic tuition. We'll be able to ascend much faster than if we'd been in the water at two hundred feet for half an hour, okay?'

'Okay,' said Gallen, pulling on the fins and throwing Saleh's laptop bag over his shoulder. The water would damage the computer but military technicians could still retrieve the data from the harddrive. 'So how long to get to the top?'

'About four minutes,' said Ford.

'You know how long it's been since I did the divers' course?' said Gallen, spitting on the inside of the mask's glass and rubbing it. 'I haven't held my breath for four minutes since I was twenty-five years old, and that was about two thousand cigarettes ago.'

'It's been a while for me too,' said Ford.

'You're a clearance diver, Mike,' said Gallen, trying to keep fear out of his voice. 'You do this for a living.'

The elevator clanked as it made its way to the surface. In a few minutes, the place would be crawling with Baathist militants.

The two men looked at each other, nostrils flaring.

'There's only one way out of here, boss,' said Ford, his accent hardened, the opposite of his usual sing-song Aussie twang. 'That's the way I'm going, and I have no intention of leaving you here.'

Gallen gulped, looked away. Two hundred feet to the surface—no air, no dive school instructors, no safety net. It was too far on one breath and the mere idea of it was overwhelming him.

'We'll do it the RAN way, okay?' said Ford, talking about the Royal Australian Navy.

'Remind me.'

'We break every operation into its smallest component parts, make a step list, take the mystery out of it.'

'Sounds like the Marines way,' said Gallen, perking up. 'This is doable?'

'Sure is. First thing we have to do is oxygen-up,' said Ford. 'Thirty seconds of diaphragm breathing, but no hyperventilation. Just relaxed breathing.'

'Don't we have to force it in?'

'No,' said Ford. 'You run the risk of getting the oxygen and CO_2 levels out of whack, and then the metabolism gets confused, makes you gasp for air before you really need to.'

'What about decompression?' Gallen asked.

'Not really an issue with free diving,' said Ford. 'That's more about breathing air while you're at pressure. But you'll probably need to equalise.'

The elevator hit ground and they could clearly hear feet shuffling out, lots of boots on concrete.

'Equalise?' said Gallen. 'Remind me—that's getting air out of my sinuses?'

'At two hundred feet, you're likely to feel the air in your sinuses compressing, and it will hurt,' said Ford, adjusting his mask to his hairline. 'So we'll use the Frenzel method, okay? Close the throat—as if you're straining—pinch the nostrils and then make a "K" sound.'

'Shit, Mike,' said Gallen, getting nervous.

'Repeat it for me,' said Ford as the soldiers drew closer.

'Close the throat with a strain,' Gallen said, making a face. 'Pinch the nostrils and make a "K" sound.'

'Correct,' said Ford. 'And take my lead for the ascent, okay? I don't want you getting a shallow water blackout.'

'A what?' said Gallen, just as the first soldier ran down the stairs and raised his rifle.

Gallen's lungs started to ache at the one-minute mark, his brain urging him to break free of Ford's timetable and just kick to the surface. Ford had asked him to maintain eye contact, to help him stay focused. The flashlight shone from Ford's chest webbing and Gallen tried to keep eye contact. But then his upper chest started to burn and he could feel the panic rising.

Ford let some bubbles go from his mouth as they flipped languidly with the fins. It wasn't fast enough for Gallen—he was running out of air.

Slowly they ascended, Gallen starting to squirm. He looked at his G-Shock again: 1.43, not even halfway.

He wanted to scream at Ford, countermand him, give an order, but it wasn't going to help him. The darkness and cold closed in, and the panic rose, overwhelming his conscious knowledge that Ford was the navy commando, he knew how to do this. A growl built in him as they passed the two-minute mark, and he knew he wasn't going to be able to hold on for another two minutes. Pushing away from Ford, Gallen kicked free, swam upwards into the blackness, his legs thrashing and arms pulling him up. His chest ached, his temples bulged and a low moan rose up in him from somewhere deep.

The light of the surface became clearer, he was getting there. He thought about the time he went through the ice on the creek at the bottom of the farm, jumped though it intentionally to save his older brother; did it against the express instruction of his dad, who'd said if anyone ever went through the ice, you should leave them, there being no point in two people dying. But Gallen had jumped through and pulled out his brother, and both of them had been so scared to tell their parents that they'd made up some story about how they were horsing around and got in a water fight. Years later, Tom was a banker in Denver who never spoke to Gallen or Roy because he felt he'd moved on from all that. Gallen remembered that afternoon: his older brother coaching him all the way back to the house, warning him that he'd be in more trouble than Tom himself because he'd disobeyed Roy. As a younger boy he'd stayed quiet because he wanted to save himself from a punishment; as an adult he'd kept the story to himself because of what it said about his character.

The water swept across Gallen's mouth, the light got stronger, the ripples giving it an arty effect. And then he slowed, and he couldn't kick any longer and he was falling into a sleep, so warm, so comfortable . . .

CHAPTER 47

The scream was inches away and came with a resounding slap. It shook Gallen's head on his neck and then someone was forcing air into his lungs and he could feel a man's stubble on his face, taste old beer and cigarettes.

Gallen's chest heaved and water erupted from his nose and mouth, his face on fire as he gasped for air. Hands rolled him sideways and he was now face down in grass, convulsing and retching, his eyeballs wanting to pop.

Slowly regaining his composure, Gallen looked around, wiping the puke off the side of his face with his hand. He felt weak, in an altered state.

'Hey, boss,' said Mike Ford, still in his wetsuit. Winter sat beside him, lighting a cigarette. The sun was warm but not hot and he could hear children's voices shouting from the water. Sitting up, he saw a few other people around him, watching intently.

'What happened?'

'Shallow water blackout, Gerry,' said Ford. 'Told you—can't rush it from that depth. You get to the shallows and the ease in pressure makes the oxygen–CO_2 levels change too quickly, the brain can shut down.'

'Where's Cole?' said Gallen, groggy.

Winter shrugged. 'Haven't seen him. We picked you up in the boat, now he's nowhere.'

'Mike tell you?'

'Told me there's a full crew loading the nukes outta there,' said Winter. 'We saw the bird come in about an hour ago.'

Gallen turned, saw where Winter was pointing. A dark green Chinook helicopter was about to lift off from an area on the side of the road, about two hundred yards away.

Gallen nodded. 'Guys, I need to speak with Chase. We got a phone?'

Winter produced his, and told the audience to scram.

Dialling from memory, Gallen made the call, feeling water run out of sinuses.

Lang picked up on the second ring.

'Chase,' said Gallen, coughing slightly. 'Gerry Gallen. I'm calling in that nuclear haul.'

Lang took the coordinates. 'You okay, Gerry?'

'They've just loaded five or six of them into a Chinook,' said Gallen. 'They've got a small army down here. They're about to clear out.'

'We're on it, Gerry,' said Lang. 'By the way—that dude Cole? We just picked up a radio intercept: he's called for back-up, he's gonna arrest you and the crew.'

Gallen turned and saw the FBI Land Cruisers parked under the trees. Special Agent Cole had a group of security guys around him as he spoke into a handset. Gallen caught Cole's eye. Cole stopped abruptly and the bodyguards turned as one, hands reaching inside windbreakers.

'Time to go,' said Gallen, standing.

Winter stood with him. 'What's up?'

'Cole's trying to arrest us,' said Gallen, nodding at the FBI guys.

'That tub working?' said Ford, pointing at the FBI launch that was pulled up on the tiny beach.

'Last time I checked,' said Winter, jogging towards the vessel. He leapt onto the bow first, ran for the bridge, while Ford and Gallen pushed it off the sand. The hull slid back off the beach and they dived for the bow railings, dragging themselves up as the beeping sounds of an outboard motor sounded and Winter shifted it into reverse. Oil fumes drifted across the water and the first bullet hit the hull about two feet above the waterline as Gallen landed on the bow decking and moved back to the cockpit.

Shifting into forward, Winter raised the revs and the launch went ass-down, digging into the water as it powered up to a plane. The hull slapped the small waves as they gained speed and Winter yelled over the wind, 'What now, boss?'

'Where's the road?'

'Runs across the dam top,' said Ford, pointing behind the boat, 'then north, up that side of the Tigris.' He gestured to the far bank of the dam.

Gallen's first rule was to survive. But looking around the dam, as they got too far for the FBI's handguns, Gallen asked Winter to ease off. As the boat slowed, they felt the throbbing sound bouncing off the water, filling the sky. The Chinook—the huge, twin-rotor freight helicopter—lurched from the valley where it had been loaded and flew across the FBI agents on the sand, towards their boat.

'Here comes trouble,' said Winter, unholstering his Beretta.

The Chinook accelerated across the lake, its nose pointing down slightly. A smaller Black Hawk followed, soldiers in their dark fatigues looking down on Gallen, Ford and Winter with homicidal interest.

As the two helos flew across the lake, Gallen turned back, saw the agents standing on the beach. They had a couple of minutes before the FBI could get a chopper to them.

'Bunch of vehicles over there.' Winter pointed to another recreation area on the opposite bank. 'Could pay a visit, leave an IOU?'

Gallen didn't like to requisition vehicles from civilians, especially poor ones, but he didn't see an alternative. 'Let's do it, Kenny,' he said, sitting back in one of the white Naugahyde seats. 'Just try some of that famous charm, alright?'

'Can do, boss.'

'So, you always travel with a thousand dollars cash in your back pocket?' said Ford, trying to read a map in the front seat of the ten-year-old Nissan delivery van.

'I got some money from the ATM last night,' said the Canadian. 'Seemed like a fair price for the van.'

Blue smoke erupted from the broken exhaust and the top speed of eighty-five kmh suggested the vehicle had already had a hard enough life.

'A grand for this, it's perfect,' said Gallen, looking out the back window for the hundredth time. Once the FBI had seen them land on the other side of the lake, they'd have been in their own Land Cruisers and giving chase. And they'd be doing it much faster than eighty-five downwind.

'We got a plan?' said Winter. 'Gas is below one quarter, we can't drive all day.'

The countryside of Kurdistan was lush, well tended, as if the farming techniques of the rest of Iraq had been altered for this area of the north. It wasn't unlike parts of the rural United States, thought Gallen, with professional fencing and new tractors.

'The only plan I got is to stop Tookie running away with the nukes,' said Gallen. 'And for that, we gotta stay alive.'

'Let's hope the FBI agrees,' said Winter, looking into his rear-vision mirror. 'Here they come.'

Looking through the back window, Gallen could see three Land Cruisers about a mile back and closing the gap quickly, lights flashing.

'They want me,' said Gallen. 'You boys drop me, get to Turkey.'

'You can go, Kenny,' said Ford. 'I'm feeling nosey.'

'Yeah, Mike,' said Winter. 'I was curious about the colour of your blood.'

Gallen sighed. 'No heroes on my watch, boys.'

'No pussies, neither,' said Winter, throwing the van into a sideways slide in the middle of the highway. The van slid to a halt so it straddled the road. Jumping from the vehicle, they took their places behind the van, watching the road.

The first Land Cruiser crested the rise at what Gallen thought was a buck-fifty. The driver's eyes were wide as he saw the van and hit the brakes, the nose plunging and the front tyres dragging the big Toyota sideways as its ABS brakes tried to kick in. The second Land Cruiser was going even faster, and hit the first in the rear door, flipping the first vehicle onto its roof and causing it to slide into the scrub.

Gallen and Winter closed on the second Land Cruiser, guns drawn as the occupants reached for theirs.

'Hands in the air, fellas,' said Gallen, walking up to the driver, whose bottom lip was bleeding from the air bag deployed in his face.

The third Land Cruiser came to halt on the other side of the road and the personal security detail emerged, guns drawn.

Gallen could see Special Agent Cole in the back seat of the Land Cruiser in front of him.

'Get out,' said Gallen. 'Time to talk.'

'The fuck you think you're doin', Gerry?' said Cole, carefully stepping onto the dirt and dropping his handgun to the ground. 'Where's Jim?'

'Jim was double-crossed by his business partners,' said Gallen. 'They shot him down there, under the dam.'

'Who shot him?' said Cole, taking in the stand-off.

'Tookie Saleh's crew.'

Cole shook his head. 'You've got it wrong, Gerry. They weren't business partners.'

'No?'

'Jim was setting a trap.'

'Well, he's the one got trapped,' said Gallen.

'Who said the trap was for Saleh?' said Cole.

'What?' said Gallen. 'There was only FBI and Baath Party down there, Cole. We saw them do the deal, saw the nukes being loaded out. They're on a Chinook outta here while you chase me playing Keystone Cops.'

'We've known since oh-three that the Saleh clan—probably Tookie, but maybe some others—were going to try to restart the whole shooting match,' said Cole. 'The Baathists weren't the big fish.'

Gallen looked at Winter, who shrugged. 'I don't follow, Cole. Who was bigger than the Baathists?'

'Jim wanted the US intelligence clique that dealt with Saeed Saleh, gave him the nukes and the guidance systems, and took the billion bucks.'

'Billion?' said Gallen. 'Thought that was accounted for?'

'Where?' said Cole.

'It was found in a Baghdad reservoir tank; they leaked the information into the networks that the billion dollars was there.'

Cole smiled. 'Shit, Gerry. You think the US government would leave a billion dollars sitting in a reservoir tank in the Baghdad suburbs?'

Gallen shrugged. 'It was a honey pot, wasn't it?'

'That *was* the honey pot,' said Cole, laughing. 'That was a pile of counterfeit C-notes and they were bad ones. The point was to flush out the people who knew what came with the money stolen from the Central Bank. And true to form, they took the black bags, not the pallet of money.'

'You've lost me,' said Gallen.

'Thing is, Gerry, elements of our intelligence community have been pandering to the Iraqis for a long time,' said Cole. 'Jim had pieced together the puzzle, had evidence linking US intelligence to the Baathists.'

'Yeah, yeah,' said Gallen. 'They supplied the nukes. But who was the big fish, if not Saleh?'

'Jim was trying to get a money transfer from Tookie for the nukes,' said Cole. 'But he knew the money was ultimately coming from the people who'd been guarding it for him for almost a decade.'

'Who?' said Gallen.

Cole smirked. 'You know, Gerry, the FBI prosecutes just as many federal employees as it does known felons.'

Gallen paused. 'Jim thought Tookie had Americans helping him?'

'Jim was about to pounce,' said Cole. 'Tookie's transfer would have blown the lid on the real story of Saddam's secret weapons.'

CHAPTER 48

The Kiowa gunship slipped over the horizon so low that when Cole turned to see Chase Lang smiling in the co-pilot's seat he jumped back half a step.

'They here for you?' shouted Cole as his shirt rode up his back.

'Guess so,' said Gallen.

'Drop your weapons, gentlemen,' said Lang over the loudspeaker system on the Kiowa. 'That includes you, missy.'

The personal security detail looked to Cole, who nodded as the dust rose and people had to protect their eyes from the high-speed grit.

The PSD—the female agent included—dropped their weapons and allowed Gallen, Ford and Winter to walk to the helos, Lang gesturing for Gallen to get in his gunship, pointing the other two to the second ship.

The Kiowa pulled away, powerful and safe, as Gallen strapped into the harness in the rear compartment beside Daly.

'Got a lock on these assholes,' said Lang, enjoying himself. 'They're heading over the border. Can you believe these Towelies?'

'To Turkey?' said Gallen, surprised. Turkey was more hawkish about volatile Arab behaviour than the United States. It wasn't where Baathist revivalists should feel at home.

'No,' said Lang, gesturing for Gallen to put on the helmet with the earpieces. 'Iran. They're crossing into Iran.'

'Iran?' said Gallen, his stomach feeling like a block of ice just hit it. 'What the hell?'

'I know,' said Lang, grinning. 'Makes you realise why folks like you and I always have a job, huh, Gerry?'

'Iran?'

'Some situations don't need nothing but a double-tap and a shallow grave, right, Gerry?' said Lang, turning back to the windscreen. 'As it happens, I can accommodate that.'

The flurry of incoming and outgoing radio contact was being routed through Diego Garcia, as far as Gallen could tell. The conversations he could overhear seemed to be of a 'whole of theatre' nature, usually meaning that someone in Chase Lang's position was talking with a US Navy comms lieutenant, who was looking at satellite imagery and ATC data.

'I need clearance,' said Lang for the fourth time. 'I need an IFF for the Iranian air force.'

An IFF code—Interrogation Friend or Foe—was a vital piece of collateral to carry with you when you were a black ops US military aircraft crossing from Iraq to Iran. Gallen thought Lang was a bit macho, but liked his caution.

'That's the border,' said Daly as they flew over a range of snow-capped peaks. 'So I guess Chase got the clearance.'

The country on the other side of the mountain ranges was breathtaking, a panorama of dark green agriculture, rivers and valleys.

'Shit,' said Gallen. 'If I had a hundred acres of this ground back home, our problems would be over.'

They came in lower and a large city came into view on the horizon, to the west of a lake that stretched further than Gallen could see.

'Urmia,' said Lang, turning to face Gallen and Daly. 'We've placed Saleh at a large tobacco plantation to the west of the city. Let's surprise him.'

Gallen felt the atmosphere tense as Daly handed him a Kevlar vest and pointed to the gun racks. There was a selection of various Colt assault rifles: Gallen took the M4, checked it for load and safety.

They flew fast and low over the lush greenery, some of the farm allotments in the same families for centuries. It occurred to Gallen that if things had been different politically then perhaps this would have been one of the richest parts of the world, certainly one of the most productive. A line of tobacco trucks motored towards the Iranian city, carrying the biggest cash crop in the region.

Gallen watched Lang touch the pilot on the upper arm, the pilot flick a switch. The latest Kiowa, in standard US gunship form, could carry a range of missiles, machine guns and rockets, but it sacrificed its rear seat for the firepower. Lang used the old variety, with a rear passenger compartment, but he'd kept the fixed-forward .50-cal heavy machine gun mounted under the pilot's seat.

Lang tapped the pilot's arm again and gave a quick thumbs-up. The pilot nodded and banked hard into a dive, and as the Kiowa came around the view filled the cockpit glass. On the loading areas in front of a collection of large agricultural sheds, the Chinook was being rolled away by a small tug. The Black Hawk already had its camo webbing thrown over it.

Gallen's pulse rose, his jaw clenching as they banked. Men ran from the shed of the tobacco plantation, firing machine gun rounds at the Kiowa. One was obviously a heavy machine gun, Gallen noted as tracer rounds flew past the helo. A round struck a panel of the aircraft and Lang—who'd had his hand raised beside the pilot—now dropped it.

The pilot's thumb went to a trigger on the side of the cyclic, pushing down. The rhythmic booma-booma from under the fuselage indicated a .50-cal machine gun at full cycle. The ground exploded under the feet of the shooter on the ground and as the pilot brought the nose up, the fusillade tore a line through the hangar the Chinook was being wheeled into.

Pulling up the nose, they circled, watching Lang's second gunship make its pass and hammer the Black Hawk with a withering volley of .50-cal machine gun fire, which sent Saleh's troops scattering and collapsed the Black Hawk's arches by shooting out the landing gear, dropping it on its belly and relieving it of its glasswork.

Gallen's helo circled in a tight bank and came in again. This time a soldier with a SAM launcher on his shoulder came to the open area of the hangar but the pilot got in first, the ground chewing up in a line across the gravel drive area, hitting the soldier in the chest, sending the SAM flying.

'Leave the Chinook,' said Lang as they circled again, the soldiers jumping into vehicles and fleeing the airborne assault. 'That one,' said Lang, pointing at a Nissan Patrol being driven wildly down the main drive of the plantation.

'Buzz it, then pull it over,' said Lang.

The pilot made a line of .50-cal fire two feet to the right of the fleeing Patrol and then banked and flared in its path. The Patrol stopped in a cloud of dust as the Kiowa hovered in front of it. Three soldiers burst from the vehicle, hands in the air.

Lang gestured for the pilot to put the helo down and told the other Kiowa to stay in the air. Gallen looked up as he jumped from his helo, saw Winter leaning out the side of the airborne Kiowa, aiming at the buildings on the ground.

Gallen and Daly followed Lang over to the soldiers, where Lang pulled Daly forwards, asked him to translate. Gallen observed the ground, saw numerous buildings and dwellings, any one of which could be hiding a shooter. He didn't like it, wanted to be behind cover.

'Says the boss has gone,' said Daly.

'We'll see about that,' Lang responded.

They walked up the drive to the hangar, where another bunch of soldiers walked out with their hands in the air. It was the same story: boss gone.

Gallen walked to the Chinook, went up the rear loading ramp and took in the load space. 'Empty,' he said, moving back into the sunlight.

'This boy says Saleh is on his way to Lake Urmia,' said Lang, lighting a cigarette. 'Took the cargo with him.'

'Ask him, tobacco truck?' said Gallen.

Daly did the asking and the soldier nodded.

'I saw those trucks,' said Gallen. 'They were heading east as we flew in.'

They found the three tobacco semis as they wound into the urban area of Urmia, finally turning into a freight hub. The Kiowa circled as the trucks drove into the hub, parking and unhitching their loads.

'You tracking this?' said Lang to no one in particular.

'Yes,' said Gallen and Daly at the same time.

'We cleared for this?' said Gallen into his mic.

'Well, we ain't not,' said Lang. 'What that one doin'?'

The tobacco trailers got new semis within ten minutes and were out on the main road within fifteen. The Kiowa stayed on their tails as they manoeuvred through the streets. When they got to the northern suburbs of the city, the three semis closed on a four-way intersection, each truck taking a different route.

Lang decided to take the lead truck, following it west along an expressway that pointed towards Turkey. As they left the city behind, Lang mouthed something terse into the mic, before looking back.

'This isn't totally kosher, okay? But we can get away with it.'

They hovered in front of the truck, which pulled over to the shoulder of the expressway. The truckie got out, confused. Gallen walked to the truck as Lang questioned the driver. The driver opened the rear doors, let them search it. After five minutes of Daly sweeping the tobacco stacks with his Geiger counter, they confirmed that there were no nukes onboard.

Lang grabbed the radio as he climbed back into the Kiowa. Shouting, he looked back at Daly, shook his head.

'It was the one that drove up sixteen,' he said. 'It's got a half-hour start on us.'

Highway 16 through northern Iran was a purpose-built road, not any worse than many of the nationals Gallen had driven in the north of the United States. It wended north from Urmia and then hooked eastwards across a long causeway over Lake Urmia. The Kiowa ate the miles, but there was little chance of finding the tobacco truck in such a wide area; there was no guarantee that it had even stayed on the highway. They swept off the eastern end of the causeway into Iranian East Azerbaijan, and almost straight into the mountain known as King Island, so named because it was once an island in Lake Urmia before the water receded and made it a mountain. They followed 16 around the base of King Island, but there was no sign of the truck.

'Overran it,' said Gallen. 'It couldn't have come this far.'

Lang made a circular motion with his index finger and the helo banked, followed 16 back to the causeway. There were occasional roads into the bush and farmland on the slopes of King Island. There was one road that looked new.

'Can we look at that one?' said Gallen.

Hovering, they saw a collection of construction equipment and earth movers in a cleared section of the foothills. One of the machines was unusual.

'Take us lower, please,' said Gallen, and the helo came further down. Now he could see the enormous white machine, the size of a round railway locomotive, twice as long and seemingly mounted on a sled-like arrangement. The red words on the side of the machine said Terratec, which triggered a memory for Gallen.

'I know that name,' he said, clicking his fingers.

Then the picture formed. It was an entry on one of Saleh's spreadsheets: it had said, Terratec—tunnelling, something like that.

'Chase,' said Gallen, 'it's a tunnelling machine. There's a tunnel around here—and you know what the Iranians use tunnels for.' Anyone in special forces knew that Iranian tunnelling was usually a front for a nuclear program.

They landed, then alighted and walked carefully up the slope towards a concrete arch built into the side of King Island. Walking towards the tunnel, they stayed close in formation, rifles ready. Gallen heard the other Kiowa land behind them.

The tunnel was well lit, about the size of a four-lane freeway tunnel, and it was deserted except for a lone tobacco truck parked about fifty yards inside.

The lights went down and the attack came in, fast and vicious. Gallen felt a hand on his shoulder, saw Winter beside him, beckoning, the tracer rounds lighting up the dark as he followed the Canadian to a line of pick-up trucks with a construction company insignia on them. Gallen panted for breath as he lay beside Winter, counting heavy machine guns among the assault rifle volleys.

Further down the line of trucks, Daly stood slightly and aimed his grenade launcher. As he fired, he took a round in the upper arm and swivelled. The grenade hit a mezzanine gantry against the wall and killed several men in one go. The scaffolding fell against the tobacco truck and Gallen could see a man running from the truck further into the tunnel. Giving chase along the cover of the tunnel wall, he realised he'd picked up Daly as a buddy.

'See him?' said Daly, right hand clasped over his bleeding bicep. 'That's Tookie.'

As they broke from behind the pick-up trucks, Gallen dropped to one knee and shot at the legs of the men hiding behind the tobacco truck. Screams pierced the gloom, and Gallen followed Daly further into the construction zone. It became quiet as they left the fighting behind, Chase Lang's voice ringing out, telling the enemy to drop their weapons, that the jig was up.

Gallen and Daly moved into wet clay up to their knees, and as they waded deeper into the darkness, Gallen sensed movement to their right. Looking, he saw Tookie Saleh, a stupid grin on his face, holding a frag grenade. He was only twenty feet away. Gallen and Daly froze, guns trained on their man.

'So, the Americans who couldn't leave well enough alone are still here, even in Iran?'

'The fuck is this about, Tookie?' said Gallen. 'You were supposed to be a Baathist, remember? Now you're selling nukes to the Iranians?'

Tookie smiled. 'They pay me, and pay me well.'

'Iran is run by ayatollahs, Tookie,' said Daly. 'You're secular socialists!'

Tookie feigned throwing the grenade, which made Daly and Gallen flinch. 'Ha! The brave men of SOCOM are now scared of their own weapon.'

'What do you want, Tookie?' said Gallen.

'I was a child when they smuggled me out of Baghdad on the night of the invasion,' said Tookie, tears welling in his eyes. 'The missile that killed my uncle and his bodyguard? From a US Navy destroyer in the Gulf.'

'There were a lot of missiles flying around that night,' said Daly. 'You were unlucky.'

'No, Mr Daly, it was superior technology. The best avionics, the best guidance systems, the best explosives, the best satellite tracking. They targeted Saeed Saleh's convoy, and they got him. From five hundred miles!'

'It was war,' said Gallen. 'Saddam had his chances.'

'Yes, and Saddam had been given the world's most powerful nuclear warhead,' said Tookie. 'The W85, which had been turned into a bomb called the B61. But he never got to use it.'

'So you lost the bombs—Uncle Saeed had hidden them so well you couldn't find them?'

'Something like that,' said Tookie, a smile tugging at the side of his mouth.

Daly sounded confused. 'So if we had the blueprint, how did you find Badush Dam? How did you know there was a freight elevator into it?'

'Ha?' said the would-be reincarnation of Saddam Hussein. 'Ask my protector. Everyone needs a protector!'

Tookie threw the grenade and Daly and Gallen threw themselves into the mud, squirming their faces and torsos as deep into the wet slime as they could. The last thing Gallen thought was: I hope those Marines instructors weren't full of shit.

CHAPTER 49

The air-conditioning was louder than the storm that raged outside, such was the thickness of the glass at FBI headquarters in Quantico. Gallen thanked the woman for his coffee and turned back to Special Agent Cole, who sat behind a desk.

'After what you did for us over there,' said Cole, 'I want to give you what I can, Gerry, but why this?'

'I need to talk to him,' said Gallen. He'd pulled on his cleanest jeans and dress boots and had bought a new shirt in Cheyenne before the flight. He thought he was presenting okay.

'Lemme think about it,' said Cole. 'But first: your turn. How'd you connect this with Amundsen?'

Gallen shrugged. He'd already written his report for the Defense Intelligence Agency and for the State Department, for its ongoing apologies to Iran. 'When I saw a list of bank transactions in Tookie's laptop, a bunch of names leapt out at me. I felt I was looking at a pattern, but I didn't know what.'

'The pattern?' said Cole, turning a pen end over end.

'This word "protection", "protector" and what have you, and too many Nominees and Associates,' said Gallen. 'Then, before Tookie blew himself up, I asked him how he knew about the Badush Dam cache if he didn't have the blueprint.'

'And?'

'And he said to ask his protector,' said Gallen, sipping the coffee, hooking his ankle over his knee. 'So while I was waiting for a flight out of Baghdad, I was mucking around on the internet in the US embassy apartments, and I did a lot of searches on names that equate to "protection" and "protector".'

Cole smiled. 'We need you here, Gerry.'

'I was just mucking around, and then I see this strain of Norse names: lots of different variations that mean protector, but the one that kept coming up was Amundsen.'

'Shit,' said Cole, shaking his head and looking at the snow driving almost horizontal. 'That one insight unpicked years of corruption and arms dealing.'

'And it was an FBI collar?'

Cole leaned forwards on the desk. 'Sure was, but, you know, the CIA is usually very good with rotating people out of their comfort zones, moving them on before they can do this sort of stuff.'

'But not Barry?'

'I think it was his overlapping expertise,' said Cole. 'He had Arabic, Farsi and a few Caspian dialects, and, of course, he was a Middle East arms and WMD expert. The Agency moved him on, but never far from his last posting. He was too valuable. He moved from Tel Aviv to Damascus and then to Cairo and Riyadh. That sort of thing.'

Gallen nodded. 'You worked out yet what he was actually doing?'

'He found Rogers, who was annoyed at his unglamorous job as a nukes accountant, and suggested a way to make a lot of money and enjoy some importance.'

'Amundsen organised the theft of the B61s from Turkey?'

'With Rogers and Saeed Saleh,' said Cole. 'There was a moralistic spin put on it about balancing power in Persia, but Amundsen wanted cash.'

'So, Saleh pays him once and then—what? Amundsen goes back for another go when he realises that the nephew doesn't know where the nukes are being hidden?'

'Sure,' said Cole. 'Only now he knows about the billion dollars stolen from the Central Bank by Saeed Saleh on invasion night, and he wants some of that.'

The two men looked at one another.

'So that's the ancient history,' said Gallen. 'But I'm thinking about the future, and what happens to a farmer who shoots down a US military helicopter.'

'Talking about the Little Bird, at Badush?'

'The only one I can think of,' said Gallen.

Cole grinned. 'Wasn't our military, Gerry. It was registered to Aviation Associates, an aircraft leasing company in Cyprus. Amundsen's front in Singapore leased it.'

Gallen shook his head, couldn't help it.

'You know, Jim was good people,' said Cole, leaning back. 'He taught me a lot, saved me from my own bad mistakes. We all miss him.'

Gallen drank his coffee.

'So tell you what,' said Cole. 'I'll give you some paperwork, you go see Barry.'

The drive to Petersburg took slightly more than an hour, and when Gallen presented himself at the prison watchtower at ten to midday, his paperwork from the FBI was well received.

'It's all in the system,' said the woman at the desk. 'Let's see some ID, we'll do a quick search, and I'll take you up.'

The smells of lunch wafted around the prison as Gallen waited in the visitation rooms. The place looked friendly enough, but he noticed there were U-bolts in the concrete beneath the bolted-down plastic seats and the whole place was set up like a goldfish bowl.

The door opened with a hiss and Barry Amundsen walked in, dressed in whites. Taking off his hair net as he stopped in front of Gallen, he smiled but didn't offer his hand. The escorting officer took a seat two tables away, opened a *WWF* magazine.

'They gave you a white uniform, Barry,' said Gallen. 'Nicer than the khakis everyone else has to wear.'

'I've got food service duty,' said Amundsen. 'It's not a bonus or anything.' He looked away then looked back, hostile. 'The fuck is this, Gallen? Huh? This a shake-down? Well don't waste your time, the feds cleaned it all out, bankrupted me, the kids out of school, sold the house, the whole nine yards.'

Gallen stared at him.

'Well?'

'It sort of gnawed at me, Barry,' said Gallen, determined to control himself. 'I couldn't work out how Tookie Saleh got to the Badush Dam freight elevator so fast. He knew where to go, he had a crane and a Chinook waiting to load the B61s.'

'So?' said Amundsen.

'So, he didn't have the blueprint, and even with you seeing it and describing it to him, there was no evidence on that blueprint of an elevator shaft running independent of either the police station tunnel or the air lock.'

'Hmm,' said Amundsen, pursing his lips. 'You got a real Agatha Christie going on there, Gerry.'

'And then it occurred to me,' said Gallen. 'Barrowman knew about the elevator shaft because he did some old-fashioned intel work with a man in a workers' village called Pawan.'

Amundsen drummed the table with his fingers.

'You see, Barry, Pawan worked on that tunnel from the police station to Badush Dam, and he told Barrowman about it. When you made your sweep in Barrowman's wake, Pawan decided not to tell you about it. He just didn't like you, Barry, that right?'

Amundsen's eyes were as clear and pale as Gallen remembered them, but a spark had gone, replaced by resignation. 'I may have spoken to some people nearby, sure.'

'You'd remember Pawan,' said Gallen. 'You smashed both his hands with a nine-pound hammer, and when he told you to go fuck yourself, you dragged his son into the room, tore off his pants and threatened to cut off the boy's testicles with a penknife.'

Amundsen looked into his hands as if they held the secret to life. He cleared his throat. 'Well, Gallen, that's quite a story.'

'Finding nuclear warheads for dictators can be a distracting thing, which is why you wouldn't have noticed that Pawan was the only breadwinner in that family.'

'I'm sure I don't know what you're talking about,' said Amundsen, checking over his shoulder, signalling the officer to take him away.

Gallen held up his piece of paperwork. 'I'm conducting interviews for the Federal Bureau of Investigation,' said Gallen. 'That's why I'm here, that's why I didn't have to wait for visiting hours, Barry. I own you.'

Amundsen slumped, moved his gaze to the window, smoothed his thin hair down towards his face. 'Okay, look,' he started. 'When you're in the field . . .'

Gallen smiled, raised his eyebrows, and Amundsen stopped.

'Barry, Pawan can't work with broken hands, and you'll never guess it, but his two sons dropped out of school to bring in money, and that pushed the enrolments at their little school so low that the Iraqis are closing it, and all the kids in that village now have to be bussed forty miles away.'

Amundsen pinched the bridge of his nose.

'And, I didn't know this before, Barry, but when school takes too much time out of the day, the Kurds withdraw their daughters because all the travelling messes with their home duties.'

Amundsen meshed his fingers and leaned his chin on them. 'What do you want, Gallen?'

The officer was engrossed in his wrestling magazine, and Gallen flicked a small piece of paper across the formica table top. Amundsen's hands dropped smoothly and caught it.

'It's a small American-run NGO that operates social infrastructure in Jordan, Iraq and Syria,' said Gallen. 'It's run by a friend of mine—a doctor. She's the real deal, and she's interested in the story of this village.'

'And?' said Amundsen.

'And she's expecting a deposit of five hundred thousand dollars in the next seven days, into that bank account.'

Amundsen laughed. 'Oh, really?'

'Yes, really,' said Gallen, standing. 'People like you and me, we spent a lifetime dropping into people's lives, turning them upside down, and then walking away to our safe lives in the States.'

'I'm paying my penance; where's yours, Gallen?'

'I'll think of something,' said Gallen. 'But money ain't it right now.'

EPILOGUE

She was four minutes late when Gallen received the call on his phone. Alison needed some muscles to shift a sofa, align the refrigerator. Could he meet her at home instead of the cafe?

He walked half a block to her apartment in Logan Circle, a trendy part of Washington DC, where Gallen noticed men holding hands and small dogs dressed in plaid coats against the winter wind. He paused at the apartment building, an old renovated two-storey brick place that was once an ironworks or stonemason's. He was nervous: they'd spoken on the phone a couple of times before his trip to Washington, and she'd filled him in on her NGO plans. But she hadn't sounded exactly warm—he wondered if he'd got things wrong. Maybe that night over the Atlantic was a mistake for her?

She wore her honey-coloured hair high in a ponytail, and she wasn't dressed to go out. Gallen didn't know whether he should kiss her or give her a hug. She seemed a bit off, slightly arch. So he held out his hand, called her ma'am.

'Shit,' said Alison, putting her hand on her hip.

'What?' said Gallen. He could feel his cheeks filling with hot blood.

'I was going to give you a telling off, know that?' she said. 'Christ—we had a date, and I was in Aspen!'

'Umm.'

'Yeah, poor little farm boy,' she taunted. 'Ride them broncos but run a mile from a woman?'

Gallen looked around, embarrassed. 'I'm sorry, Alison, it's been a tough month.'

She sighed, tension running out of her as she let her arms drop at her sides. 'Yep, it has been that.'

They'd drawn closer, Gallen could smell her perfume. It was floral but not too sweet. 'So, I guess you don't want lunch?'

They looked at each other for two seconds and Alison started laughing, couldn't help herself. 'Oh, boy,' she said, as she composed herself and Gallen put his hands on her waist. 'I spent almost twenty years getting away from fricking Des Moines and I come all the way back to guys like you, Gerry.'

Gallen pulled her in, she reached up, put her hands around his neck.

'I'm going to live in DC,' she said, her face coming closer. 'And you're on the farm in Wyoming.'

'Yes, ma'am.'

'It might be okay for us,' said Alison, her lips parting as she kissed Gallen on the mouth. He kissed her back, feeling her small waist and the push of her hips against her Wranglers. Her arms gripped harder around his neck and they fell to the sofa, Gallen landing under her and their lips not parting.

As they came up for air, Alison propped herself on her elbow and looked into Gallen's face. He saw a beautiful woman.

'You kiss like a teenager,' she said.

Gallen flinched. 'That a good thing?'

She smiled. 'You don't know women very well, do you, Gerry?'

'That obvious?'

She leaned away, unbuckled his pants and pulled them down. 'How's this bullet wound?'

Running a finger around the purplish hole in his thigh that darkened to black in the centre, she nodded. 'Healing, no infection. You're a lucky man, Gerry, know that?'

He pulled her on top of him, tried to kiss her, but she pushed him down. 'I can do this,' she said. 'If you can.'

'I can,' said Gallen, his hands resting on her butt, trying to pull her in.

'There's just one thing,' said Alison, her eyes sparkling with desire.

'What?'

She brought her right hand to his nose and flicked her fingernail hard against the space between his eyebrows.

'Ow!' he squeaked, his eyes squeezing shut and his face screwing up with the pain. 'What was that for?'

'I'm falling for you, Gerry Gallen,' she said, stroking his hair back from his face. 'But don't you ever duck one of my voicemails again.'

'Yes, ma'am,' said Gallen.

The falling sensation was the best thing he'd felt in a long time.